THE BOOKSHOP
BY THE BAY

Also by Pamela Kelley

Nashville Dreams

The Wedding Photo

Gilded Girl

The Hotel

Court Street Investigations series

The Nantucket Restaurant series

Nantucket Beach Plum Cove series

Montana Sweet Western Romance series

Waverly Beach Mystery series

THE
BOOKSHOP
BY THE BAY

Pamela Kelley

ST. MARTIN'S GRIFFIN
NEW YORK

*In loving memory of my mother, Marcia Claughton,
and my grandfather Ken Ford, for their enthusiastic
support and encouragement*

First published in the United States by St. Martin's Griffin,
an imprint of St. Martin's Publishing Group

THE BOOKSHOP BY THE BAY. Copyright © 2023 by Pamela Kelley.
All rights reserved. Printed in the United States of America.
For information, address St. Martin's Publishing Group,
120 Broadway, New York, NY 10271.

www.stmartins.com

Library of Congress Cataloging-in-Publication Data

Names: Kelley, Pamela M., author.
Title: The bookshop by the bay / Pamela Kelley.
Description: First edition. | New York: St. Martin's Griffin, 2023.
Identifiers: LCCN 2023002017 | ISBN 9781250861610
 (trade paperback) | ISBN 9781250283573 (hardcover) |
 ISBN 9781250283580 (ebook)
Subjects: LCGFT: Novels.
Classification: LCC PS3611.E4432528 B66 2023 |
 DDC 813/.6—dc23/eng/20230208
LC record available at https://lccn.loc.gov/2023002017

Our books may be purchased in bulk for promotional, educational,
or business use. Please contact your local bookseller or the Macmillan
Corporate and Premium Sales Department at 1-800-221-7945, exten-
sion 5442, or by email at MacmillanSpecialMarkets@macmillan.com.

First Edition: 2023

10 9 8 7 6 5 4 3 2 1

Chapter 1

H̶ow do you know when a marriage is truly over?
Jessica Coleman stared out her kitchen window as she sipped her morning coffee and half listened to her best friend, Alison Page, tell her about the amazing dinner she'd had the night before at the Impudent Oyster. She and Alison had been best friends since they were children living in Chatham, Massachusetts, and even though they'd lived a thousand miles apart for many years, they still spoke by phone at least once a week, usually early in the morning.

"We had the oysters Rockefeller, which had lobster, too, and a creamy spinach sauce. You would have loved it."

It was their favorite restaurant in Chatham, the small Cape Cod village where they'd both grown up. Alison had never left, while Jessica had moved to Charleston, South Carolina, many years ago, after graduating from law school, and marrying Parker.

"Jess, you still there?" Alison had stopped talking and Jessica hadn't even noticed. She felt the beginnings of a stress headache, brought on by thinking about the best time to have an uncomfortable conversation with her husband. Something they'd both been avoiding.

"Sorry, I've been miles away. A lot on my mind. Nothing new, just wondering what to do about Parker."

"No gold stars lately, I take it?"

Jess laughed. "That's an understatement." She'd once joked to Alison that she should put a gold star on the calendar for the rare occasions that she and Parker had sex. By her calculations it was almost a year now. It just wasn't a priority anymore, for either of them. They'd met during her junior year at Charleston College, and she'd never really been serious with anyone else. He hadn't, either. After graduating from law school and getting married, both took jobs at Parker's father's firm in Charleston. They'd settled in Mount Pleasant, one of the area's nicest neighborhoods, and three years later had one daughter, Caitlin, who recently turned thirty.

"I'm sorry. Have you talked to him about it? Do you want to try to save the marriage?"

Jess wasn't sure there was anything left to save. She and Parker had been madly in love, many years ago. They both worked long hours and it seemed like the only thing they had in common anymore was work.

"It's like we're roommates. It's been like that for a few years, we've really sort of drifted apart. And I feel like something has shifted in the past few months. Just a funny feeling that I have."

"You think he might be having an affair?" Alison sounded surprised, and Jess didn't blame her. Parker was the least likely person to have an affair. He worked long hours and they worked together. She knew his schedule and didn't see how it was possible. But still, the feeling wouldn't go away.

"I don't know. Maybe not. Maybe we've just both come to realize this isn't working anymore. Something just feels different."

"You need to talk to him."

"I know. I catch him looking at me sometimes, like he wants to have the conversation, too, but neither one of us wants to bring it up first. It's just easier to ignore it and keep going on the way we have, I guess."

"That doesn't sound healthy, Jess. Time goes by too fast. If this isn't working anymore, either try to fix it, together, or move on. It's not so bad being single. It might be good for you." Alison had been married for ten years and single for more than twenty. And she was best friends with her ex. It was like they got along better since they divorced. Jess had asked her a million times if they might get back together, but Alison always insisted that it wasn't like that with them.

"You're right. I know you're right. I think I might finally be ready. I've never really been single as an adult. It's going to be a change."

Suddenly single as a woman in her mid-fifties in Charleston was an intimidating thought. It was a city full of beautiful, young Southern women who never left their house without full hair and makeup and always dressed impeccably. How could she compete with that?

"Why don't you take some time off?" Alison suggested. "Come to Chatham for a month, at least. You haven't taken more than a week or two off in years."

The idea was very tempting. And Alison was right. Jess's mother would be thrilled. At seventy-eight, she was an active widow, and the family house in Chatham had plenty of room.

"I'll think about it." She glanced at the time and took her last sip of coffee. "Allie, I have to run. I'll keep you posted."

❧

Parker was already up and out. He'd developed a new habit in recent months of heading to the gym before work and then showering and dressing there. The law firm was just a few blocks away from the gym. If he had an early-morning client meeting, he brought his stuff with him and hit the gym at lunchtime or right after work instead. He'd decided recently that he needed to lose twenty pounds and, much to Jessica's annoyance, achieved his goal a month later. He just immediately stopped overeating and skipped breakfast and lunch, eating one meal a day. Something Jess could never imagine doing; she never missed a meal. Not that she was overweight, but her weight tended to go up and down by ten or fifteen pounds, and dieting was never that easy for her.

The drive into the office wasn't far, less than ten miles, but with rush-hour traffic it usually took almost forty-five minutes. Jess pulled her navy BMW sedan into the office building parking lot at a quarter past eight. Parker's car, a black Range Rover, was already there.

Jess's executive assistant, Miriam, was taking her coat off when Jess walked off the elevator. The office receptionist, a temp, hadn't arrived yet. But the office didn't officially open for another fifteen minutes. Miriam smiled when she saw her.

"I was just about to grab a coffee, would you like one?" Miriam asked. She was an older woman, in her early sixties, and had a motherly quality that Jess appreciated. She was also always two steps ahead of Jess, and great with clients. They'd worked together for years. She knew that Miriam was thinking about retiring soon, though, and she dreaded having to train someone new.

"That would be great, thanks so much." Jess settled at her desk, fired up her computer, and dove into her emails. She had a busy day, a booked-solid schedule of client meetings. She saw Parker briefly, to say hello, and then didn't see him again until the end of the day, as she was wrapping things up. He poked his head in the door before heading out. His assistant, Linda, was beside him, and as she pulled on her jacket, the front of her shirt lifted up a few inches and Jess saw something that she hadn't noticed before.

There was a familiar swelling across Linda's middle. Parker's assistant was pregnant. Linda was a fairly new assistant. She'd been with the firm for just under a year and was maybe a year or so older than their daughter. She'd replaced an older woman who had retired, and Linda came highly recommended. So far, Parker had said she'd been doing a great job. Jess couldn't remember any mention of a serious boyfriend, though. She guessed by the size of the swelling that Linda was maybe four or five months along.

She was a slim girl and usually wore dresses or long tops that covered her waist. Jess wondered if Parker knew. They'd have to start thinking about a replacement when she went on maternity leave and also consider the possibility that she might not return. About half the time, they didn't, even when they adamantly said that they would.

"Heading home?" Jess asked with a smile.

"No, actually. We have that Lions Club thing tonight. I thought I mentioned it to you. They're giving us their yearly check for the food pantry. Linda and I are going. I know you hate those things and thought it might be fun for her."

Jess did hate those dinners and usually tried to get out of them. The organization was a wonderful one, but the evenings dragged on for several hours. Both she and Parker were active volunteers and committee members for their church's food pantry, and every year the Lions Club and other organizations donated several thousand dollars to help fund pantry operations. She didn't mind at all that Linda was going in her place. It was the last thing she felt like doing after a long day at the office.

But then Linda absentmindedly patted her stomach, and Jess caught the look on Parker's face as he watched her. It was fleeting, but for a moment she'd seen it—pure adoration—and then she knew.

And when Parker met her gaze, he knew she knew. The telltale sudden flush of red across his cheeks confirmed it.

She just stared at him. "When you get home tonight, we need to talk."

Chapter 2

Caitlin Coleman had beaten out hundreds of applicants for the job at Middleton's. She knew that because Mary Middleton liked to remind her of it with the unspoken threat that if things didn't work out, she'd be easy to replace. Middleton's was a high-end department store, the Charleston equivalent of Harrods in London. Some compared it to Nordstrom because of the famous chain's legendary service, but Mary Middleton scoffed at the comparison. Middleton's was much more expensive than Nordstrom.

Caitlin had been there for two months and thought things were going reasonably well. Her role was on the floor, in sales. Many of their customers came in for the Middleton experience, which was on the store's upper level, where the most in-demand designer clothes were found, and included complimentary champagne in the dressing rooms.

Caitlin was expected to upsell—to suggest entire outfits when a client brought a single piece into the dressing room. Caitlin had thought that seemed overly pushy at first, but was surprised by how effective it was. These women wanted to know what she thought, and she didn't hesitate to tell them. She thought that they valued her truthful opinion.

"What do you think of this one?" Helen, a woman about Caitlin's mother's age, twirled in front of the three-way mirror in a sequined evening gown that cost more than Caitlin's last car. It would be a huge sale and a big commission for Caitlin. But it didn't look as good on Helen as a few other dresses she'd tried.

"That's a lovely dress, but I'm not sure it's as flattering as the other two you just tried. I'd recommend going with one of those."

Mary Middleton happened to walk into the dressing room area a moment earlier and heard everything.

"Oh, dear," Helen said. "I really do love this one. That's disappointing to hear." She bit her lower lip and stared sadly at her reflection in the mirror. "I think maybe I'll just hold off for now. Thanks so much, dear." She quickly disappeared into her dressing room.

"We have some other things you might love," Mary immediately suggested. But Helen stayed silent until she emerged a few minutes later, dressed in a Lilly Pulitzer pink floral print dress.

"Maybe another day. I'm just not in the mood anymore." She scurried off, and Mary turned her attention to Caitlin. Mary's expression was icy, and Caitlin braced for what she suspected was coming.

"Caitlin, we've been through this before. There's such a thing as being too honest. That dress might not have looked as good as the others, but it still looked fine—and more importantly, that was the dress that she loved. That she wanted. You cost us a huge sale and disappointed an important client. I'm afraid this just isn't working out. I'm sorry."

"I'm sorry. I can do better," Caitlin began. She felt terrible. Mary had only mentioned this as being an issue once before. And Caitlin really thought that she'd been helping by steering Helen to the most flattering dress. That kind of honesty was what Caitlin would have wanted to hear, so she'd just assumed their customers would feel the same way.

But Mary Middleton was done. "This isn't the place for you, Caitlin. I wish you all the best. Please leave your badge in the office when you leave today."

❦

Caitlin felt numb when she walked out of Middleton's at a few minutes past five. She'd been so excited to get that job. And Mary had seemed so wonderful when she'd first started working there. She'd told Caitlin how much she loved her look, and that clients would be excited to work with her. And that was why she'd beaten out all the others who were desperate to work there.

Caitlin had always loved fashion. For a brief time, she'd toyed with the idea of modeling. She was certainly tall enough, at five ten, and her naturally reddish-blond long hair was her best feature. But she was too big-boned, and if she was being honest, she knew that she wasn't pretty enough. She was Charleston pretty, with small features and big blue eyes, but there was nothing remarkable about her bone structure. She just wasn't that photogenic.

Working in fashion seemed like a great alternative. She'd tried just about everything else over the years, including waitressing and bartending. Working as a secretary—that was a disaster. Attention to detail—other people's schedules—was not a strength. She'd tried an entry-level job in finance as a mutual-fund accountant. Those big companies hired fresh graduates from any major and trained them. But when Caitlin sent a wire with an extra zero and accidentally sent a million dollars instead of one hundred thousand, she was let go, understandably.

She temped for a while after that and worked in customer service at a call center. She'd thought she'd finally landed the ideal job at Middleton's, and now it looked like she would have to sign on with a temp agency again. It was depressing. All her friends had their lives figured out, building careers, and most at this point were married. Caitlin hadn't managed to do that yet, either.

She'd come close a few times, but just didn't feel like any of them were "the one." Now that she'd turned thirty, though, it seemed like there was more of a sense of urgency about getting married. In Charleston and the South in general, women tended to marry early. Though Charleston wasn't quite as bad as some areas. She remembered visiting Nicole, a college friend, in a small Louisiana town the year she turned twenty-five and feeling like an old maid for the first time.

When she went to a house party with Nicole, just about all of her friends asked, "Where's your husband?" As if they assumed that she must have one and he was maybe outside or something. It was the most bizarre experience she'd ever had. And Nicole explained that just about everyone there got married by the time they were twenty or twenty-one at the latest. Nicole had married at nineteen and dropped out of college at the end of her sophomore year.

But Caitlin cheered up a bit as she drove to Fleet Landing, the restaurant where she was meeting Prescott, the man she'd been dating for exactly one year. It was their anniversary, and one of their mutual friends had told her that Prescott had mentioned that he had something big to tell her tonight, but he didn't know what the news was. Caitlin didn't want to get her hopes up, but she was pretty sure Prescott was going to propose, and she was inclined to accept. He ticked almost all of her boxes. He was tall and blond, handsome but not too good-looking. She'd dated a few guys over the years who were too hot for their own good and knew it. That never ended well.

Prescott had boy-next-door good looks and he was good company. They had a lot of the same interests—they'd met at the country club and both liked tennis and blues music and she liked his friends. She could imagine they'd have a good life if they did marry. And he was from an old Charleston family. Prescott did real estate development, mostly flipping houses, which gave him a flexible schedule. The only downside was that he didn't make her heart race. She liked kissing him, sleeping with him even, but his touch didn't make her tingle. But everything else was there; maybe in time that would come?

Prescott's Jeep was parked near the front of the restaurant when she arrived. She walked inside and he was waiting by the reception desk. They were seated right away, at an outside table. Caitlin ordered a glass of chardonnay, and Prescott got a local draft IPA. They both ordered the shrimp and grits. The weather was beautiful. Soft breezes lightly blew over them as they watched sailboats go by. They chatted easily, and Prescott told her all about the deal he'd closed that day.

"We did even better than we expected. The market right now is nuts. We held off on all showings until the open house yesterday and collected multiple offers. We ended up accepting a cash offer, fifty thousand over asking and they waived the home inspection. We close in three weeks with a profit of almost two hundred thousand."

"That's awesome, Pres." Caitlin was happy for him. She couldn't fathom making that kind of money so easily. And it really did seem to come easily for Prescott. He had a knack for finding undervalued houses that people weren't interested in because they looked like they needed too much work. But it was usually cosmetic stuff, and he had a contractor buddy who evaluated all potential flips and let him know what it would take to fix them up. He then painted them in neutral colors, soft grays and blues, and made the kitchens all-white with the latest quartz countertops, stainless appliances, and subway tiles—the latest looks that people wanted.

He told her all about it as they ate, and she never did have a chance to tell him how her day went. She didn't want to spoil the mood, either, as he was on such a high from the sale. It could wait. Maybe she'd have something else lined up soon, too, so it wouldn't be too depressing a conversation.

When they finished, their waitress cleared their plates and asked if they wanted dessert. Caitlin almost never ordered dessert, so Prescott looked at her in surprise when she asked for the dessert menu and then ordered the vanilla bean crème brûlée.

"Do you want to share?" she asked.

He laughed. "No, I'm good." He ordered a coffee, though, and sipped it while Caitlin enjoyed every creamy bite of the delicious custard. When she finished, a more serious look crossed his face.

"There's something I wanted to talk to you about," he began.

She smiled. "Happy anniversary."

A confused look flashed across his face. "Oh, right." He paused, and Caitlin suddenly had a sinking feeling. If he didn't even remember that it was their anniversary, a proposal was unlikely.

"What is it?" she asked softly.

He forced a smile. "Here's the thing. I've always wanted to travel. To spend a year abroad, going everywhere. With this latest deal, it gives me a cushion to do that and not have to worry about anything. The timing is perfect."

"You want to travel? For a year? When?"

"I just booked my first flight today, to Spain. I leave the day after we close."

"Okay." *So, what does that mean for us?* She didn't ask the question, just looked at him, waiting for him to continue.

He sighed. "I think you're great, Caitlin. But, I'm not sure I'm ready to settle down, with anyone. I hope we can still stay friends, though?"

He looked as though he really did mean that. Caitlin nodded and fought back the tears that threatened to overflow. Intellectually, she knew it was probably for the best. He obviously didn't feel the butterflies either, but still, it stung to lose both her job and her boyfriend the same day. Especially when she'd actually thought he might propose. A thought occurred to her. Her mind was still spinning, as he'd taken her completely by surprise with his news.

"Is there someone else?"

He looked offended by the question. "Are you serious? No.

You know me better than that. This just feels like something I need to do."

"Okay." Caitlin shivered, as the air felt suddenly colder, and she wished she were home, snuggled in her bed, and would wake the next morning and this awful day would be just a bad dream. She was glad at least that Prescott had waited until they were done eating and almost ready to leave. He paid the bill and walked her to her car, then hugged her goodbye. She allowed it for just a moment before pulling back.

"Goodbye, Prescott."

Chapter 3

Alison Page was in her happy place. She looked around the bookstore and breathed in deeply. The smell of books had always been intoxicating to her. Everything about books, actually. She'd stopped into Chatham Books on her way home from work at the magazine. It had been a somewhat stressful day. They all knew that more layoffs were likely, it was just a matter of when. And Jim, the magazine owner and general manager, had been in his office all day with his door closed, which was unlike him. Through the floor-to-ceiling glass walls of his office, she had watched him talking on the phone and pacing back and forth. So, when five o'clock came, she'd bolted and gone straight to the bookstore. It was on the way home and she needed a dose of happy. The shop, with its light pickled-oak floors, creamy white walls, and pale blue bookshelves, gave the space an airy, beachy feel that always made Alison want to linger.

As she always did, Alison walked straight to the new-releases table to see what had arrived since her last visit. She stopped in every week or two to feed her habit. Both she and Jess were big readers. Though with Jess's job, Alison knew, her reading had slowed down some over the years, but Alison still read at least a book or two, sometimes more, every week. And this bookstore held so many happy memories. Her mother had worked at the store, part-time, for as long as Alison could remember—until she passed just over ten years ago. When Alison was young, she used to love to go to work with her mother—it was such a treat. Jess would often come with her and they'd head there after they got out of school and would spend hours giggling and reading and snacking in the back of the store.

Ellen Campbell, the store owner, looked up when Alison walked in, and smiled.

"A new Harlan Coben came in today. I know he's one of your favorites." Ellen nodded toward the new-releases table.

"Thank you! I knew he had one coming soon, but didn't know it was out yet." Alison loved the dry humor that was in his suspense books, which she'd always found impossible to put down. She picked up another new one, too, a Manhattan-set historical saga by Fiona Davis, another favorite author. Alison read widely across several genres and always loved discovering new authors, too.

She took the books to the counter and got her credit card out as Ellen rang up the sale. She signed her charge slip, and then Ellen handed her the books in a glossy, mint-green paper shopping bag with the distinctive gold Chatham Books logo on the side.

"Here you go. Happy reading."

Alison took the bag and was about to turn to leave when Ellen spoke again. "I don't suppose you know anyone that might want to buy a bookstore?"

Alison's heart jumped. Owning a bookstore had long been a dream, but she'd never had the savings to invest in something like that.

"You're looking to sell?" As long as she could remember, Ellen had been a fixture at Chatham Books.

Ellen nodded. "I think it's time. I don't have the energy that I used to. And I'd like to do some traveling, go visit the grandkids down south, go on a cruise. Just sit at the beach and read a book."

Alison guessed that Ellen was well into her mid-seventies. It was understandable.

She shook her head. "I don't know of anyone. It sounds like an incredible opportunity, though. If I think of anyone, I'll have them get in touch."

"Thanks, honey. I'm just starting to think about it and get the word out."

Once Alison stepped outside, she took a long look back at the shop, at the pretty green awning, the three flower boxes that spilled over with pink, white, and yellow flowers, and the rounded bay windows with the white panes and the thoughtfully chosen display of new and old books. It would be absolute heaven to own that shop.

But it was also an impossible dream, so Alison took a final look before pushing the thought out of her head. There was no point obsessing over something that could never be. Instead, she would think about what to make for dinner and how it might be a good idea to update her résumé in case those layoffs happened sooner rather than later.

✽

Alison had always loved a good storm. It was the hours before the storm hit that she liked the most—when the temperature dropped and the wind picked up and the air felt slightly damp and more alive, somehow. Later that evening, a little past seven, she and her ex-husband, Chris, were sitting on her back deck, which overlooked a marshy pond. They could smell the ocean in the distance even though it wasn't visible. They'd just had dinner, a couple of steaks that she'd thrown on the grill, and now they were relaxing over a second drink, wine for her, beer for him.

Since the divorce, she and Chris found they actually got along better, and she considered him one of her best friends. Behind Jess, of course.

"You seem unsettled lately," Chris said. "Do you think it might be time to move on from the magazine, and do something else?"

Alison sighed. He'd always been able to read her well. "I might not have a choice soon. I think another layoff might be coming." Alison had worked as an editor and sometimes writer at *Cape Cod Living* for over twenty years. It had been her dream job when she first started, and she still loved the work, but the magazine world was very different now. Revenues were down every year as people moved to consuming their content online instead of in print.

"Why not get ahead of it then? Find something else. What do you think you'd want to do, stay in editing/writing?"

"There aren't a whole lot of options for that on the Cape. Anywhere really. It's a dying industry."

"So, what else then? Maybe it's time to try something totally new. Is there anything else that interests you?"

Alison told him about her conversation with Ellen. "I've always dreamed about running a bookstore, opening my own shop. But that takes money. More money than I have."

"Plus, everything is online these days. It's so easy to place an order and a day or two later, it arrives on your doorstep."

Alison made a face. "Yes, but there's nothing like browsing a bookstore. Smelling all those books, flipping through the pages and choosing the perfect one for your mood at that moment."

"True. And even the small store here always has people looking around when I stop in. But, like you said, that takes money. If I had it, I'd help, but I don't have that kind of money to invest either. Maybe you could see if she needs to hire help?"

"I could. But that would likely be a minimum-wage kind of job. I was thinking if I do get laid off, maybe I could look into freelance editing. I have a friend that does that and has clients from all over the world."

"That sounds good. You'd have to build that up, though. It's not like walking into a job."

She nodded. "Right. I think I probably have a few more months before the next round of layoffs. But it could be sooner, so just to be safe, I'll probably update my résumé." The thought of having to drum up clients was a bit terrifying. She was confident in her writing and editing skills, not so much in her sales ability.

"Sounds like a plan. Where's Julia tonight?" Chris asked about their daughter, who'd recently turned thirty.

"She was heading to the Squire to meet some friends after work." Julia had a tiny shop on Main Street that sold jewelry, much of it custom designs that she made herself. She'd opened the shop two years ago, after working in Hyannis for five years at a big jeweler in the Cape Cod Mall. Alison and Chris were both proud of how well she was doing. Julia wasn't getting rich, but she was able to support herself and loved her work. It helped that she still lived at home while she was getting the business up and running. But that was about to change. She'd just signed a lease on a condo and was moving out in two weeks.

"Is she still seeing that guy?" Chris frowned as he lifted his beer to take a sip.

"Kyle? Yes, she is." Alison wasn't a fan of Kyle's either. He was always polite to her, but there was something about him that she just didn't warm up to. He was quiet, almost too quiet. And he rode a huge Harley, not that there was anything wrong with driving a motorcycle, but she cringed whenever Julia joined him and climbed on the back and wrapped her arms around him. Alison had been afraid of motorcycles ever since she saw a terrible accident years ago, where a guy going a little too fast didn't see a divider and plowed into it. She read the next day that he didn't survive. So, she couldn't help the irrational fear every time she saw Julia on the back of his motorcycle.

"Well, at least she's not moving in with him, yet. There's that," Chris said.

"True." Alison had been pleasantly surprised when Julia said she was moving out but getting her own place. "She says he's a great guy, and we just have to give him a chance. Maybe once we get to know him better, we'll like him."

Chris said nothing in response, just picked up his beer and took a sip.

"I talked to Jess this morning. I think she might come for a longer visit this summer, hopefully a month or so." She hoped her best friend really would come for an extended visit. Jess sounded more stressed and miserable each time she talked to her. It would do her good to get away.

"That will be nice for both of you. It's been a while since I've seen Jess."

Usually she made it home at least once a year, if not during the summer then around the holidays. But they'd skipped last year; work and schedules didn't align.

"I think she really needs it. Hopefully, she will bring Caitlin, too."

"And Parker, of course," Chris added.

Alison shook her head. "No, I don't think Parker is on the guest list for Chatham this year."

Chapter 4

"ere you go. See how it fits." Julia Page handed the custom-made gold wedding ring to Amy, her client. Julia held her breath while Amy slipped it on her finger and then turned her hand to inspect it closely. The ring was a wide solid-gold band with a hammered and sculpted wave design set with two full carats of diamonds, with a big one in the center and small ones surrounding it. The wedding bands matched perfectly with a similar wave design. Julia thought it was the most beautiful design she'd made yet, and she hoped that Amy would like it.

Amy looked up and her eyes were damp. "Oh, Julia, it's perfect. I don't want to take it off."

Julia laughed. "You don't have to. It's your wedding ring. I'm so glad you like it." Amy's fiancé, Steve, had proposed with a cheap costume-jewelry ring and then sent her in to see Julia to design the ring of her dreams. Julia packed up the jewelry box and a few cleaning cloths in a small bag and handed it to Amy. "When is the wedding?" she asked.

"Three months from this Saturday. I think I'm all set, but it seems like there's always one more thing to do. But now that I have the rings, I can relax. All the big stuff is done."

"Well, enjoy and thank you. Please thank Steve for me, too."

She'd have to thank Kyle again when she saw him, since Steve was his friend. This was her most expensive custom sale yet. And it had come just in time. It had been a slower than usual month and Julia had thought she might need to dip into her savings, but now she wouldn't have to.

She opened her small shop on Chatham's Main Street two years ago, after working for a national jeweler at the Cape Cod Mall for years. She'd worked her way up to store manager and she'd learned a lot. That job had taught her the business side of things and paid the bills, while she made jewelry on the side.

At first the jewelry making had been a fun hobby. But often when she wore one of her pieces, friends and sometimes even strangers asked where they could buy them. So, she began to sell a little here and there. After a few years, her income from the jewelry hobby was a bit more than her salary as the store manager. She'd managed to save some money, since she'd been still living at home. Once she had enough saved, she decided to take the plunge and open her own shop.

It was a much better fit for her, as Julia wasn't the corporate type. She preferred to dress more creatively, and the first thing she did when she left the big jewelry store was to dye the bottom half of her curly blondish-brown hair a pretty turquoise. It was a fun color and it made her happy when she caught a glimpse of it in the mirror. She'd put her own stamp on her small shop, too, and gave it a fun, funky feel with vases of bright pink flowers on the counters and paintings on the walls from local artists.

She had jazzy Norah Jones music playing in the background, and she made the jewelry right there in the shop, while sitting behind the counter, and occasionally glancing out the window to people-watch. She was happy in her small shop, and though it was a little scary at first to clean out her savings to start the business, it was going well—well enough that she'd been able to pay herself back and finally move out of her mother's house to her own place.

There were still ups and downs, though, as she was better at making the jewelry than marketing it. As much as she enjoyed running her own business, the pressure of generating a steady income, one that would pay all the bills every month, was stressful at times.

Her stomach growled as her phone rang, and she was surprised to see that it was nearly two. She'd lost track of time and worked right through lunch, again. She was working on a spec piece, a very expensive sculpted gold bangle bracelet that she was going to enter into a contest of sorts. It was a bit of a risk, though, as the materials were expensive, and if her bracelet was selected, she wouldn't be paid for it. One of the biggest celebrity fashion influencers, Kaia Kensington, was going to select her favorite piece. Kaia wearing the jewelry would give Julia, or whoever won the contest, exposure on Kaia's Instagram and other social media.

Her boyfriend, Kyle, had told her she was crazy to work for free when she'd floated the idea of entering the contest, and she hadn't mentioned it again. But she had a gut feeling that if her piece was selected, that kind of exposure could be huge for her little shop.

"Hey, just checking in. We're still on for dinner tonight? I told Kevin we'd be over at seven."

"Right, of course." Julia had completely forgotten about the dinner that Kyle had mentioned weeks ago. She liked Kevin, and his girlfriend, Sue, was one of her close friends. Though she hoped they wouldn't ask when Julia and Kyle were going to get engaged. It seemed like everyone was asking that lately, and Julia was sick of it. Especially because Kyle already had asked, just a few weeks ago, and she'd said, "Not yet." She just wasn't ready to make that commitment—and she hadn't mentioned the proposal to anyone because she didn't want to be questioned about why she didn't accept.

They'd only been dating for a year. She liked Kyle a lot. On some days she even thought she probably loved him. But she wasn't sure she was "in love" with him. She'd never actually been in love before, though, so sometimes she wondered if she would recognize the feeling when it happened. Maybe this was love. Her gut told her there was something more, though, and she just wasn't feeling it yet. She hoped that in time she would. Because she really did like Kyle.

She knew neither one of her parents was crazy about him, but she thought that they just hadn't spent enough time with him. Once they did, she was sure, they'd come around.

On paper, Kyle did seem perfect. He was handsome, they usually had fun together, and he had a good job—he worked in product engineering as a technical product manager for a software company. One of the few software companies on Cape Cod.

Julia thought back to the night she and Kyle met. She'd been out with Sue and a few other friends for after-work drinks at the Chatham Squire, their favorite local restaurant-bar. It was right on Main Street, just a few doors down from Julia's shop. The food was good and there were always live bands on the weekends. It was a Friday night and the bar was packed. She'd gone to the bar to get her first beer of the night and when she'd turned around Kyle literally walked into her and her beer spilled all down the front of his shirt.

It was his fault, but she still felt awful that she'd drenched him with the beer. He mopped himself up and insisted on buying her a new drink. He was there with friends, and while he was ordering their drinks, she'd noticed that he was cute, too. They'd ended up chatting most of the night and before he left, he asked for her number, and they'd been dating ever since. She smiled at the memory.

There were times, though, when she felt like she only knew one side of Kyle—he was sometimes moody and distant. When she questioned him on it, he usually just said he was thinking about work and sometimes there was a lot of pressure that went along with his job. The moods never did last long. It was too soon to know if he was the one, but she hoped that he might be.

Chapter 5

Jess pulled a cozy fleece blanket around her and snuggled into her favorite plush chair in the living room. The TV was on, but she couldn't focus on the show. She'd tried to read a book earlier but that was no easier. She reached for the mug of chamomile tea that had long since grown cold. It was supposed to relax her, make her sleepy. But she couldn't go to bed until Parker got home. She glanced at the clock, a few minutes past eleven. He didn't usually stay out this late. But Jess suspected he dreaded coming home and finally having the talk they'd both been putting off.

She'd known that their marriage was in trouble and had been for a long time. But she hadn't expected that Parker would actually cheat. She really thought she'd imagined that worry, as it hadn't made sense before. She was always with Parker, either at work or home. He sometimes stayed late or went to the gym after work, but never for more than a few hours, so she'd had no real reason to suspect he was being unfaithful.

But now it all made sense. She'd never thought twice about him working late or taking a long lunch, because she was right there. But so was Linda. It was such a cliché, having an affair with his secretary. But, she supposed the opportunity was hard to resist. She understood it, even though she thought it was weak and despicable of him.

All night, while waiting for him, she'd replayed the scene in the office over and over in her mind—seeing that swell of Linda's stomach when she lifted her arm and her shirt rose up. The look of sheer adoration on Parker's face when he watched her touch her stomach. And then horror when he realized Jess had seen it, too.

She'd called Alison as soon as she got home, and they'd talked for over an hour. Jess quickly agreed when Alison suggested again that she take some extended time off and stay with her mother, in Chatham.

"You're always welcome to stay with me, of course. But I'm sure your mother would want you with her."

"Yeah, and I owe her a visit. And I think Caitlin will probably come with me. She had a rough day, too." She told Alison how her daughter had lost both her job and her boyfriend within a few hours.

"Oh, the poor kid." Alison laughed. "I know she's not a kid, she's the same age as Julia, but they'll always be our babies."

When they hung up, Jess called her mother and gave her a brief version of what had happened. She smiled as her mother's immediate response echoed Alison's. When Jess finished the call, she got online and checked out flights to Boston. JetBlue was having a good sale and it seemed like a sign. She reserved two one-way tickets, figuring they could figure out when they wanted to come back later, when they were ready. Before she confirmed the flights, though, she went upstairs and knocked softly on Caitlin's door. Caitlin called to come in, and Jess stepped inside.

"How would you feel about going to Chatham next week and staying for a month or so? You don't have to rush back for anything, do you?"

Caitlin sat up and looked confused. "A month? What's going on? Is Dad coming, too?"

Jess hesitated. She didn't want to get into too much detail with her daughter, especially as she hadn't talked to Parker yet.

"No, your father is not joining us."

Caitlin nodded sadly.

"You're getting a divorce, aren't you?"

"We haven't discussed that," Jess said truthfully. "I could use a longer break. I didn't take any time off yet this year other than a long weekend. And we missed going last year."

Caitlin nodded. "I'd love to go and get away for a while, too. I need to think about what I'm going to do next."

"Good. You can think about it in Chatham. I'll book our flights."

Jess went back downstairs, opened her laptop, and confirmed two one-way tickets to Boston. She'd pick up a rental car there and drive to the Cape. When they were ready, in a month or so, they could book their return trip.

She made herself a new cup of hot tea and returned to her seat. A moment later, the front door opened. Parker was home.

He walked into the living room, glanced her way, but she said nothing. He sighed and collapsed into his favorite recliner. He looked at her again and rubbed his eyebrows hard, his usual tell when he was stressed. She waited and finally he spoke.

"Jess, I messed up. I don't even know what to say. I've been wanting to come clean for a while, but I just couldn't bring myself to have the conversation."

"When did it start?" Jess asked.

He seemed surprised by the question. "I don't know, maybe five or so months ago."

"So right after Linda started?"

"I guess so. Not too long after that. But, it doesn't mean anything. I don't know what I was thinking. You know things were off with us. We'd grown apart, distant, but I never meant to hurt you."

Jess made a face. "Well, it's a little late for that."

"I know. I'm so sorry. I want to make it up to you, though. I swear it won't happen again."

Jess stared at him. "You really think this is fixable? You didn't just sleep with someone else. You're having a baby together. What does she think is happening?"

Parker's cheeks flushed red.

"She thinks you're going to be together, doesn't she?"

He said nothing, just looked like he wanted to crawl away.

"Parker, I agree that things were off with us, but I didn't expect this of you. She's not much older than Caitlin."

"She's three years older."

Jess shook her head in disgust. "So, here's what's going to happen. Caitlin and I are going to Chatham next week and we're staying for a month, at least."

"You're leaving? What does that mean for us? I really want to work things out, Jess. I love you."

She shook her head. "You have a funny way of showing it. I'm going to officially take a leave of absence from the office. We'll talk further in a few weeks. I just want to go sit on the beach, drink a piña colada, and not think about anything."

He nodded. "Okay."

Jess stood, ready to head upstairs. "You can sleep in the guest bedroom tonight or on the sofa, your choice."

He stared after her, looking sadder then she'd ever seen him. She held it together until she closed her bedroom door behind her and collapsed on her bed. The tears she'd been holding in came hard and fast, and she cried for the marriage she'd once thought would last forever. It made her even sadder that Parker said he wanted to work things out. She didn't see how that was possible. How could she ever trust him again?

Chapter 6

Caitlin met three of her closest friends for brunch on Sunday. She and her mother were flying to Boston on Tuesday. She was looking forward to it; her friends were less enthused.

"What are you going to do in Chatham for a month?" Meghan asked.

Caitlin glanced around the table at her three friends. They were at 82 Queen, one of their favorite downtown restaurants. Everyone looked great. Meghan was a natural blonde and quite proud of it. Her hair fell to her shoulders in casual beach waves that she'd spent close to an hour to perfect. She was the newlywed of the group and the one who was most focused on appearances.

"Nancy's party is coming up soon. You don't want to miss that. Everyone will be there and there should be some eligible single men," Meghan added. Nancy Hannigan's summer party was always a highlight, and everyone who was anyone in Charleston would be there. Caitlin couldn't bring herself to care, though.

"Meghan's right," Ashley agreed. "Don't you want to get right back out there? I'm hearing Match.com is pretty good lately." Ashley and Beth, her other two friends, both married their college boyfriends, and she knew they were disappointed for her. They'd all expected Prescott to propose. They were both pretty brunettes and almost looked like sisters with their similar shiny, long bobs and Lilly Pulitzer sundresses.

"No, I really don't want to get right back out there," Caitlin said. "I want to eat lobster rolls, go to the beach, and not think about anything. It sounds heavenly to me."

"But what about getting a new job? Won't it be harder if you wait?" Beth added. "Plus, I'll miss you. Do you really have to go for a whole month?"

That made Caitlin smile. Beth was a sweetheart. She'd miss her, too, but she needed this time away.

"It's not like I have a defined career track. I was planning to just sign up with the temp agency again and I can do that anytime."

Beth frowned. "What's really going on? You're not telling us everything."

"You're right." And so Caitlin told them. It was going to come out anyway, but she made them promise to keep it to themselves.

"Okay, now I get it, why you both want to get away. Your poor mother," Beth said. The other two nodded and looked sympathetic.

"Things haven't been good with them for a while, so I wasn't surprised to hear that my mother was thinking of separating, but neither one of us expected this. My father is an idiot. She's only three years older than me."

Meghan reached for her mimosa and took a sip before saying, "Maybe it's a midlife crisis. That's what men that age do. My father did something similar a few years ago. But he and my mother worked it out. Maybe your parents will, too?"

"I doubt that. But you never know, I guess." Caitlin couldn't imagine her mother getting past what her father had done, especially with a baby involved.

♥

And yet, her father told her the same thing, that he hoped to work it out with her mother. They sat at breakfast the next morning, and over coffee her father finally addressed the situation. He hadn't said a thing to her yet and it was getting awkward, as almost a week had gone by and they were leaving the next day.

"So, I guess your mother told you what's going on?" he finally said.

"She did. It was disappointing to hear." Caitlin wasn't going to let him off easy. It was a huge disappointment. She loved her father and thought he was better than this.

"I'm sorry, honey. I don't have a good excuse. Things weren't great with your mother and me, but still, it never should have happened. I told your mother I want to work things out. I hope she gives me another chance."

Caitlin felt her eyes well up. The whole situation was just so sad. Even though her father had been an idiot, she still felt badly for both of them, though she also felt mad at her father, too. He really had blown it. She didn't know what to say to him. So, she just gave him a hug.

"I think it's good that we're getting away for a while."

He nodded. "I'll miss you both."

Chapter 7

Jess and Caitlin left Tuesday morning for a 7:00 A.M. flight to Boston. Parker offered to drive them to the airport but Jess wanted no part of that. She and Caitlin took an Uber, had a smooth flight, and soon after landing in Boston picked up their rental car and set off for the Cape. It was early enough that they missed the rush-hour traffic going through the city. The sun was shining and it was a nice drive.

A little over an hour later, they reached the Cape Cod Canal, and though it had been many years since Jess lived on the Cape, she still breathed a sigh of relief when she crossed the bridge that separated the mainland from Cape Cod. This time she felt it a little more strongly than usual—that sense that she was almost home.

Forty-five minutes later, they pulled into the driveway of her mother's Chatham house. Where Jess had grown up. The house wasn't directly on the water, but it was on a hill and had some pretty, distant views of the ocean. It was a big, square house, white with gray shutters. There was a wraparound farmer's porch and there were two floors, four bedrooms total. She was surprised to see that her mother's car wasn't in the driveway. She had told her what time they were arriving.

But Jess had a key. Maybe her mother had just run to the store.

They brought their bags in and went upstairs. Jess put hers in her old bedroom and Caitlin in the guest bedroom that she always used. Jess unpacked a few things and put them away, then stopped when she heard the front door open.

She and Caitlin went downstairs to see her mother standing by the front door wearing knee-high rubber boots and long shorts, with her big camera hung on a wide strap around her neck. Her whitish-blond hair was in a ponytail and she had several stray leaves on her sweatshirt. She looked like she'd just walked out of the bushes. She pulled them both in for a hug when they reached her.

"Have you been here long? I'm sorry I wasn't here when you arrived. I lost track of time."

"Where were you?" Jess asked.

Her mother smiled. "I heard there was a family of geese down at the cranberry bog and I wanted to see if could get some good shots. Take a look." She held the camera out so they could see the image.

"Oh, that's adorable," Caitlin said.

"It really is," Jess agreed. It was a gorgeous shot. Her mother had a gift for photography. She'd always dabbled in it when they were younger, and then somewhere along the way it turned into a career. She had developed quite a following for family portraits and local scenic pictures that she sold online and at galleries in town.

Her mother pulled off her boots, brushed the leaves off her sweater, and carefully lifted her camera and set it on a side table. Then she looked back at her daughter and granddaughter. "Are you hungry? I have chicken stew in the slow cooker."

It wasn't quite five yet. "I'm not starving yet," Jess said, and Caitlin nodded in agreement.

"Well, how about a glass of wine, then? We can sit on the porch and catch up. Caitlin, why don't you grab that bowl of nuts, in case we feel like nibbling on something?"

Her mother poured a glass of rosé for each of them and they

settled on the front porch around a glass-topped blue wicker table. Caitlin set the nuts in the middle of the table. They talked about everything under the sun except the situation with Parker. Jess had already told her mother everything, and neither one of them wanted to rehash it in front of Caitlin. So, instead her mother filled them in on all the local gossip.

"Remember Lavinia O'Toole? She's back in town. Moved home a few months ago. Her mother's not well, and I think she's either separated or divorced now, not sure which."

Jess did remember Lavinia. They'd been in the same year, and she was the last person Jess would have expected to move home to sleepy Chatham. The Cape was a wonderful place to grow up, but outside of tourism, opportunities were somewhat limited and many kids couldn't wait to get "off the Cape" once they graduated.

Lavinia had been the class valedictorian and homecoming queen. She was a pretty blonde, type A, and had always been sort of stuck-up. Last she'd heard, Lavinia had a high-powered job in Boston and was married with several beautiful blond children. Though Jess supposed they were probably around Caitlin's age by now. Grown-ups.

"I'm surprised she came back," Jess said.

"I don't know the details, but she's going through a divorce. Too bad you two weren't close. I bet she could use a friend."

"Yeah, too bad," Jess said. She was too busy feeling sorry for herself to worry about Lavinia, who had never given her or Alison the time of day. She was looking forward to spending time with her best friend. "Have you seen Alison around town at all?"

"I ran into her just last week actually, at Stop and Shop. I know she's excited to see you. You should stop in to her daughter's store while you're here, too. I was there a few weeks back and bought a lovely bracelet. Julia is very talented. I bet she'd love to see Caitlin."

Jess glanced at her daughter and Caitlin just smiled. She and Julia had never been close. Jess and Alison had hoped their daughters would be best friends, and every year when they saw each other, they waited for it to happen, but it never did. Their girls were just too different.

Caitlin was a typical Southern girl, always with perfectly done hair and makeup and impeccably dressed—she'd loved fashion for as long as Jess could remember. She'd also loved going to the country club with them and took lessons in both tennis and golf from a young age. And she'd always been popular with the boys.

Julia was the complete opposite. She was not a girly-girl. She was more artsy, and Jess thought she had never set foot in a country club and likely had no desire to. Her boyfriends had always been artsy, too, musicians or writers. The two girls just didn't seem to have anything in common, much to Jess's and Alison's disappointment.

They had a little more wine, and eventually got hungry and went inside for big bowls of chicken stew before settling in the living room, continuing to chat and watch TV for a bit. Jess was glad to see that her mother looked well. She was almost seventy-nine but looked nearly ten years younger. She was in good health, other than the year after Jess's father had died, when her mother dealt with some depression. It was a hard adjustment for all of them, but especially her mother, who'd lost her partner of more than fifty years.

But that was nearly ten years ago now and her mother seemed to be thriving. She still worked as much or as little as she wanted to and she kept busy socially, too. She was in several groups that met regularly and had a circle of friends that she saw often. Jess suspected that she might actually be dating, too, but she hadn't admitted it yet.

Just recently when Alison went out to dinner, as she left the restaurant she'd noticed Jess's mother and a gentleman at a cozy table for two. They were deep in conversation, so she hadn't wanted to interrupt them. Her mother hadn't mentioned anything to Jess, so she hadn't brought it up either. She figured if her mother wanted to mention it, she would.

And right now her mother's attention was on her granddaughter. "So, Caitlin, how are you doing? You're quieter than usual. Are you just tired from traveling?"

"Partly. It's been a hard week, Grammy." Caitlin filled her grandmother in on losing both her job and her boyfriend on the same day. Jess's mother reached out and gave Caitlin's hand a squeeze.

"You're better off without both of them, dear. I know it's hard to see it now, but everything really does happen for a reason."

Caitlin sighed. "I know. I thought of you actually and I've been telling myself that. I think it's just hard now because all of my friends are settled in their careers and I'm the last single one of the bunch. They're all married." She smiled and sniffled a little at the same time. "I kind of feel like a loser lately, to be honest."

"Oh Caitlin, that's ridiculous. You're lucky to be single. There's no need to rush," Jess assured her.

Caitlin shook her head. "You always knew what you wanted to do. And you got married at twenty-four, four years after meeting Dad. You knew." Caitlin's eyes were suspiciously red and she sounded utterly miserable.

"I'm so sorry, honey. I didn't realize you were so upset. I do agree with your grandmother. It just wasn't your time, for the job or the guy. And I do understand. Yes, I got married young, but maybe it was too young. Most of my friends that married young have divorced."

"There's a lot to be said for waiting until you're a little older and really sure," her grandmother added. "You weren't madly in love with this one, though, were you?"

"No. I wasn't. But he was pretty perfect on paper. Good family, and job, handsome, easy to get along with. And we'd been together exactly a year. It seemed like the next logical step."

"Love isn't logical, honey. Did you feel sparks? Think about him all the time?" her grandmother asked.

There was a long pause before Caitlin finally chuckled. "No, the sparks were never there. I thought maybe, in time, they'd come." She looked at Jess. "Did you and Dad have that spark?"

Jess smiled. "We did. We were pretty much inseparable all through school. I don't regret marrying your father. We just grew apart over the years. It happens."

Jess's mother looked at both of them. "I'm so glad you're both here and that you're not rushing back. Take some time to just relax. Go to the beach. Jess, you always loved spending long afternoons on the beach. I don't remember the last time you did that. We're always so busy it seems when you come to visit, trying to do so much, see so many people." She took a sip of her wine and smiled. "Slow down, both of you, and just let the sun make you feel better. And good food of course."

❦

Caitlin was a night owl and stayed up watching TV long after Jess and her mother went up to bed. But the next morning, while Caitlin was sleeping in, it gave Jess and her mother a chance to talk over coffee in the kitchen.

"How are you really doing? I know things weren't great with the two of you, but this is a disappointment. I wouldn't have expected it of Parker," her mother said.

Jess took a sip of her coffee. It was a smooth dark roast and exactly what she needed. "That's a good word. We had our problems, I just didn't think he'd ever cheat. And with someone so much younger. She's only a few years older than Caitlin."

"Will he marry her, do you think?"

Jess shuddered at the thought. Would he?

"He says he wants to work things out with me. But, I don't see how that's possible. I had been thinking of asking him for a divorce or maybe counseling. It's too late for that now, though."

Her mother looked thoughtful. "Some people do make it work, but with a baby coming, that could be challenging."

Jess laughed. "Impossible, really. I am going to ask for a divorce, but I'm not going to do anything right away. I figured I'd make him stew a bit."

"I don't blame you. No need to rush into anything. Take some time off and just relax. You haven't taken a real vacation in a long time."

Her mother was right. "No, I haven't. I am looking forward to hitting the beach and playing tourist. Maybe taking a drive to Orleans. Alison said she found a place there that has the best fish tacos."

"Guapo's."

"You've been there? Maybe we could go there for lunch today— me, you, and Caitlin. That could be fun. Do a little shopping after. That boutique you like, If the Shoe Fits, recently moved to Chatham, right on Main Street."

Her mother smiled. "I'd love that."

Chapter 8

Alison grabbed a coffee on her way to work. There was a kitchen in the office and company coffee, but it was terrible. Other than the coffee, though, she had no complaints. She'd felt lucky to get her job at the magazine many years ago and still enjoyed it. It was a nice group of people that worked there, too. Many had been there almost as long as Alison, and it felt like family. Jim was a big reason for that. He was a little older than Alison, and he and his father had started the magazine together.

In its heyday, the magazine did very well. The pages were thick and glossy and gorgeous. Many local businesses, and national ones, too, advertised. Some of the construction and real estate firms took out full-page ads that were beautiful and effective for them. But over the years, the magazine's circulation shrank, and in-store purchases were way down. It was now half the size that it used to be.

Alison knew it was the same all over the country. People were just moving away from print and consuming most of their news online. She walked by Jim's office on the way to her own and noticed that he was on the phone again with his door closed, but she could see his expression through the glass pane and he looked upset.

There had been other calls like that lately, and Jim seemed

stressed in general. He never said much to her, but she could tell he was worried about the health of the business. They all were.

She settled at her desk, opened up her laptop, and started checking email. She had a lot to do, and before she knew it several hours had passed. She was thinking of going out for a sandwich when Jim popped his head in her office.

"You busy?"

"Not right now. I was going to grab some lunch. What's up?"

"Want some company? I need to get out of the office and stretch my legs. We could run over to the Squire?"

"Sure." Jim almost never went to lunch. Alison wondered what his earlier call had been about and if it had anything to do with his mood now, which was unsettled and pensive.

He drove, and a few minutes later they were sitting in the Squire, sipping sodas and waiting for their clam chowder and fish sandwiches.

"It has been a week," Jim said. "Our accountant called this morning and the numbers are not good. They've been trending down each quarter."

Alison sensed where this was going. "You have to do more layoffs?"

He sighed. "I really don't want to. We're down to a bare-bones staff now. I've been wrestling with this for a while, trying to figure out another way. Realistically, it doesn't look like revenues are going to increase any time soon."

Alison just nodded. She didn't know what to say. He looked so miserable, and he was a good man. She knew it pained him to let people go. But she didn't have answers for him. Eventually, she supposed, he wouldn't have a choice.

"I wanted to bounce an idea off you. It won't work for everyone, depending on their situation, but maybe for some, it could be a way to avoid a layoff. I was thinking maybe we could go to part-time with some roles. With the decrease in sales volume, there is less to do overall, so it could work, if people were on board."

"That might be a possibility for some." Alison thought of her own situation and how she'd considered taking on some freelance work if she had to. "How soon were you thinking?"

"Oh, not immediately. Not for at least a month or two. Do you think anyone would go for it?" He looked nervous asking the question. She knew that some wouldn't be able to consider it and would probably start looking immediately. She also knew there were a few that really needed that job and might have a hard time replacing it. She could probably get by if she went to part-time. She had some savings, and though it would be stepping out of her comfort zone, she could try to get some freelance editing work.

"It's hard to say. It definitely won't work for some. But there's a few that might be okay with it."

He nodded. "That's what I thought. I figured I'd chat with everyone and feel them out before I make any decisions."

Alison took a deep breath, debating for a moment whether it was smart or not to volunteer herself. It would be easier for her to stay, and she loved working at the magazine. But for some of the others, this would be a crushing blow. It felt selfish not to offer. "I'd be okay going to part-time. I've been thinking about starting to do some freelance work and this would free up time for that." For a brief moment, the bookshop flashed in her mind's eye—an image of herself behind the register where Ellen Campbell had been earlier. Alison sighed. Maybe someday that dream would come true, but for now it looked like freelance editing was in her future.

Jim looked surprised and a bit relieved. "Are you sure? It wouldn't be for at least another month or so, and depending what's going on, there could be more to do some weeks."

Alison's workload had slowed quite a bit in recent months. If she organized her time well, she could probably still get most of it done, and if not, there were others who could help.

"I'm sure. I think it's a good solution, Jim. It will let you keep more people working, even if it's in a reduced capacity."

He relaxed a little. "I never wanted to lay anyone off. Never imagined that I'd have to. Business was booming for so long." She understood his frustration. Who would have imagined that the internet would kill the magazine business? Newspapers, too, though they had adapted better to online sales. Jim had tried to launch a digital version of the magazine, but it never really took off. People looking for decorating and real estate ideas went other places online, like Houzz and Realtor.com.

They changed the subject as their food arrived and spent the next half hour laughing and talking about a range of subjects. Alison had always found Jim easy to talk to. They shared a similar outlook on local politics and the arts and he was an accomplished writer, too. She'd always enjoyed his monthly column in the magazine, and he'd been talking about writing a book for as long as she'd known him.

"How's the book coming along?" He hadn't mentioned it lately.

"Funny you should ask. I actually started writing again recently. Not a lot, but a few pages here and there. It's a historical mystery set here in Chatham involving a shipwreck." His eyes lit up as he spoke, and Alison smiled.

"That sounds right up your alley. I'd love to read it, when it's ready."

He laughed, and then his gaze held hers, his look warm and appreciative. "It may be a while. But eventually, I will need an editor."

Chapter 9

On the way back to Chatham, after lunch at Guapo's in Orleans—and they really were the best fish tacos Jess had ever had—Alison called and invited them all to dinner that night. Her mother already had plans to visit a friend, but Jess and Caitlin were happy to go. They decided to stop downtown and walk around Main Street a bit, to window-shop and pick up a bottle of wine to bring to dinner.

Main Street in Chatham looked like it was straight out of a Hallmark movie—the quintessential small-town street packed with cute shops and happy tourists walking along taking in the sights. Jess felt a bit like a tourist herself, as it had been a few years since she'd strolled down Main Street. She noticed there were some new shops to explore in addition to her old familiar favorites.

"That's Julia's shop," her mother said as they drew near the bookstore. Just before it was a tiny jewelry shop.

"Let's go in and say hello." Jess opened the door, and her mother and Caitlin followed her inside. Julia looked up from behind the counter and smiled when she saw them. She was helping a customer, so they roamed around and explored the store. It was small, but lovely. Soft jazz music was playing in the background and there were green plants and vibrant pink flowers here and there.

The shop had a pretty, welcoming feel. But it was Julia's jewelry that was the star.

"That's like the bracelet that I got." Her mother pointed to a gold bangle bracelet that looked like sculpted waves. It was gorgeous. Caitlin found a pair of earrings that she loved and Jess saw a bracelet that was similar to the one her mother got, but with a different design. When Julia finished with her customer, they made their way over to her.

"Hi, honey," Jess said. "My mother told me your store was lovely. She's right."

Julia came out from behind the counter and gave Jess a big hug.

"Thank you. It's great to see you all. Mom told me you were coming for a month or so." She nodded at Caitlin, who smiled back.

"Your stuff is gorgeous, Julia. It must be exciting to have your own store," Caitlin said.

"It is," Julia said as she went back behind the counter. "Business has been steady, so I'm feeling very lucky and relieved," she admitted.

"Well, your work is beautiful. So I am not surprised at all. We both found a few pieces we'd like to get," Jess said. She pointed them out, and Julia boxed them up and Jess put it on her charge card. Caitlin tried to give her cash, but Jess waved it away. "It's my treat, this time. We both deserve something nice, I think."

Caitlin looked grateful. "We do. Thank you."

"My mother called just before you came in and invited me over tonight. She said you're coming as well?"

Jess smiled. "We are. We will see you soon, then."

Caitlin took a final look around Julia's shop before they left. She was impressed. Her shop was full of beautiful things, many of them pieces that Julia had actually made. It must be nice to have that kind of talent and be able to make a living from it. Caitlin felt a pang of envy and frustration, as she was still so far from figuring out what she should be doing with her life. And Julia was the last person she would have expected to be this successful doing something she loved.

Though Julia still looked as unconventional as ever, with her long, wavy brown hair—and the turquoise tint on the bottom six inches. It was a very artsy, creative look, and Caitlin had to admit Julia pulled it off. But it would never fly with her crowd in Charleston. Caitlin couldn't imagine showing up in public with turquoise hair color. She'd never live it down—and probably never be invited out again. There were certain expectations, and everyone she knew wanted to make sure they met them.

They stopped in the bookstore next door to Julia's shop. Jess had always loved browsing the shelves of the bookstore, which had been in Chatham for as long as she could remember. And Ellen Campbell, the store owner, was behind the register, smiling as she rang up a sale and handed change to a customer. Her hair was a preppy, snowy-white, chin-length bob and she had a pencil stuck behind one ear and reading glasses on a chain around her neck. She smiled when she saw Jess's mother. They'd known each other for years. Ellen had to be in her late seventies and she looked tired.

"Well, look who's back in town. Nice to see you all," Ellen called out to them. Another customer went to the register, so they made their way around the store. There was a good selection of books, all the newest bestsellers as well as interesting nonfiction and a whole section for local authors. Artwork hung on the walls from local artists, too, which gave the shop a creative and artsy feel.

Jess's mother and Caitlin wandered off to browse, and Jess went straight to her favorite spot—the magical hideaway in the back of the Chatham bookstore where almost no one went, but where she and Alison had spent so many afternoons reading and dreaming about their futures, while Alison's mother worked the register.

They used to lie on the floor, each holding a romance novel

they weren't supposed to read because they were too young but Alison had grabbed off the shelf when no one was looking. Her mother would not be happy if she caught them.

They often discussed what they wanted to be when they grew up.

Even then, Jess had known what she wanted to do—at least when it came to her career.

"I want to be a lawyer, I think. Yes, definitely, a lawyer. What about you?"

"Maybe I'll own a bookstore someday. How cool would that be?" Alison would rip open a bag of Goldfish, the snack they had almost every day without fail, washed down with Diet Cokes.

Jess could see it clearly, even though it was so long ago. Alison absentmindedly playing with one of her braids. Jess remembered when they were twelve and Alison had just had six inches cut off her hair, but it still hung in a long braid halfway down her back. Jess was a little envious of that hair; it was thick, stick-straight, and blond. She and Alison were complete opposites in looks. Alison was small and blond, while Jess was tall, and her dark brown hair was long, too, but it was a tangle of wild curls that did what they wanted.

"I could see that. Or maybe you could write a book. You're good at writing," Jess said. Alison always got A's in English.

"I do like to write, but I don't know about a book, maybe a journalist or a teacher. I do know that I'll be married and have four kids by the time I'm thirty-five."

Jess laughed at that. "Really? Four kids? I don't ever want to get married or have kids. Well, maybe one, but I don't know."

"You don't want to get married? Why not? Everyone wants to get married."

"Not me. I want to have a career that I love, and to travel all over the world. But I think I'll want to mostly live here in Chatham or on the Cape, at least."

Jess's family had moved to Chatham from South Boston when

she turned ten. She didn't miss the crowded city with its smelly traffic and cement everywhere. She'd fallen in love with Chatham instantly—with its green lawns and trees and the fresh scent of the ocean. She loved the soft sand of the beaches and the cute Main Street with all the shops—where the bookstore was.

"I love Chatham, but I don't see myself staying here. I bet I'll go to school far away and live on the West Coast. I've always wanted to go to California." Alison had been born in Chatham, so she didn't know anything different. Jess could understand that she'd want to see what else was out there.

"Well, if you do move to California, you still have to come to Chatham every summer to visit me. Better yet, just stay in Chatham and we can live near each other and be best friends forever." Jess hated the thought of Alison living far away.

"Who knows where we'll end up. But even if we don't live near each other, we'll still always be best friends," Alison said.

♔

"Jess, are you ready to go?" Her mother walked over and Jess shut her memories down and picked up a few books she'd been wanting to read and brought them over to the register. Caitlin was already there and had a similar stack. They tended to like the same books and usually swapped them when they were done.

"My stack at home is towering, I'm good for a while," her mother said.

They got in line to pay for their books, and as Ellen rang them up her phone buzzed. She answered and turned her back to them so they couldn't hear what she said. When she hung up and turned to hand Jess her charge slip, she did not look happy. "That was my main employee, Brooklyn. She broke her leg and won't be able to come back to work for a few weeks." She sighed. "I think I am getting too old for this. You don't know anyone that needs a job by chance? I need to hire some part-time help right away."

Jess felt for her. She looked stressed out and exhausted. Her mother shook her head. "I'm sorry, I don't know of anyone. Maybe put an ad on that Craigslist?"

Ellen nodded. "That's a good idea."

"If you just need someone temporarily until Brooklyn comes back, I could help you. I've never worked in a bookstore before, but I've worked retail. And I love books." Caitlin volunteered herself to help, much to Jess's surprise.

"You don't have to work while you're here, honey. This is supposed to be a vacation for both of us."

Caitlin smiled. "It still will be, but I'll have plenty of time available while I'm here. I'd love to keep busy and do something. I think it could be fun."

Ellen looked relieved. "If you're sure, I'd love the help. And you're right, if you've done any retail, you can pick this up quickly. Loving books is the most important skill set. You could come in tomorrow at ten, if that's not too soon?"

"That's perfect." Caitlin glanced at her grandmother and Jess. "I'm sure I could borrow a car, or get a ride in. Or maybe even walk. I could use the exercise."

Jess smiled. It was over five miles from the bookstore to her mother's house. A long walk. "We'll figure that out."

Chapter 10

I know you said you've been liking rosé lately. I haven't had this one, but a woman in the wine store said it's really good." Jess handed the chilled bottle of wine to Alison. Her eyes lit up when she saw the label.

"Thank you. Whispering Angel is one of my favorites. I was about to open another bottle but let's have this one instead." She poured a glass for each of them. "Julia should be along any minute."

They took their drinks out onto Alison's patio, where she had a platter of guacamole and chips on a big round table. Alison's ex, Chris, was manning the grill and looked up when they stepped outside. He came over and gave them hugs.

"Great to see you both. How's Charleston?"

"Same as ever." Jess wasn't sure how much Alison had shared with him and didn't want to get into any details, so she just smiled. "How are things with you?"

"Good. Can't complain. How do you ladies like your steaks done? Medium okay? These are just about there."

"That's perfect," Jess said, and Caitlin agreed.

Chris moved the steaks off the grill and onto a platter and covered them with aluminum foil. "These need to rest for five minutes or so and then they'll be nice and juicy." He got himself a new beer and then joined them at the table. Julia arrived a few minutes later and helped her mother carry bowls of potato salad and corn on the cob from the kitchen to the patio.

They all helped themselves and then settled around the table. Jess thought it was interesting how comfortable Chris was at Alison's house. Sometimes it almost seemed like they were still married. She understood why they'd divorced, but she couldn't help wonder if things could be different now with them. They got along so well. But the few times she'd mentioned it to Alison she always laughed it off and said they were more like brother and sister now or best friends. There wasn't any hint of a romantic spark between them. Yet as far as Jess knew neither of them was dating anyone else.

The conversation flowed easily and there were plenty of laughs as they ate. But when they were just about done eating, the mood shifted as Alison told them about her lunch and that her job would be going part-time in a month or so.

"So, I thought I might try to build up a freelance-editing business," she said.

Jess frowned. "Is that what you really want to do?"

"Well, if I could do anything, I'd love to open a bookstore. That's always been a dream. But I'd need to win the lottery for that to happen, so this is my second-best option. It might be fun."

"It's too bad you can't buy the bookstore. Mrs. Campbell told me a few weeks ago that she'd love to retire if she could find someone to buy the business," Julia said.

"She's older than my mother. I really felt for her when she got the news that her employee broke her leg. She looked like she was so over it," Jess said.

Caitlin had already told them all over dinner that she had volunteered to help out at the store.

Alison looked thoughtful. "She mentioned to me when I

stopped in recently that she wants to sell the business, too. I wonder if there's any possible way that I could make that work?"

"You'd probably have to get a loan," Chris said.

"Right. That might be risky to take on, especially with my own job going part-time. What if the bookstore fails and then I'm stuck with a loan I can't pay back?"

An idea came to Jess. She wanted to mention it, but didn't want to get Alison's hopes up. She had some money saved. Depending on what Ellen Campbell wanted for the business, maybe it would make for a good investment and she could either co-own with Alison or give her a loan to take the business over. But, first she needed to talk to her accountant and run some numbers and make sure it made sense. And then she'd talk to Alison. She might not go for it still. Jess knew Alison was risk-averse, and even if it was Jess loaning the money, she might feel uneasy about taking on any loan.

"What's going on with the empty store next to the bookstore? Didn't that used to be a coffee shop?" Jess asked. She'd been surprised to see that spot empty, as it was right on the corner.

"Ellen owns that building, too. There is a small apartment above the coffee shop that is occupied. The owners of the coffee shop skipped town owing her several months' rent. She hasn't wanted to deal with re-renting it yet. She said ideally she'd like to sell the whole building, which is her shop and the café."

"Well, there's no way I could ever afford that," Alison said.

But Jess found that news even more intriguing. "That could be a good investment for someone," she said. "Depending what kind of business they wanted, they could make it one big space." Her mind was already busy thinking about the possibilities. It would mean an even bigger investment, but potentially more profitable.

"It would be cool if the bookstore and the coffee shop were connected. Like you could roam from one to the other. Buy your books, then go settle down with a coffee and read for a bit," Caitlin said.

"There's not many places along Main Street to get a good cup of coffee," Chris said. "I'm surprised that place didn't make it."

Julia made a face. "Their coffee really wasn't very good. Their pastries were stale and their prices were too high. I don't think they really knew what they were doing. They also weren't very friendly. I went there almost every day, and they never remembered me and I almost always got the same thing."

Alison looked deep in thought. "I think a coffee shop could do really well there," she said. "And I love Caitlin's idea to have it connected to the bookstore. So it could get walk-in business for coffee and traffic from people buying books. And people getting coffee might wander into the bookstore, too. That actually sounds heavenly to me." She sighed. "Maybe someday. . . . It will be interesting to see what happens to it."

"Wasn't there a different coffee shop there before that one?" Jess asked. "I remember they had pretty good coffee and raspberry bars that were delicious."

"That place was really busy all the time," Alison said. "I think the people that owned it sold the business to the ones that just left."

"Mrs. Campbell said they overpaid for it and had cash-flow issues. It was a married couple and now it looks like they might be getting a divorce. I think they just bailed on it, and will probably file for bankruptcy or whatever you do when you can't pay a loan," Julia said.

"Well, that's another consideration, too." Alison laughed. "My cash flow these days is pretty sad."

Chris caught Jess's eye and smiled. "Maybe you need a good partner. Imagine if you and Jess bought it together?"

Alison laughed again. "That would be awesome. I'm sure we'd have a blast. But Jess has her own life, and a career in Charleston. Maybe in twenty years when she retires, we can open a bookstore together."

Jess chose her words carefully. She wanted to be impulsive and say she was going to seriously consider it, but thought it best to hold off until she knew for sure whether she could swing it. She smiled big. "I'd really love that. I think we'd have a blast working together. I don't know when we can make it happen, but I'm in, at some point!" Jess lifted her glass and tapped it against Alison's. "To our future bookstore!"

"Oh, I'll drink to that!" Alison clinked her glass against Jess's and the others all chimed in, clinking glasses as well. Meanwhile, Jess's mind was spinning, mentally checking her bank balances and running some calculations. Depending on what Ellen Campbell wanted for the business and the building, there was a real chance this could work.

Chapter 11

For the first time in a very long time, Jess woke up excited for what the day might bring. She drove Caitlin to the bookshop at ten, and an hour later, when her mother went to run some errands and Jess had the house to herself, she called Mrs. Campbell to see if she was serious about selling.

"I did mention that to Alison the other day, and yes, I'm quite serious. I'd love to find a good buyer. I'll admit I'm slowing down some and I wouldn't mind sitting around and reading more myself."

"Well, I am interested, but I'm not sure if I can afford it. Did you have a price in mind?"

Mrs. Campbell mentioned a price that seemed fair and was in the range Jess had imagined it would be in. She'd done her research online to get a sense of what a fair price could be for both the building and the business. She also researched what a typical bookstore could expect to earn, though there was a wide range for that, too. Ellen also said she'd be happy to email over financials from the past few years for Jess to review. Jess still wasn't sure if she could swing it, but she felt a sense of hope that it might be possible.

"I'm very interested. I need to talk to my accountant and make sure the numbers work for us. If it does, what are you thinking of for timing?"

Mrs. Campbell laughed. "Honey, if you tell me you're seriously ready to buy this, we can close as soon as you want, and I'll start my retirement. I'm ready."

Jess smiled. "I'll get back to you in a few days, or sooner, once I know what I can do."

She ended the call with Mrs. Campbell, and pulled up her banking information. She looked over all of their accounts. She and Parker had always had separate bank accounts and also a joint account where they each contributed the same amount of money for all of their shared expenses, house, utilities, etc. They both always liked having their own accounts for personal spending and savings. They had access to each other's accounts, and Jess knew roughly what was in them. They were similar amounts, but she wanted to be sure before calling her accountant.

She checked her own account first, and the amount was as she remembered. There was enough there to buy the bookstore and have a good cushion, but she wanted her accountant, Lee's, blessing, especially given that she was getting divorced. She needed to make sure Parker's amount was still similar—so that when things got divided, the bookstore could come out of her half.

She didn't anticipate any surprises in Parker's account—but she supposed that she should have. He had two sizable withdrawals in the past two months—a check and then a much larger wired amount, both made out to Stern Realty Group, a local real estate firm they'd done lots of work with over the years. It looked like Parker had been buying property as well. Her mind spun, instantly assuming that he'd bought a house or condo for Linda and the baby—was he planning to live there, too?

Her first instinct was to call him and demand to know what the money was for. She reached for her phone, searched for his number, and then set it down on the desk. She was pretty sure what he'd done with that money. Did she really need to hear him say it? And did she want to invite the question as to why she was looking in his account? She didn't want him poking around in hers until she was ready for him to know about the bookstore. If he found out now, she worried that he might try to prevent the sale from happening.

❧

Two hours later, the email from Ellen Campbell came through. Jess opened the folders and looked over the financial statements. The income for the store was steady and healthy, though for the past few months the amount was a bit lower. Jess chalked that up to Ellen admitting that she was slowing down and hadn't been doing as much as she used to do. Once she and Alison took over, they could start those things up again, and she was sure it could be a great move for them.

So, she took a deep breath and called Lee, her accountant in Charleston, who was also a close friend. Lee did their taxes and advised on financial investments. She told Lee about the bookstore, what her investment would be, and that she'd be sending over the store's financials to review. At first, Lee was confused why Jess wanted to buy a business in Chatham, until Jess filled her in about Parker.

"I haven't told him yet, but I will be filing for divorce at some point."

"I'm sorry to hear that. So, you'll be moving to Chatham, then?"

"No! This is just an investment. I'll probably stay here through the summer and then head back to Charleston." It hadn't crossed her mind to do otherwise. After living there for over thirty years, she felt that Charleston was home.

"I'm going to have a business partner. We'll start it together and Alison will be able to run the business when I leave."

"So, you'll be going back to the law firm at the end of the summer?" Lee asked.

Jess realized she hadn't fully thought this all through. She'd assumed she'd go back to the law firm, but now she really couldn't picture working there with Parker, and his visibly pregnant assistant.

"No, I don't think I'll do that. I'll go to another firm, or maybe start my own. I still have to figure that out."

"Jess. Are you really sure about this bookstore investment? It's a lot of money and maybe the timing isn't the best. Maybe you want to be a little more settled and actually divorced before going in on something like this. It feels a little impulsive, and risky."

Jess sighed. "I know it sounds a little flaky, like I'm all over the place, but I really am serious about the bookstore. I'd like to do it. I just want to make sure I'm not overextending myself. I think the numbers work."

"You're probably right. I'll look this all over and shoot you an email with my thoughts in the morning."

"Great, thanks, Lee."

The next morning, a little before eight, Lee's email arrived.

> Jess, I went over everything and you're in a good position to do this, if you really want to. It will take a good chunk of your savings, but you'll still have a cushion and I'd advise you to pay cash and then get a line of credit on the business, so you'll have operating cash to work with. Her sales have been consistently steady—except for the past few months as you mentioned. I meant to ask yesterday, what does Parker think of this? You'll want to make sure you have his blessing or things could get messy once you do file for divorce—if he wants to be difficult.

Jess sighed. She knew Lee was right, but she didn't want to involve Parker. Not yet. They had a joint checking account and they each had their own savings accounts—and though she knew a court might disagree—she considered that money hers. Plus, when they divorced, she imagined they'd just split everything and she knew his savings was about the same size as hers. So, it should work out fine.

But, before she called Mrs. Campbell to make her an offer, she needed to talk to Alison. She needed to be fully on board if Jess was going to do this.

She texted her friend, Can you meet me for lunch at the Squire? I have some exciting news.

The text back came a second later: Love to. Meet you there at noon?

Alison was the first one to arrive at the Chatham Squire. The hostess showed her to a table and left two menus for them. Alison glanced at the menu while she waited for Jess, who she knew would be along any minute. Jess was always on time and Alison happened to be a few minutes early. It was so slow at the magazine that she'd jumped at the chance to get out for lunch and she was very curious about what Jess's good news might be. She'd picked up a sense of excitement, so she was pretty sure it was nothing relating to Parker. Jess came rushing over to the table a moment later.

"Have you been waiting long?" Jess glanced at her phone to check the time as she sat.

"No, not at all. I just got here. I'm dying to know, though, what's your big news?"

Jess smiled. "I think you'll be excited. At least I hope you will."

"Hi, ladies. Can I get you something to drink?" A waitress stood at the foot of their table, interrupting Jess's announcement.

"I'll just have water," Alison said.

"Same for me." As soon as the waitress walked off, Jess resumed talking.

"Okay, so you know how we were talking the other night about how we'd like to run a bookstore someday?"

Alison nodded.

Jess leaned forward, and her eyes lit up. "What if someday was now? What if I offered to buy Mrs. Campbell's shop and we could be business partners and run it?"

"Are you serious?" Alison felt a thrill as she imagined how fun it could be. But then reality came crashing down, and she sighed.

"How could we be business partners? I don't have any real money to contribute to a partnership."

"I know you don't. But I do. I heard from Lee this morning and I have the funds to do this, and when I leave at the end of the summer, I'll be leaving it in your hands to run. So I'm putting in the money and you'll put in the muscle. What do you think?"

Alison laughed. "I think you've lost your mind. I would love to do this, but it's too much. I can't let you spend all your money on my dream. I love you for even thinking of it, though."

The waitress returned with their waters and they put their food order in. They both ordered the same thing, cups of chowder and salads with grilled chicken.

Jess laughed when they'd finished putting their identical orders in. "See, great minds think alike. We have to do this. I need something good to focus on and you know you want to do this."

"I would love to do this," Alison admitted. "But it doesn't feel right that you're putting up all the money."

Jess smiled. "It's just money, and I have it, so let's use it. We can work out the numbers so they make sense, a management salary for you and a monthly payment to me for the initial investment, and we'll split any profits after expenses. Tell me you're in?"

It's just money. To Alison it was such a foreign way of thinking. Jess just always trusted that there would be more money coming, plenty of money, and so there was. Whereas for Alison the fear of not having enough had at times been a very real thing. Maybe she needed to change her outlook and take a chance, say yes to an opportunity that might not come her way again.

"If you really want to do this, and you're sure . . . then, I'm in."

Jess grinned. "Good. I'll call Mrs. Campbell when I get home. Alison, I think this is going to be amazing."

❦

Later that afternoon, Jess called Mrs. Campbell and made an offer that was immediately accepted. They worked out a closing date three weeks later. Her first call after hanging up was to Alison to give her the good news. Alison sounded excited but also a bit in shock that Jess's idea had turned into reality so quickly.

"I'll be part-time at the magazine by then, so I'll be able to work as many hours as we need."

"Perfect. And we have Caitlin, too. And by then hopefully the girl with the broken leg will be back. We'll have to hire more people for the coffee shop, too—we'll need someone with experience to take a lead role there," Jess said.

"We can put an ad with the *Cape Cod Times* and maybe online with Craigslist," Alison suggested.

"Great idea. Let's meet for coffee tomorrow morning to make a list of what we need to do and what we want to say in the ads."

Jess shared the news with Caitlin and her mother over dinner that night at the Impudent Oyster. It was Jess's favorite restaurant and a bit of a splurge—perfect for a celebration.

Her mother took the news calmly with just a raised eyebrow as she reached for a sip of her chardonnay. Caitlin looked at her in confusion. "That's great, I guess, but I am still not planning to stay here much longer than a month. Beth just messaged me this morning asking when I'm going home. There's all kinds of things I'm missing out on."

Jess sighed. "I don't expect you to stay longer than you want to, honey. I just hoped you'd both be happy for me and for Alison. This is her dream, to own a bookstore."

Her mother leaned forward. "*Her* dream. Are you sure it's what you want to be doing with your money? It's a big investment. It's not too late to rethink this. You haven't signed anything yet."

Jess understood her mother's concern. She had always been very conservative when it came to financial matters. Her mother was on the frugal side, not much of a spender at all, and she had a healthy bank account because of it.

"I'm very sure. I'm excited about it. I think it will be a good investment and it will be good for me to have a project like this to focus on."

"All right then, if you're sure. Congratulations." Her mother lifted her glass and smiled at Jess and Caitlin.

"Thanks, Mom." Jess tapped her glass against her mother's and Caitlin's.

Caitlin seemed happy for her, too. "Congratulations. It is a pretty cool store. I'll help as much as I can, while I'm here."

Soon after they got home, Beth called to chat and Caitlin told her about the bookstore.

"Your mother bought a bookstore? Seriously? What is up with that? Are you guys moving there?"

"No! I'm not, anyway. I think my mother may be having a mid-life crisis. She says she's not staying here either and just needs something to focus on. I think the situation with my father really threw her. They were on the verge of separating, but still . . ."

"I know. I can't imagine. Hurry up and come home, though. I miss you."

Caitlin smiled. "I miss you, too. And Charleston. I might be here a little longer than planned, though. My mother closes on the store in three weeks, which is when I was planning to head home. But I don't feel right about leaving before she takes it over. I told her I'd help some."

"Ugh. Well, just hurry, would you?"

Caitlin laughed. "I will. You know, you could always come here for a long weekend. Have you ever been to Chatham or Cape Cod? It's beautiful here. And much nicer weather than Charleston in the summer."

"No, I've never been north of Virginia. Maybe I will look into it. I'll call you next week."

Chapter 12

Are you sure about this? You and Jess are best friends. Going into business together, especially if she's the one putting up all the money, seems a little risky. I'd hate to see you jeopardize your friendship." Chris took a sip of his beer as Alison stared at him in surprise. They were sitting in her backyard enjoying the sunset and an after-work cocktail. She'd expected him to be thrilled for her good news.

"I thought you liked this idea when we were all sitting around the table at dinner recently?"

He laughed. "Sure, when it was just pie-in-the-sky dreaming. Why not? But real money is a different thing."

"Well, I don't think I need to worry about that with Jess. As you said, she's my best friend. This is something she wants to do, and I think it could be really great. I thought you'd be happy for me."

He sighed. "Of course I'm happy for you. I just worry for you, too. I've seen solid friendships end over business before."

"That won't happen with us." Alison smiled. "I think it seems meant to be. The timing couldn't be more perfect. I'd already told Jim that I would go to part-time and now I'll have the hours to put into starting this business, yet still have some money coming in."

He frowned. "Jess isn't going to pay you?"

"Or course she will. But if I'm an owner, we'll both be putting time in that won't be compensated until the business is up and running. When she goes back to Charleston, I'll be getting a management salary and we'll split any profits after her investment is paid."

"That sounds complicated. But as long as you're happy, then congratulations."

"Thank you."

"What are you celebrating?" Julia walked toward them, holding a glass of chardonnay. Alison had invited them both for dinner and to share her news. She filled her daughter in.

Julia grinned. "That is so awesome, Mom. I'm really happy for you and for Jess. And I think it will be great having you both next door. I'm happy to help out, too. Maybe with marketing. I'm no expert, but I've learned a few basic things since I opened the shop."

Alison felt her eyes grow misty as she gave her a hug. After Chris's less than enthusiastic initial reaction she was grateful for Julia's offer. "Thanks so much, honey. I'm sure we'll be glad to take you up on that."

◆

The next few weeks flew by. Jess and Alison both met with Ellen several times, spending an afternoon or a morning with her while she walked them through how she ran the store, the software she used, how she ordered from various vendors and publishers, and how to manage returns.

"I used to do more author events, signings, talks, that kind of thing," Ellen said. "I haven't had the energy for it these past few months. But you two should start that up again. People love it and it drives traffic into the store. The story hour for the children is popular, too."

Ellen didn't have nearly as much information to share with them when it came to the coffee shop, though.

"Go ahead and poke around in there. I never had anything to

do with it, so I can't help there, but I think I saw a drawer full of paperwork, vendors they used, that kind of thing. See what you can learn."

They found the drawer Ellen was talking about. It was mostly full of bills—and from the look of it, some had gone unpaid—from local suppliers for coffee and other products. Jess made a list of people to reach out to once they closed on the property, to begin establishing new vendor relationships. She guessed that given the failure of the most recent occupant some of the vendors would insist on payment up front, but that was fine. The bones of the store were good; it was mostly coffee, juices, and baked goods that they would need to purchase.

She had done her research online there, too, and both she and Alison had waitressed when they were in high school and college at local coffee shops and restaurants. Growing up on the Cape, they were lucky that there were lots of opportunities in hospitality. Their first jobs were cleaning hotel rooms. They worked as a team, listening to music as they cleaned, and for two young teens, the money was good. As soon as they were old enough, they got restaurant jobs, which with the tips paid even better. Jess quickly learned that the key to doing well as a server was to be friendly and fast—the more you turned your tables over, the more money you made. Alison hadn't enjoyed the work as much, though, and after a summer or two, she found an internship at a local magazine, which later turned into her first real job after college.

Given their experience, though it was long ago, Jess felt confident that they could make a go of the coffee shop. And Caitlin had done a bit of waitressing, too. If Jess recalled, she'd done well with it, but then another opportunity had come along, with the call center, that seemed like it had more growth potential.

"Is the ad going in today?" She and Alison had put an ad together for coffee shop help.

THE BOOKSHOP BY THE BAY

"Yes, it starts today in the *Cape Cod Times* and tomorrow on Craigslist. Hopefully, we'll get some bites."

"Maybe we can bake some of our own stuff, too," Alison said as she looked around the coffee shop. It was a cute space, with big windows that looked out over Main Street and a long bar and stools that lined the walls of the entire store. So customers could people-watch as they sipped their coffee and ate their bagels or muffins.

"I hadn't really thought about that." Jess had assumed they would buy their bagels and pastries from a vendor. "What did you have in mind?"

"Oh, I don't know. Maybe cookies or muffins." She looked lost in thought for a moment, before adding, "What about my gluten-free muffins and black bean brownies? I'm sure I'm not the only one eating gluten-free and it's hard to find good options."

"I actually really like that idea—for the gluten-free stuff. Maybe start with one option per day, so it's not too much for you, and see how it goes? If it does well, we could also look for vendors that have gluten-free options, too, so you don't have to do as much baking. It might get old after a while." Jess knew she'd hate to have to bake all the time. Once in a while it was fun, especially around the holidays.

"We'll see." Alison smiled. "You know I love to bake, though. I find it relaxing."

"Yes, you've always loved it." Jess looked around the coffee shop and pictured the counter full of freshly baked bagels, muffins, and Alison's brownies. She could see it doing well. But they had a lot to do to get to that point.

Chapter 13

W hat's that you're working on?"

Julia jumped at the sound of Kyle's voice. She'd been so lost in her graphics work that she hadn't even heard him walk up behind her. It was Sunday morning and last she knew he was still sound asleep in her bed. She was an early riser and had been on her computer since a little after six, and it was already nine thirty. Time had flown, but she'd gotten a lot accomplished.

"It's some ads and marketing materials for the bookshop and café. For their grand re-opening."

Kyle shook his head. "Are you sure that's a good use of your time?"

Julia didn't like his tone. "What do you mean?"

"Well, neither one of them have ever even worked in a bookstore. I'm just surprised that you're encouraging it." He was in a mood for some unknown reason.

"Of course I am. They love that bookstore and it's always been my mother's dream. And Jess is an attorney, a good business person. I'm sure she knows what she's doing."

"I'm sure you're right. I would just never want to buy a business like that. Most new businesses don't make it."

Kyle smiled and she saw his mood shift. Julia sensed that whatever was bothering him had nothing to do with the bookstore.

He did have a good point, though. "You're right," she agreed. "But Jess looked over Ellen's numbers and she has a solid business. She also never advertised much, and I have had some luck with that and social media. So, there are things we can do to grow the business."

"'We'? You sound like it's your shop, too."

Julia laughed. "I know. I just want them to do well. I'm excited for them. And I'm looking forward to having that coffee shop open again. Even though I didn't like the coffee from the old place that much, it was convenient."

"You could just put a coffee maker in your shop," Kyle said sensibly.

"I have one. But sometimes I like to just stretch my legs and take a little break, go for a quick walk down Main Street. Though if Mom is going to have her brownies there on a regular basis, that could become a bad habit."

He nodded. "Your mom is a good cook."

She looked at him closely. "Are you okay? You seem like something is on your mind."

He sighed. "I should have said something sooner. I wasn't ready to talk about it this week, and just didn't want to bring the mood down over the weekend. I guess I didn't want to deal with the bad news yet." He paused, and she could see that he was struggling with something.

"What is it?" Kyle hadn't mentioned anything in recent weeks. As far as she knew, all was well in his world.

"I had a meeting with my boss on Friday. They announced on Monday that they are moving the company to Nashville. Rents are cheaper there and it's where his parents live."

"What does that mean for you? Will they let you work remotely?"

Kyle shook his head. "No. Even though my job could be done totally from here. He doesn't believe in remote work. Says it's important to the company culture to have everyone on-site, in the same office. I can keep my job—if I relocate. So, it's a big decision."

Julia's jaw dropped. "It is. You'd seriously consider moving—to Nashville?" Kyle's family, like Julia's, was in Chatham. "Couldn't you get another job here, instead?"

"Not easily. There's not a lot of demand on the Cape for what I do. I could probably get another job, but it would be in Boston—and that's a hell of a commute from Chatham." It would be a minimum of two hours, and that was with no traffic.

"What if you moved closer to Boston? That's not as bad as Nashville. And maybe you could find a company here that would let you work remotely."

"I thought about that. But you're not going to want to move closer to Boston. So, what's the difference if I go there or Nashville? At least going to Nashville I'd get to keep my job. I wouldn't have to start over. I'll also get a promotion and a pay increase. It's hard to say no to that." Kyle had been waiting for that promotion. She couldn't see him turning the opportunity down.

"So, you've decided then? If you go to Nashville, what does that mean for us?"

"I haven't decided. Not fully. But I am leaning toward it. I've already asked you to marry me, Julia. And you said no. If I give up this job and try for something in Boston, then I'm giving up a lot. If you're serious about us, then we can make this work long-distance. You can fly down on the weekend, or I can fly up. Maybe it will help us move forward. Maybe you'll miss me." He sounded wistful and sad.

"Of course I'll miss you." Julia felt the rug was pulled out from under her. She wasn't ready to commit to marriage with Kyle, but she wasn't ready to say goodbye to him yet, or to have him move to Nashville. But, she also knew it wasn't fair for her to ask him to stay. "How soon is the move happening?"

"Soon. Two weeks. I'd go the week after that once they are settled. All but two people are moving. Barbara's staying, of course. She was close to retiring anyway. I'm the only one that hasn't decided yet. He was pushing me on Friday for an answer. What do you think I should do?"

That was a loaded question. Julia took a deep breath. "I don't want you to go. But it's not fair for me to ask you to stay. You have to do what feels right for you and your career. If you go, we can try to make it work."

Kyle relaxed a little and smiled again. "Maybe Nashville won't be so bad. It's warmer there and there's great music. Could be we fall in love with it. You could always move your business there, too. People buy jewelry in Nashville."

Julia didn't see that happening, but she wanted to remain open. "I can't make any promises, but I'll visit, and we'll see how it goes. If you go."

"I think I have to. I love my job and I don't want to give up that promotion and start over again with a new company in Boston."

Julia was a little disappointed that he didn't even want to try to find something locally. But she understood it, too. Kyle did love his job and the people he worked with. It would be a lot for him to give up, especially a promotion and pay raise. She didn't feel right asking him to stay for her.

"It's a bit of a shock, but I understand. It will be a new adventure for you—for us." She smiled. "I have always wanted to visit Nashville." That was true. She loved country music and had thought Nashville could be a good location for a vacation. She'd make the best of it—and see what happened.

Chapter 14

Have you heard from Parker at all?" Jess's mother surprised her with the question over breakfast. Jess had just poured a cup of coffee and joined her mother at the table. It was early, just past seven, and Caitlin was still sound asleep. Her mother, like Jess, was an early riser.

"Not really. A few emails here and there wondering when we're coming back and wanting to talk when we do."

Her mother scowled at that. "You're not going to try to work things out?"

"No. I'm not. But I'm also not ready to have any kind of discussion with him. Once the store is open and I can slow down a little, I'll see about filing for divorce. I figured I'd head back there at the end of the summer. Caitlin will probably go sooner."

Her mother nodded. "She's anxious to get back to her friends."

"She is. She said she'd stay another week or two after we open, though."

"That's good." She looked wistful as she stirred a little more sugar into her coffee. "Maybe Chatham will grow on her, the longer she's here."

Jess doubted it. Caitlin had reminded her several times that she was eager to get back to Charleston, and she couldn't blame her.

She had a life there, friends, and she needed to focus on finding a real job.

Jess changed the subject. "What are you up to today, Mom?"

"I have a tennis lesson at eleven, and then I'm meeting Betsy for lunch at the Land Ho! in Orleans. Glenda might join us. You could, too, if you're not busy?"

"I'm meeting with Alison at noon. We're going over some résumés that have come in. I didn't know you were interested in tennis."

Her mother shrugged. "It's something to do. My doctor suggested I move more. Tennis sounded fun."

"It is fun. Once you feel comfortable, we'll have to play." Jess loved tennis and had played often at the country club in Charleston. It was good exercise.

"We'll see. I'll let you know how the lessons go." She sounded a little nervous.

"I bet you'll love it."

❧

Later that morning, after she'd dropped Caitlin off for her shift at the bookstore, Jess printed out copies of the résumés that looked the best, to bring over to review with Alison. She used her mother's printer in her small office and did a double take when she saw the framed picture above the printer of her, Parker, and Caitlin when she was about eight. Things had been really good with them then. They looked so much younger, and happier. Jess had been doing so well. She'd felt like she was handling the situation as best as she could and had mentally prepared herself to file for divorce. She thought she was okay.

But when she saw that picture and the reminder of how things used to be she felt a sharp, physical pain in her gut. Her eyes immediately welled up and her nose felt stuffy as the tears fell. There was no one home, so she gave in to it. She grabbed the oldest, softest throw on her mother's sofa and curled up in a ball, pulling the soft fleece around her as she cried loud, messy, ragged sobs. It had been years since she'd cried anywhere near that much. She had to stop and grab a tissue at one point. The tears slowed but then came rushing back for a second round, until finally she felt cried out, and exhausted.

She went and looked in the mirror and laughed. She looked an appalling mess. Her eyes were pale and tearstained and her nose was red and raw. Her hair was a tangled mess from rolling around on the sofa. She ran a brush through it, splashed cold water on her face, and added a bit of concealer and rosy blush to give her cheeks some color. She felt better now that she'd had a good cry.

✧

Ten minutes later, she pulled into Alison's driveway, grabbed her folder of résumés and her purse, and headed to the door. She thought she'd cleaned herself up pretty well but when Alison took one look at her she knew something was wrong. She opened the door wide.

"Come in and tell me what's going on. You look awful. Did you talk to Parker or something?"

Jess followed her into the kitchen and sat at one of the chairs around the kitchen island. It was their usual spot when she visited.

"I didn't talk to him." She told Alison about the picture in her mother's office. "I thought I was fine with all this, but it just hit me. I guess I wasn't all cried out after all."

Alison pulled her in for a hug. "I'm sorry. I know it's not easy. It's like a death in a way—the death of a relationship. And you never know what might trigger the feelings. But it really does get easier as time goes on."

"I hope so. I know you've been through this. You and Chris are in such a good place now."

"We are. He didn't cheat, and we both wanted the divorce, but it was still really hard."

"I'm so glad you suggested we come here this summer. It definitely helps being around you and my mother and Caitlin. They've both been great, too." Even though she and Alison had talked pretty much daily over the years, it was so much better spending time in person. And the distraction of the shop had taken a lot of her energy and given her something good to focus on. So, her breakdown this morning had surprised her.

"It's normal to feel this way. I went through it—the whole range of emotions, including wondering if I was making a mistake. You're not, by the way."

Jess laughed. "Thanks. I do know that much, at least. What hit me this morning was just seeing how happy we used to be. We haven't been like that in so long. Parker shouldn't have cheated, but we should have done something about this sooner. It was just easier to stay together."

"I get it. Divorce is messy and hard. But once it's done, you'll be glad you did it. Even if it doesn't feel that way now."

"My head knows you're right. My heart is just sad. But I'll be okay." She opened the manila folder she'd brought with her and handed Alison a few résumés to review.

Chapter 15

Caitlin smiled as a familiar face walked into the bookstore. She didn't know the tall, dark-haired man, but he seemed to be a regular. He'd been in several times since she'd started working there. It was just after four on a Tuesday and the store was busy with a few moms and their children. Several young girls were browsing the romance section. Three old men stood by the magazines chatting about wooden boats while Caitlin watched the dark-haired man head to the mystery row.

She rang up a few customers, and eventually the man made his way to the register to buy two mysteries. Both were by Dennis Lehane, one of her favorite authors. She'd read the two books he'd chosen, *Gone Baby Gone* and *Mystic River.*

"Have you read any of his others? Those are both great."

He smiled, and the corners of his mouth and his dark brown eyes crinkled in that way that looks so good on men.

"Not yet. I saw the movie for *Mystic River* a while ago and was curious to read the book. It's usually better."

She nodded. "It is. That book is amazing. But the movie was good, too."

His phone rang and he glanced at it, and frowned before answering, "Jason Brinker."

And a moment later, "Stu, I didn't recognize your number. Can I call you back in a minute? I'm in a store paying at the register. Thanks." He ended the call and shoved the phone in his back pocket and grinned. "Sorry about that. I don't normally take calls in public."

"No problem. What kind of work do you do?" She was curious and couldn't tell by how he was dressed. He wore a plaid work shirt, well-worn jeans, and a navy Red Sox baseball cap.

"I'm a plumber. Brinker Plumbing, that's my company."

"Oh, nice to meet you. I'm Caitlin."

"I can see that." He glanced at her name tag and she blushed.

"Right, of course."

He grinned again. "I'm just teasing you. Are you new to town or just here for the summer?"

"Just here for the summer. My mother is from Chatham so we usually come every year. She and her best friend actually just bought this store, so I'll be here a few more weeks, helping them get it going."

"Really? Mrs. Campbell has had this place forever."

"Yes, she has. And now it's time for her to retire." Caitlin jumped at the sound of Ellen Campbell's voice behind her. She hadn't heard the older woman walk behind the register.

Jason laughed. "Well, I don't blame you. But, you'll be missed."

"Thanks, honey." She nodded at Caitlin. "Jason's one of my best customers. You need to take good care of him."

Caitlin smiled. That wouldn't be hard. "Of course." She handed Jason his charge slip and a paper bag with the two books.

He signed the slip and handed it back to her. "Thanks. I'm sure I'll be seeing you again, soon."

Caitlin watched as he left, and when she turned her attention back to the register, Mrs. Campbell eyed her with interest. "He's single. Jason. About thirty-five, I think. Has a good business here in town. I use him for all my plumbing here and at home. He's fast

73

and reasonable with his rates. Keep him in mind . . . if you need a plumber."

Caitlin smiled. "I will—and will pass it on to my mother and Alison. Not that I'm looking, as I'm heading back to Charleston soon, but you mentioned he's single?"

"He is. Was engaged until recently, when he came to his senses. I wasn't too fond of his fiancée. Merry Andrews has a ladies' clothing shop down the street—a little snooty and overpriced if you ask me. But that's Merry. She's dating a lawyer now, someone older and richer. Jason is a catch, though. If I was forty years younger . . ."

Caitlin laughed. "So, what's the first thing you're going to do once you're officially retired?" She wondered if Ellen Campbell was going to miss being at the store at all.

"I'm going on a cruise! With two of my girlfriends. We're doing the Bermuda cruise out of Boston for a week. I've always wanted to do that. When I come back I have a whole list of projects I want to tackle. I might take a class or two, join a gym, maybe even try golfing again. But I'll tell you what I'm not going to do."

"What's that?"

"I am not going to work, ever again. I'm not going to worry about getting to the store on time, or deal with fussy customers or any of it. Don't get me wrong, most of the customers are wonderful and I have loved owning this shop. But I'm really ready for what's next."

"Well, a cruise sounds fun. You'll have to stop in when you get back and show us your pictures."

The older woman's face lit up. "Oh, I'll definitely do that. And I told your mother she could always call me if she gets stuck or has any questions. I'm just a few miles up the road."

"I'm sure she'll be in touch with some questions. We all still have a lot to learn."

"I'm looking forward to when she reopens the coffee shop. There's definitely a need for that downtown." Ellen shook her head.

"It really amazes me that the last two that bought it managed to bungle it so badly."

"I'm going to help them get that up and running, too. I waitressed a bit and worked at a coffee shop for a while, during college. It was actually fun. I liked making all the fancy coffees and swirling designs in the foam."

"I don't think I've ever seen that done. You'll have to make me one and show me what you mean. I do like a good mocha with lots of foam."

Caitlin laughed. "Well, come find me when we open, and I'll make you the best mocha you've ever had."

Chapter 16

The closing went off without a hitch. Jess and Alison met at their attorney's office, where Ellen Campbell happily signed all the paperwork and accepted the large bank check for her properties. She reminded Jess that she was available for any questions.

"If you get in a jam, let me know and I can try to help. But not for at least a week. I leave for Bermuda tomorrow."

"Have a wonderful trip. I may have a question or two for you at some point, but I'll try not to bother you unless I really have to," Jess assured her.

Ellen Campbell smiled. "It's not a bother. I spent most of my adult life managing that store. I want to make sure it does well—and I think it will be in good hands with the two of you, and Caitlin."

After all the paperwork was finalized, Ellen handed over the keys and Jess and Alison went to the bookstore. Caitlin was behind the register and congratulated them when they walked through the door. The shop was quiet. There were just a few customers browsing. They walked up to the register to chat for a moment before heading next door to the coffee shop, where there was still a lot of work to be done before they could open.

"Will you change the name of the bookstore?" Caitlin asked.

"I don't know. Will we? I haven't thought about that," Alison said.

But Jess had thought about it. "I think it might be a good idea. To show that we are under new ownership. What do you think of Mothers' and Daughters' bookstore?"

"That's interesting . . ." Alison said. "Everyone knows it as Chatham Books, though."

"Well, I was just thinking since it's kind of a group effort, with Caitlin working here and Julia helping with the marketing. The store is in Chatham so that part of it is kind of obvious. But we don't have to change it if you don't want to. It was just a thought," Jess assured her. She knew Alison often needed to process things, digest ideas before making a decision and getting excited about them.

"You may have a point. And it does have a nice ring to it. Sounds friendly. I like it," she said.

"I like it, too. Though I'm not going to be here much longer," Caitlin reminded her.

Jess smiled. "But you're here now. So, it's all good. We'll sleep on the idea." She glanced at the time on her cell phone. "Alison and I have our first interview in ten minutes, so we'll be in the café. Holler if you need us for anything."

They left the store and Jess unlocked the coffee shop. There was a stack of boxes by the front door. Supplies that she had ordered that had been delivered over the past few days. Ellen had kept an eye on the deliveries and made sure they were all brought inside. So far, it was mostly nonperishable items, dry goods, and whole-bean coffee from a local roaster. She and Alison had done some tasting from various vendors and settled on this coffee and also on a local baker and bagel maker.

Her mother had recommended a contractor to handle cutting an entryway between the bookstore and coffee shop, so customers could easily go from one to the other without going outside. He was scheduled to meet with them later in the day.

The rest of the day was busy with back-to-back interviews and the meeting with the contractor. They'd both liked Sam McGregor, and after assessing the space and measuring, he said he could probably finish the work in a day and a half.

"I'll need to get a permit first, though, and that will take about two weeks."

He also suggested that they do pocket doors, which would let them open and close the entryway versus having it always open.

"I'm assuming you'll be opening the coffee shop earlier in the day than the bookstore, and that way you can keep the pocket doors closed until it's open," he'd said.

Jess and Alison had exchanged glances and both felt a bit silly that neither of them had thought of that.

"That sounds perfect, Sam. Thanks so much," Jess said.

After he left, they had time to go over the notes they'd each made from the five people they'd met. They needed to hire three to four people initially to cover the different days and shifts for the coffee shop. Caitlin had also said she'd help out there. The bookstore itself was almost fully staffed now that Brooklyn was back full-time and both Alison and Jess were able to take shifts.

"We probably should hire at least one more person for the bookstore—who can take over Caitlin's hours when she leaves," Alison said.

Jess knew she was right. She was still hopeful that Caitlin might decide to stay longer, through the summer, but she knew she couldn't count on that.

"You're right. Especially as we'll be using her on the coffee shop, too. We can go through some of the other résumés that came in from the ad and see if any of them could be worth a call."

"That's a great idea. I liked almost everyone we met today, except for the last woman. When I asked for a weakness, she said she wasn't very good with people and ideally preferred to work alone," Alison said.

Jess laughed. "I think we're in agreement there. Let's call the others and see if they can start training this week."

The goal was to be open in three weeks. At least for a soft opening. They had everything they needed, except for the perishable goods and the carpentry work.

Alison made the calls to the candidates, and everyone accepted. Sally and Joan were both in their early sixties and were looking for part-time work. Both were early risers and wanted to work a few days a week. Everly and Samantha were college students, attending Cape Cod Community College, and were more interested in weekends and a day or two during the week.

"Maybe we should hire a few more people," Jess said. "Just to make sure we have plenty of coverage and in case some of these first hires don't work out."

"We have a few more résumés that have come in that we can call and see if they can meet with us tomorrow," Alison said.

"Good, let's do that. We're almost there."

☙

Sam got the permit exactly two weeks later and spent the next two days putting in the pocket doors and they were gorgeous. Jess and Alison decided to open the coffee shop that Sunday, figuring it wouldn't be as hectic a day and there might be people out strolling along Main Street.

Alison made her black bean brownies and a gluten-free apple cake, which she cut into slices and wrapped individually. They displayed them in a big clear cake dish on the counter, right by the register. Caitlin made three different kinds of coffee: a light roast, a dark roast, and a flavor of the day—hazelnut. They also had a row of flavored syrups people could add and a list of coffee drinks like lattes and cappuccinos.

Caitlin, Sally, Alison, and Jess waited anxiously to serve their first customers.

Alison and Jess really didn't know what to expect. Jess had been half worried that they might be too busy on their first day, but that turned out not to be the case at all. For the first few hours it was painfully slow. No one seemed to realize that they were open.

A few people straggled in, but nothing like what they'd hoped for even on a soft opening. Jess really thought they'd be busier. Alison looked worried and Caitlin glanced out the window to see how busy the foot traffic on Main Street was. The people were there. They just weren't stopping in.

"I have an idea," Caitlin said. "How would you feel about doing some samples?"

"Coffee samples?" Jess wasn't sure what her daughter was referring to.

"No, not coffee. We want them to come in and buy that. I was thinking some of the baked stuff. I could chop up a few brownies and slices of cake."

"Sure, if you think that might help." Jess wasn't sure it would do much if no one was in the store.

But then she realized what Caitlin had in mind. She put toothpicks in the pieces of cake and brownies, put them all on a paper plate, and stepped outside and kept the door open. It was warm out, so an open door was a good idea and something they should have thought of.

Within a few minutes, people started coming into the store after trying a sample. They sold coffee, bagels, and baked goods. When she ran out of samples, Caitlin made up another plate and went back outside and they were off and running.

Once people realized that they were open, traffic was steady for the rest of the afternoon. A lot of people who came in were curiosity seekers—locals who wanted to check out the newly reopened store.

Jess was happy that everyone had good things to say. An older couple both had coffee and shared a slice of the gluten-free cake, then came to the counter to offer their feedback.

"We both think your coffee is much better than what was here before," the man said. He held out his hand. "I'm Todd McIntyre and this is my wife, Elaine. We live right around the corner. You'll be seeing us again."

His wife nodded. "That cake was excellent, too. I'll tell my sister to stop in. She has a hard time finding good gluten-free options."

By four o'clock, the flow of customers had trickled to a stop. All the baked goods were gone and people seemed excited that they were open again. Caitlin locked the front door after the last customer left. Sally took off her pink apron and tucked it in her purse before saying goodbye and that she'd see them the next day. Caitlin poured herself a coffee and flopped onto one of the stools.

"So, I think overall, that went well," she said.

Jess nodded. "It was a shaky start, but thanks to your sampling, we turned it around."

Alison went to the register, opened it, and fished around in the dollar bills for a moment before pulling one out and holding it up. Jess noticed there was a red mark on one corner.

"This is the first dollar we made in the coffee shop. It stood out to me because of the red mark. I think we should put it up on the wall, for good luck. Julia did that in her jewelry shop. I figure we need all the luck we can get, right?"

Jess laughed. "Yes, absolutely." She opened a drawer and handed Alison a roll of tape to stick the dollar bill on the wall. Alison positioned it right above the register and secured it with tape on all four sides. She poured herself a coffee and joined Caitlin at the counter.

Jess didn't want coffee this late in the day—she knew it would keep her up late. She grabbed a bottle of water instead and leaned against the counter, facing the other two.

"So, we did it. Day one is in the books. Now, we just have to clean up and come back and do it again tomorrow." She smiled. "I think it went pretty well, all things considered."

"It's a great start," Alison agreed.

"I'm not scheduled to be in the store tomorrow. I could open the shop and get things going if you like?" Caitlin offered.

"I won't say no to that. Thank you, honey. I'll be in the bookstore all day tomorrow, so just holler if you need anything," Jess said.

"And I'll be in tomorrow afternoon. I'm at the magazine in the morning," Alison said.

Caitlin lifted her coffee mug. "Here's to a great first day."

Jess and Alison joined the toast. "And a great team effort," Jess added.

Chapter 17

How'd the first day go for the coffee shop?" Jim added sugar to his freshly made cup of coffee as Alison waited for hers to finish brewing. They were in the office kitchen early the next morning. The office felt so quiet these days. No one else was in yet, and Alison knew that Jim had worked out arrangements with several others to go down to part-time hours. So far, he'd lost only two people, who needed to find a more secure situation. Jim was hopeful that he wouldn't have to consider any more reductions in staff for at least another year or two—if things went well. Alison was both excited and relieved that she had the bookstore now.

"It went well. A bit of a slow start, but I suppose we should have expected that. No one really knew that we were open until Jess's daughter Caitlin went outside and lured people in." She told him about the sampling and he laughed.

"Well, that's not surprising. You are a good baker. I'm sorry I wasn't able to come by. I'll make sure to stop in this weekend."

"How was the writers' conference?" Jim had spent the weekend in Boston and she knew he'd been looking forward to it.

His face lit up. "It was great. There were some good workshops and I had an encouraging meeting with an agent. I told her about my project and she wanted me to send her some sample chapters. So I emailed those off last night."

Alison was happy for him. "I'm not surprised to hear it. I look forward to reading it, too."

He smiled. "I should have something to show in another month or so. I'm nearing the finish line, and then of course I need to go back through it all again. But, I'm getting there."

Alison grabbed her coffee, and she and Jim headed back to their desks. Jim stopped when she reached her cubicle.

"You know, with Wendy leaving, we need someone to take over the monthly restaurant review. Would you be interested?"

Alison grinned. "Yes, I'd love that." She didn't think she'd be considered for it since she'd gone to part-time.

"Good. I know you wanted to cut your hours back, but you were the first person I thought of. It should be a fun assignment. I thought maybe we'd do that new restaurant that opened last month, Neptune. Have you been there yet?"

"Not yet. I've been wanting to go, though."

"We can chat about it more before you go, but plan to bring a friend or two, so it won't look strange if you order lots of food. Make sure you all order different things and save your receipt."

"I will. Thank you." Alison was excited about the new assignment. She'd take Jess, of course, and maybe Julia or Caitlin would want to go, too.

She watched him walk off toward his office as she settled into her seat. Jim hadn't mentioned Marian, the woman he'd been dating for over a year, lately. She wondered if they were still together. Jim had been working longer hours, she'd noticed, but she'd chalked that up to trying to keep the business going. It just crossed her mind now that if he and Marian were no longer together, he might be looking to fill his time, too. She'd always thought they were an odd couple. Jim was so laid-back and nice, and Marian, well, she was more of a type A. Always beautifully dressed, with perfect makeup and not a hair out of place.

Though Alison and Jim had become close friends over the years, he'd never confided in her about his relationships and she'd never had anything to share in that regard. For the longest time, Jim had thought she and Chris were back together, but she'd explained that they were just friends. She knew that many people assumed they were together or heading in that direction, but she valued Chris as a friend and both of them had talked about it and decided they worked better that way. Chris hadn't dated anyone seriously in years either. Alison knew he dated occasionally, though. Friends reported back when they saw him out with someone new. But he never mentioned it and Alison never asked.

She figured if he wanted to talk about that, he'd bring it up. She'd been content with what they had, and enjoyed his company. But she knew Jess was right, and spending so much time with Chris, even though it was just as friends, was keeping her from meeting someone new and having a real relationship. She'd promised Jess that she'd get out more, but the thought of it was a bit terrifying.

Still, she'd agreed that they would go out together soon for a night out to hear some music at the Squire. That seemed less intimidating than putting up a profile for online dating, though she knew plenty of people had success with that, too. Maybe she'd see if Jess wanted to have dinner first at Neptune; then they could head to the Squire for an after-dinner drink and to hear some live music.

Chapter 18

Julia felt mixed emotions as she watched Kyle put his overnight bag in the trunk of his car. It was Saturday morning and he'd stayed over the night before—their last night together before his big move to Nashville. The movers had come the day before and cleared out his apartment and were making another stop to fill up the truck today and would then meet him there.

"You booked your ticket?" Kyle asked before giving her a final goodbye kiss.

She nodded. "I arrive two weeks from tomorrow, Sunday afternoon, and fly back on Tuesday." She'd just close the shop a little early on Sunday for a few days. She hated to close at all, but Kyle had pointed out that Mondays were her slowest day and she hadn't taken any time off at all since she'd opened. And Nashville was a place she'd always wanted to visit, so it could be like a mini vacation. She also knew Kyle wouldn't want to take time off so soon after starting in the new role.

Julia still wasn't sure how she felt about Kyle, though. She'd been on the verge of ending things with him when he announced the big move and promotion. So she'd decided instead to see how things went. She suspected the distance might make a breakup happen more naturally if it was meant to be. But as she looked at

Kyle, with his hair slightly damp from his shower and his smile as he leaned in to kiss her, she felt a stir of something she hadn't felt in a while and wondered if the time apart might actually be good for them. Maybe she would miss him?

"Drive safely," she said as Kyle climbed in and closed the car door. His window was down.

"Will do. I'll text you when I get there."

She watched him drive off, and when he was out of sight she went back inside and made a fresh cup of coffee. She felt unsettled, and unsure of what would happen next with them. It was almost nine, so as soon as she finished her coffee, she'd jump in the shower and then head to the shop to open by ten. With Kyle gone, she had the evening free, though she didn't have plans. She figured she'd probably work, then head home and have a quiet night in, maybe watch a Hallmark movie or read for a while.

Her phone rang as she took her last sip of coffee.

"Hey Mom, what's up? Are you working in the store today? I was just about to get in the shower."

"I'll be there all day. I just dropped off some brownies and cake slices at the coffee shop and am heading over to the book side now, but wanted to give you a quick call. Do you have plans tonight? Kyle's gone, right?"

"He left earlier this morning. What did you have in mind?"

"Want to come to dinner? Jess and I are going to that new restaurant, Neptune. It looks good. And it's on me—well, on the magazine actually. I'm doing a review."

"You are? Sure, I'll go."

"Great. We'll plan on six thirty then. I'll see you before then at the store."

Julia ended the call and smiled as she stepped into the shower and relaxed as the hot water streamed over her. It would be fun to have dinner with her mom and Jess. Her mother seemed in such a good mood lately. Ever since Jess bought the bookstore and they

started working together, her mother seemed different somehow, more energized. And she'd sounded excited about doing the
restaurant review. Julia was happy for her.

◈

Julia popped into the bookstore later that afternoon, after hanging
a sign on her shop door saying she'd be back in fifteen minutes.
She did that on most days during the midafternoon period when
traffic was the slowest. She wandered into the coffee shop first.
Caitlin was behind the counter and smiled when she saw her.

"Hey there. Do you want your usual?"

Julia nodded. "Yes, please. How's it going? Have you guys been
busy today?" It was the first Saturday the coffee shop was open.
She watched as Caitlin expertly made the caramel macchiato the
way Julia liked it, with lots of foam and a hint of caramel drizzled
across the top. There was a good energy in the store. Two people
followed her in and were waiting their turn in line. Several others
were sitting at the two small tables by the door and were sipping
coffee and eating muffins. Caitlin noticed that there were only
two of her mother's cake slices left and half of the brownies were
already gone.

Caitlin handed her the coffee and rang it up. She'd originally
tried to give Julia free coffees when she came in, and Julia allowed
it once, but insisted on paying after that. She didn't want to feel
like she was taking advantage, and she liked taking her daily afternoon break and walking around for a bit.

"It has been pretty busy. We were packed earlier. Each day this
week has been a little busier than the day before, which seems like
a good sign. I think word is starting to get out." Caitlin handed
Julia her change.

"That's great! I'm going to head next door and say hello."

She took her coffee and walked through the pocket doors that
led into the bookstore. Jess was behind the register ringing someone up, and Julia's mother was putting new books on a shelf and

chatting with one of their customers, an older woman. Julia walked over quietly, sipping her coffee and browsing nearby books.

"So, I think you'll like that one. Mary Higgins Clark has always been one of my favorites and *Where Are the Children?* is her first book. It will keep you on the edge of your seat."

The older woman thanked her and headed off to the register. Julia's mother looked her way and smiled.

"Hi, honey. I didn't even hear you walk over."

"I didn't want to interrupt. How is it going?" Julia glanced around the bookstore and felt a little nervous for her mother and Jess. It was Saturday and there were only a handful of people in the store. She'd popped in each day since they opened almost a week ago and the store just didn't seem to be very busy. Julia had never paid much attention to it before, but now it was more noticeable and she'd hoped that weekends would be busier for them.

Her mother sighed. "It is a little slower than we thought it would be. I knew it would be quieter during the week, but today has been surprisingly slow, too."

Julia nodded. She didn't want to alarm her mother, but she was concerned and wanted to try to help. "Well, we can chat about some marketing ideas over dinner tonight. Brainstorm some things to get people coming in."

"We'd welcome any ideas you have. Neither one of us knows much about marketing."

◈

"I'm not worried, yet." Jess reached for one of the hot crusty rolls that had just arrived, ripped it open, and smeared a generous amount of butter on before taking a bite. Truth be told, she was a little worried, but she didn't want to make things worse by verbalizing it too soon and worrying Alison and Julia. Ellen Campbell had told her that sales were a little down these past few years but that overall, the store was profitable. Maybe she should have looked more closely at the numbers, especially this past year. She hadn't thought too much of it, though, because everyone knew that people's buying habits had changed and bookstores weren't as busy as they used to be. But since they were the only store in the area, she believed the business was there.

"I think it might just take some time to build things up. I know Ellen used to do more events and those brought people in. Maybe we can look into doing things like that?" Julia suggested.

"That's a great idea!" Jess agreed.

"Ellen did used to do a lot of author signings and story hours with the children. That would bring parents and kids into the store, maybe on a regular basis," Alison said.

"What if we did an event that combined the coffee shop and the bookstore? A monthly book club? Everyone signs up ahead of time, buys the book, and then comes into the store and discusses it over coffee?" Julia suggested.

Alison's eyes lit up. "I love that idea. How can we get the word out?"

"I could make up a flyer for us that we could post in the store, and we can put something on Facebook. The bookstore doesn't have a Facebook page, that needs to change," Julia said.

"If you could do that for us, that would be great," Jess said. "I ordered a new sign for out front. It should be here next Monday. Maybe we can have a grand reopening of both the bookstore and coffee shop? We can do it on a Saturday afternoon and offer cookies and buy-one-get-one coffees or something like that to get more people in?"

Julia pulled her phone out and started typing furiously on it. "I'm getting all of this down, so we won't forget anything."

"I can send a press release to the local paper, so we can get a mention for the grand reopening. Should we shoot for next Saturday?" Alison asked.

Jess thought about it for a moment and nodded. "I think that should work. The sign comes on Monday, and we'll get that up. And we can work on putting these other ideas into place. There must be some local authors we can invite in for a signing. Do either of you know of anyone?"

"I'll check with the library. They will probably have some suggestions. Jim is working on a book that sounds great. I'd love to have him in for a signing once he gets his published," Alison said.

"Your boss is writing a book?" Julia sounded surprised.

"He is. A mystery. I'm going to edit it once he's done with the writing." Alison sounded proud of him, and something in her tone made Jess wonder about their relationship. She spoke about her boss often.

"Is he single now?" She thought she remembered Alison mentioning something about a breakup.

"He is. I never thought they made a good couple." Her nose wrinkled with distaste, and Jess almost laughed.

"Why not? What happened with them?" she asked.

"She dumped him for someone else. Someone more successful. A real estate developer, I think. She never appreciated him and I don't think he was especially happy with her. It was just easier to avoid a messy breakup, I suppose," Alison said.

"He's not dating anyone else then?" Jess was intrigued.

Alison looked a bit nervous. "Why? Are you interested?"

And this time, Jess did laugh. "No, silly. But I thought maybe you might be."

"Oh! He's great, but he's my boss. I've never thought of him . . . that way." She seemed a little flustered, though.

Jess shrugged. "I don't think that is necessarily an issue. You're down to part-time now. And if the shop does well, you could do it full-time."

Julia smiled. "You do talk about him a lot, Mom. Something to think about."

Alison blushed a little and looked relieved when the server approached the table to set down their appetizers. She got out her phone and turned on the camera and changed the subject.

"I need to get pictures of these for the magazine before we dive in."

✧

Alison took a deep breath. The questions about Jim had taken her by surprise. She really hadn't ever thought of him that way. She liked him, admired him, but he was her boss and until that changed, she didn't think she could see him in any kind of romantic way, if ever. Plus, if she was being truthful, the thought of being in a relationship with anyone was a bit scary. Even though they were strictly friends and neither of them wanted more than that, it was just easier to spend time with Chris. Though she knew that was the biggest barrier to taking the step into finding a real relationship with someone else. Somehow, she'd just put it off, and the years had passed, so quickly. It felt like it was time for that to change, though. Things felt different, with Jess and Caitlin here. Change was in the air, and she needed to be open to it.

She snapped photos of their appetizers, the delicate tuna tacos, diced fresh tuna tossed in a creamy spicy mayo and topped with bright green seaweed salad and a sliver of avocado and tucked into a mini crunchy taco shell. There were also clams casino, small local clams roasted with diced bacon, garlic, butter, and bread crumbs, and cups of lobster bisque, decadently rich and creamy, laced with sherry and big, sweet chunks of lobster.

They shared everything and it was all delicious. Their salads arrived next: a classic Caesar; a tossed garden salad with the homemade house dressing, a creamy cross between Greek and ranch; and a Bibb salad with pears, toasted walnuts, and cranberries. Even though they only nibbled on the salads, by the time the entrees arrived, Alison was feeling almost full.

Jess groaned as their server set down more platters of food. "I think I know what I'm having for lunch tomorrow," she said.

Alison laughed. "I know. It is fun, though, to try everything." She'd ordered the restaurant's signature baked stuffed lobster, and it was presented magnificently, with the lobster claws already removed from the shell and placed on top of the mound of seafood stuffing that was dotted with scallops and shrimp. Julia ordered a filet mignon with a side of béarnaise sauce and Jess chose another house special, a baked scallop casserole, which was plenty of sweet Cape scallops dusted with bread crumbs and cooked in butter and white wine.

They tried everything and enjoyed it all. And they all laughed when their server cleared their food away to pack the leftovers into to-go boxes and asked if they wanted to see a dessert menu.

"I couldn't possibly," Julia said.

"I don't think I can do it either," Jess said.

Alison was about to agree, and then remembered she didn't have a choice.

"I'd like to see the dessert list. And I bet I can talk these two into it. We'll take three menus." When their server walked away, she reminded the other two that she had to try everything. "We need to order three desserts and I need to have a bite of all of them. You don't have to eat them."

Five minutes later, a vanilla bean crème brûlée, a flourless chocolate lava cake, and the dessert of the day, a lemon layer cake, arrived. And though Jess and Julia had said they were too full, they all managed to take a few tastes of everything.

"I'm glad your first restaurant review will be a good one," Julia said. "Imagine if you hated the food!"

Alison laughed. "That would be awful. This will be a fun one to write. We really liked everything, right?"

"Yes, except for the Caesar salad. It was a little too garlicky for me," Julia said.

"I thought so, too, but I'm sure some people would love it that way. So, I can just describe it as heavy on the garlic and let people decide if that's a good or bad thing."

"Julia, do you want to come with us to the Squire? I told your mother we're going out on the town tonight," Jess said.

Julia hesitated. "I actually think I'm going to pass. It's been a long day and I'm so full, I just want to go home, get into my sweats, and crash on the sofa. You guys can tell me all about it tomorrow."

"Are you sure, honey?" Alison worried that Julia was sad about Kyle leaving. She hadn't mentioned him once all night and she hadn't wanted to bring it up.

Julia smiled. "I'm sure. It should be fun, though. They usually have a good band on Saturday nights."

"Okay, I'll call you tomorrow."

Chapter 19

Jess's first impression when they walked into the Squire at a few minutes past eight was that it was loud. The restaurant was still busy, serving dinner, and the bar was full of people talking and drinking. The band was setting up and looked almost ready to start playing. A waitress walked by holding a tray of fish and chips, and the scent of the fried fish wafted over them. Usually the smell would make her hungry, but she was so stuffed from the huge dinner. Jess watched the bar closely and spotted two people paying their bill and headed toward them, with Alison right behind her. They reached the bar just as the couple stood to leave, and as soon as they walked away, Alison and Jess slid into their seats.

The bartender came over a few minutes later and they both ordered chardonnay. They'd only had one drink with dinner, and Jess figured they'd have one here and maybe a coffee after that if they wanted to stay out longer.

"I'm still so full," Alison said when her wine arrived. It was a generous pour.

Jess agreed and glanced around the room. As they chatted, she noticed that the dining room was starting to empty out and, just since they'd sat down, quite a few people had come in and made their way to the bar. She guessed that the band would be starting any minute.

"Have you heard them before?"

Alison shook her head. "No. It's been ages since I've been here. Their name sounds familiar, though. I think Chris saw them not too long ago and said they were good. I wouldn't be surprised if we see him tonight."

Jess frowned. She hoped not, as the whole point was for Alison to meet other people.

"Did you invite him?"

"No. I did mention that we were coming here, though. Chris stops in here regularly."

Jess sighed. She'd long suspected this was a big reason why Alison hadn't found a new relationship. She already had a very comfortable one with Chris, and anyone who saw them together would see them as a couple, not best friends. "Well, let's choose somewhere that he doesn't go next time we go out—and don't tell him. You'll never meet someone new if Chris is by your side."

Alison nodded, and Jess could tell she understood why it was a problem. "I know. I just didn't think anything of it when he asked what we were doing."

"Well, maybe he has other plans tonight. Do you see anyone here that you know?"

Alison looked around and shook her head. "No. Like I said, though, I don't get out much, and most of the people I know well work at the magazine."

The band began to play, and they were good. They covered everything from Tom Petty to Pearl Jam and even Stevie Nicks. Jess enjoyed the music and didn't even notice when the seat next to her emptied out and someone new sat down—until Alison smiled.

"Hey, Chris! You got lucky finding a seat at the bar."

He grinned. "I know. How was dinner?"

Alison filled him in while Jess tuned out and gazed around the bar, people-watching. There were all ages from early twenties to mid-seventies. She noticed a group of guys close to their age on the other side of the bar. They looked like they might have been golfing earlier. One of them smiled when he caught her looking, and she quickly looked away. She wasn't trying to attract attention for herself, and it was a shame that Alison was completely oblivious and chatting away comfortably with Chris.

Jess really didn't understand their relationship. She listened as they talked and paid attention to how they communicated and finally came to the conclusion that it was as Alison said, they were just best friends. There wasn't any romantic flirting or tension or anything of the sort between them. She'd often wondered, over the years, if there might be more to it. She and Alison talked all the time, but only saw each other once a year, if that. And given how much time they spent together, it wouldn't have been surprising if they'd explored the possibility of a reunion. But what she saw was just a very strong friendship: brother-sister, best-friend vibes. She wondered if she and Parker could ever have that. She couldn't imagine it, though.

The band played for almost a half hour before they took a break. Jess noticed that Alison had barely touched her wine and was yawning nonstop. Jess still had more than half left of hers, but she was slowly sipping it as she enjoyed the music. She looked forward to hearing the band's next set. It was still early, barely nine o'clock. Alison yawned again and apologized.

"I'm so sorry. I hate to do this, but I think I need to go home. I can barely keep my eyes open. I think I ate too much." She got her wallet out, and Jess shook her head.

"I've got this. I can finish up and head out with you."

Alison stood and reached for her coat. "Why don't you stay? You still have half a glass of wine. And you could finish mine if you want. Enjoy the music and relax. I don't want to cut your night short just because I'm ready for bed."

Chris smiled. "Yeah, stay, Jess. This band is great. Would be a shame to miss their next set. I'll keep you company."

"No one will bother you with Chris next to you," Alison agreed. Jess knew she was right about that.

"Okay, I'll stay a bit longer. This band is really good."

"I'll call you tomorrow." Alison grabbed her purse and headed out. A few minutes later, the band returned and played another set. They were just as good, and Jess felt herself unwinding and, for the first time, just being present in the moment without the cloud of Parker and a pending divorce hanging over her. She finished her wine and pulled Alison's abandoned one over and took a sip. She didn't usually have more than two glasses of wine when she went out, so she didn't intend to drink much of it. When she could get the bartender's attention she'd order a coffee.

She was pleasantly surprised that Chris hadn't tried to chat while the band was playing, like he had with Alison. Instead, he'd looked far off, lost in the music, too. When the band took another break, he finally looked her way and spoke.

"Good, huh? Saw them a few weeks ago and made sure to stop in when they were playing again."

"It's been a long time since I've gone out and heard live music. I forgot how fun it is," Jess admitted. Parker had never been much for going to hear bands. He'd been more into sporting events or dinners out. And Parker had expensive taste. Jess enjoyed a good meal, too, but liked things a little simpler.

"How are you doing? Is it good being back in Chatham?" Chris's eyes were kind, and Jess suddenly felt a wave of emotion. She fought back tears and took a deep breath, annoyed with herself to feel so fragile at the mere mention of what had happened. She needed to toughen up. It was hard, though. She realized her emotions were still so close to the surface and it didn't take much to bring them out.

"Thanks for asking. It is helping, just being here. Chatham has always been my happy place."

He nodded. "I get that. Will you stay now that you've bought the bookstore? You don't have to go back to Charleston, do you?"

Did she? Jess had assumed that she would. She smiled. "Well, Charleston is home. I'll probably head back there in mid-October, when things start to slow down."

"If you do get divorced, even if you don't move back here, it will be nice having you around more. Alison loves having you here."

Jess grinned. "It's been great spending so much time with her and with the bookstore, too. It worked out well that Ellen Campbell was thinking of retiring."

"Meant to be," Chris agreed.

Jess thought about what going back to Charleston meant. Would she want to keep the house? Or sell it and get something smaller? It would be hard to stay in that house, with all its memories. And going back to the law firm was out of the question. She'd have to think about what to do next on the work front. The thought of trying to find a new job in Charleston was a bit daunting. And she didn't know how she truly felt about any of it. Charleston was home now, but everything else was changing. Her emotions were all over the place, veering from deep sadness to anger to fear and even an occasional fleeting sense of excitement. It was overwhelming.

It would be hard to go work for someone else at this point in her career. It might make more sense to hang out her own shingle. But would it be difficult to get clients once word got out about the divorce? Parker's family was so well established. She lifted her chin. It might not be easy at first, but she was a good attorney and it could be done. But was that what she wanted to do?

"You look deep in thought," Chris said.

Jess snapped her attention back and laughed. "Sorry, I was just thinking about what you said . . . figuring out all the things I'll need to do when I go back to Charleston. It's a bit exhausting," she admitted.

"Well, don't think about it just yet." He smiled and glanced toward the band, which was getting ready to play what she guessed was their final set. "Just enjoy each day as it comes and worry about all that later."

Jess took a sip of wine and let herself relax again. "You're right. I have plenty of time to sort that out. Tell me more about you, what's going on in your life? Are you dating anyone?"

Chris chuckled at the question. "No, I'm not dating anyone right now. Things are going well overall. It's just hard to meet someone that you want to be serious with."

"You and Alison seem so good together. I always wondered if you might get back together?" She was curious to hear his thoughts on that.

His eyes grew warm again. "Alison's great. We love each other, but it's a deep friendship, not a romance. The romantic spark just isn't there but she's one of my best friends. People have a hard time understanding that. She feels the same way, though."

"She does. She told me the same thing. I guess I just hoped maybe it could be more. I want to see you both happy."

"I do, too. I've been encouraging her to date," Chris said.

"Me, too. She needs to get out and about more. It was my idea to have drinks here tonight."

Chris was quiet for a moment before shaking his head. "Sorry if I ruined that. I didn't realize. I should have. You both looked great tonight. Well, of course, you always do."

"No, it's fine. Next time we go out we won't go have a huge dinner first. I think she would have been happy to go straight home."

"Not you, though? You always were more of a night owl, if I remember."

Jess laughed. "Yes, always. I'm not a morning person the way Alison is."

The band started to play again, and they both turned their attention back to the music. Chris's hand brushed against hers a few minutes later when he reached for his draft beer and she pulled her hand away quickly, startled by the sensation. There'd been a tingling that she hadn't felt in a long time and it took her by surprise. Suddenly she was aware of Chris in a different way.

She noticed how the deep hunter green of his button-down shirt made his brown eyes look a little green and how the dusting of gray in his almost black hair looked so good on him. How when he smiled, a spray of laugh lines danced around his mouth and eyes. She'd never noticed these things in the same way before. And it felt a bit wrong, though she knew it would never go anywhere. She'd never looked at Chris that way before, for obvious reasons, and she was sure it had never crossed his mind either.

When the band finished, Jess found herself fighting a yawn. She was ready to crawl into bed. She waved to the bartender for the check. But when he set it down, Chris grabbed it and handed it back, along with his credit card for both of their checks.

"What are you doing? I told Alison I'd get her drink." She reached for her wallet.

"Like you said earlier, it's just a drink. I can buy my favorite girls a drink, can't I?" He grinned, and the laugh lines worked their magic—his eyes twinkled with amusement.

Jess could tell it was useless to protest further. It was very generous of him. She admitted defeat and laughed. "Fine. Thank you."

"It's my pleasure. Thanks for keeping me company. This band will be here again in a few weeks, we should come back then."

"Sure, that would be fun." Did she imagine it, or did he hold her gaze for maybe a moment longer than he needed to?

Jess grabbed her coat and purse and stood to go. Chris signed the charge slip and they walked out together.

"Where did you park?" he asked when they stepped outside. Her car was just a few spaces over.

"I'm right here."

"Okay, drive safe then and I'll hopefully see you soon." He pulled her in for a goodbye hug, and it felt good to be wrapped in his arms for a moment. She felt it again, too, that weird tingling. She pulled away quickly and stepped back.

"Good night, Chris."

Jess drove home, and both Caitlin and her mother were in bed when she walked in the house. Her mother had left the kitchen light on for her. She put her leftovers in the refrigerator, made herself a cup of hot tea, and settled in the living room. She put an old episode of *Friends* on and wrapped herself in a cozy fleece blanket. She was tired, but not ready to go to sleep yet, and watching *Friends* always relaxed her.

She'd had a good night and an unexpected one. She felt her eyes water again as her emotions surfaced and she realized that hugging Chris was the only physical touch she'd felt in months. She hadn't realized how much she'd missed it or how confusing it was to feel attracted to someone else. Someone who not only wasn't her husband but was completely off-limits. Though she knew she didn't really want to do anything about it. She just missed the closeness that she used to have with Parker.

She knew that she needed more time, a lot more time, to get over her marriage ending before she could begin to think about starting anything new, with anyone. Until tonight, dating hadn't even crossed her mind. She'd been so focused on finding someone for Alison. Eventually, she'd be ready to get back out there herself, but it wasn't going to be anytime soon.

Jess yawned and took a sip of her chamomile tea. It was warm and soothing and just what she needed. A few more sips and she'd be ready to climb into bed. What she needed to focus on, starting tomorrow, was finding a way to turn things around at the bookstore. To start generating more sales. Julia had some good ideas, and Alison, too. Now they just had to work together to make sure the store was a success. Jess wanted to be able to leave in the fall for Charleston and let Alison handle it for the winter, and not have to worry that sales were too slow. She hoped they could get there.

Chapter 20

Caitlin arrived at the coffee shop at a quarter after six to open up. She was surprised by how much of a morning person she'd become. Her friends would find it hard to believe. But since she'd been in Chatham, she'd slept better—she went to bed earlier and woke up feeling energized. When she'd mentioned it to her grandmother over dinner, she'd attributed it to the clean, crisp salt air. Her mother added that Caitlin was getting more exercise, too. And she was right about that.

Caitlin was on her feet in both the bookstore and the coffee shop for most of her shift, but since her mother and Jess started working in the bookstore, she spent most of her time in the coffee shop, and that was even more active. On a busy day, she didn't stop moving. And much to her surprise, she enjoyed it.

She liked getting there before everyone else, when everything was quiet and still. She got everything stocked and ready to go—making three giant thermoses of coffee, the regular dark, a lighter blend, and a flavor of the day. She made the dark roast first and poured herself a cup to enjoy while she worked.

They opened at seven, and at a quarter to, Alison arrived to drop off the baked goods. Sometimes, she stayed for a bit, depending on how busy they were—and other times, she went home and came back when the bookstore opened at ten, if it was a day she was working.

"Who else is on with you today?" Alison asked, handing Caitlin the box of brownies, cake slices, and muffins.

"Sally just walked in. She's getting changed in the back."

"Okay, good. I'm going to work on some editing this morning. If you need me, though, just text me and I can come help."

Caitlin smiled. "Will do. I'm sure we'll be fine, though. Sundays are a little bit of a later day. We seem to get busy around eleven, and we have Joan coming in then, too."

When Alison left, Caitlin unlocked the front door and flipped the CLOSED sign to OPEN. Sally tied her pink apron over her white button-down shirt and went behind the counter. She'd be manning the bagel and muffin station, toasting orders as they came in, while Caitlin chatted with the customers and rang them up.

They didn't have to wait long. Their first customer of the day, a regular now, walked in a moment later. Ed Thompson was an older gentleman. Caitlin guessed he was somewhere in his eighties. He broke into a big smile when he saw her.

"How's the world treating you today, Caitlin?" Ed was full of energy and always in a good mood. His attitude was infectious, and Caitlin couldn't help but smile back.

"It's all good now that you're here, Ed. Are you having your usual?"

He thought for a moment. "I think I might change things up a bit. I'll have my usual medium coffee extra sugar but I'll try an onion bagel instead of plain. Just to spice things up. What do you think?"

"I think that's an excellent choice."

Sally toasted up his bagel and poured his coffee while Caitlin took his money and handed him back his change. He dropped a dollar in the glass tip jar by the register. "Keep up the good work, girls," he said as Caitlin handed him a paper bag with his bagel. One of the things Caitlin had grown to like about working in the coffee shop was recognizing so many of their regulars—many came in every day and they seemed to love that she remembered not only their names but also what they liked to order.

The rest of the morning was a little busier than usual. Caitlin and Sally didn't stop until almost eleven, when there was a brief lull before Joan arrived, and then it was nonstop again until early afternoon, when it slowed enough for Sally and then Caitlin to take a short break. She made herself a bagel with cream cheese, grabbed a bottle of water, and headed outside for some fresh air.

It was a gorgeous, warm and sunny day. Caitlin walked around the corner to where there was a bench under a tree. She sat and inhaled her bagel. Just as she was about to head back inside, her phone beeped with a new text message, from Beth.

> Nancy's party is coming up. She told me to tell you that you're absolutely invited. Is there any way you can get back here for it? Could you fly home for a long weekend? You don't want to miss this. . . . and it has been too long!!

Caitlin knew that her mother was really hoping that she might stay longer, until she went back in October, and she'd been considering it, since she had no job in Charleston to rush back to. But, she did miss her friends and her life in Charleston. And wondered what she was missing out on.

Nancy's party was the biggest event of the summer—and as her friends had reminded her more than once, all the most eligible men they knew would be there. It might be a lot of fun, and she was curious to see who would be there. Maybe they could manage without her for a weekend if she could get enough coverage. She'd run it by her mother and let her know she'd be willing to stay longer. Hopefully that would do the trick. As much as she was enjoying

Chatham, Beth's message made her homesick and she was eager to get back to Charleston—for at least a few days.

♛

At about two thirty, Julia walked in. Caitlin knew Julia liked to take an afternoon break and she'd stopped in every day so far. She always got the same thing, a macchiato with extra foam and a hint of caramel. Caitlin told Sally what to make as soon as Julia walked in and it was ready for her so quickly that she laughed.

"Thank you. You guys are amazing. Has it been busy?"

"Very. It slows down in the afternoon, though. How are things in the shop?"

"Good. I had a flurry of customers this morning and around lunchtime, a friend of my mother's came in and booked a special order, a gold bracelet."

"That sounds expensive," Caitlin said.

Julia grinned. "It is! It should be gorgeous, though, when it's finished."

"How's Kyle liking Nashville?" Caitlin knew he'd been down there a little over a week.

Julia's smile disappeared and she took a long, slow sip of her coffee before answering. "He says he likes it. It's hot, though. I'm going for a visit next week, closing the shop for a day or two." She didn't sound all that excited about the trip.

"Oh, that will be fun. You must miss him."

Julia hesitated. "It's been quiet since he left. I haven't gone out as much. But, a friend is having a party tonight and our friend Tim is in a band, and I guess he and his band will be playing there, so that should be fun."

Caitlin thought it sounded like a great time. She hadn't done anything like that since she'd left Charleston. Hopefully she could get away for that weekend and catch up with her friends.

Julia looked at her thoughtfully. "What are you up to tonight?

If you don't have any plans, you could come with me, and meet some of my friends."

Caitlin didn't hesitate. "I'd love that."

"I'll text you my address. Why don't you come by around six and we'll head out. It's a casual backyard cookout, so maybe bring a sweater or jacket in case it gets cold later. They'll probably get a fire going, too."

"Perfect. I'll see you then."

❦

Julia usually closed the shop at five, but on Sundays she shut things down a bit earlier, at three. She brought her coffee back to the shop and sipped it slowly as she gazed out the window and watched people walk along Main Street. She'd checked her email several times, looking for word on the contest. She thought she might have heard something by now. She tried to tell herself that maybe no news was good news. It had been a good day overall, though, and she was ready to head home.

When she pulled into her driveway, she saw something on her front steps and realized it was a huge bouquet of red roses. From Kyle no doubt. It was the second time he'd sent flowers since he left. The first time was after they'd had an argument on the phone that was totally his fault. He'd been in a bad mood; she'd picked up on it instantly when he'd argued with her about something stupid and wouldn't let it go. That had irritated her and she'd ended the call abruptly. He'd called back and she'd let it go to voice mail. The next day the flowers had arrived, along with an apology. He said he'd been stressed about work. The new job came with more pressure and responsibility than he was used to. She'd sympathized, to a point. But it didn't make her miss him. If anything it made her glad that he was far away.

Julia had been a little distant with him ever since, and he'd been on his best behavior. So, she wasn't surprised to see more flowers.

She picked up the card and read the note. "Missing you. Can't wait to see you on Sunday. Love, Kyle."

She was looking forward to going to Nashville. She hoped that they'd have a great time. He'd promised to show her all around and to go to some of the writers' nights, which were where aspiring songwriters had a chance to sing and showcase their material. Kyle said he had it all planned out for Sunday and Monday night.

She took the flowers inside, set them on the kitchen table, and called Kyle to thank him. He picked up on the first ring.

"You got the flowers?"

"Yes, they're beautiful. Thank you. How's everything in Nashville?"

"Hot. Good, though. I played a little golf with one of the guys from work this morning and just took a swim in the pool. Did you just get home from work?" Kyle lived in a condo complex that had a pool and a gym. It sounded nice enough.

"I did. It was a good day, busy." She told him about the new commission from her mother's friend.

"Nice. What are you up to tonight? Just hanging in and watching Hallmark movies?" Kyle always liked to tease her about watching the feel-good movies. It was what she usually did on a Sunday night.

"No, actually. Sue's having a cookout and Caitlin and I are going to head over around six. Tim's band might play a little, and they're really good."

"With Caitlin? I didn't realize you two were friends now. You always said you had nothing in common." He was right. She did used to say that.

"It's been almost two years since I've seen her. She seems a little different now, more serious and grown-up. And I know she doesn't really know anyone here." Julia had realized after Kyle left, and she'd been grateful for the friends that she had, that it might be sort of lonely for Caitlin. And they were the same age, after all.

Kyle was quiet for a moment. "That does sound fun. Hey, I have to go, I think my pizza guy is knocking at the door. I'll call you tomorrow."

Julia set her phone down and stared out the window, taking a moment before she had to go get ready to meet Caitlin. She'd noticed that her phone calls with Kyle seemed to be getting shorter lately. He was busier now that he was settling in and making new friends. She was happy for him but was a little surprised that he seemed to be adapting so quickly. He raved about Nashville nonstop, and it didn't seem like he missed the Cape much at all. She knew he missed her, though. But Julia had a strong feeling that Kyle had no intention of ever moving back to the Cape. Nashville was his home now. And she wasn't entirely sure how she felt about that.

Chapter 21

"You look nice, honey. Where are you off to?" Caitlin's mother asked. She and her grandmother were sitting in the kitchen sipping a glass of wine and flipping through takeout menus. Caitlin had spent the last half hour trying on a half dozen different tops before settling on the pale blue scoop-neck cotton sweater. She paired it with her most flattering jeans and comfy leather flip-flops. She hadn't even heard her mother come home. She'd been at the bookstore all afternoon.

"Julia invited me to go to a cookout."

Her mother looked thrilled to hear it, which was no surprise. Caitlin knew her mother and Alison had always hoped that their daughters would have a close friendship. Caitlin had been surprised and pleased by the invitation. Since she'd started working at the coffee shop, she found herself looking forward to her daily chats with Julia and felt like she was finally starting to know her. She'd always thought they were too different and didn't have anything in common, but she realized she shouldn't have assumed that.

"How fun! Do you want to borrow my car? Your grandmother and I are in for the evening. We might have a pizza delivered."

Caitlin smiled. "Thanks. Grams already said I could use her car." She'd been using her grandmother's car more often, especially on the days she went in early to open the store. Her grandmother insisted that it was no bother and that if she needed to go somewhere, she could always use her mother's car. So far, it was working out well enough.

Caitlin headed out and found Julia's place easily. It was small but neat and had an artistic feel to it. Colorful paintings hung on the walls and pretty throw blankets and pillows in soft blues and greens accented a plush cream-colored sofa. Julia's kitchen was all white, with a gray subway-tile backsplash and white granite countertops that were streaked with gray, which gave it a gorgeous marble look. A butcher-block-topped island sat in the center of the kitchen. It was a perfect size for one or two people, and Caitlin felt a pang of envy as she admired it. She was long overdue to get her life together and move into her own place.

"Are you ready to go?" Julia asked. Caitlin nodded. She also admired Julia's outfit, which was both edgy and flattering. Julia wore jeans that were fashionably distressed with a flowy green top with zigzag cutouts that showed a cream lace top beneath. Her hair was down and wavy, with the turquoise tips shimmering where the light hit them.

Caitlin followed Julia to her car, an older-model Honda Civic. Julia had made a plate of brownies and Caitlin had brought a bottle of chardonnay. When they arrived at the cookout, there were already quite a few people there. Julia parked on the side of the road behind a truck.

"I didn't realize this was going to be such a big party," Caitlin said as they walked toward the house.

Two more cars pulled up behind them as Julia glanced around. "I thought it was just going to be a small gathering. That's what Sue said. Word must have gotten out that the band is playing." She grinned. "Hopefully, she invited the neighbors so there won't be any noise complaints."

They went inside and Julia introduced her to Sue and Tim, who played guitar in the band. She knew they were both two of Julia's best friends. Tim had a regular day job, too, as an accountant with a Hyannis firm.

"We play nights and weekends all over the Cape. Whoever will take us," he explained. He introduced the other band members, who were all in the kitchen, leaning against the counter and drinking beer. Caitlin nodded as introductions were made and hoped she could remember all of their names.

"And this guy. He used to be in the band. Got too good for us," Tim teased as someone walked over that Caitlin recognized. It was Jason, the plumber she'd met in the bookstore.

"I know Caitlin already," he said. "Nice to see you again."

"You used to play in the band, too?" She wondered why he stopped.

"I used to sing a little. The late nights and early mornings for plumbing didn't go so well together. It was fun, though."

"Maybe we'll get you up for a tune or two tonight?" Tim suggested.

Jason laughed. "Maybe. We'll see. I might be a little rusty."

"Let's head outside. I'll introduce you to everyone else," Sue said. She grabbed a plate of raw burgers from the refrigerator, and Caitlin and Julia followed her outside. She handed the burgers to a burly guy standing by a grill that already had a few burgers and dogs on it.

"Kevin, this is Julia's friend, Caitlin. Caitlin, my boyfriend, Kevin."

Kevin mumbled hello and took the platter from Sue and turned his attention back to the grill. Sue led them around the yard and introduced Caitlin to everyone. There were so many people, at least fifty or so with more coming in. Caitlin just smiled and said hello and gave up trying to remember anyone's name.

It was a gorgeous night, clear and warm. Perfect weather for a cookout.

"I love what you did with the lights," Julia said before Sue left them to greet new guests. Tiny white lights glittered along the bushes and trees in the backyard and hung over the back deck railing. The effect was pretty, especially as the night went on and the sky darkened. And there was so much food. Caitlin and Julia both had cheeseburgers and potato salad and shared a brownie a half hour later. They settled around one of the outside tables to eat and stayed there to listen to the band when they played their first set.

They were better than Caitlin expected, and she looked at Julia in surprise after their first song, a Blake Shelton cover. Julia laughed. "I know. They're good, huh?"

"They could do this professionally." Caitlin wondered if that was the goal.

"They've been together for a few years now and have played all over the Cape, especially in the summer. It's fun for them, but I don't think the expectations are that it will be more than that."

"Tim wouldn't mind doing it full-time. The others aren't as serious about it," Jason said as he sat down in the empty chair next to Caitlin. "Happened to overhear. Hope you don't mind if I join you?"

"Of course not," Julia said.

Caitlin looked around. There were plenty of other empty seats outside.

Julia and Jason chatted for a bit, catching up on the people they knew.

"So, Jason, Tim, and I grew up together," Julia explained when Caitlin laughed as they finished each other's sentences the way brothers and sisters sometimes did. They clearly went way back, and she could see they were all best friends.

Jason laughed. "We were inseparable ever since elementary school. We met at the bus stop, fifth grade."

Caitlin had good friends in Charleston, but none she'd known for that long. Maybe that was one of the differences between growing up in a city instead of a small town.

"Where's Kyle?" Jason asked at one point, and Julia explained about his new job. And that she was heading to Nashville to visit the following week.

"Nashville's a cool city. My college roommate is from there and I spent a few years nearby. That's where Tim should go if he really wanted to pursue music."

"I think he's given up that dream," Julia said. "And he's a really good accountant."

Jason laughed. "He is actually. He does my taxes now and for the business, too."

"Where did you go to college?" Caitlin asked. She was curious how someone with a degree ended up in plumbing but thought it was probably rude to ask.

He looked her way and smiled. "Vanderbilt."

Vanderbilt was a really good school. "What was your major?" She immediately regretted asking the question. It was none of her business really.

But he didn't seem to mind. "Business. Worked in mutual-fund accounting in Boston when I was first out of school. But then my dad had health issues and I took some time off to help out. I used to work with him during the summer." He grinned. "Turns out I like plumbing and running a small business more than crunching numbers and commuting into the city."

"Does your father still work with you?"

He shook his head. "No, he retired a few years ago. It's all mine now. What about you? Is the bookstore and coffee shop just temporary, helping your mother out?"

She nodded. "It is. Though I don't really have a job to go back to in Charleston. To be honest, I'm still trying to figure out what I should be doing."

"Most people need to try a few things before they land where they are supposed to be. You'll get there."

"Jason, they want you to join them," Julia said.

Caitlin glanced toward the band. Tim was waving at Jason to come join them.

"I guess I have to go up there." Jason stood and Tim handed him the mic as the band started playing the Pearl Jam song "Just Breathe." Caitlin recognized it immediately, as it was one of her favorites. Jason's voice was rich and deep and a little gravelly. Perfect for Pearl Jam. She was impressed.

He sang two more songs before heading into the house. Caitlin thought they'd seen the last of him, maybe. But he reappeared a few minutes later, with a new beer, and settled back at their table.

"You haven't lost your touch," Julia said. "That was really good."

"It was," Caitlin said. "You could probably sing full-time if you wanted to." She could picture it. Though he didn't seem like he was interested in that.

Jason laughed at the thought. "I doubt it. I really don't think it's that easy. And I have no interest in moving to Nashville. Fun to visit, but I like the Cape."

"The Cape really is great. It's been fun being here all summer. We usually just come for a week or two, if that. Last year we didn't make it."

"You're heading back to Charleston soon?" Jason asked.

"Probably in the fall."

He nodded. "That's when the big shift happens. When the tourists clear out."

"It doesn't get too quiet for you?"

Julia and Jason exchanged glances. "People always ask that. How can we stand it here in the winter?" Julia smiled.

Jason laughed. "What they don't understand is that we don't mind when the crowds go away. The Cape is beautiful in the off-season.

It's quieter, sure, but that's not bad. It means no traffic and that's a very good thing."

"I haven't been here in the winter since I was too little to really remember it. My grandmother always came to us for the holidays. I know she loves all the seasons, though. She sends us gorgeous photos year-round." Caitlin imagined it must be like a ghost town with all the tourists gone. She hoped there'd be enough local business to keep the bookstore and coffee shop busy. But she also knew her mother and was sure she and Alison had done their research to make sure the overall yearly revenue was there.

"You should see what it's like. Stay longer or come back during the winter, and see for yourself," Jason said.

"What are your plans?" Julia asked. "Do you have a job lined up in Charleston."

"No. I'll probably sign on with a temp agency while I start a job search."

"Jason!" Two guys who had just arrived stood by the band and hollered at Jason to join them.

He chuckled. "Looks like I'm being summoned. I haven't seen those guys in a while. I'll catch up with you two later?"

"Go and have fun," Julia urged him. Once he was out of earshot, she turned to Caitlin.

"It's too bad you have to go back to Charleston. Jason is a catch and newly single."

"Yeah?" Caitlin couldn't help but be curious. She'd felt drawn to Jason since he first walked into the bookstore. But her track record wasn't great and it didn't make sense to start something if she was going to be heading home soon.

"He was dating Merry Andrews for almost three years. We assumed they were on the verge of getting engaged when they suddenly broke up. I don't know more than that, but it was pretty recent, maybe six months ago. The rumor is that she cheated on him with the guy she's with now. But I don't know if that's true."

"Well, if it is, I wouldn't blame him for taking a break from dating," Caitlin said.

"I think he might be ready to get back out there. Last time Kyle and I were out at the Squire, Jason was there in deep conversation with a cute blond girl." She smiled. "He stopped by to chat with us for a minute and I asked if he was dating her and he just laughed and said 'Not yet.'"

For some reason Caitlin felt disappointed to hear it. "So, he's already found someone, then?"

Julia looked around and shook her head. "I don't think so. She's not here—if they were together, you'd think she would be."

A thought occurred to Caitlin. "Is he someone you'd want to date maybe? If things don't work out with Kyle?"

Julia laughed. "No. Jason is great. But we've been friends for years—I think of him like a brother."

Caitlin grinned. "Your very hot brother!"

"Are you sure you have to go back to Charleston?" Julia asked. Her tone was teasing but she was serious about the question.

"I have a whole life there. It's home for me," Caitlin said.

"I get it. That's how I feel about Chatham. Especially now that I have the shop."

The band played another set, and after that, Caitlin and Julia walked around a bit and mingled. Everyone was friendly, and most were year-round residents of Chatham. Many had gone to school with Julia. Caitlin found herself keeping an eye out for Jason. She spotted him chatting with a group of guys he seemed to know well—they were all laughing and having a good time. She didn't see him again to talk to until she and Julia were walking out the door. He was saying goodbye to a friend and on his way back inside.

"You two heading out?"

"We are. It was good seeing you, Jason." Julia gave him a goodbye hug.

"You, too."

He smiled at Caitlin. "And you as well." He leaned in to hug her goodbye, and Caitlin held her breath for a moment. The contact was brief, but the closeness made her a bit dizzy as his scent—just soap and maybe a hint of cologne—enveloped her.

"Good night, Jason." She walked on to the car with Julia and resisted the urge to look back. It had been a good night.

Chapter 22

On Sunday morning, Jess sat in the kitchen sipping her second cup of coffee and glaring at the bookstore's online banking page. Sales were still not where they'd hoped they would be. They were just barely breaking even. Once their hourly employees were paid, and all their expenses, there was very little left. She felt a stress headache building and didn't even realize she was rubbing her hand against her forehead until her mother strolled into the room, stopped short, and looked at her intently.

"What's wrong?"

Jess glanced up and saw the concern on her mother's face. She debated saying nothing and insisting that it was all fine. But knew her mother was smarter than that.

"I'm just a little worried about sales at the bookstore. They're not what I thought they would be."

Her mother poured herself a cup of coffee and joined Jess at the island, sliding into the chair next to hers.

"It's only been a few weeks. Maybe it will take a while to get things up and running?"

Jess sighed. "This is the busy season, though, and we took over an existing business. It's not like we were starting from scratch."

Her mother stirred a little sugar into her coffee before taking a sip. She stared out the window and took another sip before setting the mug down.

"You did look over the books before you bought the place, right? Things can't be that different, can they?"

"I probably should have looked more closely. Sales were down a little, but I assumed that was because Ellen was tired, and she was slowing down. I know she'd stopped doing some of the events she used to do."

"Okay. Have you started those things up? You mentioned something about author signings and story hour for the children?"

"Not yet. We've reached out to some local authors and a few expressed interest in setting up signings, but we haven't held one yet. And the story hours are due to start next week."

Her mother smiled. "So, you have a plan, then. I wouldn't be too concerned just yet. Wait and see how things go after you do some of these things. And maybe you can think of some other ideas, too. What about a store card?"

"A store card? You mean like a credit card?"

"No, I'm not sure what it's called, but the kind where people show their card when they make a purchase and get a discount or something like that. I'm not sure exactly how it works."

"A loyalty card. That's actually a great idea, Mom. I'll talk to Alison about that."

Her mother smiled. "Good. You'll figure it out. The coffee shop seems busy. I stopped in yesterday and Caitlin was running behind the counter. There was a line but it moved right along. I tried one of those black bean brownies that Alison makes. Didn't expect to like it, but I was surprised."

Jess laughed. "They are good. I was skeptical at first, too. The coffee shop is doing well. We're actually a little ahead of projections there, which offsets the bookstore, which is still a bit slower, but we are working on it. Caitlin's doing a great job. And she agreed to stay until October."

"She did? That's wonderful news."

"She did. The catch is she wants to fly home to Charleston for a weekend—to see her friends and go to the most important party of the summer."

Her mother laughed. They both knew Caitlin could be a bit dramatic. "Of course I agreed instantly. We can plan for her to be gone for a few days and it will be a huge help to have her stay until things slow in mid-October."

Caitlin's request had made Jess realize how much she was missing Charleston, too. Missing the normal, everyday life she'd had, before she saw Linda's baby bump. Things hadn't been right with Parker for a long time, but Jess had otherwise enjoyed working and living in Charleston. She'd had an active social life there and missed seeing her girlfriends for lunch or playing tennis at the club. It seemed like another world away, and she was suddenly filled with sadness. But then, her mood shifted again as a tiny robin flew by the window and landed on a hanging plant. It was a gorgeous, sunny day. A perfect beach day, actually. Maybe she could sneak out for a bit and bask in the sun's warmth.

"Maybe you won't want to go back at all?" her mother suggested. Jess knew she would love it if Jess moved home for good. But it wasn't something she'd seriously considered.

"I've built a life in Charleston. I'm not sure I'm ready to give that up, just yet. Though, some days it is tempting," Jess admitted.

"You have a lot to sort out. Go back there for a while and see how it goes. Chatham is always an option. Maybe you could split your time between here and there, six months both places?"

"Maybe." Jess couldn't imagine how that would be possible if she continued to practice law in Charleston, but it was fun to dream about. Winters down south, and summer and fall in Chatham. That would be nice.

❧

Alison sipped her coffee and looked around the bookshop. They'd been open for a half hour and not a single customer had come into the store yet. It was an absolutely gorgeous day—perfect beach weather. So, no doubt that's where everyone was, but still, it was a bit worrisome.

Alison didn't have to review the financials to know that sales were not where they needed to be. Thankfully, the coffee shop business was steadily increasing, but the bookshop sales were lagging, and Alison wasn't sure what to do about it. She thought the shop looked as good as it possibly could. There were some new and very pretty paintings on the wall—pastel seascapes from several local artists. They gave the room an artsy vibe.

She'd rearranged the display tables so that they not only showcased the obvious bestsellers, but also had some newer authors with books she'd read personally and thought their readers would love. She'd also found a round table and put it near the entrance so it was the first thing people would see when they walked in, and it was all local authors and books set on the Cape and the islands. Sales of those books had increased since she made the change, but it still wasn't enough.

Alison felt her stomach tighten as she worried, not for the first time, about her finances as well. They were closely linked to the bookshop, as Alison didn't want Jess to lose money on this investment, and if she lost money, Alison would, too. She also hadn't managed to pick up any freelance assignments yet. As she'd feared, getting the word out and generating assignments wasn't easy. The only extra work she'd managed so far had come from Jim, occasional articles or features that needed editing—and she knew she couldn't count on that as a steady source of revenue.

She knew that returning books that didn't sell was an option, but it didn't feel right to her to give up on those books. Maybe they could find a way to highlight them better. Julia had mentioned using social media to draw readers into the store, but Alison didn't have a good understanding of how that worked.

She thought of something she'd noticed in another bookstore last week in Hyannis and wondered if it might work for them. The store had little note cards under many of the books, with recommendations from the staff—notes on why they loved different books.

Alison looked around in the office and found a stack of yellow index cards. Maybe she could do something with that. She'd read so many of these books and enjoyed most of them. An hour later, she'd jotted her thoughts about the books on the cards and taped them on the shelves, just below each book. It wasn't high tech or especially creative, but at least she was doing something. And she believed in these books. Maybe it would bring some attention to them.

Chapter 23

S o, you're off soon," Caitlin said when Julia walked into the coffee shop on Sunday.

"I'm on my way to the airport now. My flight is at three. Thought I'd get a coffee for the road."

"And you're back on Tuesday?"

Julia nodded. "Tuesday night. I'll tell you all about it on Wednesday."

"I hope it's a fun trip for you. Take lots of pictures."

Julia could see the slight concern in Caitlin's eyes. It mirrored her own. But she was determined to think of the trip as a vacation and to have a good time.

"Thanks, I will."

She took her coffee, nibbled a bit of caramel and foam off the top, and headed to her car. She'd packed the night before, so she could leave right from the shop. Traffic to Logan Airport on a Sunday could be unpredictable, depending how bad the Cape traffic was, so she'd given herself an extra hour cushion. Fortunately, it was a hot, sunny day, which meant people stayed later at the beach and traffic heading off the Cape wasn't too bad.

Julia made it to Logan a little early, parked, and headed in. She had her laptop with her, and after she was through security she relaxed and surfed online for a bit while waiting for her plane to board. Once they were all on board, the actual flight was about two hours, and at a few minutes past five they landed in Nashville.

She looked around when she departed the plane and was surprised that Kyle wasn't there to meet her. She hadn't checked any luggage but followed the crowd down to baggage claim anyway, figuring that was where he was likely to be. Sure enough, a text message came through a few minutes later.

Sorry, running late. Heavy traffic. Will meet you outside baggage claim.

Fifteen minutes later, she spotted Kyle's truck coming toward her. He pulled over, jumped out, and came around to give her a hug and toss her bags in the back seat. She climbed in the passenger side, and they were off. She couldn't remember Kyle ever being late for anything before.

"Got held up at work. It's crazy busy right now. I hope you weren't waiting too long?"

She shook her head. "Not too long."

Traffic was light once they got out of the airport, and thirty minutes later they pulled into his condominium complex. Kyle grabbed her bags out of the back seat and led her inside. The condo was just like his pictures, neat and clean, and as Julia looked around she noticed that it barely looked lived-in.

"You need some paintings on the wall," she said. They were completely bare, and there was nothing on his kitchen counters either. She knew Kyle wasn't much of a cook, though. He mostly ordered takeout.

"I've been too busy to worry about decorating." There was an edge to his voice, and she wondered if she'd offended him.

"The job is keeping you busy? How is it going?"

He smiled and his tone grew warmer as he talked about his new role.

"It was a good decision coming here. The company is growing and I'm in a position to really make a difference. We're getting ready to launch a new product, a super innovative, subscription software offering. And it's cloud based, which gives us an edge in a crowded market. So, it's been a lot of late nights." He walked over and wrapped his arms around her and gave her a quick kiss. "I have missed you, though. It's not easy being so far away. Have you missed me?" His eyes held hers and she felt her pulse race a bit.

"Of course. I've missed you. It's not the same with you here."

He grinned. "I knew you'd miss me. Have you given any more thought to moving down here?"

Her warm fuzzy feeling evaporated quickly.

"Kyle, you only just moved here. We talked about this. It's too soon for me to make that kind of a decision."

He was quiet for a moment, then nodded. "Right. Just wishful thinking on my part, because I miss you so much." He glanced at his watch. "We should probably get going. We have dinner reservations at six thirty at the Bluebird Cafe."

Julia freshened up a bit, quickly splashing some water on her face and running a brush through her hair and adding a swipe of lipstick before they headed out. She was excited to go to dinner and experience a writers' night. The Bluebird Cafe was famous for these nights, where unknown singer-songwriters performed with the hope of getting noticed by a manager or record label.

The restaurant was smaller than she'd imagined, with about a hundred seats and a stage area, but it meant that there were no bad seats and there was an overall intimate feel. Service was good and their waiter was friendly as he described the daily specials. They decided to split an order of the fried brussels sprouts, and both went with the turkey club. The food was good, but the performances were magical.

There were five artists, and each one played three songs and they all chatted a bit about what inspired the songs. They were all so good.

"I wonder if someone we've seen tonight will go on and be discovered," Julia said to Kyle after the final performer finished. Their waiter refilled her water glass and overheard her comment.

"You never know. So many really big names have been discovered here. Keith Urban, Taylor Swift, Garth Brooks. Did you know he'd decided to leave Nashville after being turned down by all the record labels? He played here after that, got a standing ovation, and someone from Capitol Records happened to be here. They pulled him down the hall and signed him on the spot. And the rest is history!"

"Really? I didn't know that about Garth Brooks. That is amazing. Isn't that incredible, Kyle?" Julia was caught up in the excitement. There was a buzz in the air. Kyle yawned and narrowed his eyes at their waiter, who was actually very good-looking. "Amazing. We'll just take the check, thanks."

Julia was still on a music high as they walked out of the restaurant. "Can we go hear some live music somewhere else? There are other places nearby and it's still early."

Kyle glanced at his watch. "It's almost eleven, and I have to work tomorrow. We should probably head home."

"You didn't take tomorrow off?" Julia had assumed that he'd take Monday and Tuesday off while she was in town.

"I took Tuesday off, so I can bring you to the airport in the afternoon and maybe we can grab lunch somewhere. We're too busy right now for me to take two days off. I figured you could relax during the day, maybe go shopping or something, and we're going out again tomorrow night."

"Okay." She was disappointed but tried not to let it show.

"You can take my car tomorrow. The office is just a few miles down the road. You can drop me off in the morning and go exploring all day." He smiled as if she should be excited to spend the day alone in an unfamiliar city.

"Sure. That sounds like a plan. I'll do some sightseeing."

When they got back to the condo, Kyle was in a great mood again and they ended up staying up late and getting very little sleep when they did go to bed. The physical attraction between them had always been strong, and Julia hadn't realized how much she'd missed his touch and the closeness of waking up beside him. It was the same, but different somehow.

Morning came quickly, as Kyle's alarm went off a little after six. Julia was disoriented at first when she opened her eyes and saw the unfamiliar room. She yawned and stretched and rolled over, planning to wait until the last possible minute before getting up. Kyle swore softly and swung his legs out of bed and padded off to the shower. A half hour later, he called for her to get up. She slowly eased out of bed and went to the kitchen, where Kyle was drinking coffee and eating a bowl of cereal.

"What time do you have to be there?" It was only seven.

Kyle looked up. "I like to be in by seven thirty."

"Okay, give me two minutes to get changed." She pulled on a sweatshirt and jeans and put her hair in a ponytail. Still half asleep, she paid attention while Kyle drove to his office. He pulled up to the front door, handed her his keys, and told her to have a great day.

"Swing back around five thirty and I'll be waiting for you outside." He was all bright and cheery as he leaned in for a quick kiss, then almost sprinted toward the door. Julia was glad to see him enjoying his job, but couldn't help feeling a little annoyed that he didn't even try to get the day off.

She drove back to his condo, made herself a cup of coffee, and pulled out her laptop to plan her day. She wanted to make the most of it and see as much as possible. Tripadvisor recommended several trolley tours, and she decided to do one that had a ninety-minute tour with fourteen stops and a hundred or so points of interest and that she could hop on or off at if she wanted to explore more. She'd done a trolley tour like that in London and found it an interesting and convenient way to get around the city.

There was also a food tour that looked intriguing, and Julia thought that might be fun around lunchtime, followed by a visit to the Country Music Hall of Fame and Museum in the afternoon.

The trolley and food tour were great. Julia was happily full by the time the tour finished—she sampled lots of different local favorites, like fried chicken, barbecued pulled pork over grits, and, for dessert, doughnuts that were heavenly. After the museum, which was fascinating, Julia headed home and had a half hour or so to kill before she had to pick up Kyle. She gave her mother a call to say hello and see what she was up to. Her mother picked up on the first ring and sounded surprised to hear from her.

"Hi, honey. Is everything all right?" Julia heard the sound of a cash register in the background.

"Yes, it's fine. Just thought I'd check in. I just got home from sightseeing and have a little time before I have to pick up Kyle. Are you at the store? If it's busy I can let you go."

"I'm at the store, but it's not too busy. Brooklyn is at the register, so I can chat. Where's Kyle? He didn't show you around today?"

"He's working. He took tomorrow off, though."

Her mother was quiet for a moment. "Well, that's good. He must be busy with work."

"He is. He didn't want to ask for too much time off being so new in the role. I guess I understand it, but I was a little surprised," Julia admitted.

"Did you do anything fun last night?"

"We did!" She told her mother all about the Bluebird Cafe.

"Well, that sounds wonderful, honey. I wouldn't worry too much about Kyle having to work today. He did just start the new job a few weeks ago, and you said he took tomorrow off?"

"Yeah. It's fine. I was just surprised. How's everything with you?"

"The coffee shop is busier than ever. It's still slow in the store. I know Jess is concerned and I am, too—I don't want to see her lose money on this."

"It's only been a few weeks, Mom. Once you start some of the things we talked about, it will pick up. I'm sure of it." Julia hoped so.

"I'm sure you're right. Have a safe trip home, and I'll see you when you get back."

Her mother sounded a little more upbeat when she ended the call, and Julia felt a little less annoyed with Kyle. Her mother did have a point; Kyle was still new to the role and she'd never seen him so focused on work before. And she was happy for him.

At 5:30 sharp, Julia pulled the car up to the front door of Kyle's office. There was no sign of him yet. She waited a few minutes, then texted him that she was there. Two more minutes went by before he replied.

Sorry. Will be out in a few minutes, just wrapping up here.

Ten more minutes went by, and by a quarter to six Julia was full-fledged annoyed again. Finally, at ten of, Kyle came strolling out with two other guys. They were all laughing, and before he walked her way, they all gave him a high five. They were clearly celebrating something. Julia got out of the car and handed Kyle the keys when he reached her.

"I'm so sorry. But I have the best news. We just closed a huge deal. Huge!"

"That's great." Julia forced a smile before walking around to the passenger side and climbing in.

Kyle chatted away on the drive home, telling her all about his company's big deal. "This means we'll be needing to hire more people. I'll probably need two or three more on my team. And there's talk of possibly going public in a few years. My stock options might actually be worth something someday." His excitement was a little contagious. Julia hadn't seen him this animated and enthusiastic in a long time.

"That's great, Kyle. We'll have to celebrate tonight."

He turned and flashed her a grin. "Absolutely. And we can sleep in tomorrow. Tonight will be a good night."

And it was. They had a wonderful dinner, with a bottle of good champagne, and toasted to Kyle's company and the success he knew was coming. They enjoyed another writers' night at a different club. Julia couldn't believe how talented so many of the young performers were.

"How does anyone get discovered when they are all so good?" she wondered out loud after the final song.

"They're all crazy talented," Kyle agreed. "Do you want to go have a drink at another place and hear some more music before we head home? We don't have to rush back tonight."

"Sure." He took her to a nearby bar that advertised live music on a big sign out front.

"There's no shortage of places to go if you want to hear good music. You'd love living here," Kyle said as they walked in and found two seats at the bar. It looked like the band was about to start a new set. Once Kyle and Julia ordered their drinks, the music started. The band played for about twenty minutes before taking a break, and they were excellent. Like most of the performers they'd heard so far that night, they were playing country, a bluesy rock version that Julia really enjoyed. They seemed like more of an established band, a little older than some of the performers they'd seen the past few nights. These guys were all in their mid-to-late thirties.

The lead singer was mesmerizing. His voice was great, but he also had a presence about him, a charisma that drew all eyes his way. When he smiled, Julia smiled back—it was like he was sing-ing right to her, which of course he wasn't. She couldn't help but notice how handsome he was, too, with almost black hair that was a little too long and a slight stubble—it was a look she'd always found attractive. She glanced at Kyle, and he was focused intently on the music. She didn't think she'd ever seen Kyle with any kind of a shadow; he was always clean-shaven, and whenever his hair got even the slightest bit long, just at the point where she thought it looked great, he'd get it cut.

When they finished playing, Kyle started talking about the company again and how he had a chance for a big bonus at year-end if everything went the way they'd hoped.

"So, instead of renewing my lease, maybe I'll have enough for a down payment on a house."

"Do you really think you'll want to stay here long-term? A house is a big commitment." Julia had assumed this move prob-ably would be temporary, for a year or two and then he'd move home, if not to the Cape then to the Boston area.

"A house is a good investment. Even if I'm just here for a few years. But, I don't know. Nashville is growing on me already. Things have been really good so far. I could actually see myself here long-term." He took her hand and squeezed it. "Especially if you join me. I know you're not ready yet, but I hope you'll seriously consider it."

Julia nodded and tried not to feel annoyed. She didn't like be-ing pushed into something she wasn't ready for yet. She was about to answer when she felt something cool on her hand and pulled it away fast. She turned to see the singer from the band right next to her, an apologetic look on his face. He'd tipped the draft beer the bartender passed to him and it had sloshed onto her wrist. Just a small amount. Julia reached for a cocktail napkin the same time that he did.

"It's nothing, don't worry about it," she said.

"Clumsy of me. I'm so sorry." He mopped up the spill and motioned for the bartender to come over. "Please get these two another round of drinks, on me."

"Oh, you don't have to do that. It was just a few drops. Not a big deal at all."

"It's the least I can do," he insisted.

"Well, thank you. You were really great. We loved your music."

"You've played here before, I think?" Kyle added.

"Yeah, a few weeks ago. I'm Harry, by the way."

"Nice to meet you, Harry. I'm Julia and this is my boyfriend, Kyle."

"Are you local or just visiting?" Harry asked.

"Kyle's local. I'm just visiting. My first time here. We went to the Bluebird Cafe last night for writers' night. That was incredible, too. The energy was great."

Harry grinned. "That place is fantastic. We played there a few years ago and it's what led to us getting signed by a small local label. We're not big-time yet, but we're able to play music full-time now."

"Oh, that's great."

"Well, I should head back toward the band, we're going to go back on in a few minutes."

"Thanks again for the drinks," Julia said as the bartender set a new round in front of them.

Harry smiled in a slow easy way that she knew was probably irresistible to most women. "You're very welcome. Enjoy the rest of your vacation."

As soon as he walked away, Kyle picked up his draft beer and glared at her.

Julia was sure she must have imagined the fleeting expression, so she ignored it and took a sip of her new chardonnay.

But a moment later, Kyle spoke. "So, could you have been any more obvious?" He seemed furious and she had no idea what his problem was. "Kyle, what's wrong?"

"You were all over that guy. It was embarrassing." He was seriously mad.

And Julia was speechless. She just stared at him and grew mad herself. "You're out of your mind. He spilled a beer on me, felt bad, and bought us a round. Us. Not me, both of us. I thanked him and chatted politely. You're being silly."

"Sure. I'm being silly. Okay." He sipped his beer then turned away from her and ignored her for the rest of the set. He was still in a bad mood when they finished playing.

"Let's go. I've heard enough music for tonight." He asked for the bill and threw some cash on the bar before they left.

"Are you still mad?" she asked as they walked to the truck.

He said nothing until they pulled out of the parking lot and headed home. "I'm not mad. I'm just confused. You were totally flirting with that guy, right in front of me."

"I was not flirting, even remotely. I was just being friendly. He felt bad that he spilled beer on me. It was all harmless."

"Well, it looked like flirting to me. It just makes me wonder if this is what you do while I'm not around, too."

"You should know me better than that! I would never cheat on you, Kyle." His reaction was so over-the-top that a thought occurred to her. "Are you mad because maybe you've been tempted to cheat?"

He shot her a frosty look. "I can't believe you'd even suggest that."

"Well, now you know how I feel then."

They were quiet for the rest of the ride home. Once they were inside, Kyle tried to shift the mood, but for Julia it felt like too little, too late. He took her hands and pulled her to him. "I hate when we fight. It's been so long since I've seen you. Let's just enjoy the time we have together."

Julia nodded. She didn't want to fight either. But she wasn't feeling particularly romantic toward him. When Kyle tried to kiss her and pull her toward the bed, she allowed a quick peck, then yawned. "I'm really tired. I'm going to get changed and crash, I think."

Once they were both in bed, Kyle tried again, reaching for her, but before he could pull her toward him, she turned so her back was facing him, and snuggled into her pillow. "Good night, Kyle."

♥

They both slept in the next morning, and Julia wasn't in any hurry to get out of bed. Kyle's behavior the night before still annoyed her and raised all the prior doubts she'd had about their relationship. She was tempted to end things with him when he dropped her at the airport, but that felt impulsive and she wanted to make sure she wasn't just reacting out of anger. She needed a few days away to digest what she was feeling and decide how to move forward.

"You're so quiet," Kyle commented as he pulled up to the terminal. They'd just had a good lunch at one of his favorite local spots and she'd managed to smile and engage in small talk, but she couldn't wait to get on the plane and get home.

"I'm just tired. It's going to be a long day. It was a fun visit, though. I'm glad I came and saw where you live and finally had a chance to visit Nashville."

"I'm sorry I didn't get to do more of that with you. Next time you come, I'll be able to take more time off and I'll be a better tourist guide. I promise." He grinned and his eyes pleaded with her to agree.

So she did. "Sure, that would be great, Kyle. I'll talk to you soon." Julia gave him a quick kiss goodbye, grabbed her overnight bag, and headed into the terminal.

Chapter 24

I t didn't go so well. I think I'm probably going to call him this week and end it." Julia took a sip of chardonnay while Caitlin waited for her to explain. It was Wednesday night and they were having an after-work drink at the Squire. Julia had surprised Caitlin by suggesting it when she stopped into the coffee shop earlier that afternoon. Caitlin had thought she was just excited about her trip and wanted to tell her all about it. She didn't expect this.

"I had no idea he was like that. I'm so sorry."

"So you don't think it's bad that I break up with him over the phone? I almost did it before I got out of the car, at the airport, but it just didn't feel right then. I wanted to sleep on it, and be sure."

"I think you have to do what feels best for you. Maybe it's good that he took that promotion if you were already having doubts."

Julia nodded. "I know. In a way it makes it easier. I just hate this part."

"It's never easy, no matter who is doing the breaking up." Caitlin told her about her dinner with Prescott.

"Oh no! You thought you were getting a proposal. But you weren't in love with him, either?"

"No. So, while it stung because I didn't expect it and I'd almost talked myself into being okay with it, with trying to make it work and eventually get engaged. But I wasn't in love with him. I couldn't get there. So, I wasn't heartbroken. Just sad at first. He seemed perfect on paper, ticked all my boxes, but my heart never raced. That probably sounds silly. Sometimes I wonder if I'm being too picky—a few of my married friends think so."

The fire came back into Julia's eyes. "Absolutely not. Marriage is supposed to be forever and that's a long time to spend with someone who you're not madly in love with." She gazed out the window and a moment later smiled as Jason walked in.

Julia waved him over. Jason was still wearing his work clothes, his navy-blue shirt with BRINKER PLUMBING across the pocket. He grinned as he reached them.

"This looks like trouble," he teased. "Mind if I join you? Tim is on his way, too."

"Of course," Julia said.

The seat next to Caitlin was empty and Jason slid into it.

"So, how was Nashville?"

Julia and Caitlin exchanged glances.

"Nashville is a fun city," Julia said carefully. "I loved the writers' nights we went to."

"Did you go to the Bluebird Cafe?"

Julia nodded. "That was my favorite place." She told him a bit about the places they visited and her solo exploration of the city.

Jason raised an eyebrow. "Kyle didn't go with you?"

"Nope. Too busy with work." There was an edge to her voice that he picked up on, Caitlin could see it in his eyes. But he just nodded and took a sip of the draft beer he'd ordered.

"I'm not sure the long-distance thing is going to work for us," she admitted.

Jason set his beer down. "That's too bad."

"It is. But enough about that. Are you guys hungry? Will you help me eat some nachos if I order them?"

An hour later, after they'd had their fill of nachos, Kevin and

Sue arrived and settled at the bar next to Jason, who Caitlin had learned was easy to talk to, and funny. He'd cracked a few jokes that got Julia smiling, and Caitlin was glad to see her in a better mood, not as stressed. She glanced around the restaurant, which was still busy, and noticed that many of the people coming in seemed to know others at the bar or dining in the restaurant.

"Everyone seems to know everyone here. It reminds me of *Cheers*," Caitlin said.

Julia laughed. "It does. This is mostly where the locals go. It's not as fancy or expensive as some of the other places and the food is always good."

"I'm going to take the boat out this weekend. Probably Sunday afternoon if any of you are interested?" Jason addressed all of them.

"I didn't know your boat was back in the water. I'm definitely in," Sue said.

"I just put her in last night. I've been working on her for a few weeks to get her fixed up. She has a new motor and a new coat of paint. She's good to go."

"If it's later in the afternoon, I can make it. I'll close the shop around three," Julia said.

"I should be finished by then, too. I haven't been on a boat in ages," Caitlin added.

"Good. Weather looks like it will be great. Might get some fishing in, too. I'll bring a few extra rods."

Caitlin laughed. "I've actually never fished."

"Well, if you want to try it, am happy to help." His eyes were warm and friendly, but there was also something else there that took Caitlin by surprise. A glimmer of interest possibly, she wasn't sure. Maybe he was just being nice. But for the first time in ages, she felt a spark.

"Caitlin, when are you going back to Charleston?" Julia asked.

And just like that, the spark faded.

"Mid-October, I think. But I'm heading back next weekend for a few days."

"That's right, you're just here temporarily," Jason said.

She nodded. "This is the longest I've ever spent here. Usually we just come for a week or two. It's a different experience, staying longer. I didn't expect to like it so much."

"The Cape is special. I never thought I'd want to stay. When we were younger, we used to talk about crossing the bridge. Working in Boston or going to New York," Julia said. "Some of my friends did that, and I did, too, for a year or so. But, I was surprised to find that I really missed the Cape. Chatham is home."

Jason nodded. "Same. I've never been to Charleston, though. I hear it's pretty cool there. Or should I say hot?"

Caitlin laughed. "It's a great city. So much history—of course there's good and bad to that. But there are museums that explore all of it. And, yes, this time of year, it's a little on the steamy side. It will be fun to see everyone next weekend."

Jason's phone pinged, and he glanced his text messages, then finished his last sip of beer and put some cash down for his tab. "I have to run. My mom wants me to stop by and drop off a part for my dad on my way home. He's fixing their kitchen faucet . . . or having me do it when I get there."

"We'll plan on Sunday then. Should we meet you at the marina?" Julia asked.

"Yes, you know my boat. I'll be there from two or so on, so come on down when you get off work." He glanced at Caitlin. "You're coming, right?" His eyes met hers, and for a brief moment she felt a shift in the air, a new awareness between them.

Caitlin nodded and smiled. "I'll be there." She was excited to have something fun to do, and she looked forward to spending more time with Jason.

Chapter 25

The weather was perfect for boating Sunday afternoon. A little after three, once they'd both closed their shops, Caitlin followed Julia to the marina. Julia brought some iced tea and bottled waters. Caitlin wasn't sure what to bring, and finally decided on cheddar cheese and crackers. She wasn't sure how long they would be out on the boat but figured they'd want a snack at some point.

She smiled when she saw the name of Jason's boat. The *Wicked Beauty* was a shiny, royal-blue, twenty-five-foot Boston Whaler. "Love the name," she said, as Jason extended a hand to help her board. Tim, Sue, and Kevin were already there and waved hello.

Jason grinned. "Thanks. I thought it seemed appropriate. I just gave her a fresh coat of paint."

Once they were settled, Jason untied the boat from the dock and carefully backed it out. There was no wind, and the water was smooth as they headed out into the harbor.

They spent several hours cruising along the shoreline. Jason and Julia pointed out various landmarks, though Jason stayed far from the long jetties where the seals liked to sun themselves. "That's where the great whites like to hang out and I'd actually prefer not to get too close to one of them," Jason said.

"We need a bigger boat for that!" Kevin joked, and they all laughed.

Jason had some fishing gear on board, and when he found a good spot to hang out for a bit, he and Tim tried their luck. While they fished, Caitlin and Sue put out snacks and Julia passed out soft drinks. The time went by so fast as they laughed and told all kinds of stories—Caitlin realized the little group had been friends for years and they were a tight-knit, friendly bunch. She'd felt welcome and comfortable right away with them and was glad that Julia had included her.

"You look a million miles away," Jason said.

Caitlin snapped to attention and laughed. "Sorry. I was day-dreaming. I was just thinking how glad I am that I've met you all. It was getting a little boring just working and going home. And missing all my friends in Charleston. I wasn't supposed to be here this long."

"Well, I'm glad that you'll be around a while longer. The fall is my favorite time of year here. No crowds, great weather. You'll see."

"I look forward to it."

He held her gaze for a moment. "If you were home in Charleston, what would you be doing?"

She grinned. "Well, none of my friends have boats, so I wouldn't be doing this. Probably just going out to parties or dinner, maybe play a little tennis." She paused before adding, "I'd rather be on a boat."

"Me, too. I'm here as often as possible. Just about every weekend, right up until Columbus Day when she comes out of the water and hibernates for the winter."

"Jason always has a big end-of-summer cookout. Every year it gets bigger," Julia said.

He nodded. "This year is going to be the biggest yet. It's Monday of Labor Day weekend—to celebrate the beginning of the off-season."

Tim set down his fishing pole. "I'm done with this." Neither he nor Jason had even had a nibble. Jason took both poles and put them back in their spot. He disappeared into the cabin for a moment and then emerged holding a big insulated bag. "Anyone hungry? I brought lobster rolls." Everyone eagerly took one. They were buttered and toasted hot dog rolls filled with lots of fresh chopped lobster tossed with a little mayo and lemon. The rolls were no longer warm, of course, but still, Caitlin swooned at first bite.

"There is nothing like this in Charleston. This is amazing, thank you." Caitlin knew how expensive lobster was—she'd seen the price on a carton of lobster meat in her grandmother's refrigerator. It was shockingly high.

"You're welcome. A buddy of mine brought a few of his traps in yesterday and had more lobsters than expected. Asked me if I wanted any. Couldn't say no to that."

"We are spoiled here with plenty of good, fresh lobster. There's nothing worse than a lobster roll made with frozen lobster," Julia said.

"What is Charleston famous for? I'm sure you have something delicious that we don't have here," Sue asked.

Caitlin thought for a minute. "Probably shrimp and grits. I've never seen that anywhere here."

Jason made a face. "Maybe because grits are kind of nasty."

Caitlin had heard that plenty of times before. "They can be. Or they can be crazy delicious. Depends how you make them. You'd like my grits."

Jason looked doubtful. "I'm not so sure about that. What's different about them?"

"Lots of butter, cheese, spices, and plump fresh shrimp. Just like lobster, shrimp is better fresh. I'll make it for you all sometime."

"I look forward to being wrong." Jason's eyes met hers for a moment before he turned his attention back to his lobster roll. Caitlin wasn't sure if she'd imagined it but for a brief second she thought she'd sensed a vibe. But just as quickly, it was gone.

The time flew and Caitlin was surprised to see how late it was when Jason pulled out his cell phone to check. It was already a little past seven. It was still light out and they'd been having such a good time.

"I suppose we should head in," he said reluctantly.

Twenty minutes later, Jason secured the boat in its slip at the marina, and they all said their goodbyes when they reached the parking lot.

"Thanks so much for taking us out. This was such a fun day," Caitlin said. It was the best day she'd had in Chatham so far. The others walked ahead of them as Jason slowed to a stop and smiled down at her.

"Anytime. You know, if you're interested, there's a fair next weekend that might be fun to check out. I can get us tickets if you want to go?" Caitlin's heart skipped a beat. She wasn't totally sure if he meant the invite for all of them or if he was asking her on a date. And then she realized she couldn't go.

"That sounds great. I won't be here, though. I'm heading to Charleston for the weekend."

Jason's smile disappeared, his disappointment evident. "Oh, that's right. No worries. Have a fun trip."

Caitlin felt a sharp pang of regret that she'd miss out on going to the fair with Jason. She was really enjoying her time on the Cape and spending time with this group of people. They were all so fun-loving, laid-back, and easy to be with. Very different from Charleston. And she was starting to appreciate the differences.

Chapter 26

Are you coming home soon?

The text message popped up on Jess's phone, from Parker. They hadn't spoken since she'd left Charleston, and other than a similar message a few weeks ago, she hadn't had any contact with him. And back then she didn't realize she was going to buy the bookstore and stay longer. She supposed there was no harm in at least letting him know she was going to be here longer than she'd planned.

Decided to stay through mid-October. Will be back in town after that.

Oh! What about Caitlin?

Same. Though I think she's heading back next weekend for a few days. Nancy's party.

Right. She can't miss that. Let her know I look forward to seeing her?

Sure.

How are you? Can we talk soon?

Jess sighed. She didn't want to talk to Parker. There was nothing to talk about.

I'm good. Busy. Hope you're well.

She hoped he'd leave it at that.

Okay. Maybe we'll talk soon.

She chose not to respond to that and instead called her attorney's office. An hour later, her phone rang.

"Jess. It's Rebecca. Are you ready to do this?" They'd traded emails when Jess first came to Chatham and she let her know she might be needing her services and why. Rebecca had told Jess to take her time and call when she was ready to start the process.

"I think so. To at least get things started."

They spent the next forty-five minutes going over everything Jess needed to do to get divorced. Information she'd need to gather and send to Rebecca. Mostly financial information, prior tax returns, bank statements, investment details. Fortunately, Jess had access to everything she needed online and promised to gather it and send it along.

"So, there are two approaches we could take. You could ask for a forensic accounting of everything including his father's law firm since you're both partners there. That won't endear you to anyone, though—especially his family—but if you think they are hiding any assets it's the best way to make sure you get the best settlement possible. Or you can estimate what half of your overall assets are worth and aim to split everything evenly. That's the most amicable way to go and the fastest."

Jess didn't have to think about it. She didn't want to involve his family. Parker's father was still the founding partner, even though he wasn't there full-time any longer. They'd always been good to her and she didn't want to be at odds with Parker. It would be

Pamela Kelley

easier for all of them, especially Caitlin, if they could be civil and get through this with as little drama as possible.

"I'll go the amicable route. Easy and fast is good."

"Okay. Does he know about the bookstore?"

Jess hesitated. "No. I didn't want to involve him. Hopefully that won't be an issue. I only used my savings."

Rebecca hesitated for a moment. "We'll position it that way and hope he doesn't make things difficult."

"I don't think he will," Jess assured her. "Parker is usually pretty easygoing."

"Let's hope so. Divorce can be stressful, though, and people sometimes act unpredictably, so that's why I mentioned it. That's it for now. Let's touch base next week once you've sent everything to me. I'll have my assistant reach out to set a time for us to talk."

"Perfect."

Jess hung up the phone and took a deep breath. She felt relieved that she'd taken the first step to set things in motion. She made herself a cup of tea and went outside. Her mother was sitting on the porch in her favorite rocking chair, reading a Danielle Steel novel. She looked up when Jess walked over.

"Hi, honey. It's a gorgeous afternoon. Join me for a bit."

Jess sat next to her in a matching white wood rocker, and set her teacup on the glass-topped table between them. There was a slight breeze, and for a long moment she watched a bee land on the bright blue hibiscus flowers lining the porch.

"I called Rebecca." Her mother knew Rebecca. She'd been Jess's college roommate and her firm was a few doors down from Jess's office.

"I'm glad. She'll take good care of you. Have you discussed it with Parker yet?"

Jess shook her head. "He texted me today. He wants to talk, but I just don't have the energy. I don't know what there is to talk about.

He said he wants to work things out." She sighed. "But obviously that ship has sailed."

"You could text him back and let him know you called your attorney. So he knows you're serious."

"I suppose I could. Maybe I will. But not just yet. I'll wait until after Caitlin comes back. I don't want to put her in the middle of it."

Her mother looked thoughtful as she reached for her glass of water. "When is she going?"

"Next weekend."

"Oh, that's not so bad then. It can wait another week."

Jess smiled. "I think it can. I'm just glad I made the call. It feels like a weight lifted. I was feeling kind of in limbo."

"Well, you just weren't ready. It's totally understandable. Have you given any thought to moving back here? You could open a practice in Chatham, couldn't you?"

"I really haven't thought about that. Charleston has been home now for over thirty years." Jess laughed. "I can only handle so much change at once. And it's not that easy. I'm not licensed to prac- tice in Massachusetts. I'd have to apply for a license here. It would be easier, smarter to open a practice in Charleston, where people know me."

"I didn't think about that, needing a license. Oh well, it was just a thought. Or you could give up law completely and just run the bookstore with Alison?"

Jess shook her head. "That's not an option. It would be too much of a pay cut. Sales are still slower than we want."

"Well, whatever you decide, I'm sure it will work out fine." Her mother smiled and seemed so certain that Jess felt more optimis- tic, too. Things would work out, somehow.

Chapter 27

"Your review turned out great. Almost no changes needed." Alison looked up. She'd been so deep into her work that she hadn't heard Jim walk over to her desk. He handed her a hard copy of her article with a few small notes in the margins. She glanced at them, and they were very minor edits, which was a relief. Considering it was her first restaurant review, she wasn't sure if he might want more extensive changes.

She smiled. "Thanks. It was a fun night. I took my daughter and best friend and as you can see, we all liked the food."

"Right. Except for that garlicky Caesar salad."

She laughed. "Was it that obvious?"

He sat on the corner of her desk. "No. Just to me because I know you. The garlic lovers out there will be thrilled."

"How's the book coming along?" She figured something was on his mind. The only time Jim got comfortable and made a space for himself on her oversized desk was when he had something he wanted to talk about. She figured it was the book. A few other times when he'd been stuck, he'd run his thoughts by her and it helped brainstorm his way forward.

"Oh, it couldn't be better. I'm just about done with my final pass. Maybe I'll send you what I have, if you're up for a read? I thought maybe if you have time, you could tell me if I'm delusional or if it really is hanging together okay?" He looked so unsure about the whole idea that it made her laugh. She knew she'd probably love it.

"Go ahead and send it. I've been dying to read it—and I'm sure it's fine. More than fine."

"Great. Thank you. I'll get it to you before I leave today. There's something else I wanted to run by you, though."

"Oh? What's that?"

"There's a reception tomorrow night at that new art gallery that opened on Main Street. They already reached out and bought full-page ads, in the next three issues, and they invited me and a guest to the opening. I'd like to go and support them and thought maybe you'd want to join me?" He smiled. "I know you like going to those kinds of things."

He knew her so well. Alison loved going to art galleries. She'd always had a passion for beautiful art, and when she could afford it, she'd bought pretty watercolors from up-and-coming local artists—before their prices soared. She always bought what spoke to her, what she loved, but she also had a good eye for it and many of the pieces she'd bought over the years were worth quite a bit more now. Not that she wanted to part with any of them.

"I didn't realize there was a new gallery opening. And it's right on Main Street?"

"It's about five doors down from the bookstore, actually."

"No kidding? You know I am such a creature of habit lately. I drive to the shop, park in the back, and go inside. I haven't actually walked farther down Main Street in ages. So, I had no idea. I'd love to go."

"Great. I think you're working tomorrow?"

"In the morning, yes. I'll be at the bookstore in the afternoon—until about five or so."

"I'll stop in and then we can walk over from there. Sound good?"

"Perfect." She smiled, and it didn't hit her until Jim walked away that the night out could be considered a date. Was Jim thinking of it that way? Alison hadn't gotten that impression, at all. But she also hadn't been paying that close attention. She'd been excited to go to a new art gallery. It wasn't like she'd never thought of Jim that way. It had crossed her mind more than once recently, but she'd still immediately dismissed the idea since he was her boss. But things were changing at the magazine. She knew it was time for her to be open to change, too, even if the thought of it terrified her a bit.

❀

"You're in a good mood today. And you look really pretty. Is that sweater new?" Jess asked. She and Alison were both behind the register the next afternoon. Jess had just rung up a customer and the store was suddenly empty and quiet.

"It is new. I picked it up a few weeks ago at a sale." She'd fallen in love with the blue-green shade. It reminded her of the ocean.

"Well, the color suits you." Jess looked closely at her. "And you're wearing makeup! What's going on? Are you going some-where later?"

Alison felt herself blush a little.

"Jim's coming by a little before six and we're going to a private reception at a new art gallery."

Jess grinned. "Jim's coming by. You have a date! I love it."

Alison immediately felt flustered—and a peculiar mix of ex-citement and nervousness that she hadn't felt in years. "It's not like that. It's just a work thing. They are an advertiser with the magazine and gave him a few tickets to the opening."

"Mmm-hmm. And he chose you to go with him. Sounds like a date to me."

"It's really not. I promise." But Jess was right. Alison had taken more time deciding what to wear, and for the first time in ages she'd put on a little makeup. Just mascara and a bit of rosy lipstick, but when she saw her reflection in the mirror she realized it really did make a difference.

"Well, you look great. Date or not, I'm glad you're getting out. And you love art galleries." Jess paused before saying, "I have a little news, too. I called my lawyer yesterday and started the process to file for divorce." Her smile faded away and Alison's heart went out to her. And the fact that they'd been there for several hours and Jess was only just now mentioning it meant that she was feeling conflicted.

"Don't doubt yourself. You did the right thing," Alison assured her.

Jess's eyes grew damp, and she looked away for a moment, then took a deep breath. "I know. It's just hard. I don't know why I'm so emotional. One minute I'm fine and sure I did the right thing and the next I'm unsure and sad. Actually, I'm sad most of the time about this."

Alison pulled her friend in for a hug and squeezed her tight. "Divorce is sad. It's okay to give in to your feelings. You don't have to be strong all the time. I know you hate to cry, but it is healing."

Jess actually laughed, and sniffled at the same time. "I'm not much of a crier, as you know, but I swear I've cried more these past few months than I have for my whole marriage. And it has helped. I thought I was all cried out, but it turns out I was wrong. I think I'm almost done, though."

"Well, you know I'm here for you. Whatever you need."

"I know. Thank you. I don't know what I'd do without you. And my mom and Caitlin. Coming home to Chatham really has helped, so much. You were right about that."

Chapter 28

The bells at the front door chimed when Jim walked into the bookstore at a quarter to six. Jess saw him first, and before Alison turned around, she'd whispered, "He's here and he looks sharp. It's been a long time since I've seen Jim. I forgot how handsome he is."

Alison agreed. Jim looked tall, dark, and very handsome in his navy blazer, light blue button-down shirt, and preppy tie with sharks embroidered on it. Alison hadn't seen that one before.

"Jim, you remember my friend Jess?"

He smiled and held out his hand. "Of course. It's been a long time, though. Nice to see you again." He turned to Alison. "You look great."

That flustered them both a bit. "Thank you. So do you. I like the tie."

He laughed. "Thanks. I thought it was appropriate. Lightens the mood a bit." In recent years, Chatham had become so known for great white sharks that sightseeing boats took tourists out by the jetties where the seals sunned themselves. Sharks often feasted on these seals, so the hope was to catch a glimpse of a shark in the area, too—and sometimes, they did.

Jim quickly added, "You always look good, though. That's a great color on you."

Alison noticed that Jess was taking in their exchange with interest and wore the slightest smile of amusement.

"Thanks. Jess, I'll see you tomorrow." Alison came out from behind the register and grabbed her coat and purse.

"Have fun, you two," Jess called out as they walked off.

Jim held the door open as Alison stepped outside. It was a beautiful night but a little cooler than earlier in the day, and she pulled her coat on. There were a lot of people out and about, walking along Main Street on their way to dinner or stopping into the shops. It didn't take long to walk to the gallery. They were a few minutes early but there was already a crowd gathered inside, and a man standing at the door recognized Jim and waved him in.

"Glad you could make it. Thanks for coming." He was in his sixties, Alison guessed, with a thick head of silver hair and stylish, wire-rimmed glasses. He had an artistic flair about him, and was wearing a pink button-down shirt, a cream blazer, and turquoise pants. Jim introduced him as one of the two gallery owners.

"Alison, this is Blair Wheaton. He and his partner, Rich, just opened the gallery."

Blair shook her hand. "Pleasure to meet you. Rich is around here somewhere, probably pouring the champagne. Go help yourself and have a look around."

They wandered in and slowly made their way toward the back of the gallery.

"They've totally remodeled this space," Alison said. "It used to be a hair salon on this level and skin care and nails on the second floor. I wonder if they are using the second floor, too." They'd reached the bar, and another elegantly dressed man was pouring champagne. He overheard her last comment and smiled as he handed each of them a glass of bubbly.

"We're on both levels. Feel free to head upstairs and explore there, too. I'm Rich, by the way."

Jim introduced himself and Alison, and they chatted with Rich for a minute before a few more people walked up to the bar. They moved out of the way and circled the room again, sipping their drinks and taking a good look at all the artwork displayed on the walls. Alison felt a familiar thrill when she was surrounded by beautiful paintings and wanted to take some of them home with her.

A glance at some of the listed prices, though, let her know she wouldn't be able to buy any of these pieces anytime soon. She sighed. There was one in particular that really spoke to her. It was a vibrant abstract watercolor of sailboats in the harbor, and the blues and greens were so vivid. Jim followed her gaze and nodded.

"That one really is special, isn't it?"

"It is. So many of them here are. I think they will do well. It's a gorgeous collection."

"That it is. Let's go see what's upstairs."

They made their way to the second floor, which was filled with intriguing sculptures and more paintings, mostly oils, whereas the ones on the first floor were watercolors. While they stood admiring a wrought-iron sculpture, a server wearing black and white and carrying a silver tray walked over and offered them a mini crab cake. They each took one, and a few minutes later someone else came by offering stuffed mushrooms. The upstairs room was beginning to fill up, and they decided to head back downstairs and roam around a bit more.

The downstairs area was crowded now, too, and Alison noticed that one of the gallery owner's assistants was busy at the register, ringing up sales and wrapping purchased paintings carefully and putting red dots on the ones that would be delivered or picked up the next day.

"Looks like they are off to a great start," Alison said.

"They are. I'm glad to see it. They seem to know their market well." Another server came by, this time offering phyllo cups filled with spinach, cream cheese, and feta. They each had one, and they were delicious.

They slowly walked around the room again, stopping in front of the painting they'd both admired. Alison saw a vaguely familiar face coming their way. An attractive blond woman with a collar-length wavy bob that highlighted her piercing blue-gray eyes. She had thin lips but a surprisingly big smile as she recognized Alison.

"Alison? It's been a lot of years. I ran into Jess's mother at the store a few weeks ago and she said you were both in town. And that you live here year-round. I just moved back myself recently." She turned to Jim and introduced herself: "Lavinia O'Toole. I went to school with Alison and Jess." Jim shook her hand and then excused himself. "I see someone I need to go say hello to. I'll let you two ladies catch up."

He wandered off as a friend of Lavinia's joined them. "Alison, you remember Chelsea? She was a year ahead of us."

Alison nodded. Chelsea Nelson was Lavinia's best friend in high school, and like Alison, she stayed in Chatham after graduating college. She also married her high school sweetheart, Billy Nelson, who was one of the area's biggest real estate developers. Chelsea was a stay-at-home mother and lived in a massive waterfront home. And she always looked perfectly put together. Her fore-head didn't have a single line and didn't move when she smiled, so Alison assumed she had a little help with Botox. Not that she was judging, much. Chelsea was tiny, maybe a size 4, and her sleeveless turquoise dress showed off tanned and very toned arms. Her light brown hair had no sign of gray—it was shiny and straight and fell just past her shoulders. She was nice enough, though, and always said hello whenever Alison ran into her, which wasn't often.

"I was in your daughter's shop the other day. Bought a bracelet. She has some beautiful things there," Chelsea said.

"Oh, thank you. I'm very proud of Julia."

"Who is that man you're with? Is he your boyfriend?" Lavinia asked casually.

"Jim's my boss. I work as an editor at his magazine."

"Oh, so this is a work thing? He's quite handsome." Lavinia turned for another look, and Alison followed her gaze to where

Jim was deep in conversation with two men that Alison didn't recognize. When he laughed and smiled, she saw him through their
eyes—and Jim really did look good tonight. Well, he always did.
She also felt a pang of jealousy that surprised her. She and Jim most
definitely weren't dating, but she realized that she did not like the
idea of him dating Lavinia, or anyone else, at all.

Alison nodded. "The gallery owners are new advertisers for the
magazine, so Jim wanted to support them."

They chatted for a few minutes longer, and then Lavinia took
another look Jim's way. "It looks like he's an art fan, too."

Alison followed her gaze and saw that Jim was at the register
buying a painting. She couldn't see which one it was. He joined
them a few minutes later, holding the carefully wrapped purchase.

"Which one did you buy?" Lavinia asked.

Jim smiled. "It's a watercolor, of a few boats in Chatham harbor. I
couldn't stop looking at it. The colors were so vivid. I had to have it."

Alison's heart raced. He'd bought her painting. She didn't realize he loved it as much as she did.

"It sounds beautiful," Lavinia said.

Jim looked at Alison when he answered her. "It really is. Alison,
are you hungry? I'd like to get a bite to eat if you're up for it?"

"I'd love to." She turned to Lavinia and Chelsea. "It was nice
seeing you both."

"You, too. Have a good night," Chelsea said. Lavinia just nodded
and watched as Alison and Jim left together. Out of the corner of
her eye, Alison saw her whispering to Chelsea and guessed they
were discussing whether there was something going on between
Alison and Jim.

She followed Jim to his car, which was parked behind the coffee shop. He put the painting safely in his back seat.

"Where shall we go? I thought about Neptune but I know you
were just there. What about the Impudent Oyster? I haven't been
there in a while."

"Sure. I always love it there."

The restaurant was just off Main Street, a short walk away, and though it was busy when they arrived, a table quickly opened up and they were seated by a window that overlooked the street. There were still a lot of people walking by.

"Those appetizers were good, but they just made me hungry for more food," Jim admitted as a server approached their table. They decided to share a bottle of wine—a French rosé—and an order of clams casino for an appetizer. Alison went with butternut squash ravioli with scallops, shrimp, and lobster in a brown butter sauce, and Jim decided on grilled swordfish.

The wine and the clams casino—local littlenecks broiled with butter, peppers, garlic, and bacon—were delicious. As they ate, they chatted easily and Alison asked him about his plans for the painting. "Do you know where you'll put it?" She assumed he meant to hang it somewhere in his home.

"I was thinking I might bring it into the office. Our walls are a little bare and then we can all enjoy it."

His answer surprised and delighted her. "Really? I love that idea. Selfishly it means I get to see it more often," she admitted.

He laughed. "It's not selfish at all. Art is meant to be enjoyed. It will brighten up the office. I'll find a good spot for it tomorrow."

"I finished reading your pages last night."

"Already? I hope that's a good sign. I didn't want to ask. Well, I did—but I didn't want to push you. I know you're busy."

Alison smiled. "I loved them. I pretty much read it in one sitting. Until I had to go to bed. Finished it up this morning. It's really good, Jim. I do have a few questions and suggestions, though. If you are open to them?" She wasn't sure what level of feedback Jim really wanted.

"Totally open. Be as brutal as possible. I want the book to be its best before I send it in."

For the next forty-five minutes, through dinner and a crème

brûlée dessert that they shared, they talked about the book. About Alison's thoughts on how Jim could make it even better, where he could go deeper or clarify in spots. He listened intently and asked good questions. They brainstormed a few possibilities for a new scene, and by the time they finished eating, Jim seemed excited to make the changes they'd discussed.

"I made a few notes as I read, everything we discussed. I can send that back so you have it."

"Perfect. And I can't thank you enough. This is so helpful."

She grinned. "It's fun for me. And when you're totally done, I'll go through it again with my red pen and fix the grammar."

He pretended to look horrified. "What grammar issues? Just kidding. I appreciate it—it's impossible to catch all of your own errors. Especially the commas."

When the bill came, Alison pulled out her wallet, intending to split the bill, but Jim wouldn't have it.

"I invited you. It's my treat and my pleasure."

"Okay. Thank you, then."

They gathered up their to-go boxes—both had leftovers for another meal. The air was chilly and windy as they walked outside. Alison pulled her thin coat more tightly around her as they walked back to the parking lot. When they reached their cars, Jim pulled her in for a quick goodbye hug.

"Thanks for coming with me tonight. It was fun," he said.

"It was. Thanks again for dinner and inviting me to the opening."

"Anytime. See you in the morning."

Alison climbed in her car, started the engine, and drove off. Jim waited until she was on her way and then pulled out behind her. She knew it wasn't a date, but it had been a great night, and it made her want to repeat the experience—but maybe as a real date. She wondered if that had ever crossed Jim's mind. Or did he just think of her as a friend and employee?

Chapter 29

"You look pretty. Where are you off to?" Caitlin's father was sitting in the kitchen, drinking a bottled water and working on his laptop.

"Thanks. I'm off to Beth's and then to Nancy's party."

"Oh, right. You mentioned that last night." Her father had picked her up at the airport and they'd shared a pizza at home before she'd headed out to meet her friends.

"Are you working?" Her father was a workaholic but he usually took most of the weekends off.

"Just checking email. We have a new case, a big one. It's been busier than ever." He looked like he was going to add "with your mother gone," but thought better of it. Caitlin guessed that he hadn't hired any additional attorneys yet, as she knew he was hoping her mother might change her mind about going back there—about everything.

"Are you doing anything tonight?" He was still wearing his gym clothes.

"Linda and I are going to dinner and a movie. I'm sure I'll be home before you, though. We can catch up later and you can tell me if the party was worth flying home for." He grinned. "Of course,

I'm thrilled that you're here. Can't wait until you're back permanently. It's been quiet here this summer."

Caitlin felt both a bit sorry for him and annoyed at the same time. It was his fault they'd left.

"I have to run, Dad. I'll see you later."

When Caitlin reached Beth's apartment, she knocked and Beth hollered for her to come in.

"I'm upstairs. I can't decide what to wear. I need your help."

Caitlin made her way upstairs. Beth lived in an old town house in the historic district of Charleston. It was a great location. They could walk to Nancy's party, and if they wanted to they could stop at any of a dozen restaurants for a drink either before or after the party. Beth's father owned the building and had given the town house to Beth and her husband, Spencer, as a wedding present. Spencer was out of town for the weekend with his college buddies for a golf trip. Caitlin liked Spencer, but she was glad he was away this weekend—it was nice to spend the time with Beth alone and catch up.

She walked into Beth's bedroom. She was wearing a very pretty bright pink Lilly Pulitzer sleeveless dress and had two other dresses and a pair of jeans and a navy sweater on her bed. She turned to Caitlin and made a face.

"I'm not loving anything. What do you think?"

"You look gorgeous. Those other dresses are pretty, too. But the pink really flatters you."

Beth smiled. "Okay, I'll go with it then. Thank you! Let's head downstairs. I just opened a bottle of pinot grigio. We can have a glass before we go."

When they reached the kitchen, Beth poured them each a small glass of wine. They took them outside onto her balcony, which overlooked the busy street. It was fun to sit and watch people walk by as they sipped their wine and speculated about the night ahead.

"I heard Nancy's brother is in town. I haven't seen him in a few years," Beth said. Nancy had an older brother they'd all had a crush on during high school. Peter was one of those guys who had been good at everything—he'd been the starting quarterback for their football team and he'd been class valedictorian. He'd never been serious about playing professionally, though, and turned down offers from several schools to go to Yale and then to Harvard for his MBA. Last Caitlin heard he was working in finance on Wall Street. Doing what, she had no idea, but she'd heard he was doing very well.

"Are he and Marcy engaged yet?" Caitlin asked. He'd been dating the same girl for ages. Marcy was petite, blond, and bubbly. They seemed to complement each other well, and everyone assumed an engagement would be the next logical step.

Beth leaned forward, a gleam in her eye. "Not engaged and no longer together. Nancy said Marcy dumped him a few months ago and she's already engaged to someone else."

"Oh! Wow. Poor Peter."

"Well, I'm sure it won't be long before he finds a replacement. He's very single now, though, and she said he's in town all weekend."

"Does he still live in Manhattan?"

Beth nodded. "He does. But that's just a short plane ride away. It's manageable."

Caitlin laughed. "That sounds complicated to me."

"Just be open to it. He's just one of several possibilities. You really do need to hurry up and get back here. I never thought you'd spend the whole summer and beyond in Chatham."

"I didn't think I would either. We've never spent more than a week or two at a time there, so I didn't get to know it as well, until now. It's a great area. You really should try to come visit before I come back. I bet you'd love it, too, and I could play tour guide and show you all around. I bet Spencer would love it, too."

Beth shook her head. "He has golf stuff every weekend. There's no way he'll go. But, maybe I can get away for a long weekend. If you're sure you have room? I don't want to be a bother."

"Don't be silly. My grandmother's house has plenty of room."

They chatted and laughed as they finished their wine. It was a beautiful night, warmer than the Cape, which was expected, but fortunately not as humid as it often was in Charleston. They grabbed their purses and walked to Nancy's family's home, which was an impressive old mansion in the heart of the historic district. Caitlin could hear the party before they turned the corner and saw the house all lit up and the valet attendants out front, taking guests' cars and magically parking them nearby.

"Is there a band?" Caitlin could hear music and didn't think it was the radio. She could see the outside terrace, packed with people, all elegantly dressed. Tuxedo-clad servers passed hot appetizers, and there were two bars set up.

"I think Nancy mentioned there would be some live music. There she is!" Nancy spotted them as they reached the outside area, and she rushed over to welcome them with hugs. Caitlin hadn't seen her in a year, since her last party. Nancy was always perfectly put together. Her sleek black hair fell just to the top of her shoulders, and she had a cute, tiny nose and big brown eyes. She was a very pretty girl. And she was impeccably dressed, always. Caitlin knew she was a VIP client at Middleton's—she'd seen the file card on her.

"Caitlin, Beth, so great to see you! It's been too long. We should really all get together one of these days and catch up. These months just fly by, don't they?"

Caitlin and Beth both nodded. It was the same conversation they had every year.

"They really do," Caitlin agreed. "I heard your brother is visiting this weekend?"

"Yes! We don't see him often enough. He's around here somewhere. And if you haven't heard already, he's single now." They chatted for a few more minutes, until several new people walked up behind them. "I'll catch up with you both later. Head on in and help yourself to a drink." Nancy turned to say hello to the new arrivals.

They did as instructed and stopped by one of the outside bars for a glass of wine before making their way inside. It didn't take long before they spotted Ashley and Meghan chatting with Natalie, another former classmate. Their husbands were nearby, sipping whiskey or bourbon and laughing loudly. Ashley waved them over and they all gave Caitlin a hug.

"We've missed you!" Ashley exclaimed.

"You've been gone so long," Meghan added.

"I hear you've spent the summer on Cape Cod. Is it as beautiful as they say?" Natalie asked.

"Yes. I've been staying in Chatham and it really is lovely."

"Lucky you to escape this heat. It's been brutally humid lately. Though today isn't so bad," Natalie added.

The conversation turned to people they knew and all the latest gossip. There seemed to be a never-ending supply of it.

A pretty blond woman stopped by that they all knew, and they said hello and chatted for a moment. As soon as she walked off, Meghan leaned in and lowered her voice. "It's just the saddest thing. She's only been married for six months or so and there are rumors that her husband is already cheating. Can you imagine?"

And when another woman walked by, Caitlin thought she looked different but couldn't put her finger on what it was.

"Did Ginger get a new hairstyle?" she asked.

"She got a nose job," Ashley said. "I think it looked better before." They all agreed on that.

"Oh, Caitlin, Hunter Richards and Ted Royce are here and they are totally single. Do you know them?" Meghan asked.

Caitlin shook her head. "Not really. I know of them, and maybe even met them once or twice over the years, but I doubt they'd remember me."

"Well, we'll have to reintroduce you. Oh, and Peter Hannigan is here, too. Did Beth tell you he's available now, too?" Meghan added.

Caitlin laughed. Meghan made it sound like all these men were eagerly waiting to meet her.

"She did. I'm sorry to hear about what happened." If he really had recently been dumped, Caitlin doubted that he was anxious to jump back into dating so soon. But maybe it was easier for men?

"He wasn't devastated," Ashley said. "It came down to location and she didn't want to move to Manhattan and that's where he sees himself living for at least the next ten years or so."

"She obviously didn't love him enough. I would have jumped at that opportunity. He works for a hedge fund, and you know what that means. Multiple millions a year, maybe even tens of millions. I'd move for that," Natalie said.

The other girls all nodded. Caitlin was getting a little tired of the obsession with money and who was important. She'd never paid much attention to it before, because it was just how things were. She smiled, thinking of Julia and how much she would probably hate this party.

"Whoever marries Peter could end up with a house like this as their second home," Ashley said. Caitlin glanced around—the house was a mansion and very Southern in style, with the oversized porch and the high ceilings, and the outside area with the gardens was lush and beautifully landscaped. It was a house meant for entertaining. The floors were rich, dark polished wood and there were so many gorgeous paintings on the walls and custom upholstery and shimmering fabrics everywhere. As beautiful as it was, it had more of a museum feeling than a homey one, though.

"Nancy visited him over the summer and said he's living in a penthouse condo in Manhattan with stunning views of the city," Meghan added.

"I've never been to Manhattan," Caitlin said.

"Oh, it's fabulous. We should do a girls' weekend sometime, all go and see a Broadway show, and do some exploring," Beth suggested.

The others all agreed that they really should do that.

"Well, we should mingle," Ashley said. "Caitlin's never going to meet anyone standing here with all of us."

"Caitlin, if you want to come with me, I can introduce you to Hunter and Ted, and of course, Peter, too," Meghan offered. "But I haven't seen him yet. I'm sure he'll be here soon."

As Caitlin slowly made her way around the party with Meghan, they stopped every few feet to chat with someone. Meghan seemed to know everyone, and there were people of all ages at the party—friends of Nancy's parents—who were all important people in Charleston. Caitlin met a judge, a district attorney, an owner of one of the newest and best restaurants, and several members of the Junior League, which Meghan had joined a few years ago. Beth had joined, too, once she married Spencer, and they were all eager for Caitlin to join as well.

But they'd agreed it would be best to wait until Caitlin had a career established. She knew that her short stints in customer service and as a temp would not impress the selection committee. And one had to apply to join the Junior League. She had to be sponsored, and her full résumé would be carefully considered. They didn't want her to apply until it was sure she'd be let in.

"There's Nancy's mother. We have to go say hello to her, of course." Meghan led the way to Penny Hannigan, who was sipping a fresh martini and glancing around the room. She'd just finished a conversation with several women and was, for a moment, alone and available to approach.

"Mrs. Hannigan, thank you so much for having us. You remember Caitlin Coleman?"

The older woman nodded. "Of course. I saw your father just last week at the club. How is your mother?" she asked kindly. Caitlin wasn't sure how much she knew about what had happened, but guessed she knew enough.

"She's great. We've been spending the summer on the Cape, in Chatham."

"How lovely." She glanced at both of them. "And how are your husbands? Are they both here tonight, too?"

Caitlin and Meghan exchanged glances. How should Caitlin best handle such an awkward question? Before she had a chance to speak, Meghan jumped in and answered for both of them.

"All of our husbands are here tonight, except for Beth's. He's away on a golf trip."

Caitlin didn't feel comfortable leaving it at that, though. She smiled. "I don't have a husband yet. I'm quite single at the moment."

"Oh! Well, there are some interesting men here. You should try to make their acquaintance," she advised.

Meghan grinned. "We are working on it."

They said their goodbyes as several of Mrs. Hannigan's friends approached.

"I wonder why she assumed I was married?" Caitlin said as they walked away.

"Well, last year you attended with Prescott, right? And everyone thought the two of you were heading in that direction. And pretty much everyone in our circle is married by now," Meghan said, and then immediately added, "Not that there's anything wrong with being single! I miss it sometimes."

Meghan was the first of their group to marry. She and her college boyfriend, Derek, married five years ago.

"How is everything with you and Derek?" Caitlin asked.

"Oh, it's fine. Derek travels a lot for his job. He's often gone the whole week, visiting a client, and flies home on Friday. Sometimes I enjoy the break, but other times it gets a little lonely. But it's fine! I really can't complain." Derek did something in sales for one of the big software companies. Caitlin didn't think she'd like doing that much travel. She could see how it might be lonely if your partner was gone all week, too.

Overall, though, Meghan seemed content. She had a fun job with the ad agency that Caitlin had once worked at. It didn't pay well, but it didn't need to, as Derek made more than enough to support the both of them. Caitlin also knew that whenever they decided to have children, Meghan would quit to be a stay-at-home mother. It really did seem that just about everyone in her circle was settled down and knew where their life was going. Except for Caitlin.

She was almost dreading coming back to Charleston and starting over again—it was depressing to think about signing up with the temp agency and starting a new job search. She'd gone from being eager to rush home to wanting to extend her time in Chatham. It was nice to just relax there and not think about her future.

Meghan found both Hunter and Ted and introduced Caitlin to both of them. Hunter was big and burly, a former football player at Ole Miss. He was a financial advisor now at a firm in Charleston, and one of the first things he asked was if she had a relationship with a broker.

"My father handles that or rather one of his best friends does and has for years."

Hunter lost interest in talking after that and suddenly saw someone he had to go say hello to. Ted was a little more engaging. He was tall and on the thin side and almost had a professor look about him. Caitlin wasn't surprised when he said that he was a research scientist at a lab affiliated with a local hospital.

"Are you working on the cure for cancer, Ted?" Meghan asked.

He laughed. "Not at the moment. We are focusing on Lyme disease actually. Hoping to develop a vaccine." He told them a bit more about it until Meghan said they had to run to say hello to an old friend. She led Caitlin to the bar and they both got a fresh glass of wine.

"Well, we can cross those two off the list of possibilities. It's no surprise that they're both still single."

"Ted wasn't too bad," Caitlin said. He'd seemed nice enough, though a bit dry.

Meghan laughed. "Did you even understand half of what he said? Regression testing or whatever it was. My eyes started glazing over."

"Yeah, he lost me at that point, too. But still, he was nice."

"Well, you could go back and talk to him, if you're interested," Meghan said.

Caitlin smiled. "I didn't say that. I do wonder sometimes if I'm being too picky, though."

"You're not," Meghan assured her. "We still haven't seen Peter. Let's do another circle and see if he's here yet."

They found him five minutes later, outside smoking a cigar and leaning against the terrace railing. He'd been talking to two other men, and when they walked away, Meghan made her move and led Caitlin over to him. It had been several years since Caitlin had seen Peter and that had only been a glimpse of him in passing at the yearly party. He was taller than she remembered, easily six two or maybe six three. His brown hair seemed darker, almost black, and the dimples in his cheeks and chin were more defined and deeper when he smiled. He was quite striking.

"Peter! It's been ages. How are you? I'm not sure if you've met my friend Caitlin?"

Peter glanced at her as he set his cigar on a small stone table. "You do look familiar. I know you're both friends of Nancy's. Thanks for coming."

"Nancy said you're just in town for the weekend?" Caitlin asked.

He grinned. "Yes. It has been too long since I've been back and I couldn't miss this party. The whole family would kill me."

"How are you liking Manhattan?" Meghan asked.

"I'm loving it. The city is so fast-paced, it never seems to stop."

"Caitlin has never been. We were just talking about doing a girls' weekend one of these weeks, taking in a Broadway show and sightseeing."

"Oh, you should. Definitely let me know if you do come to town. I'll meet you all out for a drink." He reached in his back pocket, pulled out his wallet, and withdrew two business cards and handed one to each of them. "That has my private line and cell. Try me on either."

"We will, thank you." Meghan tucked the card in her purse and Caitlin did the same. They both noticed the two men he'd been talking to heading back toward Peter, so they said their goodbyes and went inside to find the others.

An hour later, Caitlin ran into Peter again when she went off in search of something to snack on. There was a table with cheese and crackers and other dips and finger foods near the bar. She put a few slices of cheese, some crackers, and a few nuts on a small paper plate.

"Don't forget the pimento cheese."

Caitlin turned at the sound of the familiar voice. Peter was sipping a bourbon, leaning against the wall and watching her with a look of amusement.

"I'm serious. My mother's housekeeper made that this morning and it's the best stuff ever. In fact, I think I need to have some more." He grabbed a plate and added crackers and a scoop of the spicy cheese spread.

Caitlin smiled. "Okay, since you recommend it so highly." She scooped out some of the cheese and added it to her already full plate.

"Try it. So I can make sure my recommendation didn't disappoint." He took a cracker, topped it with the cheese, and popped it in his mouth.

Caitlin did the same. She usually steered clear of pimento dip, because it was so fattening—a mix of shredded cheddar, cream cheese, mayo, and spices. It was delicious.

"It's so good!"

Peter laughed. "I knew you'd like it. So, Caitlin, tell me more about yourself. I don't see a wedding ring, so I'm guessing you might be single, like me. Unless you have a boyfriend?"

She shook her head. "Not at the moment. Completely single."

"Good. I wonder sometimes if this getting-married thing is overrated. Of course, I would say that considering that my bride-to-be dumped me. I suppose you heard about that, though?" His tone was casual, but he watched her intently to see her reaction.

"I did. I'm sorry it didn't work out."

"Don't be sorry. As my mother says, 'Everything happens for a reason.' Marcy's a Southern girl. Born and brought up here in Charleston. She came to visit me in Manhattan a few times, and she hated it. It's okay. It's not for everyone."

"I really do want to visit it someday." New York seemed larger-than-life to Caitlin. But she didn't know how she'd feel about living there either.

"Where do you live now? You're a Charleston native, too?"

"I am. But I've been spending the summer on Cape Cod, in Chatham. Have you been there?"

"No kidding? I love the Cape. I went to Nantucket a few months ago, for Memorial Day weekend. Sailed over on a buddy's boat for the Figawi. That's the big race from Hyannis to Nantucket and back. It was great. I'm actually going to be back on the Cape over Labor Day weekend. Staying with friends in Wellfleet."

"That's a great area, too." It wasn't far from Chatham.

"It's the last hurrah for the Beachcomber, right on Cahoon Hollow Beach. You should bring some friends and meet us there. It's a fun time."

"I've heard of the Beachcomber. That does sound fun."

Peter pulled out his phone. "What's your number? I'll call you when we're down and maybe you can join us there for dinner and drinks. It's casual and there's usually a decent band."

Caitlin gave him her number and he entered it in his phone.

"Great. I'll call you that Saturday. Hopefully you can make it."

"That sounds fun. I'll see if my friend Julia wants to go—she's been a bunch of times and mentioned wanting to go before they close."

"Perfect. We'll celebrate the end of summer." Two blond girls walked over and Caitlin didn't want to stick around.

She smiled. "I look forward to it." She moved aside as the girls reached them.

"Peter! We've been looking all over for you. This is my friend Misty. I don't think you've met her?"

A slow smile spread across his face. "I don't think I've had the pleasure."

❦

"You were gone for a bit. Talk to anyone interesting?" Beth asked when Caitlin returned.

"I ran into Peter again and we chatted some. Turns out he's going to be on the Cape over Labor Day weekend."

Beth's face lit up. "Did he mention getting together?"

Caitlin nodded and told her about their tentative plans to meet up at the Beachcomber. "Who knows if I'll actually hear from him. He could just be a big flirt. He was turning on the charm for two girls who joined him as I left."

Beth hesitated. "He might not be looking for anything serious right away. I'd just go and have fun. No expectations and see where it goes."

"That sounds like a good plan. Julia said she wanted to get to the Beachcomber this year, so I thought she might want to go, too."

Caitlin had been looking forward to going to the Beachcomber anyway and enjoying as much of the Cape as possible before she had to head home to Charleston. She was intrigued by the idea of seeing Peter again and in what was beginning to feel like her second home. She wondered how well Peter would fit into the Cape vibe.

No one there cared about who his family was or how much money he made. For a moment, as she looked forward to the weekend on the Cape, she thought of Jason and wondered how he was doing. She smiled, picturing him at the Beachcomber—it seemed right up his alley.

Chapter 30

So, how is your mother?" Caitlin and her father were sitting at breakfast the next day, at a restaurant near the airport. Neither one of them had mentioned her all weekend. Caitlin had been a little surprised when her father suggested the restaurant—it was one of her mother's favorites.

She took a bite of cinnamon almond French toast before answering. "Mom's good. It's actually been a really nice summer, for both of us."

Her father sipped his mimosa and quietly finished his omelet. When he was done, he set his utensils down and looked at her intently. "Aren't you getting tired of the beach by now? I don't understand why you're staying there so long. Are you really not coming home now until mid-October?"

Caitlin nodded. "I told you I got a summer job. I'm working at the bookstore and also at the adjacent coffee shop. The coffee shop has been really busy and we don't want to leave Alison short-handed. The Cape slows down by mid-October."

As soon as Alison's name slipped out, Caitlin knew she'd messed up. She hoped her father might not pick up on it, but he did.

"What does Alison have to do with it? Does she own the bookstore? Or the coffee shop?"

"Both actually," she admitted.

"Alison. You mom's best friend? I thought she worked at a magazine?"

"She does, but part-time now. They had layoffs."

He looked even more confused. "So, did she inherit some money or something?"

"Not that I know of."

She could see the wheels turn as he tried to make sense of it. "How could she afford to buy a bookstore and a coffee shop? Especially if she was laid off? Something doesn't add up."

Caitlin stayed silent and reached for her mimosa, hoping her father would drop it. Though she knew that wasn't likely.

"Is your mother involved in this? Did she lend Alison the money?"

"Not exactly." Caitlin took a deep breath. "They are partners."

"Partners? Your mother invested in this?"

"She did. It's a great bookstore and the coffee shop is doing really well."

"What about the bookstore? That's not doing well? Tell your mother to call me. I can't believe she spent our money without telling me." Caitlin hadn't seen her father this pissed in a long time.

"I'll tell her. But, Dad, she said she used her own money, from her bank account."

He threw his napkin down. "Really? Well, when people are married there is no such thing as my money or her money—it's our money."

Caitlin dreaded telling her mother about this conversation.

"Dad, can we change the subject? What else is new with you?"

☙

Jess was in the kitchen chopping vegetables for a new stir-fry recipe she was trying for dinner when a car horn got her attention. She paused and was about to resume cutting when it grew more urgent. She put the knife down and walked to the window. A car she didn't recognize was in the driveway, but she couldn't see who was driving. The horn blared again, which seemed quite rude.

Jess opened the front door and saw her mother leaning on the horn of a brand-new, baby blue Mini Cooper. She walked over to the driver's-side door, and her mother rolled the window down.

"About time! What do you think?" She smiled proudly. It was a very pretty car. Jess knew her mother had always admired Mini Coopers.

"Did you buy it?" She was surprised that her mother hadn't mentioned she was planning to get a new car.

Her mother nodded. "I leased it. Same thing. But I don't have to worry about the upkeep. I've wanted one of these for a long time and I was out running some errands earlier today and the muffler went. Maybe I hit a pothole or something because it was very sudden, and that noise is so embarrassing. I happened to be in Hyannis when it happened and saw the Mini Cooper dealer in front of me, and pulled in. Just to take a look. And here we are." She got out of the car and took another look at it. "Isn't it gorgeous?"

"It really is. Congratulations! Did you trade yours in?"

"No. They're actually putting a new muffler in and I'm picking it up on Tuesday. I figure it can't hurt to have an extra car. It's still fine other than the muffler and Caitlin can consider it hers while she's here."

"That's generous of you, Mom. I'll go with you when you pick it up and drive it back."

"I was hoping you might."

They went inside, and Jess finished making the chicken stir-fry while her mother poured a glass of pinot grigio for both of them. It was a warm, clear night and they decided to eat on the porch. Over dinner, Jess shared her update from the lawyer.

"Parker is going to be served with the divorce papers in the next day or two."

Her mother looked surprised. "Have you talked to him? Does he know it's coming?"

"Not yet. I didn't want to interrupt his weekend with Caitlin. I thought I might call him early tomorrow. I'd like to catch him before he's served. I don't want to upset him any more than necessary. It will be easier for us both if this is done as smoothly and as amicably as possible."

"I don't think I know of anyone that had a truly amicable divorce. Not while it was happening, anyway. Maybe once it's done and people make their peace with it."

"Alison did it."

Her mother put her fork down and looked at Jess. "While she was going through her divorce it was hardly smooth or amicable. Don't you remember how stressful it was for her? I think she lost fifteen pounds or more in a very short period. I ran into her at the store and she was crying in front of the iceberg lettuce. We went for coffee and she wondered if she was making a huge mistake." She paused for a moment before adding, "She must have told you all of this?"

Jess thought back, remembering. She was living in Charleston then and her mother was right. Alison did have serious second thoughts. But as they talked it out, Alison realized it was what she wanted, what they both wanted. But it was still the death of a relationship and it was normal to grieve for that—for a lost dream.

"She did. But she and Chris were never at odds, not really. They both wanted the divorce even though it was hard for them to admit that they both needed something more. I think Parker and I will get there, too. He says he wants to work things out, but I don't think he really does or he would never have started up with Linda. Change is hard, but we should have done this well over a year ago."

Her mother nodded. "And then he wouldn't be cheating. Not that I'm excusing his behavior. But I know you haven't been happy for some time." She reached over and gently squeezed Jess's hand.

"I'm glad you took the step. When it's all done, you'll be relieved and ready to move on."

Jess felt her eyes start to fill and took a breath. "Thanks, Mom. I hope you're right."

❦

Jess called Parker first thing the next day. She knew his routine and that by eight fifteen on a Monday morning, he would have just arrived in the office. But his assistant, the very pregnant Linda, informed her that he was in a client meeting and couldn't be disturbed.

"I'll let him know you called and have him get back to you as soon as possible. But he has a packed schedule this morning."

Of course he did. It was a typical Monday. He never booked anything from twelve to one, though, so she wasn't surprised when he returned her call at a few minutes past noon.

"Jess? Linda said you called and some papers arrived. A heads-up would have been nice."

Ugh . . . exactly what she'd hoped to avoid. "I'm sorry, Parker. I called first thing this morning to let you know they were coming."

"I've been in meetings all morning. When I finally got a break, divorce papers were waiting for me. I thought we were going to talk about this first?"

Jess sighed. "There's not much to talk about. I know you said you wanted to work things out, but I think we both know we're beyond that. I just want to move on."

"What's this about a bookstore and coffee shop that you bought without consulting me? Caitlin told me yesterday at breakfast."

Caitlin had also filled her in when she got home from the airport, so Jess had been expecting the question.

"It has nothing to do with you, or us. This is part of my future. I used money from my savings."

"Jess, we're still married. My money is your money and your bookshop is my bookshop. I might need to make a trip to Chatham to check out my investment—make sure it's worthy." He sounded upset, and Jess didn't really blame him—she knew she should have told him about the bookstore and warned him that the papers were coming. She'd avoided doing it because she didn't want to deal with him making things difficult—he could have stopped the bookstore sale from going through. She tried to reason with him. The bookstore was too important to her and to Alison. Jess couldn't let Parker ruin things now.

"Parker, this really doesn't need to concern you. You have an equal amount in your savings, so I figured it would be a wash once we divided things up. I'd like to keep this as simple and as fair as possible."

"Well, I still want to see it—and you at least owe me the chance to sit down and discuss everything in person. I'm going to book a flight this weekend and I'll be in touch when I'm in town. I have to go now." He hung up without waiting for a response, and Jess just shook her head. Parker was usually levelheaded and reasonable, and as her attorney had predicted, divorce could make people act unpredictably. She felt the beginning of a stress headache and fervently hoped this wasn't going to turn into a huge problem.

Chapter 31

Jess hung up the phone, grabbed her purse, and headed for the door. Caitlin was already at the coffee shop, and her mother was outside working in her garden. She looked up and smiled when she saw Jess.

"How did it go with Parker? Did you reach him in time?"

"No. He's furious with me and says he's coming here this weekend to see his new investment and to talk."

"Oh dear. I hope he doesn't make things difficult for you and Alison."

"Hopefully he won't. Maybe he just needs to digest it all and realize this divorce is going to happen." Parker tended to react first and often needed to sit with something for a while before changing his mind.

"Good luck, honey."

Jess climbed in her rental car and headed to the bookstore. Her mind was whirling as she replayed the conversation with Parker. She'd made light of it with her mother, but she was worried that Parker could cause problems with the bookstore. She was so wrapped up in her thoughts that she almost missed the back entrance to the parking lot and slammed on her brakes to make the left turn. A second later, she heard a loud crash and saw in her rearview mirror that a van had veered sharply to avoid hitting her and run into a telephone pole.

She parked and ran over to the vehicle. It was a white work van that read OLIPHANT'S OYSTERS across the side in green lettering. The front of the van where it had hit the pole was dented, but it didn't look too bad.

As Jess reached the vehicle, the driver's door opened and a brown-haired man wearing green rubber fishing overalls stepped out. He glared at her.

"You were in front of me?" he asked.

"Yes. I'm so sorry. Are you okay?"

"I'm fine. The van not so much." His stare went right through her. He wasn't happy and she couldn't really blame him. "Do you make a habit of slamming your brakes like that?" His tone immediately put her on the defense.

"No, I don't. And I said I was sorry. Do you make a habit of tailgating?"

He sighed. "I wasn't tailgating."

"Okay. Should we call the police then? I can get my insurance information."

His expression relaxed somewhat, and she noticed that when he wasn't scowling at her he was actually quite handsome, and he was about her age.

"No. I'll just call Triple A for a tow. It's not your fault. You're right, if I'd been further back, it wouldn't have happened."

Jess felt awful, because if she'd been paying better attention it wouldn't have happened either.

"Are you sure? Do you want to come in and wait inside? Least I can do is offer you coffee and maybe a bagel or something if you're at all hungry."

"You own the coffee shop?"

She nodded. "My best friend, Alison, and I bought it a little more than a month ago."

"I've stopped in a few times. It's better than the last place. I'll take you up on that offer. I'm Ryan by the way. Ryan Oliphant." He held out his hand and Jess shook it, noting that his hands were big and lightly calloused between the thumb and first finger. He followed her gaze.

"It's from shucking oysters. That's my business—we supply oysters to restaurants and seafood shops all over the Cape."

"Oh! That's great. I'm Jessica Coleman. Most of my friends call me Jess."

"Nice to meet you, Jess, though it's not really an ideal way to meet." He glanced at his dented van.

She apologized again. "I'm so sorry. Come on inside." He followed her in and called for a tow as he walked. He was on the phone for a few minutes and then gave her the update.

"Well, the good news is Triple A has a guy in the area so it won't be a long wait. They said fifteen minutes or less."

Jess made him a coffee the way he requested—tall, two sugars, no milk—and a plain bagel toasted with cream cheese.

"Do you want to eat it here or should I put it in a to-go bag?"

"Better make it to-go. I'll eat by the van, sounds like it won't take them long."

She handed him the bag and he looked at her for a long moment before asking, "Are you friends with Chris and Alison? I was trying to figure out where I'd seen you before. I think it was at the Squire maybe?"

"I am. I was with both of them at the bar. Alison was tired, though, and went home early."

"I thought so. I was with a bunch of college friends that were in town for a golf tournament."

Jess remembered the group of guys that were across the bar. One of them had caught her looking and smiled. It hadn't been Ryan, though.

"Are you and Chris dating?" Ryan asked.

Jess laughed. "No! Alison is my best friend."

Ryan held her gaze. "Right. But they've been divorced for a long time."

Jess thought back to that night and the vibe she'd gotten from Chris. Seemed like even from a distance, Ryan had picked up on it, too.

"I've known Chris forever. He's like a brother."

Ryan thanked her as he took his bagel and coffee. "Good. Well, I guess I'll see you around then. I'd better head out and wait by the van."

"Okay, again, I'm really sorry. I was a little distracted. I just filed for divorce today," she admitted.

Ryan's expression softened and she saw the sympathy in his eyes. "I'm sorry. I know that's hard to go through. I divorced a few years ago, too. We're on good terms now, but it was rocky for a while." He smiled. "It will get better."

"Thank you." She watched him walk out and sighed.

❦

"You hit Ryan Oliphant's van?" Alison was at the register when Jess walked into the bookstore and filled her in on why she was running a few minutes late.

"I didn't hit him. But I did cause his accident—sort of. He shouldn't have been so close behind me."

"He and Chris are good friends. Ryan also has retail shop that sells oysters, scallops, shrimp, and local fish caught off the day boats. We've known him for ages. He's a nice guy. Went through a difficult divorce a few years ago."

"He mentioned that, briefly. After I told him I was distracted because I'd just served Parker with divorce papers. Oh, and Parker didn't take it well. He's coming here this weekend."

"He is? Why?" Alison quickly turned to face Jess and looked both surprised and confused.

Jess hesitated, as she didn't want to alarm Alison, but since they were partners she needed to know. She told her about his anger at finding out she'd bought the bookstore without consulting him.

Alison twisted a section of hair, her usual tell when she was anxious. "Is he going to cause problems for us?"

"I hope not. But he might. He wants to talk, and I've been avoiding that, so maybe if I sit down with him I can get him to see reason."

"Let me know if there's anything I can do."

"I will."

"Speaking of Chris, that reminds me. He said to invite you and Caitlin over Saturday night for a cookout. A bunch of his friends will be there—probably Ryan, now that I think of it." Alison smiled and Jess just shook her head.

"Don't try to play matchmaker. We didn't exactly get off to a great start and I'm not ready for that yet. I'm not sure when I will be."

"Okay, but you always tell me to 'get out there.' It's not like what happened with Parker came out of the blue—I mean, you might not be ready to move on, but you both weren't happy."

Jess sighed. "You're right. Even though I thought I wanted to end things and thought that he did, too, it was still shocking to find that he'd already moved on. I guess I should at least think about it."

Alison smiled. "It's not like you have to put your profile up on Match.com. Just be open to it. . . . We'll have to go out again soon."

"Chris said that band we liked is coming back soon to the Squire." Jess had felt comfortable there. It wasn't just a bar, it was a family restaurant, too, with good food.

"We'll definitely do that. And you'll meet other people at Chris's cookout, too. It will be fun."

Chapter 32

Julia put off making the call to Kyle for over a week. She'd slept on it, talked to Caitlin and a few other friends about it and still kept putting it off. She knew she had to have the conversation with him, but she dreaded it. She probably would have put it off longer if not for the text message that arrived that afternoon while she was in the middle of making a gorgeous custom piece of jewelry. Her phone had dinged, indicating a new message, and it was the ringtone she reserved for Kyle.

> Call me when you get home. I want to come see you this weekend and need to book a flight. Maybe you can pick me up at the airport?

She needed to catch him before he booked his flight. And she most certainly wasn't going to pick him up at the airport. Logan was at least two hours away, and that was with no traffic. She'd have to take the afternoon off, and she didn't want to do that. Not now.

But she knew he wasn't going to take it well. Kyle was used to getting his way. Julia opened a bottle of cabernet and poured herself a glass. She needed a little liquid courage. She sipped the wine and stared out the window. It was a glorious August evening on Cape Cod. There was a slight breeze, the air was warm, and if it were any other night she'd be going for a long walk to unwind and enjoy an otherwise perfect summer night.

She finished the wine and poured another half glass. It was almost six thirty. Nashville was an hour behind them, and she knew if she didn't call Kyle soon, he'd be calling her. She waited a few more minutes, took a deep breath, and called him.

He answered on the first ring. "I was just about to call you!" He sounded like he was in a great mood, which only made it harder.

"I got your text message earlier," she began.

"I can take Friday off, and get an early flight. So, I thought if you can duck out early, you can zip up and meet me at the airport?"

Julia took a deep breath. "Kyle, I'm not sure that's a good idea. I hate to have you spend the money to fly back here. I've been doing a lot of thinking and I think you're great. I've loved the time we spent together, but, I think we might be going in different directions now."

After a long, uncomfortable silence, Kyle spoke and his tone was cold and abrupt. "What are you saying?"

"I think with you in Nashville and me here that the distance is too hard. I don't see myself moving and I think it will be better for both of us if we move on and see other people." That didn't come out right and Julia immediately regretted it.

"Why? Are you seeing someone else? Have you already 'moved on'? Is that what you are trying to tell me?" Kyle was instantly pissed and talking so loudly that Julia had to turn the volume down, put the phone on speaker, and walk away.

"No, of course not. I told you before. I would never cheat on you. I just don't think this is working anymore. For either of us."

"I want to see you in person. We need to sit down and talk this out," he insisted.

That was the last thing Julia wanted. "Kyle, please. You're not going to change my mind. I'm sorry, but this just isn't working for me anymore. I really think it will be the best thing for both of us to move on. You can build a whole new life for yourself in Nashville. It seems like you love it there."

"I do love it here. But I'd love it more if you were here with me."

There was a long moment of silence before Julia said, "That's not going to happen, Kyle. I'm sorry."

"So that's it then? I asked you to marry me, Julia. And now it's over? Just like that?"

"I'm sorry, Kyle."

"I have to go. This is very disappointing." The phone went dead. Julia let out the breath she didn't even realize she was holding. It was done.

♕

"So, it's really over? And you're not too upset?" Alison asked her daughter.

Jess had invited them over for a spur-of-the-moment dinner and made her famous kitchen-sink pasta, where she cooked up a box of pasta and tossed it with a little of this and a little of that, whatever vegetables she had on hand, shredded rotisserie chicken, wine, broth, and butter, and it all came together beautifully. She'd always been able to do that, just throw things together, without a recipe. As they sat outside on the porch, Julia filled them in on the conversation she'd just had with Kyle.

"I'm relieved actually. I'd been having doubts and after my visit to Nashville I knew I wanted to end it. But it was hard to find the right moment. I put it off for over a week—until Kyle texted that he was going to come visit."

"Good thing he texted first," Caitlin said. "Imagine if he'd just shown up?"

Julia laughed. "Kyle wouldn't do that. He'd want to make sure I knew so I could plan to take time off. It was okay for him to work while I visited, but I knew he'd want my undivided attention."

"Well, since it's officially over, I can go on the record and say that I was never all that crazy about him," Alison said. "Your father and I both felt the same way. Neither one of us could really say why, though. He was just never overly friendly."

"I knew you both weren't fans, but I thought you'd like him more once you got to know him. Instead, I realized as I got to know him better, that he wasn't for me."

"Do you have your eye on anyone else?" Jess's mother asked.

"No! Not at all. I don't mind taking a break from dating or even thinking about it for a little while."

"Well, if you're looking for something else to focus on, maybe you can help me put together a marketing email?" Alison suggested. "Ellen Campbell sent me log-in details for Constant Contact, where she had a mailing list of customers. We switched the billing over to us and I spent some time online this morning trying to figure it out. It's a little confusing, though."

Julia's face lit up. "I'd love to help you with that. I've been building a newsletter list for my shop and actually just sent my first sales email right before I closed the shop today, to announce a new bracelet."

"We'd love your help. We have our first author signing this Saturday afternoon. Grace Barrows will be signing from one to three. Maybe we could send an email out to let people know about that?" Jess asked.

Julia nodded. "Absolutely. And I'll get a post up for you on Facebook and Instagram, too. Oh, maybe we can tell people in the email about the loyalty cards, too? Caitlin and I were talking about that the other day. I think it's a great idea."

"How will your card work?" Jess's mother asked.

"Mom was the one that originally suggested a loyalty card," Jess said.

Caitlin smiled. "There's a little shop in Charleston that does it and I've always thought it was such a great idea, too," she said. "They give customers a card they bring in each time they shop and stamp the card for every ten dollars they spend. When they reach a hundred dollars they'll get a coupon for ten dollars to use on their next visit."

"And it turns out our software has the capability to do that automatically," Alison said. "Customers just have to show the card or give their name when they make a purchase and it looks them up."

"I love the idea," Jess said.

"And next weekend, I booked another author," Alison added. "A local historical author, Jack Higgins, who has a pretty big following. He has a new release, so that might be good for us."

"Oh, I didn't know about that," Julia said. "I'll add that in the newsletter, and email again a few days before."

"And the story hour is going to start this Saturday, too, at ten A.M.," Alison said.

Julia laughed. "And that will go in the newsletter, too."

"It sounds like you girls have a lot going on. Is it starting to get a little busier?" Jess's mother asked.

Alison and Jess exchanged glances.

"Not as much as we'd like," Jess admitted. "Although the cards that Alison made for the bookshelves have been moving more of those books, which is great. The coffee shop is growing faster. Hopefully once we get the word out more and start some of these programs, the bookstore will catch up."

Jess's mother smiled. "I'm sure it will. I'll tell all my friends to be sure to stop in and get their loyalty cards. That reminds me, I told Gladys to stop by tomorrow morning for coffee. She has a sticky legal situation she needs some guidance with. I told her you could help."

Alison tried not to laugh at the expression that flashed across Jess's face.

"I'm happy to talk to her and try to help, but Mom, I can't actually give legal advice here. I'm not licensed in this state."

Her mother didn't seem concerned about that. "Oh, I know. I just thought you could point her in the right direction."

꧁

Julia picked up her mail as she stepped into her shop the next morning. It was all junk mail and bills as usual—but an unusually thin envelope from her bank got her attention. She recognized the look, though she hadn't seen it in years, since the days when she used to be careless with her checking account. She ripped the envelope open and drew out the single sheet of white paper with INSUFFICIENT FUNDS stamped across the top.

Julia groaned. She'd let her checking account for the shop get too low, and her autopayment for the cable company had bounced. She would have to transfer money over from her savings account. It wasn't the first time she'd had to dip into her savings, but she usually caught it before it got this low.

She flipped on the lights and immediately opened her laptop to sign in to her online bank account and make the transfer. And found that she had no internet access. Julia sighed. Of course she didn't. The cable company was quick to shut off service if a payment was late. She fished out her debit card, called the cable company, and less than ten minutes later, she was back online and made the transfer.

It was a low start to her morning. She took a quick break to run to the coffee shop and treat herself to a large coffee and her favorite raspberry muffin. It was Caitlin's day off, so Julia missed chatting with her and quickly returned to her shop. She settled at her desk with her coffee and muffin and checked her emails. There was still no word on the contest. She was starting to worry that they might have made a decision and forgot to email her. With all the drama of the bounced check, she'd almost forgotten about the marketing email she'd sent the day before. Her expectations weren't high, though. She knew most people ignored those kinds of emails. At least she assumed that they did.

Her jaw dropped when she saw six replies, all with variations of the same message—"How can I buy that bracelet, now?"

Julia had fallen in love with one of her new designs—the gold hammered bangle with the beachy waves and blue shimmery stones. She'd taken a picture of the bracelet and impulsively decided to email it off to her list—which was a mix of paying customers and people who had stopped into the shop to browse. And now she had to make five more of them! Julia was almost giddy as she quickly calculated what her profit would be. Enough that she wouldn't have to worry about bounced checks for a few months.

Her mind whirled with other marketing ideas. She'd had no idea how powerful a simple email could be. Now that she knew, she could experiment with sending photos of other new pieces out. Or maybe even some of the items that were overlooked in the shop might catch someone's eye in an email if she took a good picture? And maybe she could do more with her website, blog, and social media? Julia had dabbled here and there and knew that she'd reached some new people, as they had mentioned it when they stopped into the store. But nothing compared to the results from the email.

It also gave her some ideas for the bookstore, too. Maybe she could really help them harness the power of email. Julia was excited to try. She was in the best mood now. It was amazing how she'd gone so quickly from such a low, with the bounced check, to feeling on top of the world after checking her emails.

Chapter 33

Gladys came by the house the next morning at ten sharp. Jess was in the kitchen on her laptop looking through the bestseller lists and checking to see if there were any books they needed to order for the store. She heard her mother chatting with Gladys, and a moment later they both walked into the kitchen.

"Gladys, you remember my daughter, Jess?"

Jess stood and held out her hand. "It's so nice to see you again."

The older woman smiled as she shook Jess's hand. "Of course I remember you. Thanks ever so much for agreeing to meet with me."

Jess opened her mouth to tell her mother's friend that she couldn't actually give her legal advice, but her mother beat her to it.

"Gladys, just a reminder that Jess can't actually act as your lawyer, as she's not licensed here, but she can try to help."

Jess nodded. "I'm happy to. What are you needing help with?"

"Have a seat, Gladys. I was about to make a cup of tea, would you like some?" her mother asked as she filled a teakettle and set it on the stove.

Gladys sat across from Jess at the kitchen island. "No, thank you though. I really do appreciate this, Jess. My husband has had some health issues recently. It's under control now, but it got us both thinking that maybe we need to try to protect our assets now, in case things get bad again. I read something about putting our home into a trust, so that no one can put a claim on it if one of us has to go into a long-term-care type of place. You might know what I mean?"

Jess did. Many of her clients wanted her to put their homes into trusts. Timing was important, as it couldn't be done once someone was ill enough to go into a nursing home. Jess explained generally how it worked and a few different options Gladys could consider.

"So, if you see a local attorney, someone you trust, they should be able to help you with this. It's a very common thing," she assured her.

"Thank you. I feel much better about this now. It's a pity you aren't able to do it. I'd love to give you the business." Gladys stood and shook Jess's hand again. "Thanks so much for making the time to talk to me. I really appreciate it."

"Of course. It was good to see you."

Gladys and her mother chatted for a few more minutes before she left. Once Gladys was gone, Jess's mother joined her in the kitchen and poured herself a cup of tea.

"Thanks for doing that. Gladys is an old friend and her husband's heart attack scared both of them."

"He's okay now, though?"

"Fit as a fiddle, it seems. He's not worried, but I don't blame her for thinking ahead. Speaking of thinking ahead, have you given much thought to what's next when you go back to Charleston?"

Jess frowned. "Honestly, no. I've been trying not to think about it and to just focus on enjoying the bookstore and the coffee shop and the beach. I haven't been to the beach this much since before I got married." When she wasn't at the store and the weather was good, she loved grabbing a book and walking to the neighborhood beach and soaking up the warm weather. Even with sunscreen she was more tanned than she'd been in years, and she liked how it looked. She looked more relaxed and she liked to think maybe a little younger, too. Though, maybe that was wishful thinking.

"Don't plan on me for dinner tonight." Something about her mother's tone caught Jess's attention.

"Oh, what are you up to?"

Her mother smiled, and there was a glimmer of something that Jess hadn't seen in years.

"Just dinner with a friend."

"Who?"

"Ray McGuinness."

Jess recognized the name and tried to recall who he was. And then it came to her.

"Of the McGuinness Funeral Home?"

Her mother nodded. "It's a good business. Recession-proof."

Jess smiled. "No doubt. So, is this a date? Have you gone out with him before?"

"We've gone to dinner a few times. He's good company and funny. You wouldn't expect a funeral director to have such a good sense of humor."

"I bet it helps," Jess said. "I'm happy for you, Mom. Where are you going to dinner?"

"To that new Neptune place, I think. It's just dinner. Nothing to get all excited about."

"Well, have fun. The food is good there."

When she finished her tea, her mother left to run some errands and Jess checked the clock. It was about time for her to head into the bookstore for the rest of the day. As she drove there she thought about what might come next for her in Charleston and still felt very undecided on what she wanted. Going back to Parker's father's firm was out of the question. And the thought of sending out résumés and interviewing wasn't appealing. She was somewhat intrigued by the idea of opening her own small office.

She was well connected enough that she hoped it could be a success. But part of her wondered if might be a challenge with the divorce and Parker's family being so prominent in Charleston. She knew friends of couples often took sides in a divorce. But she hoped that she knew enough people who wouldn't care about that, or who would take her side.

Starting any business was a risk. She'd have to move, too, as she didn't want to stay in the house where she'd lived with Parker for over thirty years. It was a big house and the real estate market was strong, so it should be simple enough to sell and just split the proceeds with Parker. Or maybe he'd want to keep it and buy her out. Either way was fine with her. She wanted a fresh start.

Chapter 34

Alison took a break from her computer, looked up, and smiled. The day after they'd gone to the art opening, Jim had hung the painting that she loved so much in the office bullpen, so that everyone could enjoy it. It was the first thing in her line of vision, and it made her happy every time she saw it.

She glanced at the time—it was eleven thirty and she was hoping to get to the bookshop by noon. She gave the article she'd edited a final once-over and then emailed it to Jim for final approval. She hadn't seen him since she'd arrived around eight. He'd been in his office all morning. As she shut down her computer, though, and stood to leave, his door opened, and he spotted her and walked over.

"Are you heading out?"

"I am. I just sent you the final edits on the lighthouse feature."

"Great. I'll give it a look when I get back. I'll walk out with you."

"Are you off to lunch?" Alison asked.

"I have to stop at the bank first, but yes, grabbing a sandwich after that. By the way, I ran into Chris yesterday. He invited me to a cookout he's having this weekend. Said it's going to be a big crowd—should I assume that means you'll be there?"

She laughed. "Yes. And just about everyone else I know. I'm

glad you're going. It should be fun. Chris throws a good party." She was a little surprised that Chris invited him, though.

"We've been fishing in the same spot lately. I've run into him a few times and we got to talking." Now it made sense.

"I didn't realize you were into fishing."

He nodded. "I don't seem to catch much but I like trying. It's relaxing. I head out sometimes after work for a few hours."

"Chris always loved to do that, too. Still does." She grinned. "I don't remember him catching many fish either."

"When I do, I usually throw them back. I think he does the same. I'm looking forward to Saturday."

Suddenly Alison was much more interested in Chris's cook-out, too.

"I am, too. I'll see you there."

❦

Alison was glad to see that the bookstore seemed busier than usual when she arrived. Jess was ringing a customer up at the register and there were quite a few people browsing. She popped into the coffee shop for a minute and saw they had an impressive line that was moving fast. Caitlin took orders, while Sally poured coffee and toasted bagels. Caitlin waved when she saw her, and Alison nodded a quick hello before heading back into the bookstore.

She spotted one of their regulars, Mrs. Edith Winslow, who broke into a big smile when she saw Alison.

"Hello, dear. Lovely day we're having, isn't it?" It was a gorgeous day—perfect Cape Cod August weather, warm and a little breezy.

Alison chatted with her for a few minutes before Mrs. Winslow remembered what she wanted to ask.

"I saw the *New York Times* list this morning and wondered if you have the new Danielle Steel book? I always buy her new releases or my sister does and then we share." Alison knew from prior chats that both Mrs. Winslow and her sister Ginny lived at one of the nicer assisted-living residences in the area. She'd told Alison the first time she met her that she and her sister were "Irish Twins," born less than a year apart. Edith was the oldest at ninety-two. She came in at least once a week and was an avid reader.

"We just got that in yesterday, let me show you where they are." Alison led her over to the table that had their newest arrivals.

"Thank you, dear. I'm going to poke around and see what else I might need."

Alison made her way to the register, where Jess was handing change to another customer. There was a lull for a moment, and Alison commented that the store seemed busier.

"It's been like this all morning. The busiest day that I can remember so far. It's encouraging," Jess said.

A moment later, Mrs. Winslow came to the counter with three books. Alison rang her up and told her about the new loyalty program and gave her a plastic card with an ID number on it.

"Do I need to give you this card each time I come in?"

"You could either give us the card or just tell us your name and we'll look you up. The computer will automatically track the amount of your purchase and when you reach one hundred dollars, you'll have a ten-dollar credit to use the next time you shop."

"Well, isn't that lovely. I'll be sure to spread the word for you. My sister needs her own account, I think."

"Thank you. Hope to see you soon." Alison handed her a paper shopping bag with her books and receipt.

"Oh, you will, my dear. You will!"

Once she was gone Jess commented, "I wish we could clone her. She's one of my favorites."

"Mine, too. I think we're on the right track now. I stopped in the coffee shop, and they are busy, too."

"I agree. I got an email from the tenants upstairs, though. They are giving their two-month notice. We'll need to find new renters after mid-October."

"That shouldn't be too hard, I wouldn't think. It's a small

space, but a good location. Especially for someone that works downtown."

"I agree. It should go quickly, so we can deal with that next month. We'll just have to make sure we check credit and references. One of my friends in Charleston got stuck with a horrible renter who stopped paying rent and wouldn't leave and it's difficult to get them out."

Alison had heard of that happening, too. A bad tenant could be a nightmare.

"Have you heard anything further from Parker? Do you think he's really going to pay you a visit this weekend? Or was that just talk?"

Jess sighed. "I'd say it's fifty-fifty. I'm really not sure. I haven't heard anything further from him. But I wouldn't put it past him to just show up and call when he gets here. He'll have to work around my schedule, though. Caitlin and I are both going to Chris's party on Saturday and I am not inviting Parker to that."

Alison laughed. "Absolutely not. Jim told me today that he's going, too."

Jess looked surprised. "I didn't know he and Chris were friends."

"Neither did I. Apparently they are fishing buddies. I'm glad he's going, though."

"How's he been since you went to the art show? Has he mentioned going out again?"

"Same as ever, and no. Not until today when he mentioned the cookout. I don't think he sees me as anything other than a work colleague."

"Do you want it to be more than that?"

Did she? "I really don't know. Sometimes I think maybe, but then I think I'm being silly and we're just meant to be work friends and employer-employee. Better not to rock that boat, probably."

"I think you might be overthinking it. Just see where things go," Jess said.

"That's good advice. I'll do that." Alison knew that was the practical approach, but she couldn't help feeling a sense of joy when Jim mentioned that he would be at the cookout, too. She was already looking forward to it, but now there was a different kind of anticipation, too.

Chapter 35

By Friday afternoon, Julia felt light and happy, like a weight had been lifted. Caitlin commented on it when Julia stopped into the coffee shop for her afternoon break. "You're positively glowing. You look more relaxed and happier than I've ever seen you," Caitlin said as she handed Julia her coffee.

"Thanks. I was thinking the same thing earlier—that I feel lighter. I thought Kyle would give me a harder time about this. That I'd hear from him again, but I think it's really done."

"Good. I'm glad."

"Are you up for a drink at the Squire after work today? I am feeling a little celebratory."

Caitlin laughed. "Of course. I finish up here around four and will run home and shower and change. What time did you want to meet up?"

"How about six? I actually need to run home and change, too. I managed to spill a little resin on my shirt earlier and want to throw that in the wash to soak."

"Six is perfect. If I get there before you, I'll try to save us seats at the bar."

The rest of the afternoon flew, as Julia was busy with tourists stopping into the shop. She sold more than usual and in between customers worked on a new commissioned bracelet. It was a heavy gold design with several diamonds and a wavelike pattern, a variation of the one she'd emailed about. She was still getting responses and orders trickling in from that email, which amazed her. Word of mouth was also spreading, and she was getting more referrals for these higher-end pieces, which were both profitable and satisfying to work on.

At five sharp, Julia flipped her OPEN sign on the front to door to CLOSED and headed home to change. She had just about enough time to go home, freshen up, change, and put some stain remover on her top and put it in the washer on the soak cycle. She got everything done, changed into her favorite light blue cotton sweater, ran a brush through her hair one final time, and was heading for the door when she was startled by a sharp knock just as she was about to open it. She wasn't expecting anyone but had a sudden sinking suspicion who it might be. She glanced out the side window and saw Kyle standing on her doorstep. She took a deep breath and opened the door.

"Kyle, this is a surprise. I was just on my way out."

His eyes narrowed. "I thought you'd be happier to see me."

"I wasn't expecting you." She was tempted to add "because we broke up." But she just wanted him to go away quickly and quietly.

"I told you I wanted to come see you this weekend."

"Kyle. I meant what I said the other day. It's over. We both need to move on."

He frowned, and took a step forward, with a determined look. "I thought you'd come to your senses. We need to talk about this, face-to-face."

"Kyle, I'm sorry, but there's nothing more to talk about. I really do have plans. I'm late to meet someone."

"What, do you have a date already? That didn't take long," he said bitterly.

"I don't have a date. I'm meeting Caitlin, if you must know."

"Okay, but I really do want to sit down and talk about this with you. Maybe tomorrow?"

"I'm working tomorrow and then my dad is having a cookout. We said all there is to say on the phone. There's nothing more to talk about."

He stood there, saying nothing for a long awkward moment, and Caitlin really did feel badly. She reached out and gently touched his arm. "Kyle, go home to Nashville. You seem really happy there."

He pulled his arm away and stormed off to his car. Julia waited a moment until he drove off, before locking her door behind her and heading to her own car.

Caitlin was sitting at the bar at the Squire when Julia arrived. There was an empty seat beside her. Julia rushed over and slid into it. "I'm so sorry that I'm late. I had an unexpected visitor as I was leaving." She told Caitlin about Kyle's visit and ordered a glass of wine as soon as the bartender came over.

"I can't believe he still flew up here." Caitlin seemed alarmed to hear it. "Are you sure you feel safe?"

Julia laughed. "I know how it sounds, but Kyle really is harmless. He's just very used to getting his own way. I think he thought if he flew up here and saw me in person, he'd get me to agree to go back to the way things were."

"He sounds controlling. I'm glad you broke up with him."

"He didn't used to be. Or at least I never noticed it, but his behavior lately hasn't been ideal, that's for sure. I thought I'd made it clear on the phone that we were done."

"Sounds like his ego couldn't accept that," Caitlin said.

"No. But I think I got through to him. Hopefully, he'll just visit with his family and head back to Nashville."

"I'm glad he doesn't live around here anymore. Makes it a little easier for you."

Julia had been thinking the same thing. "It definitely does. So, enough about Kyle. I'm hungry, let's get some menus."

They split a few appetizers and had a wonderful night, chatting and eating and then listening to the band when they came on an hour or so later. It was still an early night, as they were both working in the morning, but it was nice to get out and relax after a busy week. And Julia was looking forward to her father's cookout the next afternoon.

She half expected to run into Kyle again when she got home, which she knew was ridiculous but still, she was relieved when she pulled into her driveway and he wasn't there. His visit earlier had shaken her more than she'd admitted to Caitlin. There was a manic quality about Kyle that disturbed her—when he didn't get his way, or didn't like something, his mood shifted so abruptly. It was unsettling and Julia really hoped that he would take an earlier plane home to Nashville.

Chapter 36

Jess wasn't surprised to receive a text message early Saturday morning from Parker.

> Got in last night. Will stop in the bookstore around noon to have a look around. Would appreciate if you could sit down with me for lunch or coffee so we can discuss.

She seethed inwardly as she made her first cup of coffee and debated how to answer. She had no desire to have lunch with Parker. But, she knew they really did need to discuss the divorce—though she was dreading the conversation. Especially if he was going to be difficult about the bookstore.

> I'll be there all day and can take a fifteen-minute coffee break then. We can go right next door, so in case it gets busy, I won't be far.

Saturdays tended to be their busiest day, so she didn't want to leave Alison alone for too long. Brooklyn wasn't coming in until later that afternoon to cover the evening shift while they both went to Chris's cookout.

He replied back immediately.

See you at noon.

She gave Caitlin a heads-up that her father would be stopping in and when she got to the store, filled Alison in as well.

"What do you think his intentions are?" Alison asked. Jess knew she was worried that Parker could cause trouble for them, but Jess thought he was just blustering and hoping to get her to come around to his way of thinking—whatever that might be. She didn't really think Parker wanted to reconcile. Caitlin had let her know he was still seeing Linda, and with a baby coming, it seemed like he'd moved on personally, at least.

But Jess knew Parker hated surprises and he was used to getting his way. It no doubt infuriated him to discover Jess had bought the bookstore and coffee shop without consulting him. She didn't regret it, though. She knew he would have insisted on being involved—if he didn't try to prevent the deal from happening.

The store was busy all morning, and both Jess and Alison noticed that the loyalty cards seemed to be a big hit. Julia had sent an email instructing people to ask for the cards and also letting them know about the signing at one, which was another reason why Jess didn't want to be too long with Parker. She wanted to make sure that went smoothly and to be available if the author needed any assistance.

Jess was ringing up an order when the front door chimed as Parker walked in precisely at noon. He nodded her way, but took his time walking all around the store, taking it all in, and waited until Jess rang up another customer before walking to the register.

"Hi, Parker, nice to see you," Alison said. Jess knew she was just being polite, but Parker took her words to heart and smiled big.

"Great to see you, too. It's been too long!"

Jess stepped out from behind the register. "Hi, Parker." She turned to Alison. "We'll be right next door if you need me."

Parker went to pull her in for a hello hug, but it was awkward and both pulled back quickly.

"Where did you stay last night?" she asked as they headed into the coffee shop.

"I got a room at the Chatham Bars Inn. Nice place." That was an understatement. It was the nicest hotel in the area, right on the ocean, with rolling lawns, croquet, and delicious food. Of course that's where he stayed.

Caitlin looked happy but also a bit wary when she saw her father. She came out from behind the counter to give him a hug.

"What can I get you? You should try the everything bagel, Dad. You'll love it."

Parker chuckled. "If you say so, I guess I have to try it. Jess, what do you want?"

"I'll have the same, and a tall black coffee." Jess hadn't planned on eating, but her stomach grumbled, reminding her that it was lunchtime. She might as well have something. Caitlin handed them their coffees. "Go have a seat. I'll bring the bagels over when they're ready."

"Thanks, honey." Parker paid, and Jess led him to a small table by the window, where they could have some privacy. Most people coming into the coffee shop took their food and drinks to go, but there were several other tables in the back of the restaurant, near the counter, and two of them were occupied. Jess didn't particularly want Caitlin to overhear their conversation, so she chose a table as far away as possible.

They chatted about nothing in particular for a few minutes, making small talk until Caitlin delivered their bagels. Once they arrived, Parker got down to business.

"Bookstore seems busy enough. Maybe it's not such a bad investment after all." He said it in a way that implied it was his investment, too.

Jess narrowed her eyes and used her best take-no-prisoners lawyer tone. "This has nothing to do with you, Parker. It's just mine and Alison's."

He leaned back in his chair and crossed his arms over his chest. "Well, technically, no it's not. We're still married. And we could stay married, if you want to work at this. I really don't want a divorce, do you? We've built a good life together. We work together, have a child together."

"Caitlin isn't a child anymore. And speaking of children, how can you seriously talk about staying together when you have another one on the way—with someone else? What were you thinking?"

Parker at least had the good grace to look embarrassed. "I wasn't thinking. I think it was a midlife crisis, if you want to know the truth. I know things weren't good with us—I mean we always got along great, but the romance was gone. It was sort of like we were roommates."

He wasn't wrong about that. "I felt the same way. I'd debated what to do about it, to see if you wanted to try counseling, though I didn't really know if that would work. I put off saying anything because it was just easier to ignore it and deal with it later," she admitted.

He nodded. "I put off the conversation, too. But I was feeling lonely, and Linda—well, she was just there. And she seemed to like being around me."

"How did you first hook up with her?" Jess wondered how she could have missed it so completely. Parker often worked late, but he was still home every night, so she didn't know when he could have been with Linda.

"She goes to the same gym. And we had the same routine. She worked out in the morning, too, so we'd chat there. And then we had that corporate case that took a lot of our time. We worked late for a few weeks to stay on top of it and when it wrapped up, we had a glass of wine in the office to celebrate and then Linda suggested going for one more. Her condo is a block or two away from the bar and we ended up there. Both of us had a little too much to drink and one thing led to another. I never meant for it to happen, I swear."

Jess believed him. Linda was cute and obviously found him attractive and let him know. She was twenty years younger and no doubt that went to his head a little. Still, he should have known better.

"It wasn't just the one time, though?" She wasn't going to let him off easy.

He shook his head. "No. It quickly became a habit. Every Wednesday or Thursday night we worked late and as soon as everyone left, we got takeout and went to her place."

"Do you love her?"

"No." His answer was fast and seemed sincere. "I know I totally messed up. But it was a wake-up call. It made me realize how important you are to me. I don't want to lose you, Jess. Can you come back to Charleston? We can find a way to make this work—can't we?"

She looked at him in frustration. "Really? What would that look like to you? How do we move forward when you're about to have a baby with another woman?"

Parker just stared at her, speechless.

Jess shook her head. "I don't see how we can. How can I ever trust you again, Parker?" She paused for a moment, gathering her thoughts. "We should have addressed this sooner. Things weren't right with us for a long time. Both of us are at fault for that."

He nodded. "You're right. I've really made a mess of it." They were both quiet and focused on eating their bagels before Parker spoke again. "What about the law firm? We're buried with work. We really need you there, Jess. At least say you'll come back when you move home to Charleston."

"I've been thinking a lot about that. I don't think I can do it. It will be too hard to work with you all day and with her." Jess didn't want to ever see Linda's baby bump again—the image was burned into her memory as it was.

"What will you do then? Go to work for someone else? A competitor?" He clearly hated the thought.

"I haven't decided yet. I could always go on my own, hang out a shingle and see what happens."

"Do you really want to do that? Totally start over, at your age?"

That infuriated her. "At least I'm not having a baby," she retorted, and he looked as if she'd slapped him.

"I guess I deserved that. I just meant it might be hard to start over, for anyone."

"I really don't know. Part of me likes the idea. We'll see."

"Okay. What do you want to do about the house? I'm assuming you want to keep it?"

Jess shook her head. "I don't want the house. We can sell it, or you can buy me out."

"I thought you'd want it. We can sell it. The market is nuts and it should go fast. The lawyers can figure out the rest of it."

"And you'll let the bookstore go? It can just be part of my half of our assets? It should work out evenly."

"I need to think about that and talk to my lawyer. I'll get back to you."

"No, Parker. There's nothing to think about. I'm pretty sure our savings accounts were similar in size."

Parker sat up straight and seemed ready for a fight. "It's not similar now, though, is it? You bought a bookstore without telling me. That's unforgivable."

Jess laughed. "And that's rich, coming from you. Aside from the cheating and getting someone pregnant, you've also been doing a little spending, too, haven't you?"

"You looked in my account?" His surprise was evident.

"I did. I was pretty sure the amounts were about the same, but wanted to confirm. I was very surprised to see several large withdrawals recently. Both made out to a Realtor. What did you do?"

There was a long, awkward silence before she finally added, "Did you buy her a house?"

A telltale red flush spread across his face. "It's not her house. It's mine. A bigger condo, near the office. I want you back, but I also felt like I had to do something to help her, too. And I thought it was a good investment."

"Yet, you didn't think to mention it." She shook her head. Parker was hedging his bets. She didn't doubt that he wanted to try again with her, but he wanted Linda as a backup. Or maybe he truly didn't know what he wanted and just wasn't ready to let go. "I won't make a fuss about your 'investment' if you let the bookstore go. Let's just move on."

Parker sighed. "You're really sure about all this?"

She knew she was a few steps ahead of him in terms of where they were and that he had to digest the conversation and catch up.

"I'm sure. We had a good marriage for a long time. It's just over."

He nodded and looked away for a moment. When he looked back she was surprised by the sadness she saw reflected in his eyes.

"I'm really sorry, Jess. I never meant for it to happen this way."

She sighed. "I know."

"Caitlin's going to this party with you tonight?'

"Yeah, Chris, Alison's ex, is having a cookout."

"Okay. I'll go say goodbye to her then. I have a flight back in the morning, but maybe I'll see if I can get on an earlier flight back tonight."

"I should get back over to the bookstore, too. We have an author signing soon."

They gathered up their empty cups and plates and threw them in the trash.

"Chris and Alison get along great now, even after getting divorced, don't they? Maybe that will be us someday." Parker looked hopeful and Jess just shook her head.

"I don't know. I suppose anything is possible."

Chapter 37

"How did it go?" Alison asked as soon as Jess returned to the register. She filled her in on the conversation with Parker.

"I think overall, it went okay. It's sad for both of us, but he seems to have accepted that this divorce is happening."

"And the bookstore? He's not going to give us a hard time?" Alison was still concerned, and Jess couldn't blame her.

"He said he's going to talk to his attorneys to see about dividing things up fairly. We're going to put the house on the market."

Alison was as surprised as Parker to hear it. "You don't want to keep the house? It's a gorgeous house." Alison had been down several times over the years to visit.

Jess shook her head. "Too many memories there. It's a big house. I want to start fresh, with something smaller."

"And Caitlin will go with you, of course?"

"I don't really know what she will want to do. She may want to get her own place. But of course she'll always have a room wherever I live." Caitlin had told her how cute Julia's condo was and she'd mentioned several times over the past year that she'd like to get her own place, as soon as she was settled in a good job.

A pretty blond woman who looked to be in her late thirties

came up to the register. She was carrying a big tote bag and smiled when she saw them.

"I'm Grace Barrows. I'm doing a signing here today."

"Welcome, Grace. I'm Jess and this is my partner, Alison. We're excited that you're here." Jess led her to a table near the front door that Alison had set up earlier with stacks of Grace's books. She lived nearby, in Orleans, and wrote a popular women's fiction series set on the Outer Cape.

Grace settled behind the table and pulled some bookmarks, a journal, and a glass bowl out of the tote bag. She set everything on the table, and emptied a bag of Dove bite-sized chocolates into the bowl. She opened the journal and set a pen beside it. Across the top of the page she'd written, "Sign up for my newsletter."

"Would you like a coffee or water?" Jess offered.

Grace smiled and pulled a bottled water from her bag. "Thank you, but I came prepared!"

Jess laughed. "You've done this before. It's our first time actually. Do you have any tips for us, to help you?"

Grace thought for a moment. "Maybe just mention that I'm a local author when people come to the register? Otherwise everything looks good."

"I had a sign made to put outside. I'll do that now." Alison ran into the back office and returned a moment later with a stand-up two-foot-tall double-sided sign that said AUTHOR SIGNING TODAY. She'd tied two pink balloons to the top of the sign. "What do you think? The balloons are to get people's attention."

"I love it!" Grace said.

"It's perfect," Jess agreed.

The sign worked its magic as soon as Alison set it outside on the sidewalk. They had a steady stream of people wandering in for the rest of the afternoon. Grace sold out of all the books they'd ordered for the signing. Jess and Alison panicked a bit as she sold her last book at two thirty and still had a half hour to go for the signing.

"I'm so sorry that we didn't order enough books," Jess said. "We really weren't sure how to anticipate what we'd need."

"I wasn't sure either," Grace admitted. "It's a gorgeous day, though, and lots of foot traffic. I have a box of books in my car I can bring in if you'd like them. I brought them along just in case."

"Of course! I'm so glad you thought to do that." Jess went with Grace to her car and helped her carry two big armloads of books into the store. That carried them through to the end of the signing and only two were left when the signing ended.

"Thanks so much for bringing the extra books," Alison said. "We can put these last two on the shelf and get an order in for more right away."

Grace stood and started to pack her tote bag. "Thanks for having me in. This was fun and I'd love to do it again sometime."

"Absolutely. We'd love that, too," Jess assured her. Once Grace left, Jess went next door to check on Caitlin.

"Did you send people over to the signing?" Jess had noticed a bigger stream than usual of people coming into the bookstore from the coffee shop.

Caitlin grinned. "I did. I told them a famous author was signing today and they had to go check it out. How did it go?"

"Thanks for that. It went really well. And the loyalty cards are a hit, too."

"Oh, I'm glad. You know, I was thinking, we could do something similar for the coffee shop. But instead of spending a certain amount, we just track coffees so once they buy ten the next one is free? The regulars will love that."

"Great idea. I'll talk to Alison about it, but I think that could work."

Caitlin went and locked the front door of the coffee shop. Through experimenting with closing at different times, they'd settled on three as the best closing time. When they'd stayed open later, to four, it hadn't been worthwhile, as business slowed considerably after two.

"I'll see you back at the house, honey." Jess went back to the register, where Brooklyn had just arrived. Alison was folding up the table Grace had been using. A balloon dancing in the wind outside caught Jess's eye and she went and grabbed the sign and balloons and brought them into the office.

"So that was a success," Jess said as Alison carried the table in and set it by the sign.

"I took a quick peek at the daily total and this may be our best day yet!"

Jess was happy to hear it. The sign had brought a lot of people in, and there had been a buzz in the store all afternoon. "That really was fun. We need to do these types of events regularly."

"Yes. And tonight, we can celebrate."

Chapter 38

There was already a good crowd gathered at Chris's house when Alison arrived. She let herself in and dropped her plate of brownies on the table Chris had set up on the outside deck. It was filled with salads, sandwiches, dips, chips, and condiments. Chris was manning the grill, and it was loaded with hot dogs, burgers, and marinated chicken. He grinned when he saw her, and she gave him a hello kiss on the cheek.

"Did you invite the whole town?" she teased him.

He laughed. "Just about. This one has taken on a life of its own. It's all good, though. I have tons of food and people have brought stuff. Do I see your brownies over there?"

"Of course." Alison always brought her brownies. Chris loved them.

"There's some wine open in the kitchen, if you want to help yourself?" Chris offered.

"I'll do that. Do you need anything?"

"I'm good. Go have fun."

She did as instructed, found the wine and poured herself a glass. It was Santa Margherita, her favorite pinot grigio, which Chris usually kept in stock. She took a sip and surveyed the backyard. People were gathered on the deck, chatting with Chris as he cooked, and others were relaxing on the lawn, where there was plenty of seating, long wooden picnic tables and Adirondack chairs here and there. Chris had also added folding chairs and a few smaller tables.

"This place is hopping already," Jess said as she and Caitlin walked over. They chatted for a few minutes, and then Caitlin left when she spotted Julia and some of her friends arriving.

"Chris always did know how to throw a party," Jess said. It was true. When they were married, he was always the outgoing one, while Alison was quieter. "I'll be right back. I'm going to go say hello to him and grab myself a wine."

Alison watched her go, and noticed Chris's face light up and break into a big smile when he saw Jess. He put his spatula down for a moment and gave her a big hug. They chatted for a few minutes before Jess disappeared inside. She returned holding a glass of pinot grigio.

"Sounds like Chris is expecting a big crowd. He said he invited all the neighbors, too, so no one will complain about the noise. Or the cars parked up and down the street."

"He always does that. Ever since a neighbor called the police on us years ago for being loud. It was ridiculous, though. It wasn't even a party. He'd just had a few guys over to watch football and they had a drink outside when the game ended. One of the guys had a loud voice, though, and Chris had to keep asking him to keep it down. Sound carries near the water." Chris lived on a marshy river that led out to the ocean.

"I think I remember you telling me about that. When the police arrived everyone had already left?"

Alison nodded. "We were actually sitting inside eating cake and watching TV. The police apologized for disturbing us—said a neighbor had called in a loud party."

"Sheesh."

"Right. After that, he was always super careful if we had anyone over, and if we did have a party, he made sure to invite all the neighbors."

Alison noticed Jess squinting as if trying to better see something or someone.

"Is that Lavinia? From high school?" Jess asked.

Alison followed her gaze and sure enough, Lavinia and Chelsea were there, and Lavinia was talking to Jim. Alison's Jim—she hadn't even seen him arrive.

"Yes, that's Lavinia. Chris must have run into her somewhere and invited her."

"Isn't that Jim she's talking to?"

"It is. He must have just arrived, too. She didn't waste any time. She was asking me about him at the art show."

"He looks good."

Alison had to agree. Jim was wearing a light blue button-down shirt and faded jeans. His hair was wavy and thick and in the sunlight looked blonder than usual. He laughed at something Lavinia said, and his smile made him even more attractive.

"You need to go talk to him," Jess said.

"I will. But I'm not going to go over there and barge into their conversation."

Jess laughed. "No, you wouldn't do that. I'm sure Lavinia would, though."

"No doubt," Alison agreed.

People continued to arrive, and Alison introduced Jess to many of them. They helped themselves to food when Chris hollered that it was ready, and loaded their plates with burgers, potato salad, and chips. They settled at one of the card tables to eat. Alison looked around but didn't see Lavinia or Jim. She'd lost track of them as the backyard had filled up with people.

"I love seeing Caitlin and Julia getting along so well." Alison saw that the girls were seated at a different table with several of Julia's friends.

"I am, too. Since Julia invited her out to that party a while ago, they've been spending more time together. It's nice of Julia to include her. I think Caitlin is enjoying her time in Chatham a lot more now," Jess said.

"Mind if I join you?" Alison looked up at the familiar voice. Jim was holding a plateful of food in one hand and a beer in the other. And Lavinia was nowhere in sight.

"Of course." Alison and Jess were almost done eating, but Alison was happy to slow down a bit.

"I see someone I need to go say hello to." Jess walked off toward the house with her empty plate, and Alison knew she was just trying to give her some alone time with Jim.

"How did the book signing go today?" he asked.

"Better than expected. Luckily the author brought extra books with her, because we needed them."

Jim smiled, and his eyes were warm and happy for her. "That's great news. So, sales are picking up?" She'd mentioned that she'd been a little worried about slow sales earlier.

"Yes, finally. Some of the things we are putting into place seem to be working, which is a relief."

"It's always been a busy store. I'm sure you will both do great with it."

They chatted comfortably, and after a while Alison asked him about his book.

"How's the second half coming along? I'm ready to read whenever you want to send it."

"I appreciate that. A few more days and I think I'll be ready. I'm just tweaking here and there. It's hard to know when to stop sometimes. That probably sounds silly."

"No, not at all. You want it to be as good as possible. I think after a while, though, you have to stop tweaking. It will never be as perfect as you want it to be."

Jim laughed. "I suspect that's true. Have you thought about writing a book yourself?"

Alison shook her head. "Not fiction, no. I like doing the occasional article or restaurant review and I love editing other people's work. That's the fun part for me. Helping to make something even better."

"Well, you're very good at it. I'm lucky to have your help." Jim smiled at her and held her gaze a moment longer than he had to, and Alison felt herself blushing.

"Thank you. It's a good story, Jim. I can't wait to read the rest of it." She smiled. "Once it's published we'll have to have you do a signing in the store."

"Absolutely."

Jim finished eating and went up for dessert. He returned to the table with two of the brownies that Alison brought and handed one to her. "Did you bring these? They look like the ones you've made for office parties."

"Yes, those are mine. The semi-healthy black bean ones."

He laughed. And a moment later asked a question that surprised her. "Do you think you and Chris will ever get back together?" She thought he was teasing at first, but the expression in his eyes was serious.

"No. We've been divorced for years."

"I know, but you're so comfortable around each other. And it's rare to see two divorced people spend so much time together. He talks about you a lot."

"I love Chris and always will—but it's the same way I love Jess. They're both my best friends."

"Okay. I just had to ask, to be sure. I don't want to waste my time. I mean . . ." He hesitated and then stayed silent.

"What do you mean?"

"Well, I suppose this is my awkward way of asking you to dinner. I just didn't want to step on any toes."

Alison felt a happy glow and loved that Jim seemed suddenly nervous and unsure of himself. It mirrored her own feelings. She'd gone back and forth about whether or not this was a good idea before realizing that she was just scared, and that she'd put off dating anyone for far too long.

"You're not stepping on any toes. And I'd love to go to dinner with you."

"Really? How about next Friday then? We'll touch base before then on where to go."

"That sounds good." Alison felt on cloud nine and didn't even notice someone walk up to them.

"Jim, great to see you here." Reggie Howard was one of the magazine's biggest advertisers. Jim introduced her, and then she excused herself to let them talk and headed inside for a bit more wine.

As she filled her glass, her ears picked up the word "Jess." She turned and saw Ryan Oliphant and another of Chris's friends deep in conversation. She couldn't help but eavesdrop.

"Yeah, I met her recently. I'm pretty sure Chris is interested, though, so I'm not going there."

"I don't know about that, but yeah, maybe hold off for now."

They started talking about something else, and Alison stood there in shock. Were they talking about her Chris? He and Ryan were good friends, so it was likely. But Chris and Jess? He'd never mentioned having any interest. But then, she wasn't sure he would. Chris never talked to her about any women that he was interested in. She thought back, though, to the warm welcome he'd given Jess when she arrived.

She was a little ashamed that her initial reaction to the idea was no. She didn't want to share Chris with Jess, not that way. Alison didn't want a romantic relationship with Chris, but she didn't like the idea of him having one with Jess, her best friend, either.

She knew it would change her relationship with Chris. And she felt like a horrible friend for feeling that way. It wasn't fair, to either of them, if there was a chance that Jess might be interested in Chris that way. As much as she hated the idea of it, Alison knew she needed to talk to Jess.

❦

Jess was on the deck, leaning against a railing, and nibbling on a brownie as she people-watched. She smiled as Alison walked out of the house with a fresh glass of wine and made her way over. She raised her glass as Alison reached her. "Goes great with your brownies."

Alison smiled. "Thanks." She took a sip of her wine and looked like she had something to say.

"So I was just getting some wine and overheard Ryan Oliphant telling someone that he might be interested in you, but he's not going to do anything about it because he thinks there might be something going on with you and Chris—that Chris is interested in you." She took another sip of wine and watched Jess's reaction closely.

"Ryan said he might be interested in me?" Jess was surprisingly happy to hear it, even though she still didn't feel ready to do anything about it. She wondered how Alison felt about what she'd heard about Chris. Jess wasn't surprised to have it confirmed, as she'd definitely picked up that vibe.

"It sounds that way. But what about what he said about Chris? Is he right? If you're interested in Chris that way, you should go for it. I wouldn't want you to hold back because of me. That ship sailed long ago." Alison laughed, but Jess knew her best friend and she could see in her eyes how she really felt. She hated the idea. But she loved Jess enough to encourage her anyway. And Jess loved her for it. Even though she had felt a little spark with Chris, she knew it wasn't Chris so much as the idea of having that kind of attention from anyone. She didn't need it from Chris. She wouldn't do anything to jeopardize the friendship that she and Alison had. It was too important.

"He got that wrong," she assured her. "Chris isn't interested in me. I think he just made the assumption because we were at the Squire together after you left. Chris is like a brother to me. Ryan on the other hand . . ." She laughed. "Now, that is tempting, though I still don't feel ready to go there, with anyone. But, it's nice to know someone was interested."

Alison's whole expression relaxed and it was like the tension melted off her. "I thought there was probably nothing to it. You should go talk to Ryan, though. Just get to know him. You don't have to rush anything."

"If I run into him here, I'll definitely do that."

They turned at the sound of a loud, angry voice. Jess didn't recognize it, but Alison clearly did when the voice called, "Julia!"

"That sounds like Kyle." Alison's brow furrowed as she looked around nervously for Julia. "And I know he wasn't invited."

Chapter 39

"Your dad looks like he's having a blast," Tim said. Julia glanced toward the back deck, where her father was still manning the grill, cooking burgers and hot dogs and laughing with his friends. She was sitting at one of the long picnic tables, with Caitlin, Sue, Kevin, and Jason. They'd finished eating a while ago and were just talking and laughing. The sun was just starting to go down and the air felt a little cooler. It was still a gorgeous night, though. She was thinking about going to get one of her mother's brownies when a loud, familiar voice carried across the yard.

"Julia!"

"Is that Kyle?" Sue sounded as surprised as Julia felt.

Kyle spotted her sitting with everyone, and she jumped up and ran over toward him to avoid a scene.

"Kyle, what are you doing here?" He had a manic look about him and his cheeks were slightly flushed. When he spoke she could smell the beer on his breath.

"We need to talk, Julia. You said you'd be here and you left me no other choice. We can do it here in front of everyone, or we can walk out front and talk privately. It's up to you." He wasn't drunk, but he'd definitely been drinking and he was right about one thing—she didn't want a big scene.

"All right. Let's go out front and we can talk for a few minutes."

"Everything okay over here?" Her father walked toward them still holding his spatula and wore a concerned expression.

"It's okay, Dad. Kyle and I are just going to have a little chat. He's not staying."

"Okay." He stood watching as she led Kyle to the front steps. She sat, but Kyle stayed standing and paced back and forth.

"I just don't understand it, Julia. I thought things were good with us. What happened?"

Julia sighed. "Kyle, I never got to where I needed to be to marry you. And now with you in Nashville, it just doesn't make sense anymore. I don't want to move to Nashville, not now, not ever." Though she knew if it was the right person, and they were in love, she'd find a way to do it. But it seemed mean to say that, so she didn't.

"So, there's nothing I can do? And you swear there's no one else?"

Julia shook her head. "I swear. And no, there's nothing you can do. It's just not there for me. Not the way it should be. Not the way you deserve."

He nodded, and finally it seemed to be sinking in.

"I guess I'll just go then, if that's it." He turned to leave, and Julia reached out her hand and grabbed his arm.

"Kyle, I don't think you should drive. It's too dangerous."

"I'm fine." He tried to shake her off.

"How many beers did you have before you came here?"

"I don't know—four, maybe five."

"Kyle, the last thing you need right now is a DUI. You know the cops are all over the roads this time of year. Let me get Tim to drive you home. I'll follow behind."

He sighed. "Fine."

"Stay here. Promise me you won't leave?"

"Just go. Get Tim."

Julia ran over to get Tim and filled him in. He took charge and took Kyle's keys and drove him home. Julia followed, and fifteen minutes later they reached Kyle's parents' house. Julia got out of her car and walked over to meet them and say a final goodbye to Kyle.

"So, this is it then?" Kyle said.

"I'll be in the car." Tim left them alone and climbed into the passenger side of Julia's car.

"Yeah, this is it. Goodbye, Kyle." For a minute she thought he might give her a hug goodbye—it looked like he considered it—but instead he took a step back.

"Bye, Julia." He turned and walked into the house, and she let out a breath she hadn't realized she'd been holding.

Her eyes watered as she walked back to her car, and she felt a rush of sadness. Even though she'd wanted the breakup, it was still sad for both of them.

She got into the car, started the engine, and backed out of the driveway.

"Are you okay?" Tim asked. They'd been riding along quietly for a few minutes and Julia was lost in her thoughts. She didn't have any doubts about the breakup, but she did feel a little guilty that she'd never felt the way Kyle had. She'd tried, but just never got there.

"I'm okay. Breakups suck, even when you're the one that wanted it."

"Yeah, they do. Kyle will be okay. You will, too."

She smiled and hiccuped at the same time, which made them both laugh. "Thanks. I know it just takes time. I probably should have given Kyle more of an explanation before this, I know it was frustrating for him. But I didn't have one. It just wasn't right anymore. He got to the love part faster than I did, and I hoped I'd catch up. But it never happened. And I finally realized it wasn't going to. That's the confusing thing."

"What's confusing?"

"How do you know if love will come? I tried to get there. I really did."

Tim stayed quiet for a long moment as drove along in silence.

Finally, he spoke, and she felt his gaze as she kept her eyes on the road. "I don't think love is supposed to be that hard. It shouldn't take that long to realize you love someone. I think most people realize it a lot sooner, and then fight that feeling because it seems too fast."

Julia relaxed and laughed. "You're probably right about that."

She glanced his way and he smiled reassuringly. "Don't stress about it. He just wasn't your guy. He's out there somewhere." A moment later, he added, "Maybe you've already met him."

That made her smile. Being around Tim always made her feel better. She loved spending time with him. "You know, I'm not worried about that. I'm not in a hurry to do this again anytime soon." Jumping into another intense relationship was the last thing she wanted.

"I hear you. Just hang out with your friends and have fun. Enjoy the rest of the summer." She slowed to a traffic light and looked his way. Tim's eyes were warm as they met hers. She noticed the tiny spray of laugh lines around his eyes and mouth as he smiled.

Julia took a deep breath and suddenly felt lighter, freer. "That I can do." She looked forward to spending the rest of her summer with good friends—like Tim.

Chapter 40

So, the New York girls' weekend is a go. Can you meet us there this Friday? I could fly back to the Cape with you on Sunday for the rest of the week?" Beth suggested.

Caitlin had been sitting on her grandmother's porch Monday afternoon, relaxing with a book and soaking up the last few hours of the sun, when Beth called.

"I'll have to double-check to make sure I can get coverage, but that should work. As long as you don't mind entertaining yourself for most of the days when you're here. I won't be able to take off that much time if I go away for the weekend."

"Well, you're free at night, right? And you said you finish up around three? You can just join me at the beach."

Caitlin laughed. "Perfect. I'll confirm and hopefully see you in Manhattan this weekend."

Caitlin's grandmother drove her to the Hyannis airport on Friday. Her grandmother was excited to take the Mini Cooper out for a spin, and Caitlin had to admit it was a really cute car. They had lunch first, at Baxter's on Hyannis Harbor, and watched the ferries and other boat traffic go by while they split a fried clam platter and a lobster roll.

"It's been a million years since I've been to Manhattan," her grandmother said later as she pulled up to the airport terminal. "I bet it's even bigger and more exciting than I remember. There's an energy in the city that I've never experienced anywhere else. I can't wait to hear all about it when you get home."

"Thanks so much, Grammy. I'll take lots of pictures and Beth and I will fill you in when we get back."

"I'll be here Sunday afternoon to pick you up."

Caitlin gave her grandmother a final hug goodbye and grabbed her overnight bag and wheeled it into the terminal. The JetBlue flight was the only nonstop option, and it was a quick flight, just over an hour. She left at a quarter to three and landed at ten of four.

The flight was smooth and went by in a flash. When Caitlin exited JFK Airport, she quickly got a cab, but traffic was heavy—it took a full hour to reach the hotel in midtown. As they drove along, she gazed out the window at the steady stream of people walking by. And so many tall buildings. It seemed both busier and so much bigger than Boston.

They were staying at the Marriott Marquis in Times Square, which was a great location. Beth had done the research for them and said that the rooms were big for New York and had two queen beds. Caitlin and Beth were in the same room, and Meghan and Ashley were sharing another. When Caitlin reached the hotel, the receptionist said that Beth and the others had already checked in. She gave Caitlin a room key and directed her to the elevators.

She didn't have to wait long for one of the many elevators to come available and went up to the twenty-third floor. The hotel was huge, with more than twice that many floors. Caitlin walked down a long hallway to the room and let herself in. Beth squealed as soon as she saw her and ran over to give her a hug.

"We just got here fifteen minutes ago, and they upgraded us to connecting rooms! How fun is that? We were just talking about where we should go for dinner."

Caitlin set her bag down and followed Beth into the adjacent room, where Ashley and Meghan were sitting on one of the beds with a stack of paper menus between them. They jumped up and gave Caitlin a hello hug, then settled back on the bed.

"Which one did the concierge recommend?" Beth asked them.

"Ernie said there're so many good ones and gave us all these menus, but he thought we might really like Becco. It's walking distance from here, on Restaurant Row," Ashley said.

"He said the pasta is amazing," Meghan added.

So, they decided to go there. And to go somewhere else the next night. They were planning to see a Broadway show the next day and were hoping to get half-price tickets at the kiosk in Times Square where they sold leftover tickets at a deep discount.

"We should call Peter to meet us for a drink. Do you want to call him, Caitlin? Or should I?" Meghan asked.

Caitlin didn't hesitate. "You can call him. You know him better." Caitlin didn't want to seem too eager.

"I'll make sure he knows you're with us."

Meghan made the call, and they couldn't hear both sides of the conversation but it sounded like Peter was going to meet them. As soon as Meghan ended the call, she filled them in.

"He has to work late, so can't join us for dinner, but he'll meet us after for a quick drink. He can't stay long because he has plans later tonight, and tomorrow night."

"Well, that's perfect. At least we get to see him for a drink," Beth said.

"And Caitlin has a chance to make an impression again." Meghan looked far more confident than Caitlin felt about the matter. But she was glad Peter was going to meet them.

They went outside after that and explored the city for a bit. Meghan led them to 260 Sample Sale, on Fifth Avenue in the No-Mad area, which she explained meant North of Madison Square Park. It was about a half-hour walk, but worth it. The featured designer that day was Rag and Bone, and they had a blast looking through all the clothes, shoes, and purses. They all found something, and Caitlin was excited about her purchase, a two-hundred-dollar pair of jeans that she got for just thirty dollars.

They made one final stop on their way back to the hotel—the M&M's chocolate-candy store in Times Square. It was a huge building, several floors, and so fun. They all got some M&M's to snack on and headed back to the hotel to shower and get ready for dinner.

The restaurant was as good as Ernie said it would be. They all got the same thing, the unlimited three-pasta special and Caesar salads to start. Ashley was the one who knew the most about wine, so they let her choose, and she went with an Amarone, a type of wine that Caitlin hadn't had before. It was red and smooth and delicious.

The pasta stole the show, though. There were three different types and their waiter explained that they changed every night and that they could have as much as they wanted. Tonight's offerings were spaghetti with tomato and fresh basil, orecchiette with roasted bacon and cabbage, and semolina gnocchi with Grana Padano cheese sauce. They were all delicious, but the orecchiette was Caitlin's favorite.

Different servers kept coming around offering more of the various pastas, and they all had second helpings—and if they weren't so full, they would have gone for thirds. They passed on dessert and were all glad to walk rather than take a cab to where they were meeting Peter.

They didn't have too far to go, though, as they were meeting him at a piano bar, the Rum House, that was on Forty-Seventh in the Hotel Edison. The bar was dark, with polished wood and live jazz music. Peter was already there, and even though the bar was crowded, he was seated at a table in the corner, chatting with the server, a pretty young girl who looked college-aged. He waved when he spotted Meghan, and they made their way over to him. He stood to greet them, and they settled around him at the table. Meghan sat on one side of Peter, and Beth nudged Caitlin to sit on his other side.

"Have you been waiting long?" Meghan asked.

"No, I just got here maybe five minutes ago. Kylie was kind enough to reserve this table for me."

"Well, you are one of our favorite people," Kylie teased him. She looked around the table. "What would you all like to drink tonight? If you haven't been here before I suggest any of the rum drinks—Trader Nic's Mai Tai, pineapple daiquiris, and the Hotel Nacional are my favorites. If you like ginger and cinnamon, the Tortuga is also delicious."

Meghan glanced at Peter's drink. "What are you having?"

"I always start with Nic's Mai Tai. Can't go wrong with that."

Meghan nodded. "I'll have that."

Ashley and Beth both went with pineapple daiquiris, and Caitlin decided to try the Tortuga.

"So, what do you think of the city so far?" Peter asked.

"We love it," Meghan said. She told Peter about their bargain hunting earlier and raved about their dinner at Becco.

He laughed. "I can't say I've been to a sample sale, but I have been to Becco's many times. Great place to go before a show."

"We're doing that tomorrow night, hopefully," Caitlin said.

Kylie returned with their drinks, and once she set them down, Peter lifted his. "To a fun weekend in the city," he said, and they all clinked their glasses together.

"Do you always work this late on a Friday?" Meghan asked.

Peter nodded. "Not always but more often than not. The hours are long, but I love the job. Our fund just posted record earnings." He grinned. "That means everyone is making a lot of money. The owners are having everyone over to their home tomorrow night for a dinner to celebrate. It should be epic—they have a private chef and an insane wine cellar. He has some bottles that cost thousands."

"That sounds amazing," Ashley said. Caitlin liked wine but

couldn't imagine what would make one worthy of costing thousands. It seemed so over-the-top extravagant. But she supposed it was nothing to people that wealthy. Beth had told her that some of these hedge fund managers earned many millions if their funds did well. They typically earned a percentage of the money invested as management fees and an additional twenty percent of profits. It was mind-boggling.

"Do you like living in the city? Do you miss Charleston at all?" Caitlin asked.

"Sure, I miss Charleston. But I like it here more than I thought I would. I love the energy of the city. Everything is fast-paced and on a bigger scale. It's exciting, and challenging. And there's always something going on, no matter what time of day." He smiled. "Charleston has good restaurants and nightlife, but nothing compares to Manhattan. Everything you could ever imagine or want is here." Peter's whole face lit up as he spoke, and his energy was contagious. Caitlin looked around the table. The other three girls were leaning toward him, hanging on his every word. Peter, like the city, was larger-than-life. He always had been. There had never been any doubt that he would go far.

Kylie came over to check on them. Caitlin had hardly touched her cocktail, she was still so full from dinner. But the drink was delicious, with the sweetness of the rum and the spicy kick of cinnamon and ginger. Kylie was holding a glass of ice and a bottle of a liquor that Caitlin didn't recognize. She waved it over Peter's almost empty glass. "Are you ready for the 21?"

Peter nodded. "Yes, please." Kylie set the rocks glass on the table and poured with a flourish. Peter clearly appreciated the dramatic touch.

He glanced around the table. "That's a special high-end rum—the El Dorado 21, aged for twenty-one years. I usually start with a mai tai and then switch to this." He lifted his glass and took a sip and closed his eyes for a moment, savoring the taste. When he opened them, his eyes met Caitlin's and he smiled.

"I think I remember you said you'd never been here before. What do you think of the city, so far?"

"It's bigger than I imagined. And busier. Everyone seems in a hurry."

He laughed. "That was my first impression, too. And it's true."

The girls had more questions, and Peter told them stories about his life in the city and his job. It sounded stressful to Caitlin, but it was obvious that he loved it. "It is long hours," he said. "We all probably average seventy or so hours in a week, but everyone does it."

His phone buzzed with a text message. He glanced at it and frowned.

"I'm sorry I can't stay longer. That was my buddy Dave, asking where I am. His place isn't far from here and everyone else is there now except for me—it's poker night." He waved Kylie over and asked for the check. "And another round for the girls." He took another big sip of his drink, then set it down and pushed it away. He still had quite a bit left.

Kylie took Peter's credit card and returned with another round of drinks and his credit card slip. He signed it and said his goodbyes, turning to Caitlin before he stood. "Are we still on for the Beachcomber on Labor Day weekend?"

"Yes, of course. I'm looking forward to it."

"Excellent, I'll call you when I get there. We fly in Friday night, so we'll plan on Saturday or Sunday night."

"Sounds good."

Peter took a final swig of his drink, stood, and a moment later was gone.

"Well, that worked out well," Meghan said. "I'm so glad we got to meet up with him. And Caitlin, he definitely wants to see you again. I'm excited for you."

"Imagine if it works out and you move here?" Ashley said.

"I'm not sure I like the idea of you living here," Beth admitted. "But I am excited for you to see him again, too. Peter is such a catch."

Caitlin laughed. "I don't know about living here, I think it's a little soon to even think about that, but I am looking forward to seeing him on the Cape." However, she wasn't sure if Peter was the right catch for her—assuming he was even interested. His world was so different. The girls were all dazzled because he epitomized what they all aspired to—money, prestige, and glamour. New York was a perfect fit for Peter, but while Caitlin enjoyed her time in the city, she was also feeling anxious to get back to the Cape, where it was calmer and felt more like home. And she realized that she wasn't feeling that same urge to rush back to Charleston, which was interesting.

The rest of the weekend flew by. They saw a Broadway show the next night and got a great deal on the tickets and had another delicious dinner at a nearby restaurant. Sunday morning they had breakfast at Junior's restaurant across from the hotel, and Caitlin got two of their famous cheesecakes to bring home for her mother and grandmother.

She texted her grandmother from the airport when they were about to board, and when they arrived in Hyannis a little over an hour later, she was in her Mini Cooper, waiting for them. Caitlin gave her a big hug and introduced her to Beth. Once they were settled in the car and heading out of the airport, her grandmother glanced at both of them. "Okay, I'm ready to hear all about your trip. Tell me everything."

Chapter 41

I can see why you love it here so much," Beth said. She and Caitlin were at the beach in Chatham late Friday afternoon. Beth had spent most of the day there and Caitlin joined her when she finished up at the coffee shop.

"Thanks. It's been really nice spending the whole summer here. I never fully appreciated it before," Caitlin said. "I can't believe you're already going home tomorrow," she added.

The week had flown by, and it had been fun playing tourist with Beth. Caitlin took her to all of her favorite places, and they drove up to Orleans one day to do some shopping. They had lunch after, and Caitlin introduced her to the fish and shrimp tacos at Guapo's.

They also went out a few times at night for dinner or drinks, and Julia came with them earlier in the week, and was meeting up with them tonight, along with Tim, Sue, Kevin, and Jason. They were all going to see the band play in the park. Every Friday night all summer, the town sponsored a band to play, and it was an all-ages, family night that always drew a big crowd. The weather was supposed to stay warm and gorgeous, and Caitlin thought it would be a nice last night for Beth. She'd also hoped to have her meet some of her new friends, especially Jason, to see what she thought of him.

"I hate to leave, but I'm starting to miss home and my husband a little, I have to admit," Beth said.

"Do you think Spencer would like it here?" Caitlin asked.

"If I could ever tear him away from his golf, yes. I think he'd love it. If we plan far enough ahead, maybe next summer we can both plan to come for a week—during the time you'll be here. You usually come every summer, right?'

Caitlin nodded. "Yes, usually. Though we didn't make it last year. Both of my parents were too busy with work."

"It will probably depend on what you and your mother are doing for work next year, too. Things might be very different, depending on what kind of job you end up with. Will your mother go to another firm, do you think? I imagine she's not going to stay where she is."

"No. I don't blame her for wanting to leave the firm. I wouldn't want to see Linda and her big belly every day. I still don't know what my father was thinking. I can't imagine it will last. She's just a few years older than me."

"Has he talked about it with you?"

"Not really, only that he messed up. He wanted to work things out with my mother, but of course that's not going to happen. I think she's going to open her own office."

Beth looked surprised. "In Charleston?"

"Of course. Where else?"

"Right. I was just thinking, well, you know how people are. She'd be leaving a well-established Charleston firm. Parker's father started it and they know everyone. It might make it challenging for your mother to go against them."

Caitlin thought about that for a minute. "I know people often take sides in a divorce, but my mother knows tons of people, too, and has been there for over thirty years. I think she'll do fine, if that's what she decides to do."

"Oh, I'm sure she probably will. I'd just be too nervous to do it.

But I'm sure your mom will do great. Have you given any thought to what you might want to do?"

Caitlin sighed. "Honestly, no. I've been completely avoiding even thinking about it and trying to just enjoy the summer. I can't really do much job-searching-wise until I'm back in Charleston. I'll probably sign on with the temp agency again while I look. Sometimes they have interesting temp-to-perm opportunities, too."

"If I hear of any openings anywhere, I'll let you know. Though my agency lost a big client and had layoffs a few weeks ago, so I don't think there will be anything soon there."

"I'm actually really liking managing the coffee shop. I'm not sure if it's because it's my mom's place or just that it's a no-stress, social kind of job, but it's been fun. I like chatting with all the regulars that come in. There's a lot of them now."

Beth made a face. "That's fine for a temporary summer job. But you went to a good college. Working at a coffee shop kind of seems like a waste of that. And you know you could never do that kind of work in Charleston. Especially if you wanted to join us at the Junior League."

Caitlin thought about that. "I suppose they'd think that kind of work was beneath them."

Beth laughed. "Absolutely. And it is. You know that. You're just having fun, in vacation mode. When you come back to Charleston you can focus on finding a real job."

"Right." Caitlin found the thought—of returning to Charleston and starting the hamster wheel of job searching and temping again—downright depressing. But Beth was right. This was just fun because it was temporary and she was helping her mother and Alison, and it felt good to be useful and contribute to making the business successful. Maybe she'd have better luck this time in Charleston and find a really great temp job.

Chapter 42

Thanks, Tim. I really appreciate it. I didn't want to bother Jason for something so small." Julia's toilet kept running whenever she flushed it and it was driving her crazy. She had to keep jiggling the handle to get it to stop and didn't always remember, so sometimes she went out and came home and it was still running.

She'd been meaning to call Jason but kept putting it off. Tim came by to pick her up, as they lived a few streets apart and were planning to ride into town together to meet the others at the park. When he noticed it running longer than it should, he offered to look at it.

"It's nothing. I don't think Jason has to worry about losing any business to me, but I did learn a few things from him. Your chain is twisted, so I just unstuck it and that should hopefully do the trick." Jason and Tim had been roommates for several years before they both got their own places.

Tim drove, and they reached the park fifteen minutes later. Usually it wouldn't take that long, but traffic was heavy. The Friday-night concerts were a big deal in Chatham—they drew lots of tourists as well as the locals, and Julia read recently that crowds were often over five thousand people.

The plan was to have a picnic in the park as they watched the show. Everyone was bringing lawn chairs and takeout. Julia and Tim picked up an order of chicken wings along the way, and the others were planning to bring pizza, snacks, and beverages. They parked in Julia's spot behind her shop and walked to the park to meet the others.

They spotted Sue and Kevin first. They were spreading out a big blanket as they walked over to them. Jason arrived moments later carrying a six-pack of beer and a pizza. And soon after, Caitlin and Beth joined them, with an assortment of cheeses and crackers and a bottle of Bread & Butter chardonnay, which Julia knew was Caitlin's favorite. Sue and Kevin had a big box of pizza with them, too, and once they all set their chairs up, they put the food out and everyone helped themselves.

Caitlin introduced Beth to everyone, as so far she'd only met Julia. Beth had bought one of Julia's bracelets and was wearing it. She gave Julia a hug when she saw her. "I love this bracelet so much. I keep staring at it. Do you sell online, too? I might want to order more for Christmas gifts."

Julia was thrilled to hear it. Beth had bought one of her new and favorite pieces and one of her most expensive, too. It was solid gold and had blue turquoise stones atop wave-line swirls.

"I do. We add new stuff to the site all the time and I'm happy to ship anywhere."

"I can email you the web address," Caitlin offered.

"What do you all do for work here?" Beth asked at one point. "Caitlin mentioned that the Cape is busy with hospitality-type jobs, but that a lot of people have to go to Boston for more opportunities."

"I work in accounting," Tim said. "People always need their taxes done and I do a lot of work with the area businesses, hotels and restaurants as well as individuals."

"Kevin and I are partners in business, too. We run a real estate office," Sue said.

"I used to work in finance, but a few years back I gave that up and run the family business now. I'm a plumber, always a need for that, too."

❦

Beth nodded, but Caitlin had caught the quick look of distaste that crossed her face at the word "plumber." Caitlin loved her to pieces, but Beth could be a bit of a snob at times.

"What do you do?" Sue asked.

Beth leaned forward and smiled. Like Peter, Beth enjoyed her job, thought it was glamorous and loved to talk about it. "I work in marketing at the biggest ad agency in Charleston. Caitlin used to work there, too."

Caitlin made a face. "I did. Until I was fired when they lost a big client." It was the one time when she'd done absolutely nothing to deserve it. They'd always praised her work. But they didn't have a choice. When the client decided to move their business elsewhere, there were no other openings in the company for her.

Beth looked sympathetic. "That happens often when the agency loses a client. It's just bad luck when you're on that client team."

"What will you do when you go back to Charleston?" Sue asked.

"I'm really not sure. Start a new job search and see what's out there."

"You do a great job at the coffee shop. Maybe look for something similar there?" Jason suggested.

"I think Caitlin can do better than that!" Beth said. There was a sudden awkward silence before Jason spoke again.

"I never imagined I'd like plumbing either. I went to school for business. Sometimes it takes a while to see where you fit."

Beth looked like she was going to object again, so Caitlin hurried to speak. "I'll likely temp while I look and explore lots of different options. Hopefully something interesting will work out."

"I'm sure it will," Jason said. "Anyone want more pizza? There's still lots of pepperoni left." He held up the box and Caitlin grabbed a slice.

The band began to play around eight, and they settled in to listen. She caught Jason's eye, and he smiled before turning his attention to the band. She was glad he'd spoken up and changed the subject before things grew more awkward. She'd also noticed that he was looking even more handsome than usual. His tan had deepened, probably from fishing more lately, and he was wearing a Nantucket-red button-down shirt that looked good against his dark hair. There was no one as interesting back in Charleston. Other than Peter, who wasn't really there anymore.

The girls were excited about his potential, but Caitlin wasn't as sure. She liked him and of course was impressed by his career and wealth, but they hadn't even had a real date and she got the impression that Peter had his pick of women to date. She also couldn't really see herself living in New York City. She understood why Marcy had broken things off. It was a wonderful city, but it was intense and she felt more comfortable in a smaller city like Charleston or even a smaller town, like Chatham.

Caitlin could see herself living in a Charleston suburb possibly, depending on where she found a job. She always felt stressed out thinking about it, though, so for the rest of her time in Chatham, she was going to think as little as possible about her future plans.

The evening was fun as they listened to the band play a wide range of music. People of all ages got up and danced, and the weather cooperated and stayed warm with a slight breeze. They played until a little after nine thirty. Caitlin and Julia gathered up all of their trash, and then Caitlin and Jason took it to the nearest trash can. As they walked back, he slowed his steps and a serious look crossed his face.

"Don't be swayed by what Beth says. If you like the kind of work you're doing now, don't rule it out." He smiled. "You could always decide to just stay here, that's always a possibility. Didn't you mention that your mother needs to find new tenants for the apartment above the shop? What if that tenant was you?"

Caitlin stopped and considered what he said. She'd seen pictures of that apartment and it was cute, really the perfect size for one person. She'd have the perfect commute if she moved in there. But that would mean not going back to Charleston, and that was impossible.

"That sounds awesome, and I have to admit it's tempting. But Beth is right. I'm really on a long vacation and when it's over, I need to go back home and back to reality—and find a real job."

❦

The next morning, Caitlin drove Beth to Hyannis to catch her flight home—first to Boston, then on to Charleston. Beth hugged her goodbye outside the terminal. "This has been such a fun week. Thanks again for having me. I can see why you love the Cape so much. I'm totally going to talk Spencer into coming here next summer."

"It was a great week. Seeing New York for the first time was a blast, too."

"I knew you'd love it! I'll talk to you soon. Can't wait till you're back in Charleston."

Caitlin watched her go and waved back as Beth turned and waved a final time before stepping inside. It had been a fun week, but Caitlin was ready for a return to the peace and quiet. Now she understood why her mother used to say that she always loved having company, but was happy when they went home, too, and she had her house back to herself.

Chapter 43

We have company for dinner tonight," Jess's mother announced as she walked through the front door with a surprise guest—Ryan Oliphant. Jess almost dropped the wooden spoon she was using to stir the risotto. She didn't even know her mother knew Ryan.

Ryan stepped into the kitchen and smiled when he saw Jess and Caitlin. Jess was making a big pot of chicken and mushroom risotto, and Caitlin was grating fresh parmesan to stir in at the end.

"I know you weren't expecting me. I'm happy to just stay for a drink and be on my way."

"Nonsense. There's plenty of food. Caitlin, pour Ryan a glass of wine, or would you rather have beer? I think we have some somewhere." Her mother opened the refrigerator to check for beer.

"Wine's fine, thank you."

Caitlin poured him a glass of chardonnay while Jess's mother explained that they'd run into each other at the pier. "Ryan was fishing and I was trying to get a shot of the blue herons that sometimes hang out by the rocks. They're pretty elusive, though. I didn't have any luck today, but I did get some nice shots of the harbor."

"I know your mother from the seafood shop," Ryan added.

"Ryan wasn't having much luck fishing, so we got to talking. He

243

told me about the incident with the van and I figured the least we could do is feed the man." Her mother had a gleam in her eye and Jess groaned inwardly at the blatantly obvious attempt at match-making.

"I told her that was completely unnecessary, of course," Ryan said.

"How is the van? Were you able to get it fixed?" Jess still felt guilty about that.

"I did. I had Triple A tow it to a friend's auto body shop. It was minor damage. He was able to bang the dent out and it's good as new now."

"Well, that's good news, isn't it?" her mother said brightly.

The risotto was just about done. Caitlin added the grated par-mesan to the pot, and Jess stirred it in with a splash more broth and a knob of butter. A few more stirs and it was ready. Jess had used leftover rotisserie chicken and it came together quickly. It was one of her favorite ways to use up leftovers. Creamy, cheesy risotto made everything taste good.

"Let's eat on the porch," her mother suggested.

Jess plated the risotto and they took their food and wine outside.

Her mother acted like she and Ryan were best friends as she encouraged him to talk about himself.

"You didn't grow up here, but you moved here at a fairly young age if I recall? Once you graduated college? How did that hap-pen?" her mother asked.

"I grew up in New Jersey actually, but my family summered here for years. When I graduated from college, I had a summer job working with an oyster fisherman. I was going to have one last fun summer in Chatham before I started my job search in the fall."

"What were you intending to do for a career?" Caitlin asked.

"I didn't have any specific plans. I graduated with a liberal arts degree. A bunch of my friends went into entry-level financial-services jobs, customer service, fund accounting, that kind of thing. I figured I'd probably do the same. But then I had an unusual opportunity fall into my lap. Don, my boss, wanted to take a year off and sail around the world. He asked me if I'd consider holding down the fort for a year. Said I could stay rent-free at his house since he wouldn't be there and in return I'd feed his cat and keep an eye on the place." He grinned. "I couldn't say no to that."

"That does sound fun," Caitlin said.

"It was an incredible year. And I saved a lot of money since I didn't have any expenses. When Don came back he had a proposal for me. He'd fallen in love with the Florida Keys and wanted to move there and start a new oyster business. If I was interested, he'd sell me the Chatham business. The price he wanted was fair and by then I realized I didn't want an office job. I like being outside. I used some of my savings as a down payment on a business loan and my father was good enough to cosign. And here I am."

"And Ryan's divorced, too," her mother added. "Jess will be divorced soon. You two have that in common."

"Do you have any children?" Jess asked.

He nodded. "One son, Tyler. He had no interest in the family business. He's the principal at the Chatham high school."

Jess wondered if his ex-wife was still in the area and why they divorced. But she didn't feel comfortable asking.

"Ann is somewhere down south, isn't she?" her mother asked.

"My ex-wife lives outside of Asheville in North Carolina. Her family is from there. We met at Boston College and married a year after graduating. She was never thrilled about my occupation. She was a teacher, too. We just grew apart, I guess. By the time we got divorced I think we were both relieved. It was still hard, though."

Jess could certainly relate to that. "It was similar with my husband, Parker."

"Not that similar. Parker behaved badly," her mother said.

"He did. And I'm not defending that. But things weren't good with us for a long time and neither one of us made an effort to do anything about it. I think we both wanted to, but dreaded the conversation, so we just ignored it. And then Linda happened."

"My father slept with his secretary, who is just a few years older than me, and got her pregnant," Caitlin explained.

"Ouch," Ryan said.

There was a long awkward silence until Jess threw up her hands and laughed. "And now you know all our ugly secrets."

"You don't have anything to be ashamed of. His bad behavior is on him," Ryan said.

"Ryan's right," her mother added.

"Parker actually said he wants to try and make things work," Jess said.

"Obviously that's not possible," her mother said indignantly.

"No," Jess said sadly. "It's not. Maybe if we'd tried counseling before this happened, but I don't even know if that would have worked. I think maybe it's just like you and your wife, Ryan. We met in college, too, and married young. It works for a lot of people, but it didn't work for us."

"I just saw my friends from home last weekend. They're all married and I'm the only single one in our circle. That used to bother me, but I don't care about it that much anymore. I'd rather wait and get it right, if I can," Caitlin said.

"You're only thirty, Caitlin. Still so young," her grandmother said. "You have all the time in the world."

Caitlin laughed. "Well, not all the time. But yeah, I'm not in a rush anymore."

"Caitlin, why don't you help me clear the table?" Jess's mother asked. "Does anyone want coffee? We have a Junior's cheesecake I can open, too. Caitlin brought two of them home from New York and we've already eaten one. You must have a slice."

Ryan patted his stomach and smiled. "I'll never say no to cheesecake. No thank you on the coffee, though."

"I'll just have cheesecake, too. Thanks, Mom."

As soon as her mother and Caitlin went inside, Jess apologized to Ryan.

"I am so sorry for the obvious matchmaking. My mother can't seem to help herself."

Ryan chuckled. "I don't mind. We got to talking on the pier and when she mentioned she was your mother, I was intrigued. I knew her by face of course but didn't make the connection that she was your mother until she told me."

"And that didn't scare you off?" Jess teased him. "I do still feel badly about your van."

"Well, don't. The van is fine. Didn't cost me a thing. My buddy owed me for hooking him up with oysters and clams for a party recently."

"Good. That does make me feel better."

"So, there was something I was wondering, though. I was actually glad that I ran into your mother. I'd hoped to see you at Chris's party, but when I tried to find you there, I think I might have just missed you."

Jess had tried looking for him, too, after her conversation with Alison, at least to just say hello. When she found him, he was deep in conversation with Lavinia and the last thing Jess wanted to do was interrupt. She'd wandered off and found Alison and Chris and chatted with them and left soon after.

"You must have. I was going to go say hello to you but you were talking pretty intently with Lavinia, so I didn't want to be a bother and interrupt."

"It would not have been a bother, trust me. Lavinia's great, but she can be a little intense. So, anyway, I was hoping to find you and see if you might be interested in having dinner sometime?"

The question took her by surprise, and she fumbled for the right words to say and couldn't find them. When the moment stretched on a little too long, he added, "Or if it's too soon for you, then no worries. We can revisit the idea at another time, or not."

"It's not that I'm not interested. It is too soon for me, though. I only just served Parker with divorce papers a little over a week ago. I'm just not ready to go there yet." Jess felt a pang of regret, because the man sitting beside her was the first person she'd felt any kind of chemistry with other than Parker. There was the fact that she lived in Charleston, too. A long-distance relationship would be even more difficult to navigate.

"I'm heading back to Charleston soon, too. So, that's another reason why this probably isn't a good idea."

"You're definitely going back to Charleston, full-time? Have you thought about splitting your time between here and there? So you could be more involved in the bookstore and coffee shop?" Ryan suggested.

Jess smiled. "My mother asked me that, too. I'm not sure how easy that would be to do with a law practice. I still need to figure out what I'm doing with that, too."

"Fair enough. You have a lot to sort through. They say timing is everything . . . maybe another time."

"Things are very up in the air with me right now. Hopefully once everything calms down it will be different."

Ryan nodded as Caitlin and Jess's mother came back to the table with plates of cheesecake.

"Did I miss anything?" her mother said as she sat back down and picked up her fork.

"Not a thing," Jess assured her. "Ryan and I were just getting to know each other." He smiled and caught her eyes for a moment and she felt another moment of regret, wondering if she'd made the right decision. But she knew in her gut that it was too soon. Parker might be able to move right on, but Jess wasn't ready. Not yet.

Chapter 44

Alison didn't think much of it when Jim asked her to come to his office soon after she arrived Monday morning. She'd just made her coffee and settled at her desk when his email flashed through. Maybe it was about the newest article she was working on. Or maybe he had an update on his querying. She'd given him her notes on the second half of his book and read his edits and told him to go ahead and start emailing agents with his query letter to see if they might be interested.

Things were going well with them, too—they'd gone out twice so far, lovely dinners and good conversation. She enjoyed spending time with Jim and was glad that he was happy taking things very slowly. She stood and took her coffee into his office with her.

Jim glanced up and she immediately saw that something was bothering him. His eyes had a pained expression as he asked her to have a seat. He absentmindedly dragged his hand through his thick, usually well-tamed wavy hair—but this morning it was a bit of a mess. He had bags under his eyes like he'd had a horrible night's sleep.

"Jim, what's wrong?"

He sighed. "I miscalculated, again. I thought I'd made enough cuts to buy us time to turn things around, but advertising is still declining as more local businesses are going to Facebook and other online ads. This next month's issue is half the size it was a year ago." Alison knew that advertising dictated the size of the issues—how many pages they could afford to produce.

"I'm sorry to hear it. So, more layoffs are necessary, then?" They were already down to a bare-bones staff. Alison wasn't sure who he could cut.

"Yes. Unfortunately. I wrestled with this all last night, trying to come up with another solution, but the only option is to eliminate overhead, which means several positions need to go. And as much as I hate to do this, yours is one of them. I know you're already down to part-time, but even that is too much, I'm afraid."

Alison nodded. She was stunned but understood at the same time. She knew this wasn't easy for him. "What will you do for editing?"

"I'll have to do it myself, for now. If things pick up some, then I could consider outsourcing some projects. If you'd be open to that? I wouldn't blame you if you didn't want to have anything to do with it. I'm so sorry. I really tried to avoid this."

"Jim, it's okay. The bookstore is starting to do better. The goal was for me to go there full-time eventually, so now I'll just do it sooner. I'm also doing quite a bit of the baking for the coffee shop, so that's a little extra income. I'll be fine." Though it was a little scary to lose the cushion that the part-time role gave her. Juggling the editing, the baking, and working in the store was a lot. Maybe this was a blessing in disguise—the push she needed to really go for it with the bookstore.

"You're not as upset as I thought you might be. I'm glad to hear the bookstore is doing better."

She nodded. "The news was a surprise, but I'm not upset. Now I can spend more time at the bookstore, so that is a good thing. And the coffee shop is doing great."

"Well, I'll confess, that's a relief. I still have two more people to talk to and their jobs are full-time, so I feel just awful about that. But it can't be helped."

Alison reached out and squeezed his hand. "You're doing the best that you can. That's all anyone can ask of you."

His eyes shone with gratitude. "Thank you. I worried, too, that this might change things with us. Just when it seemed like we were off to a great start. At least I thought we were?"

Alison smiled. "We are. And this doesn't have to change anything. I'm not going anywhere. I'll still be here in Chatham, just not in your office every day. It will work out."

⚜

"What's wrong?" Jess asked as soon as Alison walked into the bookstore that afternoon. It was a few minutes before one. She'd run home after she finished up at the magazine and had a quick lunch—a turkey sandwich—before heading downtown. Alison stayed quiet; she'd debated not telling Jess, as she didn't want to worry her by adding more pressure when they were just barely profitable now. But she'd never kept secrets from Jess before— and her face was always an open book. She couldn't lie if she wanted to.

Jess and Brooklyn were at the counter, and Brooklyn was ringing up a customer. As soon as she finished, Jess suggested that Brooklyn take her lunch break. Once she was out of earshot, Jess turned to Alison. "Okay, out with it. What's going on?"

"Nothing is wrong, but I did get laid off this morning. I knew it was going to happen eventually. But not this soon. It was a bit of a surprise. But it will be fine." She smiled. "Now I can spend more time here."

Jess looked concerned. "If he laid you off, things must really be bad for him. I'm sure he had no other choice."

Alison nodded. "That's what he said. He was really sick about it. He has to let two others go, too—and they're full-timers that have worked for him for years. Those will be painful conversations."

"I can't imagine," Jess agreed. "Are you upset with him? Will this change anything for you two?'

"No, of course not. I think he was concerned that it might, but I know he didn't want to do this. Like you said, he had no other choice."

"That must be so stressful. I can't imagine. The magazine business has really taken a hit."

"Our issues used to be two to three times the size that they are now. Advertisers and readers are going elsewhere. It's a shame because it is a beautiful magazine."

"Well, if you're able to spend more time here, we'll have to figure out a way to get you more money—I've been thinking about this anyway, for when I leave in October and it's just you here. We'll work out a salary that seems fair, and of course any profits, above and beyond other expenses, will be split. We'll get there. Take a look at last week's numbers—they are encouraging."

Jess pulled up their financial software and showed Alison a graph of the shop's daily revenues. For the past two weeks they were slowly and steadily creeping up. Which was a relief.

"That *is* encouraging."

"And the coffee shop is doing even better." Jess pulled up those numbers, and the difference was startling.

"Wow. The coffee shop is making more money than the bookstore!"

Jess nodded. "And a lot of that is due to Caitlin. She's doing a great job managing the shop and she seems to like it, too. Whenever I pop in over there, she's chatting with the regulars and they seem to love her."

"She is," Alison agreed. "We probably need to think about how we will replace her when you guys leave. I don't know if any of the others are able to take that on."

"I know. I've been thinking about that, too. I'm going to talk to Caitlin to ask for her input, but I know she thinks Sally, Joan, and the two college girls are doing a great job. Maybe some of them might want more hours. If not, we'll have to think about hiring a more experienced person to manage it. We still have some time, though, before we have to worry about that."

"We need to get an ad up soon for a new renter for the apartment, too," Alison said.

"Right, we need to get on that. Labor Day is right around the corner and then only six weeks until the current tenants' lease is up and that's when we leave, too. It seems like it's coming faster than I expected," Jess said.

♛

"Can you recommend a good mystery?" The familiar voice sounded amused. Jess had her back to the register while she was talking to Alison and didn't see who had walked in. But she recognized the voice. She turned around to see Ryan standing there with a big smile. She guessed he was on a lunch break, as he was wearing a work shirt with OLIPHANT'S OYSTERS embroidered across his pocket.

"I have to head into the office for a minute." Alison walked away to give Jess some privacy.

Jess smiled. "What kind of mystery did you have in mind?"

"I like a good suspense story with some mystery. Harlan Coben is a favorite. Good sense of humor and fast-paced. Anyone come to mind?"

"Two actually. Follow me." She led him over to the mystery section and pointed out the authors she had in mind. "Joseph Finder and Linwood Barclay. Both remind me of Coben's fast-paced stories." She handed Ryan a copy of Finder's book *Vanished*. "This is the first one in his Nick Heller series."

Ryan took the book and glanced at the back cover blurb. "Looks good. I'll take the other one you mentioned, too."

"Linwood Barclay?" She grabbed his newest stand-alone suspense book, and Ryan took that one, too.

They headed back to the register, and Jess rang him up and ran his credit card. He signed the slip and handed it back to her. "So, there's another reason I stopped in here." He reached in his pocket and pulled out two movie tickets. "One of my customers gave me these today. Wondered how you felt about movies?"

Jess laughed. "I love them, of course. Who doesn't?"

"Okay. Good. Any interest in seeing a movie with me? Tonight? Possibly getting a bite to eat first?" His eyes were big and warm, and full of hope.

Jess hesitated. It was tempting, but she'd already said she wasn't ready to date.

But Ryan anticipated that, too. His dimples popped as he smiled and said, "Oh, and by the way, this isn't a date or anything. Just two new friends that like to see movies. No harm in that, right? And we have to eat."

She laughed. And appreciated his good humor and willingness to go at whatever speed she needed. "Well, when you put it that way, how can I say no?"

He grinned. "Excellent. I'll swing by around six, if that works? Movie is at seven thirty and we can find a place to eat first."

"Okay. I'll see you then."

Ryan left with his books, and Jess was still in a daze when Alison returned. She filled her in on the conversation, and Alison looked pleased.

"Good, I'm glad you're going out with him. Even if you don't call it a date. It totally is, you know. But that's okay."

"No, it's really not. I was clear about that. We're just going out as friends."

Alison smiled. "Sure. Well, have fun and tell me all about it tomorrow."

Chapter 45

"A re you wearing mascara?" Caitlin asked as Jess came into the
kitchen. Jess almost never wore mascara, but she didn't expect that her daughter would notice when she did. Jess's mother
looked up and smiled. "You look nice. Where are you off to?"

"I'm going to the movies with Ryan."

Her mother looked thrilled at the news. Caitlin seemed surprised. "I thought you weren't ready to date?"

"It's not a date. We're just going out as friends."

Caitlin raised her eyebrows. "Right."

"Really. It's just a movie."

"You're not getting dinner first?" Her mother sounded disappointed.

Jess sighed. "We are going to get a bite to eat. I don't know where
yet. It's not a big deal."

There was a knock at the door, and Caitlin grinned. "Your 'friend'
is here."

Jess opened the door, and Ryan poked his head in and said a
quick hello to her mother and Caitlin before they headed out. Even
though it wasn't a date, Jess had changed into her favorite rose-
colored sweater and faded jeans that were the most flattering that
she owned. And she'd put on mascara and a hint of lipstick.

Ryan looked good, too. His hair was still a little damp in the back and he was freshly shaved and smelled good. He was wearing a navy button-down shirt and jeans.

"Do you like burgers?" Ryan asked as they pulled out of the driveway.

A burger actually sounded good. Jess didn't have red meat often, but every now and then she craved it.

"Sure. I could go for a burger."

"Have you been to the Red Nun? That's my favorite place in town for a burger and it's right near the movie theater. We can walk over after we eat."

"I haven't been there. I keep meaning to try it."

"All right, the Red Nun it is."

The restaurant was busy when they arrived, but they were seated right away and Jess's stomach rumbled as she read the description for the burgers—they used three kinds of meat, ground short rib, brisket, and sirloin. They both went with the Nun Burger, which was topped with sautéed mushrooms and onions, cheddar, bacon, lettuce, and tomato grilled on a giant English muffin.

Ryan was easy to talk to, and it felt like she was out to dinner with a good friend—though a very attractive one. He told her more about his job, and she learned that every three to six weeks during the growing season, he'd shake the oysters up.

"We put them in batches into a tumbler of sorts and run them around in that. It sort of prunes the length; otherwise they'd grow longer and slimmer, and this way they go a little deeper so we get a nice, juicy oyster. We let them grow to about three inches long. That's what most of the restaurants want."

"Are you busy year-round with it?" Jess wondered as their server arrived with their burgers and set them down.

"It's slow in the dead of winter. I usually close the market for a few months then and reopen in April."

Jess took a bite of her burger. It was as good as it looked. "What do you do during your time off?"

"I do a lot of education then, learning about better ways to do things and buying new equipment to try. I only just got that tumbler a few years ago. I usually try to do a little traveling, too. Sometimes I go to the Keys and visit Don and check out what he's doing with his oyster place. Have you ever been to the Keys? It actually reminds me of the Cape a bit—but without the cold winters."

"I went to Key West for spring break when I was in college, years ago. Now that you mention it, it does remind me of the Cape. We went to the Hemingway house."

"With all the cats?" Ryan laughed.

"Yes!"

"I've never been to Charleston. Maybe I'll venture there one of these winters."

Jess smiled. "Well, if you do, I'd be happy to show you around. There's a lot to see there. So much history."

"You're heading back mid-October?"

Jess nodded. "I need to head back sooner, though, for a quick trip to check out some places for a possible office rental."

"You've decided to open your own office?"

"I think so. I went back and forth about it and I just don't see myself joining another law firm at this point. I kind of like the idea of a small office that's all mine, so I can take on whatever cases I want to take on—to be more of a generalist."

"Is that a big change?"

"We were pretty focused at my law firm. Not a lot of variety. My mother had a friend stop by a few weeks ago with a legal question and while I'm not licensed to practice here, I was able to answer some questions for her and steer her in the right direction. If she'd come to see me in Charleston, I could have taken her on and done the work."

"That sounds more interesting—to do a variety of things."

"I think it will be. It's a little scary, too, to start over, but I'm ready for a change."

Ryan smiled. "Well, I have no doubt you'll do great."

They finished their burgers and chatted easily. There was no shortage of things to talk about and the conversation flowed as if she'd known Ryan for ages.

Although when the bill came, she expected to split it, but Ryan insisted on paying and gave his card to the server, who ran off with it.

"I wish you would let me split this."

"I was the one that invited you out. Friends can buy friends dinner, right?"

He had a point, but it was still a bit awkward and suddenly made the evening feel very much like a date. "Well, thank you. You didn't have to do that."

He grinned in a friendly, funny way and she relaxed again. "I know. Are you ready to go?"

They went outside, and it was a very short walk to the Chatham Orpheum Theater, which was one of Jess's favorite theaters. The building was over a hundred years old and was a movie theater until the late eighties when it closed and reopened as a CVS pharmacy. Twenty or so years later, the pharmacy left and a nonprofit group was formed to restore the building to a theater. It was remodeled and now it was the best of both worlds—a modern theater in a historic building.

The movie was an edge-of-their-seats suspense thriller and they both enjoyed it. When they left the theater, Jess was actually a little sad that the evening was coming to an end. She'd had such a good time. Aside from occasional dinners out with Alison or Caitlin, she hadn't gone out much all summer.

"Any interest in getting an ice cream? I was too full for dessert earlier, but I wouldn't mind something sweet now."

Jess loved the idea. "Sure."

There were several places to get ice cream on Main Street, and they stopped into the first one that they came to. They both got an ice cream cone and this time, Jess was faster with her credit card.

Ryan laughed. "I'll just say thank you, because I can see you're determined."

They slowly made their way back to Ryan's car, enjoying their ice cream and chatting about the movie and its surprise twist ending as they walked. Once they finished eating, Ryan drove her home, and she turned to him before she got out of the car.

"This was a really fun night. Thank you."

"It was fun. Thanks for coming out. We'll have to do it again soon." He picked up his phone and handed it to her. "If you don't mind typing in your number, I'll text you back so you have mine. And whenever you feel like doing something, let me know."

Jess punched her number in and handed him her phone. He quickly typed a text message and hit send. Her phone pinged and she glanced at the screen and smiled. Ryan's text message read,

Good night Friend.

"Good night, Ryan."

Chapter 46

can't believe it's already Labor Day weekend," Julia said. It was Friday night, and Caitlin had come to the Squire after work to meet up with Julia, Tim, and Jason. Sue and Kevin were coming a little later. The restaurant was packed, but they'd managed to get the last open seats at the bar. Caitlin was sitting next to Jason, and Julia was on her other side with Tim next to her. They were at the corner of the bar, which made it easier for them to hear each other.

"Fall is right around the corner. Are you still planning to head back to Charleston then?" Jason asked.

Caitlin laughed. "Yes. My plans haven't changed."

"Pity." He grinned. He'd asked her that a few times since she'd known him, and it made her laugh each time. She was sad, though, that her time in Chatham was coming to an end soon. She'd been spending a lot of time with Julia and her friends, especially Jason. They were always in a group, though, so it wasn't like they were dating. She'd actually been a little bit surprised that Jason never did actually ask her on a real date. She'd definitely gotten that vibe from him a few times, though now that she thought about it, instead of asking her out, he'd always asked if she was still planning to go back to Charleston.

"He's not a casual dater," Julia had said at one point. "If he's not asking you out it's probably just because he knows you're leaving and he doesn't want to get too attached."

"Or maybe he's just not that into me," Caitlin said. Jason was hard to read at times and she didn't always get that vibe from him. Maybe he wasn't interested in anything beyond friendship. She hadn't given him any encouragement, either. After Prescott, Caitlin was hesitant to get into a relationship that didn't have the potential to go anywhere. She'd lost a whole year when she'd known early on that he wasn't the right one. She didn't want to do that again.

"He's definitely into you," Julia said. "I've caught him looking at you and it's clear as day, to me. Jason's just cautious. I guarantee if you ever decided not to go back to Charleston, he wouldn't hesitate."

Caitlin wondered if she was right about that. But it didn't matter, because after Columbus Day she was gone. And she was still a little curious to see how things might go with Peter. He'd texted earlier in the day to confirm for tomorrow. She and Julia were meeting him and his friends at the Beachcomber around four. Julia and Caitlin were planning to head out from work as soon as they finished up at three.

"What are you guys up to tomorrow? It's supposed to be a gorgeous day and I was thinking about taking the boat out. I already mentioned it to Kevin earlier when I saw him, and he and Sue are in," Jason said.

"Sounds good to me," Tim said.

Julia and Caitlin exchanged glances. "I'd love to, but Caitlin and I are actually meeting some friends at the Beachcomber when we get off work tomorrow."

"Who's going?" Tim asked. "Anyone we know?"

"It's a friend of Caitlin's actually."

"It's someone I know from Charleston. He works in Manhattan and is here for the weekend with a bunch of friends."

"Oh, fun. Did you get to see him when you went to New York a few weeks ago?" Jason asked.

"We did. Peter met us all out for a drink after we had dinner."

"That's great. I'm sure you'll have a good time. The Beach-comber is always fun." Jason's tone was flat. He grew quiet and didn't say much for the rest of the night. Caitlin wondered if it had anything to do with her. Maybe he was just tired. It wouldn't make sense that he'd be bothered by her meeting up with Peter, since there was nothing going on between them.

♦

The next afternoon, as soon as they both finished work, Caitlin left her car at the coffee shop and rode with Julia to Wellfleet. She was excited to go to the Beachcomber for the first time.

"I try to get here at least once every summer," Julia said, as they drove slowly along Suicide Alley—the stretch of highway on the Outer Cape that is one lane in each direction and no divider in the middle. They slowed to almost a full stop more than once. "It's a lot of fun, but the traffic is crazy on the weekends, as you can see."

Once they reached the Orleans rotary, the traffic lightened up as it expanded into two lanes, and they picked up speed. They drove through Orleans, then Eastham, and finally reached Wellfleet.

Julia turned onto Cahoon Hollow Road, which led to Cahoon Hollow Beach and the Beachcomber. One of the two young parking attendants waved them into a back lot. Once they paid for parking, which also served as a beach pass for the day, Julia led Caitlin to what used to be the lower parking lot, in front of the restaurant, which faced the beach.

The first thing Caitlin noticed was a big sign with a picture of a huge great white shark and a warning that they could be in the area. She remembered reading about a recent fatal shark attack a little farther down at Newcomb Hollow Beach—a twenty-six-year-old man was attacked while on a boogie board.

"I never go in the water past my knees here, anyway," Julia said. "The currents are too strong. That's what makes it good for surfing, but I prefer to stay on the beach, or up at the bar."

"The beach is gorgeous, though." Caitlin walked to the edge and looked down at the beach and water below. She could see the rip currents by the way the water moved, and that would make her nervous as well.

"The beach erosion is really bad here," Julia said. "This used to be a huge parking lot. A few bad storms wiped out an entire row of parking and a sinkhole swallowed up a car. Eventually they might have to consider moving the restaurant back."

They headed into the Beachcomber, and walked by a counter that sold all kinds of T-shirts, sweatshirts, and hats with the Beachcomber logo emblazoned on them. The colors were faded blues and the popular Nantucket red that Caitlin only saw in New England. It was a pretty shade, sort of a salmon red. She slowed to take a closer look.

"If you want a sweatshirt, get it when we leave. You don't want to have to lug it around and it's too warm to wear a sweatshirt now," Julia advised.

She had a good point. Caitlin picked up the pace and followed Julia into the bar. It was a very casual outside bar, which led into the main restaurant. At the far end of the bar was a raw bar, and there were several people in line for shucked oysters, clams, and shrimp cocktail.

"They also serve oyster shooters," Julia said.

"What's that?" Caitlin had never acquired a taste for raw oysters.

"Vodka, Bloody Mary mix, and a raw oyster. They're actually pretty good," Julia said.

The thought of it made Caitlin's stomach flip. "I'll pass on that."

Julia laughed. "Okay. I don't know what Peter looks like. Do you see him anywhere?"

Caitlin scanned the crowd and the bar area, which was two and three people deep in spots. At the far end, there was a group of five guys and one of them was wearing a Yankees baseball cap, so she thought maybe they could be his friends, but there was no sign of Peter.

"I don't see him out here. Maybe he's not here yet."

Julia frowned. "I thought he was getting here earlier?"

"I thought so, too, but maybe they're running late."

"Well, shall we go get in line for a drink? They have delicious frozen piña coladas here." Julia started walking toward the bar. There was an opening near the end of the bar by the group of guys, and she slid in and waited for the bartender to notice her.

There were two bartenders on and they were both busy, running from one customer to the next. One of them caught Julia's eye and nodded, indicating he'd seen her and would be over shortly. When it was her turn, Julia ordered a piña colada and turned to ask Caitlin what she wanted.

"I'll have the same."

"Colin, put those on our tab." Caitlin turned at the familiar voice. Peter was behind her wearing a welcome grin and a Beach-comber long-sleeved shirt and baseball cap. He pulled her in for a hug hello, and she introduced him to Julia.

"Nice to meet you! And thank you for the piña colada." She handed Caitlin her drink. It was frosty and white and had a cherry and a drizzle of dark rum across the top. She took a sip and savored the creamy coconut and pineapple flavors and the kick of the rum. It was the perfect vacation drink. "Yes, thank you."

"Bring your drinks over here, we've got a cocktail table." Peter led them to his group of friends and introduced Caitlin and Julia to all of them. The names went in one ear and out the other, except for Freddie, the one wearing the Yankees cap. He was easier to remember because of the hat. Peter explained that he knew them all from work. Half of them worked with Peter at his company and the others were friends who did similar work at different firms. Freddie also stood out because he was the tallest and the loudest.

"He's our top trader," Peter said. "Freddie has killer instincts and just had his best quarter ever. He flew us here last night in his private jet."

"It's still new to me. I just got it last year," Freddie explained. "But it's very cool. We flew into P-town and picked up our rental cars there."

"Provincetown is the closest airport," Peter explained. "We had dinner in town at the Lobster Pot, which is always awesome, then came straight here and continued the party at the house."

"What do you two do for work?" Freddie asked.

"I'm helping out my mother for the summer, running a coffee shop. I'll be heading back to Charleston soon, and will start the job hunt then."

"I make jewelry," Julia said.

"Do you work at a jewelry store?" one of the guys asked her.

Julia smiled. "I used to. I opened my own shop last year."

"That's very cool," Freddie said. He seemed nice enough, Caitlin thought as she listened to their conversation. The other guys all seemed to look to Freddie and Peter, she noticed. They talked about money, a lot. And they weren't shy about mentioning specific numbers. Some of the amounts they discussed shocked her.

"So, I have an offer in on that co-op on Park Avenue," Freddie said. "Maintenance fees are annoyingly high at almost ten K a month, but the unit itself is a deal at just five million."

"I hope you get it. That sounded like a good one," Peter said.

"Thanks. You were looking in that area, too, weren't you?"

Peter nodded. "Yeah, I'm looking, haven't found the right thing yet."

Julia leaned over and whispered to Caitlin, "Five million? These guys live in a different universe than we do."

Caitlin laughed. "So different."

"Anyone getting hungry?" Peter asked. There was a general chorus of yes, and menus were passed around. They decided to get a bunch of appetizers—steamers, fried calamari, nachos, chicken fingers, and fried clams—and a few of the guys got cups of clam chowder. They pulled another cocktail table over and everyone helped themselves when the food came. Even though there was a ton of food, the guys were drinking a lot. Caitlin and Julia were still sipping their piña coladas while the guys drank several rounds of beers and a few had the oyster shots that Julia had mentioned earlier.

They each had one more drink when Peter insisted but also ordered waters and didn't plan to have another drink after that, since they were eventually going to make the drive back to Chatham.

"You gotta come back to the city soon," Freddie said when Caitlin mentioned that she'd just recently been there for the first time. "A weekend just gives you a taste of it."

"You really should come back soon," Peter agreed.

Caitlin smiled. "I had a blast. I definitely want to go again. Maybe next time I can convince Julia to join me."

Peter glanced at Julia, who was deep in conversation with one of the guys. Peter's gaze seemed focused on her hair. Her turquoise tips shimmered in the sun. Julia was the only one there with such brightly colored hair. Caitlin was used to it on her and thought she wore it well. Peter seemed less impressed.

"She's more of the artsy type, your friend Julia. She could never pull that look off in Charleston. I can imagine the comments now. I'm not so sure it would fly in New York either. Well, not in the circles we're in. She seems nice, though."

Caitlin hated his snobbishness but knew he was right. Her crowd in Charleston would have things to say and they wouldn't be nice. Beth was different. She didn't judge the way the others did, but she was the exception. Caitlin got the strong impression that Peter would prefer that she didn't bring Julia to New York if she planned on seeing him. That was disappointing.

He changed the subject and was his usual charming self for the next few hours. Though he drank an awful lot. They all did, and they all kept offering to buy more drinks for Caitlin and Julia, but they stayed with water. Freddie had gone from outgoing and fun to loud and sloppy drunk, and Peter's charm was fading fast, as he wasn't far behind him. When the guys all broke into song, singing along with the Jimmy Buffett song "Cheeseburger in Paradise," Julia gestured to Caitlin that it was time to go.

"Peter, we're going to head out. How are you all getting home?" She was worried about them driving, as not one of them seemed sober enough to get behind the wheel.

"We have an Uber driver on standby. Someone Freddie knows. Are you sure you don't want to stay? There's going to be a band soon. It should be a blast."

"No, we're driving back to Chatham, so we don't want to risk it. This has been a lot of fun, though."

"Great fun. Glad you came." Peter slurred his words. "I'll call you, we'll make a plan."

"Okay. Bye, Peter." They said goodbye to the rest of the guys, who were midsong and didn't seem to fully comprehend that they were leaving, so they just waved and made their way out. Caitlin stopped to buy a Beachcomber sweatshirt, and a few minutes later they were in the car and Julia was driving home.

"So, what did you think of Peter and his friends?" Caitlin asked as they headed back to the highway.

"They seemed nice enough for a bunch of rich drunks," Julia said.

Caitlin laughed. "I get the sense the bunch of them don't do anything halfway. The saying 'work hard, play hard' fits."

"What's important is what do you think? Do you want to see him again? Start a long-distance relationship? Do you know if he's dating anyone else?"

"I have to imagine that he is. Peter has always been a big flirt and now he's an even richer one and that's attractive to a lot of women. Especially in the city. I don't know that I'll actually hear from him again and if I do, I don't think I'm inclined to pursue anything. It seems too complicated, especially with the long-distance." And even more so with his comments about Julia. Caitlin wasn't going to mention that, but she couldn't forget it either.

Chapter 47

Labor Day has come and gone. Before we know it, Columbus Day weekend will be here. And then you'll be leaving us? Is that still your plan?" Ed took a sip of his coffee, then stirred a little extra sugar into it as Caitlin put his onion bagel with cream cheese into a paper bag. She'd told him when they first chatted that she was just helping out for the summer. He had a good memory.

Betty Smith, another regular customer, was waiting in line behind him and heard his question. "Oh, dear. I hope that's not true. We'll miss you."

Caitlin smiled. "That's still the plan. I will miss you guys, too. It's been a good summer."

"Will the shop stay open?" Betty asked.

"It will," Caitlin assured her. "We'll probably hire another person or two soon to take over my shifts."

"Well, like Betty said, you will be missed. But you're not going anywhere yet. We have you for a while yet. I like to focus on the positive!" Ed took his coffee and bagel and moved out of the way so Betty could order. "See you tomorrow, Caitlin."

The store was busy for the rest of the day, and Caitlin barely had time for a half-hour lunch break. She ate her sandwich quickly and wandered into the bookstore to say hello.

Alison and Brooklyn were both behind the register. Now that she was done at the magazine, Alison was there all the time, and Brooklyn was their main employee, along with a few part-time people. Caitlin's mother worked a few shifts, but she did more of the administrative work at home. Between Alison and Brooklyn the store should run just fine with her mother back in Charleston. And once they found a replacement for Caitlin, the coffee shop would be fine, too.

She'd talked to Sally, and she was interested in picking up more hours but didn't want to be in charge. Joan had no interest in taking on more. Everly and Brooke said the same, as they were both busy with school. But Everly also said she was more flexible, as she had a lighter course load this next semester. So, they really only needed to hire one good person who could work shifts and oversee what they'd put in place. The thought of it made Caitlin sad—handing the store over to someone else. But she knew it was time to get serious about her job search.

When she got home, she took a long, hot shower, and climbed into a pair of comfy sweats and her new Beachcomber sweatshirt. No one was home. Her grandmother left a note saying she was playing tennis at the club, and she had no idea where her mother was. She made herself a cup of tea, settled at the kitchen island, and opened her laptop.

For the first time since she arrived in Chatham, Caitlin went online and searched new job listings for Charleston. What she found depressed her. There was nothing that she was qualified for other than retail; customer-service roles at call centers, which did not interest her; and administrative positions, which she just couldn't get excited about. There were temp opportunities, there always were, but those tended to be a mixed bag and she'd never found one that she'd wanted to keep doing on a permanent basis.

She sighed and went to the freezer and found her grandmother's stash of coffee chocolate-chip ice cream and scooped herself a generous bowl. She felt like a kid who was enjoying summer and dreading going back to school in the fall. The job listings were exactly what she'd expected, which was why she'd put off looking at them all summer. Maybe once she got to Charleston and signed on with a temp agency, things would seem better. Maybe one of the girls would know someone who was hiring.

Caitlin took her ice cream into the living room and flopped on the sofa. She clicked on Netflix and browsed romantic comedies until she found the one she wanted. She'd lost count of how many times she'd seen *When Harry Met Sally*, but for a gloomy mood like this it seemed appropriate and always cheered her up.

She was halfway through the movie when her phone pinged with a text message, from Jason.

> I'm taking tomorrow afternoon off to go fishing. Weather's going to be good. Want to come along? Tuesday still your day off?

Caitlin smiled and texted right back.

> Yes and yes. Though I've never fished, might need a lesson.

Jason replied back immediately.

> I can do that. Meet me at the boat tomorrow at 11.

❦

The next morning, Caitlin packed a small cooler with water, iced teas, some fresh cut veggies, and onion dip. She added a big bag of potato chips, too. Jason had texted that morning that he'd bring turkey subs for lunch. She picked up two coffees along the way as well. She met him on the dock at a few minutes before eleven and he was already aboard the *Wicked Beauty*.

He helped her into the boat, and she put her cooler in the cabin next to his. It was a sunny day but there was a slight chill in the air, so she was glad she'd brought her sweatshirt. She put it on as Jason untied the boat and then jumped back on. He noticed the sweatshirt.

"How was the Beachcomber? Was it fun?"

"It was okay. It's a great spot. Our friends had a little too good of a time, though. They were singing along to the radio as we left."

Jason laughed. "Not entirely uncommon at the Beachcomber."

"I don't know how they do it. They all work in finance and seem to bring that intensity to everything, work and play." She told him about the private jet and the five-million-dollar apartment.

Jason whistled. "That is crazy. Totally different world than what I live in."

"Me, too."

"A lot of people want that, though. It's the dream. More of everything."

Caitlin made a face. "Too much of anything isn't necessarily good. That's all a little much for me."

"Glad to hear it. So, we won't be losing you to New York anytime soon then?" he teased.

"Not likely."

He looked like he was going to say something else and then thought better of it and focused his attention on driving the boat out of the harbor. Once they were farther out and near the spot Jason liked for fishing, he slowed the motor, dropped the anchor, and went to get the fishing rods. He handed one to Caitlin.

"Okay, so there're a lot of striped bass in this area. I brought three different kinds of bait—herring, porgies, and clams. We'll try them all and see what works. No day is ever the same."

Jason baited her hook with a herring and then showed her how to cast the line into the water. Once it was in she looked to him for the next step.

"Get comfortable, now we wait."

They sat and let the sun wash over them as the boat gently

rocked against the waves. The ocean was calm, so it was more like a slight sway.

They sat like that for a good half hour or so, sipping their coffees mostly in comfortable silence. Every now and then Caitlin felt a slight tug on the line and jumped up, but it was always nothing.

"Fishing is all about patience. Many times I don't even get a nibble, but it's still relaxing just sitting out here on the water."

"It is." Caitlin had never understood the attraction of fishing before. But now she got it. It was almost meditative, just letting your thoughts and worries go and feeling the water move beneath you and the sun shine down above you. She closed her eyes and started to slip into that lovely trance state when you're almost asleep but not quite. A sharp tug on her line shook her out of her dream world, and she stood and held on tight as the pole dipped and pulled harder.

"Oh, you've got something. Try to slowly reel it in."

She did and laughed when a giant fish popped out of the water.

"That's huge! Is it a striper?"

"Looks like it. Let's bring it in." Jason stepped behind her, wrapped his arms around her, and helped her to pull the fish into the boat. The feeling of Jason's arms around her was unexpected and a little overwhelming—being that close to him. He stepped away as soon as the fish was on board and immediately put it on ice.

"You can take that home and cook it up. Or . . . if you want, we can go to my place from here and I'll grill it up for us." He grinned. "I make the best striped bass you've ever had."

Caitlin was intrigued. She liked the idea of Jason cooking. "Do you just cook it on the grill? Everything does taste better on the grill."

"Yep. But it's what I do to it, brush it with mayonnaise and my secret cracker topping. You'll see. Unless you'd rather take it home and do it yourself . . ."

Caitlin laughed. "I think I need to try it your way. Let's do that."

"Perfect. Doesn't look like I'm having the same luck and I don't know about you but I'm getting kind of hungry. Want to take a break and eat?"

They had the subs and chips and dip and ignored the fresh vegetables. After they ate, they fished a little more and neither one of them got so much as a nibble.

"Did you bring your bathing suit? I know a spot not far from here that's great for swimming. It's not too deep and the water is clear."

Caitlin had taken her sweatshirt off soon after they started fishing, as the sun warmed them up so fast. She lifted the bottom of her T-shirt to show her bathing suit underneath. "I'm ready."

Jason pulled up the anchor and found the spot he liked for swimming. He dropped the anchor again and jumped off the side of the boat. A minute later he stood, and the water was just up to his shoulders. Not too deep at all. Caitlin sat on the edge of the boat and eased herself into the water. It felt cold at first but after a minute she got used to it and swam over to Jason. They didn't stay in the water long, though. Caitlin couldn't stop seeing that image from the sign at Cahoon Hollow Beach, of the great white shark. And she knew they often came into shallow water.

"I have an app on my phone," Jason said when they were back on the boat. "It shows where the sharks are—all the ones they have tagged anyway. There's probably a few they don't know about yet." He showed her the app, and her jaw dropped when she saw all the little shark symbols indicating shark sightings all over the Cape, but most heavily in Chatham and the lower Cape from Wellfleet to Provincetown.

"It's a good thing you didn't show me that before we went in the water."

Jason laughed. "I figured as much. Want to see if we can find a new spot and try our luck at fishing again?"

"Sure."

He drove along the coast for a bit until he saw an area that he liked and dropped his anchor again. This time he used clams for bait. They cast their lines and resumed their positions. The swimming had woken Caitlin up, so she didn't feel as sleepy as the afternoon sun shone down on them. And Jason was in a chattier mood. He told her about his days living with Tim before they both got their own places.

"He was pretty serious about music for a long time. I think it's still his dream, though he's mostly given up on it and settled into being an accountant. He's a good accountant, though, and I think he likes the work well enough. It's just not his passion, you know?"

"Is plumbing yours?"

"Ouch. Touché."

"No! I didn't mean it like that. I just meant it wasn't what you dreamed of doing but now that you are, you're happier than what you were doing before. If that makes sense."

"You're right. I don't mind the work and I get a sense of satisfaction making things better for people. It's never a good thing when someone has to call a plumber."

"That's true. But you're good at it and it must be nice to have your own business instead of working for someone else."

"I do like that. A lot," he admitted.

"Do you miss having a roommate? It sounds like you and Tim had a lot of fun together."

"It was fun. Back then we were both really into the band before I got busy and it was too much to juggle."

"Tim still does it, though. Do they play at a lot of places?"

"Not like they used to. The other guys aren't able to put as much time into it either, so they don't get as many gigs. But they still do some, mostly in the summer. Tim would like to do more, but at least he gets to play out now and then." He smiled. "I do miss those days sometimes. We used to stay up late and sleep in. Staying up late isn't as much fun when you have to go unclog a toilet at seven A.M."

Caitlin laughed. "I can imagine."

They fished for another hour, and just as they were about to call it quits Jason caught a striper. But it was a half inch too short, so he tossed it back in the water.

"That's fine. We have plenty to eat with the one you caught. Let's head in."

A half hour later they pulled into Jason's slip at the marina, and he tied the boat up and carried the cooler with the fish off the boat. Caitlin followed, and when they got to their cars he gave her his address for her GPS in case she lost him. But she was able to follow him easily enough to his house, which was a small Cape-style home about a block from the beach. His house had big yard, a wraparound deck, and a distant view of the ocean.

When he led her inside, she was even more impressed. His house wasn't big, but it was light and airy, with lots of white paint and navy-blue accents. His kitchen cabinets were a deep navy and his walls and island a bright white. It gave the room a nautical feel. It was also very neat, with no clutter in sight.

Jason grinned. "It's five o'clock, would you like a glass of wine or a beer?" He set the cooler in the sink and washed his hands before opening the refrigerator.

"Sure, I'll have a glass of wine, thanks." He poured her a glass of red wine and opened a beer for himself.

"I'm going to take this outside to clean it. Want to check out the patio?"

Caitlin followed him outside to where he had a fully plumbed outside kitchen area with sink and countertop next to an over-sized Weber grill.

"Wow, this is really nice." Caitlin saw outside kitchens down south and out west, but not often in New England, because of the colder winter weather.

"Perks of being a plumber. Figured why not? Comes in handy at times like this." Jason quickly cleaned the fish, then went back into the kitchen and returned a few minutes later with tinfoil, a lemon, mayonnaise, and a bowl of what looked like cracker crumbs.

"Is that your secret topping?" she asked.

"It is. It's not that secret, though, just crushed Ritz crackers, a little melted butter, a few shakes of thyme, salt and pepper, and a splash of this." He drizzled about two tablespoons or so of his beer into the bowl and stirred it up. She watched as he turned the grill on, laid the tinfoil across it, then cut the fish in half lengthwise, and spread both halves on the tinfoil. He brushed a thin layer of mayonnaise over the fish and sprinkled the topping evenly across both halves.

"Can I do anything to help?" she asked as he closed the grill.

"There's nothing to do really. I've got some potato salad we can have with this and some leftover grilled asparagus. I'll throw those on the grill to warm up, then let's just sit and relax."

He led her to a comfy outdoor sofa. His patio looked like the most lived-in area of his house. There was the big sofa, and three matching chairs and a gas firepit with a wide ledge that could be used as a table.

The air was cooling a bit, and Caitlin was glad she'd pulled her sweatshirt on when she left the boat.

"Have you thought about where you'll live once you get back to Charleston?" Jason asked.

"Everything is sort of up in the air about that. My parents both want to sell the house and I'd love to get my own place, but until I'm situated in a new job that is secure, I'll probably stay with my mother for a bit. I don't have the best track record with jobs, so I'd hate to get a place too soon and then get fired—again."

She told Jason about her succession of failed jobs. It was a little embarrassing. "I feel like I should have this figured out by now," she admitted.

"You just haven't found the right thing yet. Some people always know what they want to do and it takes longer for others." He took a sip of his beer, and his gaze was sympathetic and encouraging. "I don't know of any of my college friends who are actually doing what they went to school for. Things change once you actually try out a job. You'll figure it out."

"I hope so."

"Focus on what makes you happy. Not necessarily what you think you should be doing. Some people get caught up in other people's expectations."

"That's so true." She'd worried about what other people thought for so long. Too long.

"I think this fish is probably about done. Do you want to grab some plates and the potato salad from the fridge?"

Caitlin found the plates, utensils, and potato salad and brought them outside. Jason loaded her plate with a big piece of fish that smelled so good. He cut the lemon into wedges, and she squeezed one over the fish. Once they had everything, they sat back on the sofa to eat. The striped bass was a firm white fish that was flaky and mild tasting, and the topping was buttery and delicious.

They chatted as they ate about the rest of their week. Jason was booked solid until the weekend, and Caitlin was working every day at the coffee shop.

"Julia mentioned something about having people over Friday night. Do you know what she has in mind?" Jason asked.

"I think she wants to have a small dinner party, but I'm not completely sure. She just said to plan on coming over Friday night."

Jason nodded. "That works for me."

Caitlin was stuffed when she finished, but she ate every last crumb. Jason offered seconds but she protested, with regret.

"I wish I could—it was so good."

"Well I'll pack up some leftovers for you. It's your fish, after all."

Caitlin helped him to clean up, and once everything was put away and Jason made a to-go box for her, Caitlin took her last sip of wine and figured that was her cue to leave. But as she was about to rinse her glass out, Jason offered her a refill.

"How about a second glass? It's still early. And it's a beautiful night. We can sit outside for a while." It was a gorgeous night and she didn't have to rush home for anything.

"Sure, why not."

He refilled her glass and opened a new beer for himself and they headed back to the patio and settled on the sofa. They chatted about everything under the sun. She loved that Jason was so easy to talk to. There were no awkward silences and there was so much to say. They touched on books and movies that they'd recently seen, and discussed how they felt about various issues like the death penalty and climate change.

"I've been thinking about installing solar panels on my roof. A friend did that and he's saving a ton on his electric bills," Jason said.

And they debated which sitcom was funnier, *Seinfeld* or *Friends*.

"*Seinfeld*, hands down. He and Larry David are geniuses. His opening comedy-show scenes are some of the funniest stand-up I've seen," Jason said.

"I love *Seinfeld*, but *Friends* always makes me laugh and yet there's a good story there at the same time."

"If you could only watch one for the rest of your life, which would it be?"

Caitlin didn't hesitate. "*Friends*, of course."

"Ugh. Well, that settles it, we can only ever be friends. That's a deal-breaker for me."

Caitlin laughed. "As if you even considered it."

Jason said nothing to that. He just held her gaze until she looked away. She took her last sip of wine. "I should probably get going. We both have to be up early." It was somehow already just after ten. She'd lost all track of time and they'd been talking for hours.

"I'll walk you out." Jason got her to-go container and walked her out to her car.

"I had a really great day off today. Thank you," Caitlin said.

"Anytime."

Jason pulled her in for a goodbye hug, but there was a look in his eyes that gave her goose bumps—a definite vibe. For a moment she thought as he leaned in that he might kiss her and she realized that she wanted him to. Very much. She held her breath in anticipation, but then Jason hesitated and instead gave her a quick hug.

"Okay, then. I'll see you Friday night at Julia's," he said.

Caitlin exhaled her disappointment and felt a bit deflated. She smiled brightly, though. Friday was just a few days away. "Right, see you then."

Chapter 48

I was chatting with Gina in the real estate office next to mine this morning and she mentioned that she has a few new office listings. One in our building and two others nearby. If you're still thinking of opening an office, you may want to get in touch with her. She doesn't think they will last long—this market is crazy." Jess listened to the voice message from her accountant Lee.

Lee was in a great building downtown. It would be an ideal spot for a new law office. And she knew Lee was right about the market. Things were going so fast lately. She had to act quickly in case there might be a chance she'd want one of those offices.

Jess booked a flight for the next morning, which would arrive in Charleston by noon. She could spend a few days and check out the listings and maybe catch up with some friends for lunch. Jess planned to stay in the house and did not want to be there with Parker, so she texted him and suggested he stay elsewhere for the next few days. She expected some pushback, but he agreed so quickly that she wondered if he'd even been staying at the house. Maybe he'd already moved himself into the condo with Linda.

She left early the next day, while her mother and Caitlin were still sleeping, and drove to Hyannis, then flew to Boston and on to Charleston. She took an Uber to her house, dropped off her bag, then drove her car to the Realtor's office to see the vacant unit. It was a beautiful building, with an ideal downtown location, close to everything. And the open unit was on the first floor. It was large and roomy, with floor-to-ceiling windows that let in plenty of sunshine. One of the walls was exposed brick, which she'd always loved, and it had ten-foot ceilings. There was absolutely nothing wrong with the office. It was perfect. But she wasn't jumping to make an offer.

"It's a big decision," Gina, the Realtor, said. She was a well-known, successful Realtor and looked the part with a bright pink suit, ivory silk shirt, pearls, and a sleek brown bob. "Let's look at the other two and then you can consider your options." The other two units were just a few streets away, so they walked over. Both units were fine but not as big or as nice as the first one.

"Well, the choice seems obvious to me. But it's your decision. We do have a lot of interest, though, so timing is everything. What do you think?"

"They're all great. I love the first one. If I decide to move forward with this, it would be perfect. I'm not ready to make a decision just yet, though. Can I let you know in a day or two?"

"Of course. You have my number."

Jess promised to call as soon as she knew what she was going to do.

She went home and felt completely out of sorts. She walked around her house, which felt foreign now, a place where she no longer belonged. Exhaustion from being up so early and traveling hit her hard, and she decided to take a long, hot bath and just soak for a while. She made herself a cup of cinnamon tea, grabbed a book she'd started reading ages ago, and brought them both into the bathroom.

She spent the next hour buried in warm bubbles, sipping her spicy tea and trying to focus on reading the book. That lasted all of about five minutes. She set the book down, closed her eyes, and sank down in the tub until her head rested on the back. It felt absolutely marvelous to just lie there and feel warm.

She let her mind wander as she considered her options. She could sell the house and buy something else, closer to the office, so she had less of a commute. Caitlin would probably like that and Jess knew she'd likely live with her for a while, until she found a job that was a keeper. And the first office really was perfect. Jess liked the idea of starting over and building something all her own, from scratch. She was normally a decisive person, and she'd surprised herself by not jumping on the office immediately. But something was making her hesitate.

It was a huge change, after all. And once she signed a lease, that meant she was committed to the new business. She was pretty sure that she wanted to do it. She just needed to sleep on it and digest the idea before moving forward. And she wanted to see her friends. She was curious what they would think about her breaking from the firm and starting her own office. Everything had happened so quickly when she and Caitlin left for Chatham that she hadn't filled her friends in on what she was considering. Other than Alison, of course.

Her thoughts drifted, and she saw Ryan's face in her mind's eye and found herself smiling just thinking about him. They'd gone out a few times now—they'd seen another movie and on a different night played trivia at a local pub, and one Sunday afternoon they went to the Chatham Lighthouse and she took some pictures before they went mini-golfing.

Ryan kept to his word, though, that until she said otherwise, they were just friends enjoying each other's company. It was nice getting to know him that way. She still didn't feel ready to officially date anyone, not until her life was more settled. But she appreciated his company. Between him and Alison and her mother and Caitlin, Jess was loving her time in Chatham.

At first it felt like she was on her usual summer vacation, but more often now it felt like she was home. Chatham was her home-town, after all, and she remembered that at one time she thought she'd always want to live there. But she was so established in Charleston, and it could be an exciting opportunity—a new chal-lenge to focus on—if she opened her own office downtown. It was very tempting.

The next day, at noon, Jess met three of her friends for lunch at the country club. She'd known Ava, Caroline, and Whitney for years. Their husbands played golf with Parker, and their children attended the same private school that Caitlin had gone to. Ava owned a successful public relations firm, and at one time Jess thought that might be a good career for Caitlin, as it seemed similar to the ad-vertising work she'd done, but Caitlin felt PR was too salesy for her.

And when Jess thought about it, she could see that. Ava spent most of her time on the phone, pitching her clients to various me-dia. Caroline and Whitney didn't work, other than volunteering for local charities. They threw great parties and fundraising events. Both of their husbands came from wealthy old Charleston fami-lies and did something in finance.

So, they had varying reactions when Jess shared what she was considering.

Ava was supportive of the new office. "That's a great loca-tion. I think it's exciting to build something new. I bet you'll do great."

"That seems awfully risky to me," Caroline said. "Wouldn't you feel safer going to a more established firm? I can't imagine starting from scratch. How would you get your clients?"

"She knows a ton of people," Ava said. "Once she announces the new business, I bet she'll have plenty of interest."

"I don't know about that," Whitney said. "Most of our friends are also friends with Parker and have been using his family's firm for years. Do you really think they'll switch? They might not want to do that. If you go to an already established firm, that won't be as much of a concern as they'll already have clients you could work with, I would think."

"It might be a little slow at first, but Jess is a good lawyer. The clients will come, eventually," Ava said.

"I agree with all of you. It is a little scary to do this. But I just don't think I have it in me to go to another firm. That is still starting over. If I'm going to do that, I think I'd rather do it for myself." Not to mention also running a book and coffee shop. Jess sometimes wondered if she was taking on too much, but it wasn't like she was doing it all herself. She had Alison and Caitlin and somehow it was all working.

Ava smiled. "Well, there's your answer, then. Shall we celebrate the new office?" She lifted her glass for a toast.

Jess laughed. "I haven't totally decided yet. I told the Realtor I'd let her know in a day or two."

"Did she tell you how crazy the market is? If you think you want to do this and you love that office, I'd call her sooner rather than later," Ava advised.

"I'll do that," Jess said.

"So, fill us in on Parker. What's going on with him and that woman and the baby? Do you think they will stay together?" Caroline asked. Jess smiled. They knew Linda's name but still referred to her as "that woman" out of loyalty.

"Are you keeping the house?" Whitney asked at the same time.

Jess brought them up to date on everything.

"I don't know for sure, but I suspect he might already be living with her. He bought a condo without telling me. Though I sort of did the same thing—I bought a bookstore and coffee shop without telling him. I knew he'd try to prevent it if I told him, and I needed something to focus on this summer."

"How is it doing? It's just an investment, right? Your friend is running it?" Ava asked.

"Yes, Alison is my business partner. It was a little slow at first but it's better now."

As they ate, Jess caught up on all the local gossip about people they knew. Two other women in their circle of friends had also filed for divorce.

"I really feel for them. Both were married for over thirty years," Caroline said.

"Like me. It is hard after that long," Jess said.

"I really can't imagine." Whitney shuddered. "I don't think I could do it. It would be too hard after so long."

Jess wasn't sure what to say to that. Given the situation, it wasn't like she'd had much of choice. Staying with Parker after what happened was out of the question. Though she supposed some women still wouldn't want to get divorced. Whitney and Caroline were both completely supported by their husbands. If they were to divorce, they'd likely be fine, but others in less secure financial situations would find it a struggle. Jess felt lucky that she had a career that could always provide a good income.

"The Fall Ball is coming up on in mid-October," Caroline said. "Will you be back for that, Jess?"

"No, we're staying on the Cape through that weekend and will head home soon after."

"Oh, that's too bad, it's going to be even bigger and better than last year. I got the most amazing dress at Middleton's," Whitney said. Her eyes clouded, though, as she added, "Though it might be hard for you to attend that without Parker by your side." She scrunched her face up in distaste. "Especially if he brings . . . her."

"It's going to be hard the first time Jess goes to any event. You know how people are," Ava said. "But after that, it should be fine." She smiled cheerily, as if trying to convince Jess that all would be well. But Jess knew there was a lot of truth to what Whitney said. The first time she attended one of those balls or charity events, there would be stares and whispers. And if Parker and Linda were at the same event . . . Her stomach flipped at the thought.

She could get through it and she'd have to, but it wasn't something she looked forward to. The thought of attending any of those events alone made her a little sad. She'd always gone with Parker, who loved to dress up and hit the town. She'd enjoyed it, too, but she didn't know how much fun it would be to go alone when everyone else she knew was coupled up.

But it was all part of starting over. And Ava was right, the sooner she did it, the better. Like ripping off a Band-Aid—it would sting at first but then it would feel better. Hopefully.

She finished lunch and told her friends she'd keep them posted and be in touch when she was back in town. When she got home, she paced the house for ten minutes, still warring internally with herself. But she knew she needed to move forward and make this decision. She picked up the phone and called the Realtor. Gina answered on the first ring.

"Jess! Great to hear from you. Are you ready to do this?"

Jess took a deep breath. "Yes, I think so. I'd like to move forward with the first office we saw. The one in your building."

Gina hesitated for a moment. "Shoot, I have some bad news on that one. Someone just signed a lease on it an hour ago. I knew that one would go fast. But the other two are still available. They're both great offices."

Jess felt a strange mix of disappointment and relief. She didn't feel the same attachment to the other two offices, but they were both fine.

"That's too bad. Is there as much interest in those other two? I need to think about this a little more. I really loved that first office."

"Everyone did. I think you have a little more time with those other two. They're probably not both going to be snapped up in the next few days."

"Okay. I'll get back to you as soon as I can." Jess ended the call and exhaled. She didn't want to think about making an offer on either of those other two offices. She was anxious to get back to the Cape and not make any more decisions just yet. Charleston was home, and yet everything felt different now. Could she really see herself starting over here? She wasn't sure at all. Maybe spending a sunny afternoon on the beach in Chatham, soaking up the warmth and letting her cares drift away . . . maybe the answers would come to her then.

Chapter 49

When Jess walked into the house the next afternoon, her mother and Caitlin were both in the kitchen, sitting at the island. They were sipping tea and chatting, and at first glance it looked like the two were plotting something. Jess smiled, wondering what they were up to. She set her overnight bag down and joined them.

"Do you want a cup of tea, honey? There's still some hot water in the kettle," her mother offered.

"That sounds great, actually." Her mother went to get up. "I can get it, Mom. What are you two up to?" Her mother and Caitlin exchanged glances. They were definitely up to something. Her mother answered with a question.

"How was your trip? Did you find an office you liked?"

Jess brought her tea over to the island and joined them.

"I found a great one, actually. It was in the same building downtown where Lee's office is and the Realtor that I met with. It was the perfect size and had lots of light and exposed brick."

"It sounds lovely." Was she imagining it or did her mother and Caitlin both look disappointed?

"Did you sign a lease?" Caitlin asked.

Jess shook her head. "No. I wanted to sleep on it. I called the next afternoon and was ready to take it, but someone beat me to it. There are two other offices nearby, but I didn't love either of them as much. They might be fine, though. I wanted to give it a few days before deciding."

"Well, it wasn't meant to be." Her mother seemed cheered by the news.

"So, what have I missed? What's going on with you two?"

Her mother and Caitlin exchanged glances before Caitlin spoke.

"I want to rent the apartment above the shop."

Jess didn't expect that. It took her a moment to process what Caitlin meant. "You want to stay here?"

Caitlin nodded. "I do. I've done a lot of thinking, especially this past week. After seeing Peter at the Beachcomber and the girls a few weeks ago, I just feel like Chatham is where I want to be. I love it here. And I really love managing the coffee shop." She lifted her chin and Jess saw a determination and a passion that she hadn't seen in a long time. "And I think I'm good at it."

"You are doing a great job." Jess thought for a moment. "Are you sure you want to rent that apartment? I'm sure your grandmother wouldn't mind if you stay here."

"Of course I wouldn't mind. But I think Caitlin wants her own space, and I don't blame her," her mother said.

Caitlin smiled at her grandmother. "She's right. And that apartment is perfect. I'll need to pick up a few things and maybe I can have my bed shipped up here and some of my other furniture, and of course the rest of my clothes."

"You might need a big truck for that," Jess's mother teased.

Caitlin laughed. "You're right. I'll probably purge a ton of stuff, though. I need to go through it all and donate to a local charity. I was thinking if I fly down a few days before, I can get it all packed up and have it brought here that Monday or Tuesday. The tenants are leaving the week before."

Her daughter had it all figured out. Jess envied her certainty. "Okay, honey. If you're sure that's what you want?"

"I'm sure."

"Okay, then. The apartment is yours." Jess had been so focused on everything going on in her own life that she hadn't realized that Caitlin might want to stay in Chatham. She'd just assumed that she would move back to Charleston—that they both would. Now that she did think about it, though, it made sense. Caitlin seemed happier and more confident and overall was thriving in Chatham. She would miss her, though. Jess would really be alone if she moved back to Charleston.

"Thank you! And you're okay with me staying on at the coffee shop?"

Jess nodded. "Of course. I just want you doing something that makes you happy. And if it's running the coffee shop, then I'm all for it. Alison and I are lucky to have you there. You've really done a great job for us."

Caitlin's eyes lit up. "I've been thinking and I've got some ideas I want to try soon, to keep the store as busy as possible in the off-season."

"I'm all ears."

✹

Julia checked her email one final time before closing the shop early on Monday to head to the beach with Caitlin and both of their mothers. She was just about to shut things down when a new email flashed through, and Julia did a double take. And then burst into happy tears. She wasn't usually a crier, but this was big, really big.

> *We are excited to inform you that Kaia Kensington has chosen your gorgeous gold bracelet as her signature piece of the season. Watch for her to wear it later today in her Instagram story and on a feature post. Get ready for a stampede of orders!*

Julia felt light-headed. She'd set the retail price of that bracelet in the low five figures. If she even got several orders, she'd be beyond thrilled. She hoped for at least one, to cover her cost of materials. Anything beyond that would be amazing.

💎

"We really should do this more often." Jess applied a bit more sunscreen to her nose, then leaned back in her beach chair and let the sun's warmth wash over her. It was Monday afternoon, typically the slowest day of the week. Julia closed her shop at noon, and it was Caitlin's day off. Jess had checked with Brooklyn to make sure she felt comfortable holding down the store so both she and Alison could have the afternoon off. She'd encouraged them to go, and Jess was grateful. They all needed the break, and it was the first time the four of them had managed to hit the beach together. And they had something big to celebrate potentially, too. Julia had excitedly shared her news at winning some design contest. Jess didn't fully understand it, as Julia wasn't being paid anything other than a mention on social media. But Julia seemed thrilled, so they were all happy for her.

Alison packed a cooler for them, with tuna and turkey subs, a big bag of potato chips, and of course her brownies. Julia brought a six-pack of water and iced teas. Jess brought ice and two bottles of chardonnay. She figured they might want a glass later, around four or five. Jess loved the late-afternoon hours at the beach the best, when the temperature cooled just a little but there were still warm breezes, and the beach was less crowded.

This was their favorite beach. It was the closest one to her mother's house, and while it was a public beach, it was never as busy as the more popular, bigger ones. It was more of a neighborhood beach. There was a jetty that went far out into the harbor and made for a fun walk when they tired of sitting. Sometimes in the late afternoons, they spotted seals sunning themselves on the rocks. When Jess was younger, they used to love to swim out to the end of the jetty and sprawl out on the rocks. But that wasn't safe anymore. In recent years, there were more great white sharks in the area, and they usually were found where the seals congregated.

"Do you want one?" Caitlin held out a stack of magazines. Jess grabbed a copy of *People*. This was part of their beach routine. One of them would stock up on all the trashy celebrity-gossip magazines and bring them along to the beach. They discussed the various actors and actresses and their relationships as if they knew them personally and always laughed at the ridiculousness of it all.

"You know I read recently that many of these relationships are fake anyway. Just PR stunts to promote a movie or new album," Julia said. Jess had never thought about it, but that did make sense.

They chatted for a while, and after a while the sun worked its magic and they fell silent, and Jess let her thoughts drift. She'd felt agitated when she woke that morning, her stomach churning with uncertainty over what to do. Did she want to rent one of those other two offices? She knew she had to move quickly or risk losing them. But the bigger question was whether she wanted to go back to Charleston at all. When she thought about renting one of those offices, she felt a sense of dread. Maybe that meant they just weren't the right offices and she needed to see more? She really didn't know. She sighed and emptied her mind completely and just let go. And fell asleep.

She woke an hour later to the sound of children laughing as they raced to the water. Alison was flipping through a magazine and Julia and Caitlin were knee deep in the water. Jess watched as they went out a little farther, ducked down quickly to cool off, and made their way back to their towels.

"How's the water?" she asked when they finished toweling themselves off and settled back in their beach chairs.

"Chilly at first, but it's not too bad. You should go in," Caitlin urged her.

Jess laughed. She almost never went in the water, especially now that there were so many sharks in the area. She'd seen the movie *Jaws* again recently, and the thought of it made her shudder. She'd dip her toes in occasionally to cool off, but that was it.

"I'm good." She glanced at the time on her phone and was surprised to see it was almost five. She'd been asleep longer than she realized. She was suddenly hungry again and reached for the bag of chips. "Is anyone ready for a glass of wine?"

They all nodded, and Jess poured a plastic cup of wine for each of them. She took a sip of the cool, creamy wine and felt a sense of happiness and relaxation that she hadn't felt in months. The nap had done her good, and just being at the beach. When Jess was younger, the beach was always where she went when she needed to work out a problem. Just letting her mind relax always seemed to bring the clarity she was seeking. Today was no exception. She didn't have all the answers yet, but she felt like they were close.

⟡

Julia took her first sip of the cool chardonnay. It was La Crema, one she hadn't tried before but knew Jess had raved about. It was silky and buttery with toasty hints of oak—delicious. She savored the flavor for a moment until her frantically buzzing phone caught her attention. She pulled it out of her beach bag and saw that it was blowing up with Instagram notifications, and she knew what that meant. She clicked onto Kaia Kensington's page and felt a thrill when she saw Kaia's story and her own gorgeous bracelet prominently displayed. Kaia encouraged her followers to visit Julia's website and order one for themselves.

Julia took a deep breath before checking her email. Kaia had just posted, so there probably weren't any orders yet. Maybe she should wait a bit before looking? But, no, she had to take a peek. She pulled up her email, and then the tears came again. Her mother, Caitlin, and Jess all looked at her in alarm.

"Kaia Kensington just wore my bracelet on social media and I already have five orders and a bunch of emails asking about other pieces."

"Already? Isn't that the bracelet that you said goes for five figures?" Jess asked.

Julia nodded.

"Oh honey, that's fantastic. I'm so proud of you," Alison said.

"Julia, that is huge. Massive. Congratulations," Caitlin added.

"Thank you." Julia felt dazed and a rush of other emotions ranging from extreme excitement to abject panic—she was going to be very busy. But that was a good thing. She wasn't going to have to worry about bouncing a check again.

❦

The next morning, after Caitlin left for work, Jess and her mother had breakfast together in the kitchen. Her mother still had that same look in her eyes, that she was up to something. Jess waited for her to say whatever was on her mind. She didn't have to wait long.

"So, after Caitlin told me what she wanted to do, I was thrilled, of course. I did a little poking around on the computer. You probably know this already, but I found that Massachusetts allows for reciprocity with lawyers from South Carolina. So, you wouldn't have to take the bar exam here. All you'd have to do is apply for a license and meet the years of experience required. And you more than meet that. Just a thought."

Jess smiled. "I don't know what I'm going to do. I know I want to start my own office. But I didn't jump on the one I loved, even though I knew it would go fast. I think it's just a huge decision."

"It is. But you'll be starting over, no matter which office you choose . . . and which state. Now that Caitlin has decided to stay . . . well, it would be nice to have you both here. Just think about it, no pressure."

"I will. I have a lot to think about."

"Okay then. Well, I'm off to meet Betsy at the gym. Our aqua aerobics class starts in forty-five minutes, so I need to get a move on."

After her mother left, out of curiosity Jess opened her laptop and searched for commercial office listings in Chatham. There were quite a few, but most of them were too big or in areas that didn't have a lot of visibility. Wherever she got an office, Jess wanted it to be easily seen as people drove or walked by. She knew that when a need came up, people often called the first name that they remembered. And the more often they saw her sign, the more likely she'd be top of mind.

Nothing that she saw fit the bill. She was about to move on to checking her email when a new listing popped up that got her attention. It had just hit the market and was a small office on Main Street. Not far from the bookstore. It looked about the right size, and as she read the description, she saw that it was already a law office, but the current lawyer was retiring and no longer needed the space. At first glance, if she wanted to open her office in Chatham, it seemed perfect.

She still wasn't sure that she wanted to do that, but found herself dialing the Realtor's number and making an appointment to see the office two hours later.

Jess met Barbara Lynch, the Realtor, at the Main Street office, and as soon as she stepped inside she felt an immediate sense of peace. There were cardboard boxes in the corner, which the Realtor explained would be gone in a day or two.

"Stan is still packing up. He's in his mid-seventies and had this office for almost fifty years. Everyone loved Stan Murphy. It's good news that you're also a lawyer." Jess had told Barbara a little about herself and what she was looking for when she'd called to make the appointment.

The office had two large bay windows that looked out on Main Street. There was a small reception area, a front desk where an assistant could sit and answer the phones and greet people as they came in and help with any paperwork. On the other side was the main office area, which had a large dark wood desk and a few lamps, bookcases, and file cabinets.

"Stan left the furniture here in case anyone wanted to buy it from him. He said he'd let it go cheaply as it would save him having to get it moved out."

Jess took a closer look. The desk was well made, the drawers deep and the wood smooth and polished. It would do just fine and would be one less thing she'd have to worry about. The office was move-in ready.

And this time, she didn't hesitate. It felt right the moment she walked in.

"I'll take it."

They worked out the details and Jess wrote a check and gave it to the Realtor.

"If you want to stop by the office on Monday, I'll have a key for you."

"Perfect."

When they left the office, Jess walked down Main Street to the coffee shop. The first person she wanted to share her news with was Caitlin.

There was a long line, but it moved quickly, and as soon as it cleared out Jess stepped up to the register.

"Hey, Mom. Are you working in the store today?"

"I was downtown, so I thought I'd stop in and say hello. I have some news. I signed a lease for an office today."

Caitlin's face fell. "Oh, that's great, Mom. Which one of the two did you decide on?"

Jess smiled. "Neither of them. This one is on Main Street."

"Oh, that's an even better location." Caitlin didn't look any happier about it.

"It is. Especially when it's Main Street in Chatham. I searched online this morning and an office just opened up that used to be a law office. It's perfect."

Caitlin grinned and came out from behind the register and gave her mother a big hug.

"That is so awesome. I'm so glad you decided to do that. I think you'll be happier here, Mom. Everyone you really care about is here." Her eyes looked damp, and Jess felt her own water up as a wave of emotion rolled over her.

"I think you're right, honey. I can't wait to show it to you. I get the keys on Monday. And I walked over from there. It's very close."

A flurry of customers walked into the shop, so Jess stepped aside and went next door to the bookstore. Alison was ringing up Mrs. Winslow at the register. When she finished, she saw Jess and knew something was up.

"What do you look so happy about?"

"I just signed a lease for a law office . . . here in Chatham. Stan Murphy is retiring."

Alison's jaw dropped. "That is incredible news. I thought you were going to say you'd signed a lease in Charleston."

"I almost did." Jess filled her in on her near miss. "Like my mother said, it wasn't meant to be. And I think this was. The office just felt right when I walked into it. Oh, and Caitlin told me last night that she wants to stay on, and I agreed to rent the apartment to her. I didn't think you'd mind."

"Mind? That's incredible news. I was getting a little worried about renting that as no one decent has applied, they've all failed the background or credit checks. And now we don't have to re-place Caitlin either. And you're staying in Chatham. Jess, I couldn't be happier about any of this." Alison's happiness was evident. She was beaming, and Jess was excited, too. Instead of weekly phone calls, she'd see her best friend all the time. It really was perfect.

"I'm feeling good about it, too. It took me a while to get to this decision but once I saw the office, there wasn't any hesitation. Remember I once said years ago that I'd be the one who would never leave Chatham? I feel like I'm finally coming home, and it feels good."

Chapter 50

Julia was looking forward to having her first dinner party. She'd
been wanting to have everyone over for a while, but her lack of
cooking skills had made her hesitate. Until she realized there was
a way around that. She still had about five minutes before anyone
was likely to arrive. Tim lived close by, so she knew he'd probably
be the first one to show up.

She wound her last section of hair around the wand of the curl-
ing iron and carefully formed the curl, then gave her head a quick
shake so the rest of the long spiral curls fell into place. She'd just
had her tips refreshed a week ago, to brighten the deep turquoise,
and was happy with how it turned out. She added silver drop earrings and a thick silver bangle bracelet with turquoise stones set
into it.

Her top was new and was a deal she couldn't resist. She'd found
it at Marshalls when she was looking for shoes and fell in love with
it instantly. It was a shimmery black fabric with a crinkle effect,
three-quarter sleeves, and a deep scoop neck and a flowy bottom.
It was flattering on her and she paired it with skinny jeans and soft
chocolate-colored leather cowboy boots.

Julia heard a knock on the front door as she came downstairs, and through the glass window she saw Tim on the front steps, holding a bouquet of flowers. She opened the door, and he smiled and handed her the flowers.

"These are gorgeous. You didn't have to bring flowers. I'll put them in water. Come on in." Tim followed her into the kitchen, where she found a square-cut crystal vase and put the flowers in it with a bit of water. The colors he'd chosen were gorgeous—vivid purples, blues, and pinks accented with white. She didn't know what kind of flowers they were, but she loved them.

"My mother told me it's proper etiquette to bring flowers when one is invited to dinner." Tim grinned and she laughed. She could totally picture his mother saying that. He had a bottle of wine with him, too, and handed that to her. "This is the one you like, I think?" It was Bread & Butter chardonnay, which was her new favorite, thanks to Caitlin.

"Thank you. I have beer in the fridge if you'd rather have that." She knew he wasn't much of a wine drinker, usually.

"Beer sounds good." She opened the fridge and handed him a bottle of an IPA that she knew he and Jason both liked.

"Thanks. You look really nice tonight. I mean you always do, but I like your top." He sounded a little nervous, which wasn't like him.

"Thanks." She glanced at what he was wearing—tan dress pants, and a hunter-green button-down shirt. It was a good color on him and made his green eyes pop. She'd never noticed how green they were before. His hair looked better than usual, too.

"You look great, too. Did you get your hair cut?"

He nodded. "Earlier today. It was unruly."

She laughed at that. His hair was anything but. Tim just liked it really short. He looked really good actually. She'd never thought of Tim as particularly tall. He was maybe five nine or five ten, but standing close to him, she was suddenly more aware of him physically. She was only five three herself, and when she glanced up at him, he seemed taller somehow—just right, really.

She felt flustered suddenly, since she'd never looked at Tim that way before, as anything other than a friend. They'd known each other for years. This was the first time, though, that they'd both been single at the same time. He'd never given her any indication that he was interested in anything other than friendship. Or were the signs there and she'd just missed them?

Julia turned the oven on and poured herself a glass of wine. She already had a bottle open of the same one Tim had brought for her.

"Do you need help with anything?" he asked.

"I don't think so. But I have a secret—you can't tell anyone, though."

He smiled. "What's that?"

"Well, you know I'm not much of a cook?"

Tim stayed quiet. She laughed and opened the refrigerator and pulled out several big plastic containers. She found a roasting pan that had never been used and filled it with meat from one of the containers.

"What are we having?" Tim asked.

"Spoon roast, butternut squash, baked potatoes, and green beans with almonds and cranberries. All from the Chatham Village Market. Well, except for the baked potatoes. I made those myself and just need to heat them up."

Tim laughed. "Your secret is safe with me. That place has great food. And I bet this is much less stressful."

"Absolutely."

Julia put everything in the oven to warm up, and threw out the plastic containers that said CHATHAM VILLAGE MARKET on them. "And now the evidence is gone." She also put out some cheese and crackers, a bowl of roasted Marcona almonds, and chips and dip, also from the market.

"Okay, everything's done. Cheers!" Julia tapped her glass against Tim's before taking a sip.

A moment later Caitlin arrived, followed soon after by Jason, Sue, and Kevin.

They all helped themselves to wine or beer and nibbled on the cheese and crackers and other snacks. When dinner was ready and everyone sat down to eat, Julia made an announcement. "So, Caitlin has some big news to share with everyone."

Caitlin looked around the table. "I do. I've decided to stay in Chatham. I'm going to be renting the apartment above the coffee shop and staying on to manage it. I really love it here. It feels like home now, and I'm so glad, thanks to Julia, that I've met all of you, too."

Julia loved the look on Jason's face. He was not expecting that news, and a range of emotions flashed across his face from shock to delight.

"Well, that's the best news I've heard in a long time. Congratulations!" Jason held his glass high, and they all leaned in to clink glasses and echo his good wishes.

They had a wonderful night after that. Everyone raved about the food, and Julia fessed up that she hadn't actually cooked it.

"I feel too guilty taking full credit for it. But it's much better than anything I would have made."

"Your baked potatoes came out awesome," Tim said.

Julia laughed. "The one thing I can cook."

"Who cares if you cooked it or not? It was delicious and we all had fun. I think it's a great idea, actually. Expect the same when I invite you all over for dinner at my place," Caitlin said.

Everyone stayed until around eleven, when Sue was the first to yawn and Kevin said they should probably get going. Caitlin and Jason decided to head out, too.

"I should probably hit the road, too. Thanks for dinner, you really did a great job," Tim said. He was the only one left but was on his way to the door as well.

"Thank you. It was a fun night. And thanks again for the flowers."

"Anytime." A moment later he asked, "Do you feel like catching a movie maybe tomorrow night? I noticed there's something new at the theater downtown that looked pretty good."

"Sure." She and Tim went to the movies often, so she didn't think anything of it. But when he gave her a goodbye hug, he held her a moment longer than he usually did. Unless she was imagining it, which was possible. But it felt a little different. Or maybe it was just that she'd noticed him in a different way for the first time. She'd never thought of Tim as a potential love interest. But since she broke up with Kyle, she had been spending more time with Tim and with all of her friends.

Julia knew she didn't have the best track record with men. She usually either fell fast for the ones who were not great boyfriends or tried to make something work that clearly wasn't working, like with Kyle. She'd never dated anyone that she'd been good friends with first. That foundation might be something to build on. If there was interest on his side. She didn't know if there was. But she was curious to find out.

✿

"Caitlin, wait up a minute."

Caitlin walked out of Julia's house just ahead of Jason. She waited for him, and they walked over to their cars, which were parked next to each other at the end of Julia's drive.

"So, when did you decide to stay?" he asked.

"I've been thinking about it for a while. After my trip back to Charleston and seeing New York for the first time and then Peter again at the Beachcomber I just did a lot of thinking about what I want and don't want and where I think I'll be happiest. If you'd told me when I first got here that I'd see my future managing a coffee shop, I would have thought you were crazy. But it's what makes me happy. And being around everyone here."

"Including me?"

She laughed. "Most definitely including you."

"So, how would you feel about going to dinner tomorrow night? Not as friends?"

"Are you asking me on a real date?" she teased him.

"I am. There's also something else I've been wanting to do for a long time. I don't know if you'd be interested?"

He leaned in closer and she caught her breath. "What's that?"

"This." He touched his lips to hers, tentatively at first, but when she leaned into him, he deepened the kiss and she felt like she was flying. She'd wanted to kiss him for so long and it was even better than she'd imagined.

When he ended the kiss, he whispered, "So, I guess you were interested."

"You could say that."

He kissed her again before saying goodbye. "I'll call you tomorrow."

Chapter 51

A lison and Jess were both surprised by how busy the bookstore was for a Friday afternoon in mid-October.

"This is always a busy weekend for the Cape, though," Alison said. "It will probably slow down quite a bit after this, I would think."

Jess pulled up their sales software and checked the daily and weekly numbers. She clicked a few buttons to make it a graph and showed Alison the screen. "Look at how much sales are up. This is our best week ever."

Alison looked at the graph and was impressed. "I think everything we've done is starting to pay off. The loyalty cards, the regular signings, and the Facebook ads and mailings that Julia has done for us."

"I think you're right. And the coffee shop is humming along, too. Caitlin says there are so many regulars that come in every day. And I had some good news from the local bank yesterday, too. I've been approved for a commercial mortgage for the business. So, I'll get my money that I invested back and we'll pay the note down with profits from the business and we can deduct the rent the business pays and put that toward the mortgage. We'll slow down some in the off-season, maybe cut the hours back a little if it makes sense to do that."

Alison laughed. "I don't really fully understand all that. But it sounds good to me, and I'm glad you're getting your money back."

The front door chimed, and Alison smiled when she saw Jim walk in.

"You sure you don't mind if I take off for twenty minutes or so?"

Jess smiled. "Of course not. Brooklyn should be in any minute and it's not busy right now. See you in a bit."

Alison walked with Jim into the coffee shop, and they got two coffees and two brownies and took them outside and sat on a bench.

"So, what's going on? What brings you downtown this time of day?" Jim rarely left his office during the day.

"Well, I got some good news and wanted to see you to share it. I now have an agent!"

"Jim! That's wonderful news." Alison knew he'd sent out a bunch of queries and several agents were reading his manuscript, but he'd been anxiously waiting to hear back.

"Thanks. It's a good agency, too. She wants me to make a few small tweaks and I agree with her suggestions. Once I do that, she has a list of editors in mind that she wants to submit it to."

"Well, I'm not at all surprised. It's a wonderful book." Alison was excited for him.

"I know we're going out tomorrow tonight, but I didn't want to wait until then. And it was good to get out of the office. It's so quiet there lately."

"I'm glad you called me. It was nice to get outside for a bit. It's been so busy all day in the store. Which is a good thing, of course."

"The minute I heard the news, the first person I thought of was you. And I appreciate your help in getting the book in shape to send."

"It was fun for me. Hopefully it's the first of many."

"I actually do have a new idea. I'm just in the making-notes stage, but I'm starting to get excited about it."

"I can't wait to hear more about it." Alison was glad to see Jim in such a good mood. He'd been quiet lately, and she knew he still felt badly about having to lay her and a few others off.

"So, about tomorrow. What do you think about taking a drive down to Provincetown in the afternoon? We can walk around and check out the shops and art galleries on Commercial Street and maybe grab dinner at the Lobster Pot or somewhere else, your pick."

"I love the Lobster Pot, that sounds great to me." Even though she was from the area, Alison had only gone there in the past year with friends who were in town. She'd always assumed for some reason that it was one of those touristy places and that the food might not be as good as some others. But she was wrong. The food was outstanding and the lobster dishes were among the best she'd had anywhere. They even had a better than usual breadbasket.

"Good. I'll plan to swing by to get you around three then."

Alison noticed the time on her phone. They'd been chatting for just over twenty minutes already. "I should probably head back into the store."

"Right, of course. I don't want to keep you." He leaned over and gave her a kiss before they walked back to the bookstore and kissed her again quickly before she stepped inside.

"See you tomorrow, Jim." Alison watched him walk off and smiled to herself. Things were going so well now with them. They went out several times a week and talked most days at least once. And Chris approved. She knew Chris and Jim had gotten to know each other fishing. She invited both of them over for dinner one night and it was a fun evening. Jim understood that she and Chris were best friends and he wasn't threatened by that. And Chris thought Jim was a good guy. She talked to Chris on the phone the next day, and he gave Jim the thumbs-up.

"You two seem like a good fit. You have a lot in common and I think it's probably better that you don't work there anymore," Chris said.

"You're probably right about that. Everything happens for a reason and now the bookstore is doing better. So, I think I'm where I'm supposed to be. And things are going well with Jim. I'm glad you two get along."

"I just want to see you happy."

"I want the same for you. Are you dating anyone these days?"

"I actually have a date tomorrow with someone I think you know. We went to school with her, Lavinia O'Toole."

That surprised Alison. She wouldn't have put those two together. "Really? How did that come about?"

"I picked her up at a bar," Chris joked. "I was at the Squire and she and a friend were sitting next to me and we got to talking. I remembered you weren't crazy about her, but I think she's mellowed out. She had a rough time of it with her divorce and seems happy to be back home. Her mother's been sick, too, so she has a lot on her plate."

"Oh. I had no idea." She'd never pictured Lavinia as having any real-life problems, which probably wasn't fair.

"We'll see how it goes. I'll keep you posted."

Alison was glad that all of her friends liked Jim. Because they knew each other for so long, it felt like they'd been together now for ages. Between the bookstore, having Jess back in Chatham, and now a blossoming relationship with Jim, Alison felt like things really couldn't be going much better in her world.

Chapter 52

Four and a half months later . . .

Jess looked up at the new sign that was installed above the door to the law office. She'd ordered it months ago, but waited until she was almost ready to open before she put it up. She couldn't open for business until her application for a law license in Massachusetts was approved, and the process took four to six months. She was lucky that hers went through as quickly as it did.

She'd put a sign in the window, though, that read COMING SOON, LAW OFFICES OF JESSICA COLEMAN. GENERAL LAW PRACTICE. She'd also put an email and web address in case people wanted to get in touch, and she'd received a few emails. It was mostly from people who were curious to learn more. But there were already a few potential clients. Ed Thompson, one of the regulars in the coffee shop, said that he'd be in touch as soon as she opened to see about updating his will. And Edith Winslow, one of their favorite clients from the bookstore, and her sister wanted to set up new trusts. They left their contact details for Jessica to get in touch when she was officially open.

So, she had a few calls to make today. And Julia was going to stop by later in the afternoon to help her with setting up some online advertising. Caitlin had joked that she should leave a stack of business cards at the coffee shop and in the bookstore and they'd both laughed at the idea, but Julia actually thought it was a good one. She'd picked up little standing card cases for Jess that could sit on the countertop. So they thought they would actually try that out.

Ed had told Caitlin that he didn't think it would be long before Jess was busy, as all of Stan Murphy's clients needed somewhere to go and it might as well be to her. Jess hoped he was at least a little right. She knew it might take a while to build up a client base. But being on Main Street should help. She loved the location and planned to pop into the bookstore and coffee shop regularly.

Jess settled at her desk and called her two potential clients and talked to both of them. Ed was available to stop in and see her that day, and they made plans for him to come by around eleven. Mrs. Winslow wasn't available until the following day, so Jess put that on the schedule as well.

She had her laptop with her and kept busy online reading up on local news and researching advertising options that Julia had mentioned. At eleven o'clock sharp, Ed walked in and looked happy to see her.

"It's official! Glad to see you're finally open," he said as he walked toward her desk.

"Thanks so much for coming in." She led him into her office and spent the next forty-five minutes listening to him discuss the changes he'd like to make. Ed also liked to chat in general, and Jess was more than happy to talk to him. She learned he was eighty-two and he had the most positive attitude. She hoped that she'd have half his energy when she reached his age.

He finally paused and said, "Well, now that I've talked your ears off, I should probably get out of your hair and let you get busy."

Jess laughed. "It's been wonderful chatting with you, Ed. I'll get right to work on this, and why don't we set up a time for you to come back to review it?"

They made an appointment for him to return in two days, and

he left with a smile on his face. Jess took a lunch break after he left, and after that she got to work on Ed's will. It didn't take long, and she was just finishing up when her front door opened and an older woman walked in.

"Is this still Stan Murphy's office? He was here for as long as I can remember, but the sign out front doesn't look the same."

Jess stood and walked over to her. "Stan retired a few months ago. I'm a lawyer, though, maybe there's something I could help you with?"

The woman hesitated. "Well, I'm not sure. My husband always told me that Stan was who I should go to." Her eyes watered up and she couldn't talk for a moment. Finally, she caught her breath. "He passed a month ago and it's been hard sometimes."

"I'm so sorry for your loss."

The woman smiled. "Thank you. I suppose it would be all right if I told you what I need help with?"

Jess smiled. "Why don't you come into my office?"

✸

At five o'clock, Jess was just about to close down for the day and head home when the front door opened and Caitlin walked in, followed by Jason, Alison, Jim, Julia, Tim, Chris, Jess's mother, and Ryan. Alison had several bottles of champagne, and Caitlin carried a giant bakery cake that said HAPPY GRAND OPENING across the top, which made Jess laugh, as most of the day she'd been alone in the office. But not as alone as she'd expected.

"We had to celebrate your first day open. This is a big deal!" Caitlin said.

"Well, thank you. I didn't expect this."

"How did the first day go?" Alison asked.

"Better than expected. Ed came in and I helped him with his will. And I actually had two walk-ins. Both people who were look-ing for Stan Murphy."

"It was worth getting this office and sitting on it for a few months," Ryan said.

She'd been so excited when she signed the lease for the office, but then had been disappointed to discover that the office was going to have to sit unused for another four months, at least until she had her Massachusetts law license. But, she agreed with Ryan that it was definitely worth it.

Ryan walked over and put his arm around her. "Congratulations. I'm proud of you."

"Thanks." She smiled up at him, and he gave her a quick kiss. They'd only just recently decided that they were officially dating. It happened slowly and so naturally that somehow they just evolved from being friends to a little bit more when Jess surprised them both by giving Ryan a kiss good night when he pulled her in for a goodbye hug one night. And just like that, they were dating.

Jess looked around her office at all of her favorite friends and family and felt her eyes water. It was incredible how much her life and Caitlin's life, too, had changed in less than a year. And how much happier they all were.

Caitlin walked over and gave her a hug. "You look deep in thought, Mom. Are you feeling okay about the office?"

"More than okay. I was just thinking about how happy I am that we decided to stay."

"I feel the same," Caitlin said.

Jess's mother overheard them and chimed in. "And no one is happier than me."

They all laughed at that. Alison walked over and gave her a big hug. "I'm so glad you're here, too. Thank you for helping to make my bookstore dream come true. And thanks for being such a good friend, always."

Jess hugged her back as Julia joined them and glanced at Caitlin.

"I'm so glad you're staying. I've known you and your mom forever, it seems, but this summer I feel like I've really gotten to know you both. You're one of my closest friends now." She and Caitlin hugged.

Jess felt tears of happiness building. She faced the other three and lifted her glass of champagne. "To mothers and daughters and best friends, forever."

Acknowledgments

Thank you to my family—my sister, Jane, and nieces Taylor and Nicole for being my early readers and cheering me on, always. To my three amigos—Cindy, Lee, and Rachel, my writing buddies, for their support and friendship. A special thanks to Cindy, for reading and offering such good suggestions, always. To my agent, Christina Hogrebe, for all of your wisdom and support. Also, the awesome rights team at Jane Rotrosen—Sabrina Prestia, Maria Napolitano, and Tori Clayton. A huge thank-you to my editor, Alexandra Sehulster, for being so wonderful to work with. Your suggestions were always amazing and made the story so much better. And for the team at St. Martin's Griffin—I appreciate you all so much, thank you for all that you do—Anne Marie Tallberg, Marissa Sangiacomo, Alyssa Gammello, Brant Janeway, Kejana Ayala, and Cassidy Graham.

About the Author

Alison Thompson Photography

PAMELA KELLEY is a *USA Today* and *Wall Street Journal* bestselling author of women's fiction, family sagas, and suspense, such as *The Restaurant* and *The Hotel*. Readers often describe her books as feel-good reads with people you'd want as friends. She lives in a historic seaside town near Cape Cod. She has always been an avid reader of women's fiction, romance, mysteries, thrillers, and cookbooks. There's also a good chance you might get hungry when you read her books, as she is a foodie and occasionally shares a recipe or two.